She Went to Paris

By the same author:

Murder at Machu Picchu

Murder in Barbados

Murder in San Francisco

Murder in New Orleans

She Went to Paris

Mariann Tadmor

Library of Congress Control Number: 2013903027
ISBN: Hardcover 978-1-4836-4491-2
Softcover 978-1-4836-4490-5
Ebook 978-1-4836-4492-9

This is a work of fiction. Names, characters, dialogues, places and incidents are the product either of the author's imagination or are used fictitiously, and any resemblance to any actual persons, living or dead, events, or locales is entirely coincidental.

This book was printed in the United States of America.

Cover artwork by John Goodnough.

Rev. date: 04/23/2013

To order additional copies of this book, contact:
Xlibris Corporation
1-888-795-4274
www.Xlibris.com
Orders@Xlibris.com
123871

This book
is for Ethan and Zackary
who went to Paris

Acknowledgements

Once more, my thanks go to Yoav Tadmor who read and commented untiringly upon my many versions of the book and who didn't ever let me off the hook; and to family and friends who thought they'd never see this final product.

Chapter 1

"What do you mean," I said.

The woman was on the edge of her seat. She leaned forward and placed a thin manila envelope on my desk.

"I mean she disappeared."

"Where?"

"In Paris."

"How old was she?"

"Thirty-six," she said. "Born 1896."

I made a quick calculation.

"She must be dead by now," I said.

"I know," she said. "I want you to find out what became of her. She went there in 1921 and sent one postcard—without an address—in 1930. Then there was silence."

I stared at her and drummed my fingers on the arm of my office chair.

"What made you come to me?" I said.

"You were recommended to me as a Francophile who speaks the language and knows Paris well. Wouldn't you enjoy spending some time over there at my expense?"

She almost smiled.

I took another peek at her card. It said Marjorie M. Robinson, Realtor, 629 Central Park West, New York City.

I'd better explain. My name is Jamie C. Prescott, I'm 42 and single. I'm six feet tall plus half an inch or so with broad shoulders, I dress with some elegance, I have real-to-goodness blond hair and a black belt in Tae Kwon Do. I have a Master's in Criminal Justice and a nose for crime. I'm a private investigator working out of quite opulent quarters on K Street in Washington, D.C.

Marjorie Robinson looked around my well-appointed office and said: "You and your husband look very successful. Your address gives me confidence."

"We're not a wife-and-husband team," I said. "Bob Makowski and I are business partners."

"I just assumed," Mrs. Robinson said.

And you're not the first, I thought.

Bob had been pestering me for a couple of years to give up my adventure as a travel agent and return to sleuthing, the life he insists I was born to. So last year I closed down the agency which was located in my Cape Cod style house in Bethesda, Maryland. Next I bought the snazzy little townhouse in Georgetown to which I've just moved my antique furniture and collection of exotic paintings.

Marjorie Robinson crossed her legs. I studied her frankly. Well-preserved. Some signs of work done on face and neck. Tailored suit, silk shirt, taupe hose on good legs in pumps, some fine jewelry on arthritic fingers.

"Who recommended me to you?" I said.

She smoothed down her silver-streaked hair.

"My son lives in town, he's with the State Department. A Martin Cook is a friend of his although, personally, I don't know him. Mr. Cook recommended you."

Martin Cook is in private business as a constable and employs a number of musclemen who serve papers on potentially violent clients. And, yes, they do exist in the nation's capital.

Martin is also my personal internet and general snoop. He's smart, 45, and until recently, divorced. He has helped me out of scrapes on various occasions most recently supplying me with a false identity in my quest to root out some shady characters in New Orleans. But that's a different story.

I've known him for years and have sometimes felt it's too bad I don't mix business with pleasure. Until I remembered he's only five-six and then I earmarked him for Topsy, formerly Bannister, who's five-four. They recently married and now live two blocks down from my new Georgetown abode.

I made a mental note to call Martin.

"My son tells me you are friends with Martin's new wife, Topsy," Marjorie Robinson said.

Let me explain again. Topsy and I have been close since Lower School at Sidwell Friends and were college roommates. She joined me in the travel agency adventure until she went through a messy divorce, met Martin Cook, re-married and decided to leave the business world. That somehow took the fun out of travel agenting for me. I was probably getting tired of it anyway and this was a good excuse for me to re-align my life.

"Can you leave for Paris immediately?" Marjorie Robinson said. "I'm told you have no family obligations."

I'm always ready to leave for Paris and except for my mother, a partner in a small law firm downtown, I am as they say, unattached. Did I mention I'm divorced? I suffered through a few years with the very French Roger whom I met and married in Paris in my senior year of college much to my parents' horror. Due to irreconcilable differences I gave up the husband but am still in love with Paris. I finished college upon my return home.

"You're quite right," I said. "I have no family obligations."

You may wonder if I date. Enter Topsy. Over the years she has set me up with a series of flawed Washington men. I could mention a fugitive from justice (tax evasion).

A supposedly divorced lawyer who returned to his wife from whom he was not even separated. A foreign embassy diplomat who was repatriated to his country by our government for undisclosed but no doubt sinister reasons. And the list goes on. Lately I've been dating a jazz saxophone player who's ten years my junior. Topsy is apprehensive but, as I say, what's to prevent me?

"Will you do it?" Marjorie Robinson raised her voice. "I'm 72 years old and I want the riddle solved."

"I will do it," I said, picked up a yellow legal pad and poised my pen.

"What was your aunt's name?"

Chapter 2

1921

"I'm the Cat's Meow."

Sterling Kirkland Sawyer gave her emerald green cloche hat a rap and a tug, smoothed down her silk dress, adjusted her long string of pearls, and sprang open the cabin door in response to a sharp knock.

The steward stepped inside, picked up her two leather valises, one under each arm, and seized her hatbox and traveling case, one in each hand. He watched her boyish figure and superior profile as she preceded him up the wide stairs to the first-class lounge.

The first-class lounge teemed with travelers. Several officers collected passports. The captain who had steered the ship safely to port in Le Havre exuded self-satisfied pride. A most divine crossing someone exclaimed. Good show, said another, the days just flew by.

"Yoohoo, Sterling, darling, over here."

Victoria Huddersfield—'Babe' to her close friends which numbered in multiple scores and heiress to a New York railroad fortune—spoke with a vague English accent carefully acquired during summer visits to her mother's family in Hertfordshire.

She dashed forward and dragged Sterling several feet towards a sofa. Here sat a deathly white emaciated youth clutching at his coat collar. He gazed pathetically at Sterling from pale blue eyes lodged in doughy skin under a blond patch of hair.

"Darling Sterling, you haven't met darling Wainwright Manners III, he's the writer I told you about, he's been under the weather, haven't you darling, up-chucking all over that luxurious cabin for days. Doesn't he look wan and wasted?"

Victoria pushed Sterling forward and left her standing in front of the wasted youth. Then Victoria sailed forth to join a group of smart women in mainly pink and mauve silk dresses, tight-fitting cloche hats, with shapely legs in nude-colored stockings, and feet in snub-nosed shoes with T-straps across the arches. They put their heads together and gazed furtively back at Sterling. Their whispered remarks stayed below their breaths.

"Her father was filthy rich."

"She keeps herself to herself."

"Who does she think she is?"

"What does she care? She doesn't need anyone."

They waved half-heartedly at Sterling who didn't wave back. She turned to Wainwright Manners III.

"You look positively cadaverous," she said. "What do you write?"

"Oh, write," Wainwright said. "It was in my previous life before I boarded this floating punishment of a schooner. Poems and stories. *The Saturday Evening Post*. And others."

"Have I seen your name?"

"Probably not. Father objects. Mommy let's me use hers, don't you know. Have to be a-anomynous. Amonimous, don't you know." Wainwright the Third had gone if possibly paler and looked on the verge of another purge.

"Sorry, must rush off to guard my valises," Sterling said and stepped away from him. "Maybe we'll meet up in Paris."

"H-h-hopefully." Wainwright leaned back in the sofa and closed his eyes.

Sterling shuddered, crossed the lounge, followed Victoria and her coterie, and joined the line which moved slowly down the gangplank to the pier. The American Express porters bustled about—interspersed with those from Thos. Cook—checked off their lists and placed travelers in taxi-cabs which would transport them from the port to the train station. It was a good twenty minute ride.

"Yoohoo, Sterling, darling, come ride with me," Victoria shouted from inside a cab where she sat obscured by a tower of valises. The porter stacked Sterling's baggage on top of Victoria's and Sterling climbed into the back seat.

The driver yanked the taxi-cab to a start in a puff of exhaust.

"Divine, isn't it," Victoria exclaimed and took off her cloche. Her black hair was plastered to her skull and she shook it free until it bounced. "Good thing we're both at the Ritz."

"Well, actually," Sterling mumbled. She pulled aside the curtains at the rear window of the taxi-cab and took a last look at the towering hull of the *SS Paris* with its three giant chimneys. Several tugboats darted about in the water blaring their horns. "Actually, I'm staying with a family friend over on rue du Berri."

"Really? You never told me." Victoria looked up sharply. "Well, send me a petit bleu when you've settled in, I'm having the smart set in for cocktails Friday at five. You'll meet some absolutely divine chaps. You do need to find a husband soon."

Victoria talked on while Sterling closed her eyes and kept them closed until the taxi-cab stopped. Yet another porter accompanied them to their first-class compartment on the boat train. Conductors shouted, travelers clamored for directions, horns tooted, and the porters rushed about.

Sterling tossed her hat into the rack on top of her two valises—her Louis Vuitton steamer trunk having been loaded into the freight compartment—and dropped into her plush seat facing forward. She placed her traveling case in the empty space beside her and kept the hatbox underneath.

Victoria flung herself at the window, pulled at the leather strap to release the top and leaned out.

"Whatever became of darling Wainwright," she said out the window. "You should have brought him, darling Sterling, I put him in your care. Can you never do anything right?"

"He's most unattractive. The last I saw of him he was preparing to spew forth again."

"Too insensitive of you, my dear." Victoria jumped up and down and shouted: "Over here you chaps, over here. Let's have a party, I'm serving champagne."

Four more bright young things crammed into the compartment, Dunhills were passed around, flutes handed about. Sterling lit up, accepted one drink but refused a second. She retreated into her seat and only occasionally during the two and a half hour ride did she join in the merriment. Her heart beat faster as she gazed in recognition at the yellow wheat fields moved by the wind into wavering valleys dotted with red poppies and blue cornflowers. The familiar gray stone houses nestled in the midst of the fields, their windows closely shuttered, the people within living unseen lives.

When the train pulled into the Gare St. Lazare a new group of American Express men were at the rank of hire-cars outside the station.

"Sterling, darling, let me drop you on Berri, it'll be my pleasure. I did promise Pierre I would look after you."

Not that I need looking after, Sterling bristled to herself.

Victoria watched as her taxi-cab filled up with her voluminous valises barely leaving room for herself.

"Spoke too soon," she said.

"Not to worry," Sterling waved. "I'll take my own."

"Stay in touch, darling, and come around at five on Friday for those heavenly cocktails. You must get over being so devastatingly shy."

"I'll do my best," Sterling said and waited for the next cab in line.

"Where to, Miss," asked the porter but Sterling leapt into the taxi and directed the driver in her fluent French.

The taxi-cab eased into traffic amid Parisian pedestrians, tramcars with noisy klaxons, slow-moving runabouts and sleek roadsters, horse-drawn carts, push-carts overflowing with flowers and vegetables, the air filled with the fragrance of Paris.

Sterling settled back in her seat.

When the cab crossed the Pont Neuf she leaned expectantly out the window. Her eyes were intensely blue under her bob of blond hair. She took in the glittering water on the Seine, the booksellers along the quaie, and the heightened clatter of horse-hooves along the Boulevard St. Germain-des-Prés. Her sense of home was instant and comforting.

The cab took the corner from rue Bonaparte down the narrow rue Jacob and stopped in front of the ten foot high arched doorway to her small hotel. Sterling breathed in deeply before entering.

"I'm the Cat's Meow," she said aloud and smiled triumphantly to herself.

Chapter 3

"Her name was Sterling Kirkland Sawyer," Marjorie Robinson said. "Her father, Samuel Sawyer—my grandfather—was the heir to a banking fortune in Cincinnati. Her mother, Eliza Kirkland—my grandmother—came from a wealthy shipping family in Boston. They married in 1895 when he was 25 and just out of law school and she was 20. Then, instead of practicing law, Samuel Sawyer moved with Eliza to New York city where he invested his fortune in real estate."

"And that's where Sterling was born?"

"Yes, she was the eldest. She was born in 1896 and my mother, Rose, was born the following year."

"So, by the time your grandmother was 22 she had two small children to care for?"

"I wouldn't call it care for. She gave birth to them and then handed them over to the servants."

"Of course," I said. I'd forgotten about the money.

"The thing was, Eliza was delicate and, also, she was Catholic while Samuel was Presbyterian."

"Probably not a good combination in those days," I said.

"Exactly. Eliza's family in Boston wanted the children brought up Catholic and Eliza sent them to her mother for months at a time. Then, in 1901, when Sterling was 5 and my mother, Rose, was 4, Eliza died after yet another still-birth. She was 26."

"Did the children stay in Boston?"

"No, they were separated. My grandfather sent my mother, Rose, to his family in Cincinnati where she grew up Presbyterian and Sterling stayed in Boston with her mother's Catholic family. That is, until she was 10, when she was sent to a convent school in France."

"How did that happen?"

"When her grandmother died in 1906, no one seemed to know what to do with Sterling. Her father was living the single life in New York, her sister was living in Cincinnati. Her only aunt in Boston had been educated in France and so the idea of sending Sterling there was born."

I thought of a ten-year old child being shipped abroad because no one wanted her.

"She had been taught French, of course," Marjorie Robinson said, "and she was already Catholic so she shouldn't have had any problems at a convent school."

Really? I thought.

"Where was the convent school?" I asked.

"My mother never said."

"It may not be relevant," I said. "Did Sterling eventually return to the States?"

Marjorie Robinson settled back in her seat and looked rather pleased.

"You won't believe this but Sterling's father remarried in 1912—someone finally managed to nail him down or rather her parents did—they took an extended honeymoon in Europe and sailed back home on the *Titanic.* And you know how that turned out."

"They perished?"

"They did," Marjorie said matter-of-factly while I, with a shudder, saw twisted metal, water rushing, and hapless passengers succumbing to the icy waters or disappearing into the depths trapped in the ship as it hurtled down to the ocean floor carrying Sterling's father and his new wife with it.

I shuddered again and caught a cold glance from Marjorie Robinson.

"My mother and Sterling became very rich," she said.

"Indeed," I said.

"Of course, my mother's money was lost in the 1929 crash," Marjorie said, "and I presume that Sterling's was, too. Maybe that had something to do with her disappearance."

"Maybe," I said and looked at my yellow pad. I'd stopped writing several scenes back. "But to get back to the beginning, did Sterling return to New York after her father died?"

"Yes. She was 16. Her lawyers set her up with an apartment in Manhattan, hired a housekeeper, a cook, and a maid, and a family friend took a parental interest in her. He was the celebrated photographer, Pierre Fast-Brown, who took those marvelous pictures of society women for all the fashion magazines of the day. You've heard of him, I assume."

"Vaguely."

"In any case, he and Samuel Sawyer were friends even though Fast-Brown was a couple of years older than Samuel. Fast-Brown studied law at Georgetown (his mother was Catholic) while Samuel went to Harvard. The interesting thing was that they both went into other fields, Samuel into real estate and Fast-Brown into photography. They arrived in New York at the same time and after Samuel became a widower they chased women together."

"And, then, what happened?" I felt as if I was watching an old movie.

"Mind you," Marjorie said, "I have all this from my mother, Rose, who also had it second-hand. She stayed in Cincinnati and never saw Sterling again. She received one single postcard from Paris without a return address."

"Hard to believe." I resumed jotting down notes.

"In any case, Pierre Fast-Brown's mother was from Boston, she was a friend of Sterling's grandmother, so Pierre knew Sterling."

"And, *voilá,*" I said, "Sterling was all set."

"Yes. Apparently she went to a finishing school in Manhattan and on to college where she got a degree in literature and wrote poetry and short stories."

"And, *voilá* again," I said, "Fast-Brown helped her get published in the best magazines."

"Exactly," Marjorie Robinson said. "I understand that she had some pieces published as early as 1917 in *The Bright Set*. But I don't know what they were about. You must have heard of the magazine."

"It rings a slight bell," I said.

We took care of the formalities. My new client signed a contract, paid a substantial retainer, and left with apologies that the manila envelope she'd handed me did not contain much more information for me to go on.

Just before the door closed behind her she popped her head back in.

"You will report to me by e-mail," she ordered. "Once a week."

"Of course, Mrs. Robinson," I said.

But little does she know, I thought, how vague my reporting can be until something substantial shows up. Fun discoveries do not happen on the dot once a week.

"If you have any more questions at all, do get in touch," Marjorie said. "I'm returning to New York this evening."

And she was gone.

After she left I opened the envelope. Marjorie Robinson had written down the entire story she'd just told me. No surprises there. There was a gap in the information between 1918 and 1920. In 1921, when Sterling was 25 she had sailed for France, ostensibly to visit an old friend of her mother, who was nameless but lived on rue du Berri in

Paris. However, upon arrival in France Sterling had dropped out of sight.

The postcard Rose had received was enclosed in the manila envelope. It had a colored picture of the Chat Noir on one side and, on the other, just five words written in a small firm hand: '*All is well here, Sterling*.' The postmark was smudged but I could just make out a faint 1930. I sifted through the scant paperwork for a photograph of Sterling. There was nothing.

An obituary in the local newspaper from 1965 revealed that the last of the Kirkland dynasty had died with the passing of what would have been Sterling's unmarried cousin, the only son of her only aunt in Boston.

Rose had died in 1980.

Marjorie Robinson, Rose's only daughter and Sterling's niece, was 72. Time was of the essence.

Chapter 4

1922

It was spring. It was the Ritz. Napoleon stood on his perch in the Place Vendôme, luxurious motorcars cruised down the rue de la Paix, the chestnuts on the boulevards were in bloom, and Pierre Fast-Brown was waiting in the palatial hotel lounge—adjacent to the equally palatial dining-room—in an opulent Louis XVI chair.

"There you are," Pierre exclaimed. "Darling Sterling, over here."

"Dear Uncle Pierre." Sterling embraced him feeling genuinely happy.

"Let me look at you. You're the Cat's Meow. Smart and stylish, love your dress, Chanel, I do believe, hangs perfectly on you. You should also try a mushroom sailor hat, they are all the rage."

Pierre beamed at her, his spare mustache twitched, his red boutonniere trembled, and Sterling tugged at her emerald-green cloche hat with the black velvet band and diamond clip and beamed back at him.

"I'm no longer a girl," she said, "and I wear cloches."

"Quite. Now, what's this all about. Your address must not be broadcast, especially to anyone in New York? And not to Victoria? Victoria who's your best friend?"

Which was when the same Victoria burst forth from a chauffeured black touring car which had glided to an elegant halt at the entrance to the hotel. She dashed through the foyer, stopped in the middle of the opulent space under a crystal chandelier and waited for all eyes to turn to her. To her slick beige jacket over a pleated silk skirt and curvy legs in nude-colored stockings. To her black bobbed hair and floating pearl necklace.

"You invited her?" Sterling stared at Pierre.

Victoria glanced at herself in the tall mirrors, sailed across the fine carpet in the lounge, threw her arms around Sterling and squeezed her a little too hard.

"Sterling, darling, where *have* you been, why did you disappear. You never sent me a single message."

Sterling disengaged herself from the taxing embrace.

"I was away," she said. "I saw it in *The Bright Set* much later. You looked perfectly lovely. And you're a Comtesse now, your distinguished husband looked very, uh, distinguished." Sterling had been about to say dissipated.

"He'll do," Victoria said. "He's going through my money at a delirious speed and Daddy is acting peevish. But the title is lovely. Get's me into some frightfully swell country homes and châteaux."

"How splendid," Sterling said.

"Would you believe," Victoria said to Pierre, "that I couldn't find her address to send her my wedding invitation. Everyone, but just everyone, came but not Sterling. Devastation."

Victoria's face crumpled pathetically. She swiped her hand at her mouth and left a red streak across her cheek.

"I'll pop into the bar. Time for a libation," she cried.

Pierre Fast-Brown hurried after Victoria and brought her back with a soothing hand.

We weren't ever best friends, Sterling thought. Best friends don't stab you in the back. They don't constantly belittle you.

At lunch—surrounded by gold-leaf and mirrors and obsequious waiters—Victoria drank a bottle of wine, Sterling had one glass, and Pierre had sparkling *Evian*. Before the dessert Victoria had dropped out of the conversation entirely and when the maître d' informed her that her Rolls was at the door she dabbed at her nose with a powdered pink pad from a silver compact and got up unsteadily.

"Uncle Pierre," she slurred, "you should know that Sterling is living in sin with a married man in a run-down flat on the wr-wrong side of the river. I heard it from a very r-reliable source."

Sterling bristled and Victoria stumbled away in a swirl of silk and a clatter of heels before the astonished Uncle Pierre could get out of his chair.

"This is not true, of course," Pierre Fast-Brown said sternly.

"No, Uncle Pierre, of course not," Sterling said.

"I would hope not," he said. "I am very disappointed in Victoria."

"Not as much as I am."

"Well," Pierre said, closing the chapter. "Today I'm seeing my hatmaker on Place Vendôme from where I'll continue to a meeting at *The Bright Set* offices. There must be someone I can photograph although the French models don't go over well at home."

"Surely you can find a suitable woman of society," Sterling said. "Maybe someone who speaks several languages. Much as you do, not only French but also Italian and German."

"Flattery will get you everywhere with me," Pierre said. "I shall have to use some flattery myself. I'll be adding a Derain to my collection of Rouaults and Segonzacs. He uses such wonderfully bright colors. You will like them, I assure you."

"I already do," she said.

"I also hope to acquire one of those Surréalist paintings by Alexandre Orgoloff. Seems to be the latest."

"I've heard of them," she said.

"And you," Pierre said, "are you still writing in French?"

"Yes. The language has come back to me forcefully. I am immersed in French literature."

"You no longer write in English?" Pierre said with a slight frown. "I have an idea for you. Send me an article every month, I'll get it published in *The Bright Set*, we'll call it *Paris Diary*. You could use any *nom de plume* you like and throw in some French phrases. Everyone reads French."

"What would I write about?"

"You could report on the fun people you meet especially the literary French and American and what they are talking and writing about and throw in a little gossip," Pierre said.

"I'm not a journalist," Sterling said. "And it would take my focus off my writing."

"It's only once a month. Try it, it'll be fun."

"I appreciate the idea, dear Uncle Pierre," she said after an uncomfortable pause, "but I fear I would be a terrible disappointment. You had better think of someone else."

"My dear child, it was a momentary inspiration—and you know I have plenty of such moments which is why my photographs are so hugely successful. But, if not you, then we must find someone else to do it. It suddenly seems to be one of my better ideas and I'm not even an editor."

Pierre squeezed Sterling's hand affectionately.

"As for my real writing," she said, "Roland Lee Rainier has introduced me to the owners of several small presses and they've read my short stories. He also introduced me to the owner of the best bookstore in town."

"In that case, I applaud him."

"*La Librairie* on Boulevard St. Michel is where *toute le monde littéraire* meets."

"Are you sure you should be involved with this Roland," Pierre said. "People are talking in New York. His reputation has been in jeopardy since he published his infamous book, *Strangers In Paris*."

"Why, I'm amazed at you, Uncle Pierre, have you read it?" Sterling couldn't help but enjoy his heightened cheek color.

"A copy came to my attention," he said.

"What did you think?"

"Four hundred and twenty-eight pages. Hard for me to read that many pages. Also, I like a story with a beginning, a middle, and an end, with well-defined and noble characters, written in elegant sentences with ample punctuation. I am not fond of depravity, that is all I can say."

"And you're not alone."

"But what's he like? We move in different circles in New York even though he writes for *The Bright Set*."

"He's perfectly charming and so is his wife."

"Didn't know he had one."

"She stays in the country and tends to her social engagements."

"Ahem."

"Claire speaks rather well of Roland's books," Sterling said.

"Claire?"

"Claire Garcia-Bonsonwell."

"Ah, dear Claire of the silver turban. I will be seeing her glamorous mother in London next week. She's appearing in that new extravagant play everyone is talking about. Where did you meet Claire?"

"At one of Effie Rousseau's dinners."

"The elusive Madame Rousseau. She paints nudes, and not in a good way." Pierre looked down his handsome nose. "How clever of Claire to have left London and the suffocating clutches of her mother. Her father, Don Miguel, has long since departed for Madrid and his baronial pursuits. Claire has inherited her mother's sense of drama and applies it to her Flamenco dancing and has her father's mysterious, dark looks. There, we've had enough gossip for one lunch."

"It won't leave this room," Sterling said.

"I should hope not," he said. "What will you be doing the rest of the afternoon, my dear?"

"Oh, this and that."

"I will be happy to take you home on my way," Pierre said. "The limousine will be here momentarily."

"Thank you, but it is not necessary. Did I not tell you? I arrived in my *Peugeot Quadrilette*, a darling two-seater, it takes me everywhere, parks easily, and I'll leave the same way."

Pierre Fast-Brown looked miffed.

"You will not forget the amusing captions you've promised the office back in New York," he said. "I was told to remind you."

"They will be on the boat-train to Le Havre in time to meet the deadline."

Sterling looked at him affectionately.

"Ahem," Pierre Fast-Brown said when coffee had been served. "I ran into Andrew the other day and I have a message for you. He's exceedingly sorry, he said, exceedingly sorry."

Sterling folded her hands in her lap.

"Please, dear child," Pierre said. He covered her hand with his and squeezed it gently. "Are you all right?"

Sterling slid down in her chair. Exceedingly sorry. Exceedingly sorry. The words thumped through her head.

"Fine," she said. "I am exceedingly fine."

Pierre Fast-Brown sat up straight. His strong-boned face with its closely shaved square jaw looked harsh. He zeroed in his very brown eyes on Sterling's blue.

"Not worthy," he said quietly. "He's not worthy of you."

Then, with a chuckle he stacked their demi-tasse cups and saucers on his napkin, whisked the napkin out from underneath leaving the stack standing. It teetered a long moment, then fell with a clatter.

The maître d' stiffened his back and Sterling laughed as she hadn't laughed in a long while. Pierre looked around innocently at bemused guests and popped the last petit-four into his mouth.

Sterling choked. "Really, you're as incorrigible as ever."

"This is nothing." Pierre said and twinkled at Sterling. "So, what else is new in Paris?"

Sterling, brightly, told him some but not all.

At the end of lunch she escaped in her perky *Quadrilette* across the river, across Place St. Germain-des-Prés to her hotel. She now had two adjoining rooms on the second floor facing the courtyard, one was her bedroom, the other her workroom. Her books were ordered in a tall bookcase, a gramophone stood on her brown and beige Louis Vuitton flat-top trunk next to a small sofa. An unframed Matisse oil hung above it.

Her traveling typewriter, the folding Corona, sat on a desk under the window. Paper and carbons were piled on top with a heap of crumpled pages flowing over the brim of a waste-basket. Within fifteen minutes she was tapping rhythmically at the Corona with two fingers, inserting fresh paper and carbons at steady intervals. She smiled occasionally at a felicitous phrase.

At eight o'clock Sterling locked her door, went down the stairs with the threadbare carpeting, crossed the street to the corner café, sat down at her customary table, ordered a bottle of house-wine, filled her glass, and waited.

"There you are," Wainwright Manners III said, tossed his straw boater on a chair and sat down. "I've been waiting for you all afternoon, where were you?"

"Nowhere," she said shortly.

"You took your car out."

"I take my car out when I want to take my car out."

"Swell. I don't know why you stay in this hotel instead of in a smart apartment on the right side of the river where everyone lives."

"I couldn't write there."

"I do it perfectly well," Wainwright said.

"Have you heard from any of the New York magazines?"

"Yes."

"You got another rejection letter?"

"Yes." Wainwrights leg jerked under the table. "I don't have your kind of connection to the almighty power-that-be, that superior editor-in-chief, Andrew Blake."

Sterling stiffened and her eyes blazed at him from a white face.

"You've crossed the line," she said and her voice was barely audible. "Do not come around here anymore."

"I'll come here whenever I want. You don't own the streets."

"That is true. Just don't come around to my place."

"And may I ask why?"

"I know why you turned up on my doorstep. You're Victoria's emissary. I call you her spy. I abhor people who pry into my private life. I must go now, I have work to do."

She put money on the table, left the café without another look at Wainwright and hurried across the street to her hotel.

Half an hour later, sitting before the Corona, she slowly picked up speed and wrote on the machine until midnight.

Chapter 5

"Are you *insane*?"

Bob leaned back in his chair and loosened his tie.

"It's just to get to Paris, isn't it? You know perfectly well you can find this woman in two shakes of a stick without going over there. You just want an excuse to stroll around the boulevards, eat crêpes, drink champagne, or whatever it is you do over there."

My partner in crime, Bob Makowski, is a former FBI agent and, for the past fifteen years, a cracker-jack private investigator. He's just what you'd expect a special agent to look like. Military crew-cut, gray suits—although not as well-pressed as in his days at the Hoover Building—and flat feet in wing-tips. He has no known skills in the martial arts or in any other exercise. He can best be described as a couch potato. And we're long-time friends.

"Yes, it's just to get to Paris. No, dear Bob, you know very well that I get to Paris anyway. But think about it. I've never had a case like this before and you know how that strikes me."

"I know, I know, it's your insane curiosity, you can't leave anything alone. What'll I do here without you. The workload isn't getting any lighter."

"It's a client like any other," I said. "One, we'll text and e-mail. Two, if you ever need me desperately I'll come rushing back. Three, I'm not leaving yet, have a lot of research to do. And, four, I really can't solve the case without going over there."

"Where are you going to start?" Bob said.

"I've got my research team set up. We're meeting in an hour at Reginald Fletcher's antiquarian bookstore in Georgetown."

"You're buying books?"

Bob feels books are a waste of time and that the sports page news is all the information anyone needs.

"I may have to. Public libraries seem to weed out books that are more than fifty years old. I'm relying on Fletcher's considerable knowledge to dig up information."

"Why do you need old books? And I know I'm a fool for asking."

"Sterling Kirkland apparently wrote poetry and short stories. She must have known a lot of writers in the 1920s both in Paris and here. Everyone in those days wrote their memoirs and someone may have mentioned her. Just a long shot."

"Seems like a very long one to me."

"Probably, but Topsy insists. We're thinking of some of the minor writers rather than the greats of the day. Certainly not Joyce."

"You're an exasperating woman. Who the hell is Joyce?" Bob looked defeated.

"Someone who was averse to actual memoirs."

Bob shook his head.

"Martin Cook is getting the passenger lists from ocean liners leaving for Le Havre in 1921."

"Does it matter which ship she sailed on?" Bob said.

"Not that as much as with *whom*. Maybe she went with friends who knew what happened to her."

"You mean someone who's now, what, a hundred and ten?"

"Fine, someone's offspring who's now, what, seventy-five."

"Could happen, I suppose."

"So you're going to be okay with this?" I said.

"Yeah, what the hell," Bob said. "Not that you need my permission."

"I know," I said.

We're equal partners but I still want to be polite.

I walked from the office on K Street across Lafayette Square where the homeless slept on benches a few steps from the White House or sat eating out of brown paper bags retrieved from trash bins. None of them asked for money but I still spread some cash around in the name of the President.

At the corner bakery I hurriedly ate a croissant and downed a coffee before getting my black Jaguar from the garage on K Street.

I stopped by the library on Wisconsin Avenue on my way to Fletcher's antiquarian bookstore to find the 1917-1920 issues of *The Bright Set*.

This occasioned some murmured discussions between the reference desk and the check-out counter. Seemed no one ever asked to take the magazines out but that there were no rules saying one couldn't. After half an hour I had in my arms four tomes of bound magazines weighing five pounds each.

At the bookstore on M Street in Georgetown I found Topsy at a table surrounded by stacks of musty books. I dumped the magazines next to her and sat down.

"Coffee or tea?" Reginald Fletcher looked in on us, his rimless glasses on a slant as usual, his light-weight brownish hair in a muss and his thin body bent over at the waist. "Come to the kitchen in five minutes."

"What've you got so far," I asked Topsy when caffeine had bucked me up and I came down from a doughnut induced sugar-high.

"Autobiographies, biographies, novels, literary critiques about the greats as well as about the lesser luminaries of the time. I'm drowning and haven't found anything yet. But I'm hoping since they all wrote about themselves and about one another."

Let me explain. Topsy has a Ph.D. in Early 20th Century American literature which makes her eminently qualified to guide me in my search. She also writes a syndicated column—with a corresponding website—through which she keeps a multitude of readers on the grammatical straight and narrow.

No one wishes to be caught dead confusing laying down with lying down. You lay down an object, while people themselves *lie* down. And confusing 'me' and 'I' is even sloppier. 'It's all the same to you and I?' No, 'it's all the same to you and *me.'* Simple Topsy test: remove 'you and' and the sentence becomes 'It's all the same to *I*,' which is nonsense.

We, her family and friends, avoid redundancies such as 'return back', 'separate out,' and 're-assemble together,' not to mention confusing advice with advise, affect with effect, capital with capitol.

"Where are you going to start?" I said.

"First, the indices in the biographies and the autobiographies. So far no mention of Sterling Kirkland Sawyer."

"And Google?"

"Done. She's only mentioned as the daughter of Samuel Sawyer."

"Weird."

I opened *The Bright Set* volume from 1917 and stopped at page 5. Offices at 352 Fifth Avenue, New York. 25 cents a copy, $3 a year.

I went down the contents page of every single issue from January to December without finding Sterling. What I did find was a poem by Roland Lee Rainier and some very elegant photographs by Pierre Fast-Brown of society beauties in lovely gowns.

There was a tongue-in-cheek piece called *Women Annoy Me*, an article about *Country Home Visiting*, and a funny piece by Roland Lee Rainier concerning *Bad Manners*.

According to Marjorie Robinson Sterling had some poems published, but I found nothing anywhere with her name. There were quite a few poems just with initials although none that said SKS.

Topsy peered at the pages over my shoulder.

"Look at those irascible drawings by *Angelo.* That would be the American satirist popular with the magazines of the day. Could Sterling have been assigned to write the captions for his drawings? No name for the author of those."

"It's possible," I said. "But why would she have been anonymous?"

"Maybe she was publicity-shy or maybe she wasn't good enough? We still haven't seen anything she wrote."

"Let's not jump to conclusions," I said. Somehow I now felt protective of Sterling Kirkland Sawyer and wanted her to be good enough.

Topsy sat down next to me.

"Look," she said and turned the pages of the many ads. "*Reduce your flesh: Medicated Rubber Garments.* I want some of those! How do you suppose they worked?"

"Probably didn't," I said. "Instead, this is what you need: 'A Corsetiére. Constraint without restraint, style without discomfort'. Or maybe this one: 'A cushion on which to rest one's long-suffering elbow during a telephone conversation. Blue taffeta'."

"How divine."

"Marjorie Robinson mentioned Sterling's college," I said. "I'll call and have someone send me the 1918 yearbook. It will have a photograph of her and give me the names of her friends."

"Might be useful," Topsy said and stuffed books in a large tote, Reginald Fletcher gave his blessing, and she left with a promise to return them all eventually.

On my way home I stopped by the deli to stock up on some smoked salmon, potato salad, a fruit salad, an extra crisp baguette, brie cheese, and a chocolate mousse. I put the stuff away on the kitchen counter—black granite, if you please—and went upstairs to slip into something more comfortable.

My newly acquired townhouse still feels new to me and each time I enter I'm surprised that this is where I now live. The livingroom, diningroom, den, half-bath, and kitchen are, naturally, on the first floor. My eclectic collection of antiques and cozy modern with splashes of Caribbean color from my paintings still look alien in the new surroundings. On the second floor I have three bedrooms and two full baths.

There's a small fenced-in yard at the back where I'm supposed to barbecue something on weekends. Some shrubs and plants hover around the five steps up to the red front door. I'm already feeling guilty for not watering these ornaments on a regular basis. Maybe I should get to know the neighbors who might agree to swing their watering cans my way. Or else forget about plants and replace them with riverbed stones.

I had two text messages. My more or less steady date, Jon Douglas, informed me that he'd accepted a six week jazz gig playing his tenor sax in Barcelona and would be leaving the following day. I texted him back but didn't tell him about Paris since I never talk about my work outside of the office. Client privilege or, maybe, my peculiar penchant for concealment which Bob Makowski calls my tool in trade.

The second message was from Martin Cook. He had found Sterling on the first-class passenger list of the *SS Paris*.

And he had recognized one other name on the list.

Chapter 6

1922

"Did you think it very beastly of me not to stay with you?"

Sterling sat opposite Effie Rousseau in her spacious livingroom on rue du Berri.

"No, my dear, you did send me a pneu the very next day so that I wouldn't worry."

"Dear Effie."

"Nevertheless, it would have been lovely to have you here, your father would have been pleased."

Effie, her hair in a Titian frizz, her smallish blue eyes helped along by Khol, squinted at the wall where a man in a large water-color portrait stared back at her. Sterling followed her glance and shuddered.

"Does that look like him?" she said. "I hardly remember him. I doubt if he would have cared one way or the other if I had moved in with you."

"My dear, he was a difficult man. I left him, you know, shortly before he remarried and I returned to Paris. I never did fit in very well in America."

"Did he want to marry you?"

"He did. Imagine, if I had said yes I could have been the one on the Titanic. Instead he fell into the clutches of that dear young woman's ambitious mother."

"It doesn't bear thinking about," Sterling said.

"And, so, we won't, my dear. Let me show you my latest painting. A lovely subject and I believe it turned out all right."

They stood together in Effie's studio and looked at the painting still on the easel.

"Where did you paint her?"

"She came here."

"She's voluptuous," Sterling said, "and she's very nude."

"She's Bernice Boch. From Buffalo, New York. No good painting a portrait when you're confronted with that body."

"Did she talk about her writing while you painted her?"

"She did and I've obtained a couple of her books for you," Effie said and handed over two handsome volumes.

"That's very good of you, thank you."

Effie looked very pleased

"She will autograph them for you this afternoon."

"You mean she will be here?"

"Yes, they will both have drinks with us."

They arrived half an hour later, Bernice Boch dressed in a flowing dress under which her body undulated and shifted alarmingly as she breezed into Effie's living room. She was followed by her husband, the Russian violinist, Pyotr Vasilevich, a well-known boulevardier, hard to miss with his flaming red hair, straggling goatee and tall stooping frame. He had a disconcerting squint to his left eye. It was impossible to know if he was looking at *you* or at the next person.

Sterling flitted about helping Effie with the gin fizzes and whiskies and Pernods and canapés and bite-size quiches all of which disappeared speedily.

"Give me another Pernod," said Bernice, "and then we'll admire the painting. I won't take it now, I'll wait until after your exhibition."

"Where you will be in good company with my portraits of Orgoloff and Louis Saint and of my darling Sterling."

"Sterling," Bernice said, "what a wonderfully stalwart name for a woman. I knew a man in Buffalo by that name."

Sterling sat down in the sofa.

"My father chose it," she said. "He was expecting a boy."

"And never found a girl's name for you?"

"He lost interest."

"Naturally," Bernice said and glared at Pyotr.

Bernice shifted her glance from Sterling's face to her hands which held two books.

"What did you bring," she said.

"Two of your books," Sterling said and hoped she wouldn't be asked which ones and whether she had read them.

"Pyotr," Bernice raised her voice. "Pyotr, lend me your pen."

She wrote her name with a flourish and from her belly emerged a highly contagious laugh. Her great big bosom heaved.

"You are very gracious," Sterling said.

"Oh, bosh," Bernice said, "Effie has told me that you are a writer in both French and English. That's something. Let me read some of your stuff, will you?"

"I will," Sterling said. I won't, she thought, she'll demolish me.

"Why don't you read to us from my book, the one with the red cover," Bernice said.

"That's a special privilege," Pyotr said. "Says her words must be read, not heard."

"Oh, bosh," Bernice said. "Why do you put words in my mouth. Let her read to us, *you* haven't bothered to read any of my books, it'll do you good to hear what I write. Get me another Pernod, will you."

"Roland Lee Rainier will be here from New York next week," Effie said. "How would you all like to have dinner here on the Thursday."

"We will come," Bernice said. "Anything for dear Roland."

Effie lit a Pall Mall and offered the cigarettes around.

"I smoke too much," Sterling said and lit up and there came Bernice's sonorous laugh again, straight from the belly.

"Now," she said. "Now read to us."

And while Sterling read Bernice stared unblinkingly at the ceiling. Once in a while she chuckled at one of her own phrases and a couple of times she said: "How about that!"

Pyotr moved around the room squinting at paintings and blowing blue smoke about.

"Oh, do sit down," Bernice said. "You distract me and how can you listen when you bounce about?"

When Sterling read the last line of the last short story and closed the book Bernice sighed deeply and drained her glass to the last drop.

"Your writing is very mysterious," Sterling said. "I was constantly on the lookout for clues while I read."

"I'm avid about clues. Especially in crime stories. They are wonderfully relaxing, get them sent over from Mudie's in London."

"So do I," Sterling said. "There are some good detective writers about.

"You bet," Bernice said. "A good writer is a good writer."

"Conan Doyle and Agatha Christie."

"I've read them."

"Very entertaining," Effie said.

"Of course, they write about *men* operatives," Sterling said. "I'm waiting for someone to have a *woman* as a *real* detective. How about Shirley Holmes and her side-kick Rose Watson. Or Madame Poirot?"

"A woman as a real detective? Maybe *you* should write it," Bernice said. "*You* could be the woman operative."

"I have a better idea," Pyotr Vasilevich said. "Make Effie your detective and call the book *The Case of the Dead Writer*."

Bernice got up abruptly and stubbed out her cigarette.

"I'll look at my painting now," she said to Effie.

Chapter 7

1922

"What else did you enjoy about her stories," Effie said to Sterling when Bernice and Pyotr had left.

"The one from Venice with the dwarf and the masked ball."

"She visits Venice often."

"That figures."

"What else?"

"The one from Buffalo—I imagine it's Buffalo, she disguises places and people—it seems autobiographical. Makes you wonder if the character is suicidal."

"Bernice, herself, has strange moods. Swings from one extreme to the other. One week she's up, the next she's down."

"Wonder what's wrong," Sterling said, "I recognized myself, I am also often blue and think of the relief it would be to end it all."

"But you will not, Sterling," Effie said. "You must be durable and strong. Like your name."

"Yes," Sterling said.

"Now, tell me, do you have a young man?" Effie trained a discerning eye on Sterling.

I did, Sterling thought, but he wasn't young and he wasn't mine.

"No," she said. "No, I don't have a young man at the moment."

"Then we must find you one," Effie said and continued smoothly, "and are you writing?"

"I can't always write every day."

"You must. That's what someone told me. But you must think it all through so that you're ready when you start to write. That's what I do before I start painting. I go for a good long walk."

Sterling nodded. "I walk down to the corner café and sit by myself while I think."

"Someone I know shuts himself off in the country. We all do it differently."

"Pierre Fast-Brown says if I write a page a day, rewritten, corrected, edited, I'll have a book in one year."

"I remember him well. He photographed me once. Said he loved my hair."

"So do I," Sterling said.

"You live alone," Effie stated.

"Yes, I am alone. I was always alone. Remember that when my grandmother died I was sent to the convent in Bourgogne. My real mother was Soeur Madeleine. She is old now."

Effie nodded and lit another Pall Mall. Sterling now saw her through a blue haze.

"Before Soeur Madeleine I had Star," Sterling said. "She was my true friend. She was always there."

"She was your imaginary friend, wasn't she?" Effie's eyes had grown warm. "Is she still with you?"

"She's gone now," Sterling said.

"I, too, had my double. I, too, was lonely and desperately needed a friend to see me through."

"Yes?"

"You'll be all right," Effie said. "It will take courage, though."

"Yes."

"Have you seen Victoria? She married for a title and her Count married for the money."

"I am sorry to say that I have cut myself off from her."

"You have done well. She is poison to you, always was."

"I couldn't avoid her in New York but in Paris I can."

"Quite true," Effie said. "Now tell me, are you comfortable at your hotel?"

"Yes. I finally have the place I need."

Sterling remembered her small room at the convent which had felt secure, where the walls had been close. She remembered her large apartment on Fifth Avenue where she had roamed around alone and had dreamed of being in control of her own fate. Now the time had come.

"I'm working on a novel," she said.

"You must bring me some pages to read."

"I will. One day. In the meantime maybe you would like to read the short story which Auguste Metier is publishing in his French magazine."

"Yes, I imagine you write in French as well as in English. How wonderful for you." Effie said.

"French is my other true language."

"You must show me your poems and I will make the illustrations for the book. You know that I started out doing pen and ink sketches before I turned to oils."

"That would be too, too marvelous," Sterling cried out. "I will bring you're the poems next week."

Effie looked at her affectionately.

"Have you run into that young compatriot of yours, Scott Winteride? He frequents Auguste Metier's bookstore down on the Boul' Mich. and that's where Laura Waverley can be found most days. I keep thinking she is wasting her time at the shop instead of writing her poetry."

"I've met Scott briefly. He was belting out his favorite aria, *O Sole Mio*, and knocked over a flower vase on Laura's desk and soaked all her letters. He takes out armfuls of books and needs a haircut."

"I hear he's become quite thick with Laura," Effie said. "He's a strange one. Don't know if I trust him."

"As always, the situation in a nutshell, darling Effie."

Chapter 8

"Here's the list," Martin Cook said. "She sailed on the French Line *SS Paris* on July 18, 1921, and arrived in Le Havre about five days later."

We were at Fletcher's bookstore waiting for Topsy.

I gawked at the photos Martin handed me of the luxury liner, built in France and launched the year Sterling sailed.

"Look at the Art Nouveau first-class dining room. Bet the haute cuisine was superb. And look at the grand staircase under the curved ceiling."

"Room for five hundred and sixty first-class passengers although they had only two hundred on this voyage," Martin said. "And she was on the list."

"Which name did you recognize?"

"Wainwright Manners III. He was the son of Manners II, of *Universal Publishing*."

"Never heard of them."

"They went out of business in 1933."

"Why do you think this Wainwright had anything to do with Sterling?"

"No reason, but I looked him up. Seems he stayed in France several years getting published here and there in lesser literary reviews in Paris. They could very well have known one another."

"What happened to him?"

"Same as to Sterling. At least that's what I got from the websites. The information about him simply ends at that point."

"Anyone else?"

"No one else," he said. "What have you unearthed?"

"I'm waiting for the college librarian to get me the 1918 yearbook with Sterling's photograph. And to see who her fellow students were. Women were apt to stay friends—witness Topsy and me—and, who knows, maybe some of them traveled with her to France. I need to find some connections to Sterling over there."

"Ah, here's my sweet wife," Martin said as Topsy staggered into the room. "What *are* you toting?"

"Hiya," Topsy said and dropped her backpack on the floor. "I had a brainwave at the library. I brought you some *Bright Set* magazines from 1914 which is the year Sterling would have been eighteen and a debutante. Wouldn't her fatherly friend, Pierre Fast-Brown, have made a big splash for her? And wouldn't that have appeared in *The Bright Set*?"

It took some time going through the society pages of six issues but there it was, in June of 1914.

"She looks thin," I said. "She's dancing with Pierre Fast-Brown. Her back is to the camera, one cannot see her face at all."

"*He* looks happy in all the photographs. Good-looking," Topsy said.

Next to this photo Sterling stood in another with Andrew Blake, editor-in-chief of one of the more prestigious magazines.

"There," Topsy said, "she looks absolutely besotted."

"Still can't make out her features except for a vague profile. But don't let your romantic notions run away with you. He looks old enough to be her father."

"Fine, so she had a father fixation. It's plain to me that she adores him and not in a daughterly way. She's standing very close to him."

I took another look and couldn't discount Topsy's take on the situation.

"Look, Pierre Fast-Brown is dancing with a real knock-out of a girl. *They* look as if they're enjoying themselves. It says here that Victoria Huddersfield, one of the year's most popular debutantes, was the daughter of the railroad king, Cranston Huddersfield."

"Sterling and Victoria must have been friends. It's a long shot that they traveled to Paris together but let me get back to the passenger list," Martin said.

Which is when my cell phone rang.

"Ms. Prescott," the University librarian said. "I looked for the 1918 yearbook and discovered that our yearbook file starts in 1935. No one has ever asked for one."

"Oh, God," I said. "Are you sure?"

"I'm sorry," she said.

"What's the matter?" Topsy said.

"Their yearbook collection starts with the 1935 issue."

"Shoot. I was getting curious to see a real portrait of her, but strictly speaking it's not that important."

"True. The names of her classmates would have been more interesting," I said.

"You wouldn't have found any of them today."

"Of course," I said. "I'll give it up."

While Martin continued to pore over the two hundred some names on the passenger list, I turned on my laptop and googled first Andrew Blake and then the Huddersfields.

Andrew Blake hadn't impressed the world with any achievements except for a prestigious editorship for a few years. Born in Boston in 1871, he was a Harvard man listed in the Social Register. He had married well and had one child.

Cranston Huddersfield, Victoria's father, was a third generation railroad magnate whose ancestors had come over from England in the early 1800s. They were a rowdy lot who went out west, gained control by dubious means of several railroads and ended up with twenty percent of U.S. rails. The money kept rolling in.

At the end of my search I scrolled down some more and found an entry containing, among other names, Victoria, Comtesse d'Auvergne, nee Huddersfield.

"Hey," I shouted, "found her," and Topsy and Martin came to lean over my shoulder and read with me.

"Victoria Huddersfield of New York City (1896-1967), in 1921 married Henri, Le Comte d'Auvergne (1890-1950), two children, Henri (1925-1975) and Marie Louise (1928-2004)."

"It's coming together." Topsy took a spin around the small room.

"And here is Victoria on the *SS Paris* traveling with Sterling." Martin, who is less exuberant than his new wife, nevertheless jumped up from his chair.

Not to be left behind I joined them in the victory round, constricted as it was. Reginald Fletcher stuck his head in through the door to observe the commotion.

"I see you found something," he said. "It always warms my heart."

"Except they're all dead," I said. "I had counted on the second generation. Victoria's son, Henri, died at age fifty just eight years after her. And the daughter, Marie Louise, died several years ago when she was seventy-six. Wonder if Victoria had grandchildren. I must find out."

But Google offered up no additional information.

"Wouldn't the wedding pictures be in *The Bright Set*?" Topsy said. "And wouldn't Sterling have been at the wedding? Maybe there's a better photograph. *Bright Set*, here we come."

And there they were in the November 1921 issue. A radiant Victoria Huddersfield, now the Countess, dancing with her Count Henri. Her father, Cranston, with his own new wife. Her mother, Priscilla, with her third husband. Victoria with her four bridesmaids.

I scoured the captions.

"No Sterling Kirkland Sawyer," I said.

"Maybe they weren't close friends, after all," Topsy said. "What about the other bridesmaids? Two Americans, two French."

I jotted down their names.

"What do we do now?" Topsy said.

"Two things," I said. "Tomorrow I'll be on my way to New York to find this Wainwright Manners III."

"Who will also be dead," Topsy said.

"Hopefully he had offspring."

"Always the optimist. Seems to me you have nothing to go on."

"I'm counting on Mel Kramer and his vast network in the arts."

"You mean the Mel Kramer you had a fling with in Barbados?" Topsy said.

"It wasn't a fling, or mostly not. When we met he was involved with an art gallery owner in Bridgetown and I was dating my perfidious lawyer. The one you introduced to me as the perfect mate. When Mel and I parted he was with a long-legged model in New York and I was involved with my British diplomat, the one whose estranged wife took a shot at me in the proverbial dark alley."

"It wasn't all my fault," Topsy said. "You've always attracted colorful friends."

"So you say."

"And after New York, what?"

"Then on to Paris, I've got a hunch that an old adversary over there might know the d'Auvergnes."

"Don't tell me," Topsy said. "Your very own former mother-in-law the thought of whom still gives you goose bumps. And you're actually planning to suck up to her after everything that happened? Never thought I'd see the day."

"Neither did I."

Chapter 9

"You are looking for a 115-year old woman in France?"

Mel Kramer looked me deep in the eyes and put his hand on my arm which made me shiver as he knew it would. He hadn't changed a bit since Barbados except for the suntan which had faded and a few new gray hairs at the temples. He was dressed in Armani and black loafers without socks. As I remembered, he likes to ease out of his shoes and walk around barefoot. And he was still six foot three which suits me well.

"Actually," I said, "at this moment I'm looking for the descendants of a hundred-and-ten-year old man whose family was in publishing in New York in the 1920s."

"Who were they?"

"His name was Wainwright Manners III, his father was Manners the Second, the company was *Universal Publishing*. Any of this ring a bell?"

"No bells ringing. I own an art gallery, I know nothing about publishing."

"But surely you know someone who does," I said.

Mel signaled to the waiter who brought us another bottle of Pinot Noir. We were at a crowded restaurant around the corner from Mel's art gallery on Bleecker Street. It was hard to keep Mel's attention since people stopped at our table every few minutes and gorgeous women flirted with him right in my face.

"Yes, I think I know someone who does," he said and punched in a number on his cell phone. He leaned back in his chair and looked at me again, hard.

"How've you been, babe," he said just as his phone call connected.

"Uncle Gus," he shouted, "it's me, Mel. Can you hear me? Turn down the TV. Fine, that's better. Yes, I'm good, working hard. Yes, I'll come see you soon. Yes, I know I keep saying that but I promise I will. Soon. Yes, I'm fine. Just working too hard."

Mel winked at me and gazed at the ceiling while he listened to the loud voice at the other end.

"Uncle Gus," he shouted again. "Uncle Gus, listen to me. Yes, I'm still fine. Got a question for you. Remember a publishing firm from the '20s or '30s called *Universal Publishing*?"

Mel listened while the voice at the other end got louder.

I leaned across the table to see if I could catch something but couldn't. I drank some Pinot Noir and waited.

"Who wants to know?" Mel asked Uncle Gus. "Jamie Prescott, the love of my life that's who wants to know. Is she gorgeous? You bet. So what'm I waiting for? Yeah, you may well ask."

Mel looked at me again, hard, and I had another shiver.

"Uncle Gus, I'm waiting for this woman to marry me. I want to spend the rest of my life with her. She's a cut above. Are we compatible? Yeah, we're both commitment-phobic. You say you want to come to the wedding? I'll ask her."

Mel looked at me with a mixture of laughter and seriousness in his dark blue eyes.

"Sure," I said. "But he may have to wait a while."

"Uncle Gus, she said yes, I think. Is she beautiful?"

Mel waited for me to blush.

"Yes, Uncle Gus, she's beautiful. She's tall, she has a black belt in Tae Kwon Do, she's in terrific shape. Her eyes are blue as bluebells, her hair's like a wheat field in summer."

"Enough already," I moaned. "What does he know about the Manners?"

Mel hung up after listening some more to the voice at the other end.

"That was my Uncle Gus," he said.

"No, really. Who was it?"

We laughed and remembered Barbados.

"So, how've you been, babe," Mel said again. He grinned and I shook my head.

"What did Uncle Gus tell you?"

"Let me explain about my Uncle Gus. He's my father's much younger brother, the black sheep of the family, went to sea at eighteen, returned in the late 1950s, wrote a book about his adventures in China, didn't have another book in him and became a typesetter. He was a great gossip, hung around in bars, knew all the reporters and writers. Salt of the earth. He's in a retirement home in Brooklyn. I must go visit him soon."

"And?"

"He remembers hearing about Wainwright Manners the Second, believes that after *Universal Publishing* went bust in New York in about 1933, Manners went to Philadelphia and started a printing press. Went out of business again and that's all Uncle Gus knows."

"And what about Wainwright Manners the Third? Did he know him?"

"As a matter of fact he did. He got quite excited and not in a good way. Said this guy was an s.o.b. Said he'd lived in Paris when he was young and affluent, returned to the U.S. when his father lost his money, but went back to France almost immediately."

"When did Uncle Gus know him?"

"Apparently Wainwright came into some money a short time later. Gus seemed to think he'd married into it. Said the wife's name was Bianca, there was a daughter, Elizabeth, and a son, Paul. Gus thinks Bianca left Wainwright and went West with the children but that the son returned to New York and lived with his father. Wainwright Manners III hung around in New York until the 1970s when Uncle Gus lost track of him."

"The daughter would most likely have married and changed her last name, she will be difficult to trace. But the son is a possibility. He would be Paul Manners, Jr. Or could he be Manners IV?"

"You got me there. But tell me again why you're looking for them. It's really about the 115-year old woman, isn't it?"

"Her name was Sterling Kirkland Sawyer, she was a writer who went to Paris in 1921 and disappeared there around 1930. I'm supposed to discover what happened to her."

I told Mel what I'd found out so far and where I was going next.

"You're going to Paris? And you're getting in touch with your ex-husband? Not that I'm feeling threatened or anything."

"No, not the ex, just the ex-mother-in-law. She's one of those blue-blooded Frenchwomen you never hear anything about and who always wanted me replaced by a blue-blooded Frenchwoman as her daughter-in-law."

"Ouch. Is that what happened?"

"I have no idea. I didn't follow up on Roger's afterlife. And speaking of afterlife, how are you doing with your model? Still together?"

"She comes and goes," Mel said. "Just say the word and she's history. How about you? Seeing anyone?"

"Off and on," I said and Mel laughed.

"I'll wait because you're worth waiting for."

"Thank you," I said. "I've got to get back to my fine hotel."

"You're an extravagant woman," Mel said. Mel who lives in a million-dollar loft on Broome with a sauna and hot tub and monogrammed towels, designer kitchen, Liechtensteins and Rothenburgs on the walls—interspersed with a few Warhols— and an odd Giacometti on tabletops. As opposed to my exotic but modest paintings acquired on the run.

"I'll take you," he said. "We'll have a nightcap. My Mercedes is at curbside."

"Thanks, Mel, I'd better grab a cab, I've got some work to do."

"Fine, we'll do it next time."

We walked to the corner of Spring Street and Broadway where Mel flagged down a taxi for me. Before he opened the door he grabbed me and kissed me hard.

"Think it over," he grinned when he felt my response. "And let me know what you find out."

In the cab I thought about Sterling. I would dearly have loved to read something she'd written. And I thought about what kind of person she might have been, about her life in Paris, who her friends had been, if she had been happy or unhappy, if she had been involved with Andrew Blake, who else had been in her life.

The hotel room sent me, as always, back to my hotel in Paris. Fleur-de-lis upholstery, silk draperies, a Louis XVI bed with satin sheets, and ankle-deep carpets. These are my weaknesses in hotel decor and I'm unapologetic.

I found several columns in the white pages with the last name of Manners. There were twenty with the first name of Paul and of those five had the middle initial W. The W could stand for William but one of them might be Wainwright.

I started calling them just after nine the next morning and my conversations went like this.

"Good morning, is this the residence of Paul Wainwright Manners?"

"Knock it off, Phyllis, what's with the Wainwright, I know it's you and you can kiss my ass."

I dialed the next one.

"Good morning, is this the residence of Paul Wainwright Manners?"

"Who wants to know at this ungodly hour?"

"This is from Dr. Connor's office. You had an appointment this morning at eight."

"No, I didn't, and my middle name isn't Wainwright, it's Witherspoon, so you've got your wrong patient. Good day."

I dialed the third one.

"Good morning, is this the residence of Paul Wainwright Manners?"

"Who wants to know?"

"This is from the Financial Services Corporation."

"I don't take marketing calls and I've listed my phone number accordingly and I don't want your crappy calls."

"But you're Paul Wainwright Manners?"

He hung up the phone.

His address was 1550 East 68th Street and that's where I headed at eleven without the benefit of breakfast.

Chapter 10

1923

Sterling stopped at the bookstalls along the quai, picked up a small volume of Paul Valéry's poems, leaned on the parapet to watch two fishermen on the steps below reel in some small fry, and took a deep breath. She closed her eyes and absorbed the sounds of barges on the river, the rumblings of horse-carts on the road, the faint voices from side-walk cafés.

She came to as two painters set up their easels and shuffled around her feet until she offered her excuses and left them to interpret, yet again, the grand cathedral of the Notre Dame. The gargoyles, hunched above the flying buttresses purporting to stave off evil, looked evil.

Crossing the Avenue des Grands-Augustins, Sterling hurried up the Boulevard St. Michel or, as they all called it, the Boul' Mich. The British poet, Laura Waverley, could be found most days at Auguste Metier's bookshop and publishing house on the right hand side of the boulevard. It sat next to a tailoring establishment and an antiquarian bookstore. For a couple of years now Laura had attracted English-speaking authors to the shop where they congregated without learning much French.

The sign swinging in the breeze from the dark green iron facade read Le Librairie and in the big store front window stood a sampling of reviews and books. There were French and British selections from poetry by Larbaud and Paul Valèry to James Joyce's *Ulysses*, T.S. Eliot's *The Waste Land,* Ezra Pound's *Cathay*, and Laura Waverley's latest collection of poems. There were a few books by American writers from Scott Fitzgerald's *This Side of Paradise*, Roland Lee Rainier's *Strangers in Paris*, a slim volume by Scott Winteride, and the latest book, in a loud red cover, by Bernice Boch.

Inside the bookshop, in front of the fireplace, stood a coffeepot perpetually heating and books were crammed on shelves to the ceiling. The shop, at the moment, was empty of people.

"Laura?"

"Sterling!"

Laura raised her tall angular body from the floor behind her desk and looked around vaguely. Her long unruly hair stood on end and she squinted through her round glasses.

"Lost my pencil," she said, "and found it. How lovely to see you, are you here to buy or are you here to gossip?"

"I'm here to gossip," Sterling said. "Tell me, has Scott Winteride been in today?"

"He should be here about now. Comes in every day like clock-work."

"Is he getting published again? He has quite a nice collection of short stories ready."

"I've read them."

"What do you think?" Sterling said.

"Between you and me?"

"Yes."

"His stories are not ready."

"Have you told him?"

"Yes. He no longer speaks to me."

"He's never angry for long. He'll take your advice."

"Don't think so," Laura said, "and I don't really care."

The bells at the front door chimed and Scott Winteride, in a slouchy felt hat and a long face, walked into the bookshop carrying a handful of envelopes.

"Rats!" he said and waved the envelopes in the air. "Nothing for me at the American Express. Not even rejections."

"I'm on my way to meet with Claire and whoever else turns up," Sterling said. "Will you be coming?"

"Maybe," he said. "Claire is ignoring me."

"Nonsense," Sterling said. "Claire adores you. And you, Laura? You never go anywhere, you must come have some fun."

Laura tried to re-arrange her long woolen sweater without much success. Her face looked pinched, her eyes faded behind her round glasses.

"I do have fun," she said. "But I'll go to Auguste and have it there. We're not the café-going types. He's almost ready for you to proof your story."

"Auguste is publishing you?" Scott said to Sterling. "Do you write in French or did he translate you? And what kind of story is it?"

"I write in French," Sterling said.

"Don't tell me you write childhood memories or, worse, adolescent drivel," Scott said. "Everyone writes those."

"No, I actually do not write about my childhood, or even about myself or about my friends," Sterling said.

"No disrespect meant," Scott said and flashed his tight smile.

"I'll return tomorrow and gossip some more," Sterling said before departing the bookshop followed by Scott and leaving Laura to tidy up her desk and prepare for a quiet evening.

They walked down the boulevard, past the shoemaker and the corset maker, and the upholsterer and the tall buildings hung with wrought-iron balconies, to Place St-Germain-des-Prés.

"You didn't tell me about Spain and the bulls," Sterling said to Scott. "I bet you could have done without the gore and pleasure killing."

"Claire made me travel with her. She danced the Flamenco in her extravagant red dresses. Her father is a bull-fight aficionado. Don't know why she thought it would inspire my writing. I left before the end. Bullfighting is hardly the stuff of fiction."

Chapter 11

1923

The golden medieval tower of the monastic church on the Place St-Germain-des-Prés soared upwards and the bells chimed. The cobblestones stretched across to the Deux Magots from where the conversations drifted to the square amid the clatter of plates and the bustle of waiters in foot-long white aprons balancing their skywards trays.

Claire Garcia-Bonsonwell sat outside at a small table with a glass of Pernod, extravagant in her red silk dress, her black bobbed hair cut closely to her head, a red rose behind her ear, her slim legs in shimmering silver hose. Her cigarette was in a long ebony holder. She paid no attention to the people around her but stared across the plaza until she saw Sterling.

Sterling paused half-way as she came across a tall angular man treading along determinedly on large feet.

"Ben," Sterling exclaimed. "Ben Vogelhut, come join us."

Ben never missed a step, just shook his head and trod on.

"Sterling, old chap, over here!" Claire pointed imperiously to the chair she had been holding and adjusted her red rose. "Let that unsociable being alone, he's on his way to the Flore where no one will disturb him."

"Too bad." Sterling said. "So much more fun here and I wanted to talk to him about my collection of short stories."

Claire turned around and waved at Scott Winteride.

"Find a chair," she said cooly.

"I hear Ben Vogelhut is publishing Sterling's stories," she said to him when he had squeezed in beside her. He parted his thin lips to show a fine row of smallish teeth. His face with its sharp nose was white, the rims of his eyes red. He ordered a whisky, gulped it down, and ordered another.

"It'll be your turn next," Sterling said.

"Ben the Vogel won't touch my stuff. He has something against me." Scott downed another double whisky and his face grew longer.

"I'm sure you're wrong," Sterling said half-heartedly.

Which is when, in a black, billowing dress and a breeze in her hair, up sailed Bernice Boch followed by a sour-faced Pyotr Vasilevich. Bernice laughed her nicotine-stained laugh and coughed.

"Darlings, make room for us," she said. "Hello Scott, why are you looking so flustered, hello Sterling, you're looking swell."

The circle had widened and Scott Winteride got up to add another table. When everyone had been rearranged Pyotr had claimed the chair next to Claire and had his arm on the back of her seat. Bernice looked at him with murder in her eyes.

"Pet," Claire drawled to Pyotr, "Sterling has a question for you."

Pyotr Vasilevich trained his somber Russian eyes on Sterling who wondered not for the first time how he managed to keep his wild hair out of the violin strings.

"What is the question?" he said.

"Yes, what is the question," everyone intoned.

Sterling looked around the table.

"The question is: How do you bring music to life in your writing? How do you describe a Chopin waltz, a

Beethoven symphony or the music Louis Saint prefers to play, without descending into trite generalities?"

"I am not a writer," Pyotr said. "I am a violinist. I cannot describe the music I play."

"But I can, old sport," Scott shouted. "When Saint plays it sounds like tomcats on a fence, scratching on washboards, cascading marbles. It's a cacophony of noise."

"It's the music of the future," Pyotr said.

"Of course, my pet," Claire said.

"It will be easy for readers to visualize tomcats and washboards and cascading marbles. But how to describe a Chopin Etude?" Sterling said.

"Describe it as *triste*, describe it as accursedly depressing," Scott mumbled.

Bernice stood up and raised her arms. Her lips parted, her square teeth glistened, her large face glowed.

"Describe Beethoven's symphonies as thundering flocks of bison on the Russian steppes, as roaring bears charging out of the forest, as a sad and deaf man's tears."

"I told you, describing music is infernally depressing," Scott said.

"Music is not for the eyes, it is for the ears," Pyotr Vasilevich said.

"Fine, I'll give it up," Sterling said. "It was just a thought."

"I'm giving up writing," Bernice said.

"What?" three voices howled.

"I was a sculptor before I moved to Paris."

"Sculptor?"

"She chiseled voluptuous female torsos from enormous chunks of Italian marble." Pyotr squinted crazily. "Self-portraits."

"I was famous in Buffalo," Bernice hissed.

"She is looking for a studio," Pyotr said.

Claire shook her head and Sterling stared at Bernice in disbelief.

"Here comes someone else who should give it up," Scott said. "If it isn't that great writer, Wainwright Manners the Third, himself, in person, and how is it going, Winny, got any stories into the women's magazines?"

Wainwright ignored the comments with some difficulty and tried to insert himself at the table next to Sterling.

"You're not invited," she hissed. "Didn't I tell you to stay away from me."

"It's a free country." Wainwright pushed at the table and accidentally knocked the glass out of Sterling's hand.

Scott stood up impersonating one of Bernice's roaring bears. He pushed at Wainwright until they stood together on the sidewalk.

"You go ahead and apologize to Sterling, you old snob."

"It's not your business, it's between her and me," Wainwright said.

"You insult a friend of mine and you insult me," Scott shouted.

"Go to hell," Wainwright muttered just as Scott's fist made contact with his face. A mighty blow and Wainwright sank to the pavement with a bleeding nose. He righted himself, coughed and wiped his face on his sleeve. He stood awkwardly and swayed in front of the company on the terrace.

"Oh, God," Claire moaned.

"Good show," Pyotr Vasilevich hissed.

"Jeepers," Bernice shouted.

"I'm in for it now," Sterling exclaimed.

"He had it coming," Scott Winteride said as Wainwright shuffled off holding his nose. "I think we're done here, let's push on to the *Bal Musette* on rue Cluny, Sterling enjoys dancing with those sweaty Frenchmen."

"We'll go get Ben Vogelhut," Sterling said.

"The fun has gone out of this," Claire said and stood up suddenly, imperious and exotic, her dark eyes inscrutable. "I'm not joining you, my pets."

"No sweaty Frenchmen for Claire," Scott said. "But you could dance with me."

"No sweaty Americans for me, either," Claire said as she walked out of the café and she wasn't smiling.

Scott stood up and took a few deliberate steps trying to catch up with Claire but she was gone. He left behind on the table a goodly stack of saucers—each denoting payment for a drink—and a goodly amount of francs. The only sign of this consumption was one bloodshot eye.

"Ready?" he said. "Let's go dancing without Claire."

They took the Boulevard St. Germain to the Boul' Mich' to Place Maubert and from there up the hill on Rue Monge. Sterling walked with Scott with Pyotr and Bernice close behind. They stopped at the corner of rue Cluny where Ben Vogelhut lived.

Scott opened the front door and treaded noisily up the stairs to the second floor—past the stinking water closets on the landings—closely followed by the others.

"My gosh," Sterling muttered and held her nose.

"Don't be so bourgeois," Scott muttered but held his breath until his face took on an unusual pink hue.

Scott knocked sharply on the heavy door but no one answered.

"Just as well," he said, "he's not home yet. Didn't feel like seeing him, anyway."

"Don't be mean. Have you seen his apartment?" Sterling said.

"Have not."

"It's small and dark with only one window. The bedroom hardly holds a bed and the toilet is right next to you here on the landing. Don't know how he stands it."

"He should move," Bernice said and coughed long and hard. "Pyotr, you must give him money."

"What? You do it. You're the one with the trust fund."

They clattered down the stairs into fresh air.

At the small dance hall around the corner cigarette smoke and sweat and sour wine breath mingled with live music provided by one musician treating an accordion and shaking a leg with bells attached. A swarthy man sold tokens for each dance.

Bernice danced with a brawny man with a fierce moustache and Pyotr grabbed a blowsy woman waving a handkerchief. A weighty Frenchman swung Sterling about in a breakneck waltz only contained by the tight quarters.

Scott Winteride set course for the bar and hung across the counter drinking and being bored and watching the crowd.

"Here," the Frenchman said and delivered Sterling to Scott.

"I don't think he enjoyed his dance," she said, "I haven't learned to let the man lead."

"Heaven forbid," Bernice said.

"Are you through dancing?" Sterling asked.

"Yes, here at least. We're moving on down to Claire's place for some food and wine. Want to come?"

"Thank you, but no. If I don't get some sleep tonight I can't work in the morning. I'm heading home."

"Now you make me feel guilty," Bernice said.

"But not guilty enough to give up Claire's place," Pyotr said.

"I'm sure nothing could make *you* give up Claire's place," Bernice shouted and they walked off together.

"A frightful pair," Scott said to Sterling. "I'll walk you home. I am nothing if not a gentleman."

"I've read your short stories" she said. "I've learned a lot about you and the way it was back in California, the people you knew, even your family, and I think you loved your mother."

"How would you know," he said. "It's supposed to be fiction."

"Nevertheless, it shines through beautifully."

I chickened out, Sterling thought, the dialogue was wooden and the plot obscure but I can't bear to hurt his feelings.

They cut through on rue Clovis and past the Pantheon where famous men were honored once they were dead.

"Did you know there is only one woman in there," Sterling said as she and Scott went across to rue Sufflot on their way to Boul' Mich. "Her name was Sophie Berthelot and she's there only as homage to her conjugal virtue."

"Meaning?"

"Meaning that she died of sorrow within an hour of her husband Marcellin's death—her only claim to fame—and was buried with him."

"And I'm supposed to do what about that," Scott said.

"Just say that you're surprised that no woman has been worthy in her own right."

"You bet. I guess. And here we are, I've escorted you home and I'll be on my way. So long, kid." Scott bowed over her hand and turned back towards rue Bonaparte. He walked very thin and straight heading for Claire's place.

The street was deserted but as Sterling rang the bell for the concierge at her hotel a movement across the street caught her eye. She turned her head abruptly.

The man disappeared around the corner and Sterling shivered as the massive oak door opened and she slipped inside.

She had recognized Wainwright Manners III even in the dull light from a distant gaslight.

Chapter 12

I had brunch at a crowded deli on Seventh Avenue and waited an hour before calling Paul Wainwright Manners again just so he wouldn't remember my voice. As a further precaution I pitched the tone to an uncomfortable level.

"Mr. Manners? Good morning, my name is Betty Johnson, I'm a free-lance journalist writing a series of articles about New York publishing firms from the early parts of the past century. Our research has brought to our attention that you may be related to the owners of *Universal Publishing*."

"What's your name again?" he said in his querulous voice.

"Betty Johnson, sir," I said respectfully and glanced at my faux business card just to make sure I was who I said I was. It gave my address as Albany, NY, with an innocuous street address which, as far as I knew, probably existed. Martin Cook supplies me with these tools of my trade and I carry cards with a variety of names and professions just to be prepared.

"You're a free-lance journalist?"

"That's right. I am wondering if you could spare me half an hour or so of your time. Are you indeed related to the owners of the publishing firm?"

"Yes, the publisher was my grandfather. Will you put my name in the article?"

"Certainly, and your photograph, too, if you wish," I said and didn't even blush.

I checked to see if I had my digital camera, and I did, and it was fully charged.

"Do you have my address?" he said.

"My researcher had it as 1550 East 68th, is that correct?"

"Yes, I'm in apartment 1008. When will you be here?"

"Would one o'clock be convenient, sir?"

"Fine, I'll see you then, Miss Jones."

"Johnson, my last name is Johnson.'

"Fine, I'll see you then, Miss Johnson."

The apartment building was one of those old posh places with a circular driveway, a revolving door, a doorman, a vast lobby, and two elderly men in green uniforms behind the counter. One of them called up to apartment 1008, got the go-ahead, and pointed me towards the elevators at the back.

Paul Manners was a scrawny little man with a faded blue cardigan over a white shirt topped off with a red polka-dot bow-tie. He had on a pair of baggy gray pants. His cheeks were pinkish as if he had just shaved.

Sometimes I feel that my six feet plus put me at a disadvantage and with a short fellow like Paul Manners I usually look around for a chair to even out the difference in height. He opened the door just enough to let me in, I shook his hand which was loose and clammy, and headed for a sofa in his large living room. There was no sign of a woman in the house but there was a good assortment of bottles on a side table.

"A drink?" he said.

"Thank you, I wouldn't mind some Seltzer," I said.

He poured me some fizzy water and himself a hefty tumbler of Scotch on ice. A drinker.

He pushed towards me a large scrapbook sitting on the glass coffee table.

"Here," he said, "this is all about my grandfather's publishing company. He started it in the 1890s and published all kinds of poets and story-writers."

"Here," he said again and flipped the pages of the scrapbook to a place marked with a yellow stickie. I leaned across and examined a faded book review dated March 1, 1917, which praised *Universal Publishing* for its forward looking author selections.

"That is very impressive," I said. "Was your father also in the publishing business working for your grandfather?"

"Yes, for a while. My father's name was Wainwright Manners III, he was the third in a long line, and I'm the fourth."

I jotted all this down in a professional looking notebook with a spiraled back.

"I imagine your father was born around 1900?"

"Yes, in 1901, as a matter of fact. He was a writer."

Paul Manners flipped some more pages in the scrapbook and showed me a photograph of his father as a young man. Quite thin, in a 1920s tight-fitting suit and a rakish straw boater with a wide striped band. He was pictured at the railing of an ocean liner and I, of course, guessed which one.

"Not sure when this was taken," Paul Manners said, "but my father did go to Paris to write in, I believe, 1921. He had quite a few stories published in magazines over there."

"Very impressive," I said.

"They all deal with an imaginary childhood because he certainly didn't grow up with all the hardships the stories described. Can't imagine where he got those ideas. They said that my grandfather was quite put out and forbade him to use his own name. My grandmother lent him hers instead."

I bent over the scrapbook and read the beginnings of a 1925 story entitled *Hard Times* which described in most Dickensian terms the sad fate of an orphaned child. No discernable influence by anyone famous.

Paul Manners was on his third glass of booze and I speeded up my interview in case his capacity was only three.

"May I?" I said and pulled the scrapbook closer. "Any photographs from your father's time in Paris? Did he know some of the famous writers from the 1920s, he's almost bound to have moved in those circles?"

"I suppose," Manners said without much interest.

There were two pages of faded photographs secured by black corners. Groups of fun-loving blades in tight-fitting suits and boaters, one party of three men and two women on what looked like a houseboat on the Seine, one group of smartly dressed women and two men at a round table on the terrace of what I recognized as the Deux Magots on Place Saint-German-des-Prés.

Paul Manners got up unsteadily and veered his way to what I supposed was his bathroom and I quickly removed the last photograph from its four corners. On the back was written 'Here we are, Scott, Bernice, and yours truly with Sissy and Pyotr. Signed: Winny (that's what they call me here.')

Under normal circumstances I would simply have pocketed the photograph—and please don't read anything sinister into that. Privately I'm a perfectly honest person—but instead I copied down the text, took a good long look at the people in the picture especially at Sissy whose face, unfortunately, was in the shade.

Reluctantly I returned the photograph to the scrapbook and was about to snap a picture of it with my digital camera when Paul Manners returned to his drink. I let the camera drop back in my pocket.

"This was a lovely group of photos, especially the last one," I said. "Your father looks very debonair in his straw hat. I wonder who the two women are, especially the one on the far right."

Manners leaned closer and his breath very nearly asphyxiated me.

"Who?" he said. "Must've been a girlfriend, don't know who she was."

"And there she is again," I said, and pointed to a second photograph.

She was in white gloves and a tight-fitting cloche hat, sitting in a smart-looking black car with tall wheels and wooden spokes. Her face was turned away. She seemed unaware of the photographer.

"Now wouldn't that be a lovely period picture for my article," I said.

"You can't take anything out of the scrapbook," Paul Manners said. He shut the album and pushed it to the middle of the coffee table, away from me.

"I understand," I said. "It was just a thought. So, what happened to your grandfather's publishing house?"

"Went down after the stock market crashed," he said.

"And your father? Did he continue his writing career? Did he by any chance write his memoirs as it seems all the writers from the 1920s did?"

"No, nothing like that. He published one book before he gave up writing, that's all."

"How did he make his living?"

"My father didn't have to make a living," Paul Manners said. "He had his trust fund from my grandmother."

"Was this where he lived?"

"Yes, we've been here since 1935."

I looked around the apartment. There were two large paintings on the back wall and I got up to take a closer look.

"Yes," Paul Manners said without waiting for my question. "Those are famous paintings, heavily insured."

"That's quite amazing," I said. "I imagine your father acquired them in Paris?"

"He did." He looked at me suspiciously. "You are not to mention this in your article or I'll hold you responsible if anything happens to the paintings."

“Oh, I promise,” I said happy to be telling the truth for once today.

We returned to our seats although I was now itching to leave but figured I’d better get back to my alleged subject.

“And you, yourself, sir,” I said, “have you been a writer, too? It would be interesting for my article to follow a third generation in a family involved with books.”

“No, not a writer,” he said. “In banking, involved with ledgers, heh, heh. Retired now. What about the photograph?”

He was slumping where he sat but I took some pictures of him in profile. I showed them to him and he looked pleased.

“Where and when will your article be published?” he said. He was actually holding his four drinks quite well.

“*The Washington Post*,” I fantasized. “Maybe the *San Francisco Chronicle*.”

I gazed at Paul Manners reassuringly.

“Which other publishing houses are you researching?” He got up and poured what would be his fifth drink.

“I’m at the beginning of my research,” I said. “But certainly *Boni and Liveright* and *Lane’s* in London.”

“Let me have your card,” he said when I got up to leave. “And let me know when you’re ready to publish.”

I hoped he wouldn’t notice there was no phone number on my card.

“I’ll be sure to call you soon,” I said.

Chapter 13

My cell phone rang at 11 p.m. that same evening just as I was enjoying a late-night snack of oysters Rockefeller and a superior bottle of Chablis.

"Listen to this," Topsy said without preliminaries. "*The Bright Set* ran a monthly *Paris Diary* for a whole year and a half from 1923 to 1925 under the byline of *CAT*."

"You think this might be Sterling?"

"Lots of French in the articles and lots of gossip about French writers such as Larbaud and Valéry and Americans such as Pierre Fast-Brown, the photographer, and Bernice Boch, the writer. She talks about a Pyotr Vasilevich and a Scott Winteride about whom I know nothing, and a Claire Garcia-Bonsonwell of whom I know even less. I'll try to find out about them. Also about the British poet, Laura Waverley, and Auguste Metier and his bookstore cum publishing house."

"Does the author of this diary write anything about him or herself?"

"No," Topsy said, "that's the frustrating part. The author doesn't come across at all. The writing is quite dry, a bit academic, nothing frivolous. Can't tell if it's a man or a woman."

"Okay."

"I'm perusing the indices of all *The Bright Set* issues from 1917 to 1925 to see who else wrote during that time. So far I've come up with Bernice Boch—who sculpted as well as wrote—Roland Lee Rainier, very amusing, and Auguste Metier, whose articles were entirely in French."

"If you were a member of the bright set French was no problem."

"Exactly. Roland Lee Rainier wrote a couple of novels set in New York and the third was entitled *Strangers in Paris*. Mainly he wrote caustic pieces in the magazines of the day. Very witty but today entirely forgotten. If Sterling was a friend of his he might have mentioned her in one of his pieces."

"I don't know how that will help me," I said.

"The only one who wrote anything near an autobiography was Bernice Boch. After that she took one shot at the mystery genre and called the book *The Woman Operative*."

"An early feminist, maybe?"

"As the title might indicate. Richard Fletcher is trying to find an old copy."

"We're really on a huge fishing expedition," I said. "The only ones who might know if CAT was Sterling and could have old correspondence in their archives would be *The Bright Set* offices. I'm right here in New York, I'll call them tomorrow."

"Fat chance," Topsy said. "*The Bright Set* closed down in the mid-1930s."

"Bummer," I said, taken down several pegs. "That's why it's not on the newsstands."

"You really slay me," Topsy said.

"I know. What are the chances of the old archives having been preserved?"

"I know of someone who's a whiz at research. Her name is Betty and I'm finding her phone number as we speak. Call her and tell her hello from me. In the meantime, I'm scanning CAT's Paris diaries and e-mailing them to you. You might find some clues which have escaped me, four eyes being better than two and all that jazz."

"Have you remembered to water my one surviving plant?" I murmured and swallowed the last shriveled oyster.

"I certainly have and I've picked up your mail, just utility bills—I'll pay them tomorrow—and a slew of catalogs."

Before falling asleep in my satiny hotel bed I googled *The Bright Set*. The magazine was started in 1911 by two literary agents and flourished until 1934 when it went quietly out of business. In its heyday everyone who was anyone clamored to be photographed for the magazine by Pierre Fast-Brown and satirized in its pages by the wits of the day.

I called Betty and told her Topsy Bannister sent me. Instead of offering me her services she suggested I call a colleague of hers, a certain Ms. Puigh who worked in the archives of a publishing firm on Broadway.

The next morning a taxi let me off at Times Square and I walked down Broadway to find Ms. Puigh. I strode in under a low awning, past steel pillars, through revolving doors, and into a grim front lobby. The only light came from the undulating ceiling panels. A couple of colorful murals on the end walls would have helped.

I had called ahead and, pleading my upcoming travel schedule, set up a last-minute meeting with Ms. Puigh in archives. I now called her office and was informed that she would descend to the lobby momentarily.

In the meantime I observed the many types parading past me on their way to and from the elevators. None struck me as writers or journalists, some were obviously photographers but most were business types in suits and an ungodly number of high-powered women were in red.

In contrast, Ms. Puigh was in green hair with a tattoo on her neck, black boots to her knees and a yellow knit dress.

"Hi," she said and shook my hand fiercely.

"Hi," I squeaked, "and thanks for seeing me at such short notice."

"Your question about articles in *The Bright Set* from Paris in 1924 sounded so fascinating that I couldn't wait to meet you. It so happens that I was at the Sorbonne two semesters last year."

"That's where I went twenty years ago," I said feeling suddenly ancient at 42. "Just two semesters."

Just two because I was married to Roger who didn't want his younger wife sitting around at sidewalk cafés drinking café-au-lait or, worse, cheap wine, in the company of young, randy students. So his mother bought us a small château a hundred miles from Paris where I spent a couple of isolated years waiting for Roger to return at night from his public accounting firm on rue du Bac expecting an elaborate meal. Not cooked by me because, as it turned out, I'd never learned to cook and seemed incapable of learning, but by a series of *femmes á tout faire* from the nearby village.

My mother-in-law—the one Topsy refers to as 'the ogre'—would have me for tea with her elegant women friends at her own nearby mansion although when it came to bridge I was entirely incompetent. Had it not been for a compassionate fellow student from my classes at the Sorbonne who sent me huge boxes *poste restante* I wouldn't have read a single English-language book.

I had a small Renault—bought for me by my parents over Roger's protests—but I drove into Paris only twice in those interminable years. The second time I left it at the airport before boarding Pan Am to Washington D.C. When it became clear that I would not be returning Roger sold the Renault and kept the money. We were divorced without any further ado.

"I found the back issues of *The Bright Set* from 1924 and 1925 at the library," Ms. Puigh said as we went out to find a table at a nearby deli. "Correspondence and other papers must have been donated to an institution. If it exists, I'll find it."

"I have no doubt you will," I said.

"The *Paris Diary* pieces by CAT are quite fascinating. The author discusses some of the most wonderful French and American poets, novelists, and painters of the time and CAT must have been on quite intimate terms with them."

"And now the million dollar question," I said. "Who was CAT?"

Ms. Puigh stuffed her mouth and squinted at me. Her green hair had taken on a brighter hue under the fluorescent tubes.

"I was wondering that myself. Couldn't find any real clues but research is my middle name so expect to hear from me," said the green Ms. Puigh whose tattoo I now realized depicted a snake.

"You're looking at my snake," she said. "It gives the wrong impression."

"Really," I said.

"I'm having it removed."

"Good call," I said.

"I'm getting one on my left leg, instead."

"Are you quite sure?"

"Depends on how painful the removal is."

Miss Puigh took in another mouthful.

"Paris is absolute heaven," she said and swallowed hard. "I used to walk around in the footsteps of all the famous expatriates of the 1920s. Gertrude Stein, Hemingway, Ezra Pound, and the like. What an exciting era, you've made me quite anxious to return."

"Call me day or night," I said. "My cell phone should work in Paris but if there's a problem just leave me a message here." I wrote down the phone number of my hotel on the back of the card and said good-bye to Ms. Puigh.

Back at the hotel I called Topsy in Washington and left her a message about my interview with Ms. Puigh after which I organized my notes including the list of names of Victoria Huddersfield's bridesmaids.

Two American and two French. If the two Americans had married French husbands and changed their last names they would be difficult to find. If the two French bridesmaids were from prominent families my chances were better. Of the family friend on rue du Berri I knew nothing, but it seemed like a long shot. There were only so many dead ends I could pursue.

I read CAT's articles sent me by Topsy. They recounted lofty literary gatherings at salons in Paris attended by a host of American and French writers and poets whose names I didn't recognize. There was mention of Thursday dinners at Effie Rousseaus with Claire Garcia-Bonsonwell, Laura Waverley, Auguste Metier, Pyotr Vasilevich, Scott Winteride, and Roland Lee Rainier. CAT gossiped about the small presses—especially Ben Vogelhut's *The Pyramid Press*—which sprang up enthusiastically and disappeared just as quickly for lack of funding.

CAT's last contribution from Paris in *The Bright Set* which appeared after 16 months in the June 1925 issue didn't mention it would be the last, and I had found no clues as to CAT's identity.

At four p.m. I was headed to Newark and Air France.

Chapter 14

1924

"Deuce! I'll beat you yet!" Sterling hollered.

"The hell you will."

Scott Winteride slammed a tennis ball straight across the court.

"Okay, I'll let you win," he shouted.

"No, no, I don't need your pity." Sterling swung her racket in menace over her head. "I'll win fair and square."

"Fine," Scott shouted back. "I'll let you have one more go at it and may the best man win."

He rushed back to the base line and served, hard and precise.

Sterling swung her backhand and sent the ball across Scott's head into the corner.

"My ad," she shouted gleefully.

"Damn lucky shot," he shouted back and served a weak ball.

Sterling waited until it bounced into her racket and delivered a flawless little lob right over the net. Scott stumbled for the ball and missed it by an inch.

"Game!" Sterling squealed and did a triumphant Charleston jig while Scott slammed his racket into the net in mock fury.

"You were lucky," Scott said.

"No, I was damned good!"

"Of course you were," he said.

He suddenly cast off his shirt exposing a good tan and a flat stomach rippling with muscles. His blue eyes reflected the sky and the sun. His thin lips parted and his teeth flashed. He draped the shirt dramatically around his shoulders, flung up his head and launched into *O Sole Mio* which made a couple of staid Frenchmen stop and stare into the court from the street.

Sterling applauded enthusiastically.

"Nice exhibition, old chap," she said when Scott finished his aria, not even out of breath, and put on his shirt. "Where did you learn all that?"

"It so happens that I trained my voice in San Francisco."

"Did you really?"

"I really did. Before I went to war in Europe."

"You never told me you were over here in the war."

Scott scowled at her.

"It's not a subject for bland conversation," he said. "It was a gruesome bloody experience. They died, and I shouldn't have lived instead of them."

"Oh, you mustn't think that for a moment," Sterling cried. "You are so brave and good. You fought for us so that there will never be another war. I know that in my heart."

"No one knows anything," Scott said darkly.

Sterling took his arm and they left the court.

"Re-match tomorrow?" Scott said.

"It's a date," she said.

They sauntered from the tennis courts, crossed the Pont Neuf and strolled down behind the Notre Dame tripping around pecking pigeons, and on to cobblestoned streets where Sycamore trunks changed colors like chameleons, past sand-colored buildings facing the embankment above the dark flat river.

The Pyramid Press was in a cramped room on the ground floor of a tall building and Ben Vogelhut's thin frame filled the entire space. A lock of dark hair fell over one eye, his black mustache barely covered his upper lip, his fingers were black with ink and had deposited a rakish smudge on his cheek.

"Sterling," he said when she edged into the room next to his ancient printing press. "Did you get my message?"

"Yes, I will bring the last pages soon."

"Pages?" Scott said.

"Ten short stories. A limited edition. It will sell through my agent in New York and Auguste Metier will have some for sale," she said.

"You have an agent in New York?"

"Well, more like a friend," Sterling said.

"I bet."

"What's this," Sterling said and picked up a manuscript sitting on the narrow table behind the printing press. "A new author?"

"Just came in," Ben said. "He said he's a friend of yours. Wainwright something something."

"Wainwright Manners III. He's no friend of mine, in fact, he is a great big nuisance and will not stop following me around."

"If you do not wish it I will not publish him," Ben said. "The writing is not that good, anyway, and I have not accepted any monies from him yet."

"Fine. Just don't tell him you discussed this with me."

"You can count on me," Ben said. "And speaking of nuisance, here he comes."

Outside the door there was a scuffle and some shouting before a disheveled Wainwright tumbled in followed by Scott Winteride.

"Are you publishing this bum?" Scott shouted and grabbed the manuscript out of Ben Vogelhut's hand. "Is this it? Here, take it back, you won't be published here or anywhere else if I can help it."

Wainwright Manners III stared first at Ben Vogelhut who turned away, then at Scott Winteride who glowered at him, and then at Sterling who said nothing but could not turn away in the small space.

"You will all be sorry," Wainwright screamed. "And you in particular, Sterling Kirkland Sawyer, you will be very sorry."

Chapter 15

1924

"Here," said Effie Rousseau to Céline, her newly acquired bumbling servant, "the *jus* needs heating."

Effie sat at the head of the table with Pyotr Vasilevich on her left and Bernice Boch at the lower end.

"Alex," Effie leaned towards Alexandre Orgoloff who was seated on her right, her smile particularly bright, her eyes ashine. "You haven't come to see me in too long a time. It's good to have you here, *mon ami*."

"And it's good to be here, *ma chére* Effie," he answered back in his strong Polish accent and they beamed at one another in exclusion of all others around the table.

"Are you still in your Surréaliste phase?"

"It is not a 'phase', my dear."

"Very well. I shall come around and choose something."

"What a delightful thought. I am well pleased with your portrait of me. No one does it as well as you do."

"High praise, indeed," Effice said.

"Alex has gone bourgeois," Bernice said to Sterling who sat in her pencil-slim black crêpe de chine Chanel dress, long, narrow sleeves reaching below her wrists—discreetly perfumed in Coco's divine No.5—next to Orgoloff. "He has an apartment on rue du Colisée and gets driven around by a chauffeur."

Bernice had an uncanny talent for carrying on her own conversation while listening in on at least two others and giving her sly comments. This evening she was in an up-beat mood, her eyes glistened and so did her large teeth.

"Is it such a bad thing to have an apartment on rue du Colisée and be driven around by a chauffeur?" Sterling said to Orgoloff. "It means you're successful and why should you live in a garret and walk everywhere?"

Orgoloff half turned to Sterling and slid his arm along the back of her chair.

"*Exactement*," he said. "And I don't know how to drive."

Sterling laughed and Alex Orgoloff looked pleased with himself.

"Are you successful, too?" he said. "You must be doing something important to be in this exalted company. Are you a writer?"

"Yes," Sterling said. "I'm a writer."

His face was sharp-edged, his cheekbones sculptured, his lips thin. His best features were his large luminous eyes—hazel with green specks—and his long serpentine fingers. His reddish hair, swept back, curled around the nape of his neck. He was dressed in expensive style. He took in her blue eyes and the perfect oval of her face framed in a whirl of blond hair.

"Ah, yes," he said.

His intense glance didn't stop at her face but dropped to her throat, to her breasts, and to the slim hands resting in her lap. He moved his hand from the back of her chair to her bare shoulder. His fingers felt alive. He looked at her face again and she knew he sensed the tremor that went down her spine at his touch.

Sterling leaned back in her chair and closed her eyes briefly. When she opened them the arm along the back of her chair had been withdrawn and across the table she caught the eyes of the tall guest who had come to the dinner with the pianist, Louis Saint, and was seated next to him.

Stefan Oxenkranz was tall even sitting down, with broad shoulders and a face like a Nordic god: deep-blue eyes, a high forehead, golden hair, a perfectly straight nose, and full lips.

His smile said that he knew how Orgoloff's touch had affected her. He observed her face with such intensity that Sterling felt her spine tingle in exactly the same way. Well, not exactly, she thought, because Stefan seemed familiar and safe although she didn't know him. Alexandre Orgoloff felt exotic and spelled danger.

Sterling reached for her wineglass just as Orgoloff upset his. Amid exclamations of dismay and a great deal of mopping up with large napkins Orgoloff shouted for the salt cellar. When he had it in hand he dipped two fingers into it and threw the salt over his shoulder. Not once, but twice.

Sterling looked across the table to the handsome man who was laughing and pretending that he, too, was throwing salt over his shoulder. He shook his head and rolled his eyes. Superstition was ridiculous—and so was Orgoloff—was his message to Sterling.

The salt having prevented bad luck, Orgoloff turned to Effie and Sterling turned to Roland Lee Rainier.

"Pierre Fast-Brown sends his great love and affection," Roland said. "I think he looks at you as the daughter he never had."

"He's a darling man," Sterling said.

"You have become an insider in the literary community here in an amazingly short time. But Pierre tells me you won't reveal to him where you live. Getting your mail at the American Express? I do think it hurts his feelings. Maybe you should reconsider?"

Roland's front teeth protruded charmingly and his pink cheeks glowed.

"I will," Sterling said. "I'm getting over it, some silly adolescent notion of wanting to be free and anonymous. I'm at the best little hotel on rue Jacob."

"I know it well. You are in good company there and around the corner on rue Bonaparte. I'll come visit."

"Oh, do, Roland, darling, have lunch with me tomorrow and tell me about your next novel. You know that you're my favorite novelist in the whole world and how I adored *Strangers in Paris*. You caught the spirit of Paris too, too perfectly."

Although, she thought, I find the main character to be a thoroughly exasperating chap, the way he can't make up his mind about anything. I would have done it differently, she thought and, suddenly, she wanted to escape the dinner party and hurry home to her writing machine.

"Tell me, now, are you writing your own great novel?" Roland peered at Sterling and sputtered endearingly. "Are you pushing yourself without getting distracted? You must write no less than three hundred words every single day even if you had a spurt of two thousand the day before. Discipline, my dear, discipline is the answer."

"Yes. In the meantime I'm having some short stories printed by Ben Vogelhut at his *Pyramid Press*."

"My dear, Pierre told me. Congratulations," Roland said. "And Ilana sends her love. My dear wife applies her discipline to her music."

"I had looked forward to seeing her," Sterling said.

"Then you must visit us in New York, our salon there is almost as amusing as Effie's in Paris. You'd enjoy yourself."

"What about your own discipline, dear Roland. When do you get any work done?"

"I write in the mornings, go about in the afternoons, and party at night. A swell life."

"Indeed."

Roland sputtered, a lock of hair fell over his forehead, and Sterling caught an amused glint in the eyes of the tall man across the table. She took note of his high color and admirably broad shoulders. He'll run to fat for sure in another ten years, she thought. He had arrived late to the dinner and had barely been introduced around before Effie called the guests to the table. Through the vol-au-vent and the bouillabaisse his eyes had been on Sterling who—as she told herself—was the only young eligible woman in the room.

She looked away from the tall man and spoke under her breath to Roland.

"Dear Roland," she said, "tell me about the mysterious guest."

Roland twisted around to get his lips in sync with her ear. Sterling shot a glance across the table but the guest was talking to the pianist, Louis Saint, who was at a certain disadvantage since he spoke rusty English and was seated next to Bernice Boch whose French was mostly non-existent.

"He's a noble fellow," Roland whispered, "landed gentry with a fearfully grand Schloss in Switzerland. Educated, I do believe, at Eton and Oxford—Balliol, no less—and at the Sorbonne but declines to manage his estate in person even though he travels regularly to Switzerland."

As if he sensed they were talking about him Stefan Oxenkranz abandoned Louis Saint and leaned across the table towards Sterling. He looked at her quite seriously.

"Louis has just told me all about you," he said.

"Or as much as he knows," Sterling said. "Which isn't all that much."

"Then I have a lot to learn. Would you let me?"

His voice was low, his face flushed.

Sterling looked down, then up, and met his gaze.

"Maybe," she said.

"Roland," Effie said, "talk to me." She had eaten sparingly except for the creamed asparagus tips, sweet peas, and the potatoes purée.

"My dearest Effie," Roland said, "as usual your food exceeds all expectations."

"It will never be quite as wonderful as what Bernice serves," Effie said. "I'm encouraging her to write a cookbook, it would be a great success."

"Yes, dear Madame Boch, you should," Roland said.

"Oh, no," Pyotr Vasilevich said, "she has time only for her sculptures but none for me and certainly not for another book."

Bernice Boch glowered at him but held her tongue. He would get the lashing later.

"He is enormously possessive and jealous of everything she does," Sterling whispered to Roland.

"I wouldn't worry, she looks as if she can throw a good punch."

Roland Lee Rainier let out a high-pitched squeal and turned his attention obediently to Effie while Sterling turned hers to Louis Saint. Louis adjusted his pince-nez which, as always, cut into the bridge of his florid nose. His face was wide, his cheeks drooped, his black suit with its bulky shoulders was out of shape and, not for the first time when contemplating him, Sterling had a vision of Van Gogh's potato eaters. Feeling simultaneously guilty and kindly, she leaned across the table and spoke to him in French and he, as always, responded in a mocking tone of voice.

After the *Péche Flambées,* Orgoloff took possession of Sterling and led her around the room to point out Effie's paintings, both her own and those she had acquired.

Chapter 16

1924

"Here's the first painting of mine Effie ever bought," Orgoloff said and stared closely at the two figures in the frame. "What do you think?"

He stood back a few paces and stared fixedly at the painting.

"*C'est ça.* This way I see it anew," he said. "I haven't been here for a while. It now looks unfamiliar in a familiar way."

"I think I understand," Sterling said. "I, too, put aside my writing for a while and see it better when I read it anew."

Orgoloff moved to stand close behind her.

"Look over here," he said. "These are my true paintings."

They were lovely, his pictures, and eccentric, entirely different from any she had ever seen. Strange objects floated on seas of blue, disconnected, unreal. There were thin bodies in flowing veils, birds with strange wings, fish with huge eyes, a starfish in the corner.

"My mascot," Orgoloff said. He pointed a slender finger at the starfish.

"Oh," she said and turned her head to find his face quite close. "Is that a dream sequence?"

"It is more than that, it is my vision of life and an image of the universe. What do you think?"

"*Trés surréaliste*," she said.

He pulled her closer and took her hand.

They were interrupted by some decidedly atonal music from the upright piano where Louis Saint sat on the bench with Pyotr Vasilevich, squinting madly, standing at his side, his red hair diving towards the strings of his violin.

"Practice for your concert," Effie said, her titian hair equally on end, while a dark nicotine laugh peeled out derisively from Bernice.

Louis Saint adjusted his pince-nez, yelped like a mad hyena, and went at the keys while Pyotr tore at the strings of his violin. The result was something very much like cascading marbles and scratching on a thousand washboards. Louis stomped his feet and Pyotr swirled around and they concluded their number with a bang and a flourish.

"Louis, *mon chér ami.* A worthy piece for your first concert with Pyotr," Alexandre Orgoloff said.

"We will hear xylophones and sirens and a mournful tuba. Probably ragtime and vaudeville."

"Louis is a genius," Orgoloff whispered to Sterling. "And to think he practices at a café piano fortified by beer and Calvados."

"I had no idea."

"Louis's playing of the new composers is akin to my paintings. We both wish to discard romanticism and impressionism," Orgoloff said.

"He's given to the absurd, the *chér* Louis Saint," Roland Lee Rainier said. "And Pyotr Vasilevich no less so."

"I'm speechless," Sterling said.

"Pen and paper," Orgoloff said and found some on top of the piano. While Louis Saint continued to play, he sketched him from the back, sitting at the piano, head bent, ears sticking out like trumpets. Then he looked at Sterling and, with a few swift strokes, sketched her slender figure into the corner—with pearls and a cigarette in its jade holder—and presented her with the drawing.

He put his arm around her shoulder.

"I want to paint you. You have the body I've been looking for, so slim, so American," he said and turned her towards him. "Will you come around to my studio tomorrow?"

"You be very careful, my dear." Roland suddenly stood between them. "Orgoloff has an eye for his models."

"And Orgoloff can't be trusted," Bernnice said from across the room.

Orgoloff tried to stare Roland down.

"I'll bring Sterling myself and stay while you paint her," Roland said. "Or maybe I should send Effie."

"No, no," Orgoloff shouted, "then I don't want her to come at all."

"Why do I feel as if I'm not in the room," Sterling said. "I don't mind sitting for a portrait and I don't need you two to defend my womanhood, much as I love you."

Roland looked like thunder.

"Tell me, Orgoloff, where is your wife?" he said.

"She's visiting with her family in Poland. But it is of no consequence if she's here or not. She does not interfere. And I do not have to ravish my models."

"No, you seduce them with those hypnotic eyes of yours," Roland hissed.

They stared at one another with loathing and seemed to have forgotten all about Sterling.

"Looks as if the evening is winding down," Stefan Oxenkranz said to Sterling. "May I take you home?"

"No," Orgoloff said, "she's leaving with me. My chauffeur is waiting outside."

Stefan Oxenkranz, in blond power, loomed a head above Orgoloff whose slighter frame now grew square. He looked as if his head was about to butt into the taller man's chest.

"This is not a bullfight," Effie said and looked stern. "And Sterling is not a trophy."

"As flattering as all this is—and I would go with either one of you," Sterling said, "the fact is that I have my own motor waiting around the corner."

"Then *I'll* ride with you," Stefan said, "and Orgoloff here will ride with his chauffeur. How is that, *mon ami*?"

Orgoloff scowled at Stefan but got the last word.

"Until tomorrow, then, come at eleven," he said to Sterling.

He glared in fury at their backs as Stefan grasped Sterling's hand and led her towards the door, past Bernice who smiled wickedly, past Effie who embraced Sterling and whispered in her ear, past Louis Saint who was collecting his black bowler hat, past Roland Lee Rainier who frowned with downcast eyes, and past Alexandre Orgoloff who smiled wickedly.

"Quick, quick," Stefan said and put his arm around Sterling to get her out the door, down the marble stairs, and into the street.

"You are not going to his studio, I trust," Stefan said.

"Oh, I think not."

They ran hand in hand around the corner to the Quadrilette. Before they entered the car Stefan cupped her face with his warm hands and brushed her lips lightly with his.

"You are going a little fast," Sterling whispered but she didn't move away.

Chapter 17

At Charles de Gaulle I stood in line an age to have my passport stamped, still feeling cramped from the agonizing experience of an economy class seat. Barely an inch wider than my hips the seat had been a veritable straight-jacket. My six feet and then some are mostly located in my legs and I need more knee room than the average person. Marjorie Robinson had booked the ticket and, although I tried, the airline wouldn't upgrade me. The ticket was that cheap. So I went.

A taxi took me straight to the most luxurious hotel in town because there was no way in the proverbial hot place I would meet anywhere else with Mme Simone Croissier, my erstwhile mother-in-law.

As it happened, when I called her she told me to come to her apartment on Boulevard Haussman but at least she knew where I was staying. Yes, very childish of me, I know, but then I was only twenty when I first knew her—and twenty-two when I stopped knowing her—and just the thought of seeing her face-to-face after twenty years had sent me into a familiar *crise de nerfs*.

The apartment took up the entire third floor of the honey-colored 19th Century building. One look at the ancient elevator had me sprinting up the wide marble staircase to the door. A butler in black delivered me to a maid in white cap and apron who deposited me in a gorgeous salon just shy of a similar one at Versailles, all blue and silver with ancestors in gilded frames and intricate tapestries on the walls.

She was as tall as I remembered her, tall for a Frenchwoman, just an inch or so shorter than me which put her at five eleven. As elegant as ever in a string of pearls hanging on her little black dress, the kind only Chanel makes—and, for all I knew, it was the same dress she wore twenty years ago. I remembered her as moneyed but disturbingly frugal, blue-blooded because her father had been a Count but plain Madame because her husband had been a plain Monsieur albeit rich as Croesus.

I had learned when I called her from Washington that she had been widowed five years ago at age sixty. We hadn't mentioned Roger and I had told her only that I would be in Paris and wanted to see her for old times' sake. She had been pleasantly surprised, she said, to hear from me after all these years and to please let her know when I arrived. When I told her where I would be staying she said 'bièn sûr,' as if there was no other hotel.

I used to call her *Maman* and she would call me *ma petite fille* but I had set the new tone by addressing her as Simone and she had followed suit by saying *ma chère Shamie.* Oh, well.

Her hair was artfully tinted and beautifully cut to frame her youthful face not much different from how I remembered her. High brow, cold eyes, tight lips. Severe when she stared in judgment but astonishingly vivacious when she smiled in approval.

That's how she smiled at me now and looked me straight in the eye as she would a dear friend though not a near relative. She hooked her arm through mine and led me—this time not to the slaughter—but to a table laid with tea for two. She poured, she offered me a paper-thin sandwich, she took a tiny sip from her cup and leaned towards me.

"Now tell me all your news," she said. "*En Français.*"

I filled her in on my education—a Master's in Criminal Justice—which produced a polite little gasp; my work as a private investigator followed by a stint as the owner of a travel agency, which produced an inquisitive frown; and my present assignment to find Sterling Kirkland Sawyer.

"You are an *agent policial*," Simone concluded.

"Private," I said and could feel my confidence slip. "Private investigator."

"*Bièn sûr*," Simone said and frowned. "I remember Roger told me some time ago."

"Roger?" I said. I had hoped to avoid his name until later in our conversation but here it was. "How did he know?"

"*Ma chére fille*, don't you know how sad he was to lose you, so sad that he married someone who looked quite like you. You were so beautiful and you are beautiful today. Age has even improved you."

"Well, thank you," I said.

Is he still married, does he have children, I thought, but didn't ask.

Simone sipped her tea and I ploughed ahead.

"The woman I'm looking for disappeared in Paris around 1930 when she was thirty-four or thirty-five years old. Her closest friend was another American heiress, Victoria Huddersfield, who in 1921 married a Count d'Auvergne, had a son named Henri who died in 1975 and a daughter Marie-Louise who died in 2004. If the daughter married I don't know her married name nor if she had children. I was hoping you could help me."

Simone put down her tea-cup on the table a bit harder than I would have dared jeopardize the dainty Limoges. She pressed two fingers to her lips.

"*Ma chére fille*," she said, "Henri d'Auvergne. I knew the dear man a long time ago when I was myself a *jeune fille*.

He did not approve of my marrying a commoner and we never afterwards moved in the same circles."

"Was he married," I said and scooted to the edge of my chair. "And did he have children who might be alive today?"

"*Mais non*, I believe he did not marry."

"And his sister, Marie-Louise, did she marry?"

"*Alors*, I did not follow the family at all, at all, and I cannot tell you."

"Is there any way you could find out?"

"*Mais bién sûr*," Simone said.

"And you will let me know?"

"But, of course, of course."

I took out my list of Victoria Huddersfield's bridesmaids. There were two French names: Robillard and Vasseur.

"These were bridesmaids at the Countess d'Auvergne's wedding," I said. "Do you by any chance recognize any of the names?"

Simone brought out a pair of bi-focals, placed them half-way down her exquisite nose, and read the names out loud.

"Let me think."

She closed her eyes and, again, I moved forward in my chair eager to catch her thoughts.

"There was a jeune fille Nicole Robillard," she said at last. "I think she married a Manon-Vasseur."

"Did they have children? If they were born in the mid-1920s or even the 1930s they may still be alive. Their last names might be either Manon-Vasseur or Robillard-Vasseur."

"Indeed." Simone furrowed her brow.

"Knowing where they lived would make the search easier. Do you know where?" I said.

"The Manon-Vasseurs lived in Provence if my memory serves me right. I must ask Roger."

No, I wanted to shout, do not ask Roger but immediately calmed down by saying to myself this does not mean personal contact with Roger.

After a few more minutes of polite conversation we took gracious leave of one another. I thanked her in advance for her most certainly valuable help and let myself be shown out by the butler. Once down on Boulevard Haussman I sighed a sigh of relief and felt perspiration gather between my shoulder blades.

I walked back to my hotel and googled the Manon-Vasseurs, the Robillards, the Robillard-Vasseurs, and any other combination I could think of without success. I gave it up for the moment.

My e-mail contained an exhortation from Marjorie Robinson to keep her updated which I did, and a few lines from Jon Douglas saying he missed me in Barcelona. I told him back that I missed him, too, and felt a slight twinge of remorse that I was in Paris without telling him. Mel Kramer sent me a message signed "Uncle Gus," and I gave him an actual update on my meeting with the ex-mother-in-law.

Then, as a treat, I spent the rest of the afternoon asleep to get over my jet lag and by five in the morning I was involved with a *café crème* and a buttered croissant when Ms. Puigh of the green hair and the snake tattoo called from New York.

"Papers from the defunct *Bright Set* were transferred to a university in upstate New York in the 1950s," she said with a note of triumph in her voice.

"And?" I said.

"And I have permission to go through the material."

"When?"

"Right now, today, this afternoon, I'm on my way as we speak."

"You're a peach," I said with feeling.

"It's my very pleasure," said Ms. Puigh.

Chapter 18

1925

"No, Claire, I'm not letting you paint my wall black with silver stripes."

Sterling stood at the tall window of her new apartment on the quai des Grands-Agustins and looked towards the river. Three low-slung barges chugging down the waterway roiled gently in the wake of a faster-moving *bateau-mouche*.

"Darling, it's only one little wall but red and gold is just as fine, in fact, darling, too too divine. And you did throw in the black coffee table and the Modigliani. We must get back to the Exposition at the Grand Palais to get new ideas. I know, I know, you cling to your outmoded Art Nouveaux but I wish to educate you most frightfully."

"But I love the flowing lines of the Beardsleys and the Gibsons, can't get used to the geometric stark lines of the likes of Corbusier, it all seems so grim."

"Move with the times, darling, move with the times, be *moderne*," Claire said. "Nevertheless, just look at your Lalique glassware and your Cartier lapel watch. Your Stefan has taste and money and I notice you wear the watch constantly, my pet."

Sterling touched her diamond-studded pendant and traced the quadrant-shaped watch at the end of it.

"Stefan is eager to give me gifts but except for the watch he has no feeling for what suits me and what I really like."

Claire eyed her carefully from across the room.

"To get what I like I must buy my own gifts. Here," Sterling said and held out her slim silver cigarette case. "Now, this design speaks to me. Stylized red florals on black lacquer."

Claire extricated a slim Dunhill cigarette from the case and stuffed it into a jade holder. Sterling lit up for them both with a matching lighter.

"This I adore," Sterling said, blew a thin stream of smoke towards the ceiling and pointed to a small statue.

"It's you, my pet," Claire said. "Divine, divine. Seems Stefan has some taste after all."

Sterling moved the small malachite base in a circle so they could admire the bronze and ivory Charleston dancer perched on top.

"Just like you at one of my wild parties," Claire said. "Look at her long legs, cute bubs, elegant arms and lacquered fingernails, the bandeau, the aristocratic nose. It's perfectly you."

"I love it," Sterling said.

"And do you love Stefan?"

"Of course." Sterling lowered her eyes.

"In your own way, you mean."

"No, no, I do, he's an awfully swell chap."

Claire removed the red rose from behind her ear.

"You love someone else better," she stated and Sterling looked startled. "It's all right, pet, you can love two men at the same time. I do, frequently."

"How did you know?"

"It's clear enough, pet, you keep yourself aloof from all men, as if you're waiting for someone. But he's not coming, is he?"

"No, he is not coming. Ever. And he's exceedingly sorry. Exceedingly."

"Is he terribly married?"

"He is married but she's not terrible. In fact, she's always tried to be like a mother to me."

"So, he's old enough to be your father? Darling, you must get over him. You need someone your own age. Someone single. Someone just like Stefan."

Sterling sat down abruptly, her shoulders shook violently, she covered her face and wept into her hands.

"I loved him so miserably," she sobbed, "and he said he loved me and then the unthinkable happened and he said I'd have to get rid of it or it would ruin his career, it would ruin his reputation, and it would ruin his marriage. He said he would arrange everything at the best clinic and I went there and I died along with the baby. He said it wasn't even a baby yet so not to worry. But I died. It was a mortal sin. I will burn in hell. I am already burning in hell. I cannot go to confession. My God has forsaken me and now I can't love anyone ever again."

"The selfish bastard," Claire said. "Don't despair. You've just confessed to me, and I absolve you. You were forced. You had no choice."

"Oh, darling Claire, that is not how it works."

"That is how it ought to work. You are most sincerely and utterly repentant, are you not?"

"Yes, dear Claire."

Sterling sat up and dried her eyes.

"If only my mother hadn't died. She would have been there for me," she said.

"Oh, my pet, not necessarily. Look at mine. She constantly belittles me, always has, always will."

"But if my mother hadn't died so young my father would not have sent me away to Boston, he would not have married, in the end, someone not much older than me, he would not have died a horrible death in the icy waters of the Atlantic Ocean."

"Would have, could have, should have," Claire snorted and stuffed a fresh cigarette roughly into the jade holder. "At least you had a loving grandmother and an aunt in Boston. But consider what happened to me. My mother had never wanted a child, it interfered with her acting career. My father returned to Spain after he finished his medical studies in London. I was five and since then I've been shuttling back and forth to Madrid. That's where I learned to dance."

"You're fond of your father, I know," Sterling said.

"My Papa has always been good to me. He re-married, retired from medicine and is training horses on his country estate. My mother is a different story."

Sterling couldn't help laughing. In London Claire had introduced her to her mother, an extravagantly dramatic actress, and to her mother's lover, a writer. Sterling hadn't liked either one of them. Claire's mother had cast a cold eye on them dressed as they were—by Claire's design—at their most outrageous in culottes and berets, butterfly lips, and eyes shadowed in black. She hadn't spared her disparaging remarks about Spain in general and Claire's Flamenco dancing in particular. Claire and Sterling had fled London the next day.

"You make my life sound idyllic. No wonder I love you to pieces," Sterling said.

Claire went to the fireplace and stared several moments at the oil painting above the mantel.

"How's Alexandre Orgoloff," she said and inhaled on the Dunhill.

"What do you mean?"

"Darling, you know what I mean. People are talking."

"People are talking?" Sterling looked pale in the light of the bright sun. "What are they saying?"

"They're saying that Maître Orgoloff has a new mistress."

"But are they saying my name?"

"No, my pet, they're not whispering your name—yet—at the Deux Magots or the Rotonde or the Select, not even at the Closerie des Lilas. And if they were talking about me, I wouldn't care, my reputation is long gone but you are not me. You still have your fine aura of innocense about you."

"Thank you, Claire, and that is how it will remain."

Sterling stood up and Claire gave her a hug. They looked at each other and began to laugh, tentatively at first, then in great heaving guffaws.

"Oh, gosh," Sterling croaked at last.

She went back to gaze out the window at another barge on the Seine while Claire re-wound her silver turban.

"Here, darling," she said. "I brought you this house-warming gift. It's a Derain, don't you love his bold colors, it'll go so well with your reds."

"Claire! Thanks most awfully," Sterling said and held the painting up against the wall. "I'm mad about it."

"And now I must push off." Claire flung a red, fringed shawl around her shoulders and re-arranged the red rose behind her ear. "Scott Winteride and I are going to the country tomorrow, I love our long walks and he loves to get away from the little writing he does."

Sterling thought of the country, of the quiet, of the hearty food, of Scott and how she hoped Claire wouldn't hurt him too badly when she rejected him which she would soon, inevitably, for someone more stimulating.

She hung the Derain above the fireplace and moved the Orgoloff to the dining room. She went to the extra bedroom where she kept her desk and her Luis Vuitton trunk. She pulled open the flat lid, quilted inside, placed the manuscript she had been working on in the tray and turned the key in the brass lock.

Then she hurried out the front door, took the slow elevator down, started up the *Quadrilette* and swung down the Boulevard Saint-Michel towards the *Closerie des Lilas.*

Chapter 19

1925

She parked in view of Marshal Ney who stood untiringly in his little patch of garden, in his fine brass uniform, brandishing his sword. The chestnut trees were no longer in bloom and the lilacs which had earlier perfumed the air were gone. The air was humid after a recent drizzle. Only one person sat outside the Closerie des Lilas and did not look up when she approached his table. Scott Winteride had his head down, his eyes half closed, his hands cupped around his whisky glass.

"Scott?"

"Ah, there you are, thought you'd stood me up."

Scott stretched his arms over his head and grimaced.

"I'll have a café crème and a brioche," Sterling said and offered him a Dunhill from her black laquered case.

"Very rich," he said. "So what's new at the quai des Grands-Augustins? I hear you are throwing your money around on swell furniture and Orgoloff paintings and going to fancy parties with your new beau."

"So you heard that I've moved? I had to. They changed the name of my hotel so I just couldn't stay."

"Really?"

"No, not really. But it was time. I needed more room," she said, down-playing the fact that she was not renting but had actually bought her apartment.

"I'll come around to your new place," he said.

"Splendid," Sterling said. "And another thing. I've heard rumors about Bernice Boch's new novel."

"I thought she had abandoned writing for sculpting?"

"The novel was finished before she switched horses."

Scott shouted for another whisky and tossed it down as soon as it was served. His face was flushed, something that didn't happen often.

"And what are they saying? Is it good?"

"I hear it's brilliant."

"What?" Scott leaned towards her and tilted his head as if to hear her better.

"That's what I hear."

"What's it about?" Scott's eyes were half closed.

"The person I'm quoting says that the main character, who's also the narrator, is called Pietro Vecino, that he is a horrible womanizer and ends up fatally ill from some mysterious disease."

"Unbelievable twaddle."

"Pietro, Pyotr," Sterling mused. "Without even reading the book I hear echoes of a very troubled marriage. And that's not all. I gather the many insider jokes will delight everyone who's not being skewered. Effie, for one, is furious."

"What did Bernice do to her. In the book, I mean."

"Seems a certain Eloise cum Effie steals the husband from the wife," Sterling said.

"Does she give this Pietro the disease?"

"Apparently."

"Doesn't sound like Effie. More like Claire."

"Now who's being cruel?" Sterling said and wondered if he'd already been replaced in Claire's affections.

"Did your source say that you're in the book?" Scott had slipped way down in his chair.

"Well, he insisted that I *am* in it although in a kindly manner. Apparently my eyes open up wide when I smile and that's in the book. Do my eyes do that?"

Scott looked at her, his expression softened and he laughed.

"I guess. Should make you proud. Am I in it?"

"Hard to say but a lot of people will surely see themselves whether it's true or not."

"Good. Then everyone will be upset."

Scott ordered another whisky.

"Speaking of novels," Sterling said. "What did you think of Roland Lee Rainier's *Strangers in Paris*?"

"Don't know," Scott said. "Some will say the main character is effete and some scenes are vulgar."

"That may well be true," Sterling said and felt a rush of compassion for this Scott who could not finish even his short stories and was no longer talking about his novel.

Scott stared across the naked lilac bushes at Marshal Ney, leaned back and emptied his glass.

"How about you?" Scott said. "When do I get to see *your* novel?"

"I've come to a decision. I'm going to start over or, rather, I'm going to write a different novel, a more immediate story in the first person. First person will suit me better. And I must be ever conscious of using my imagination to change the memory so that the memory becomes something quite unique. That is my intent."

Scott took a good look at her.

"Don't take after me," he said. "Don't dither too long. Get it out of your system if you have a compulsion. Then re-write. Then it will be good."

He got up, raised his arms high above his head and looked as if he considered a display of his favorite aria but thought better of it. He sat down.

"Do you have a title for your book yet?" he said.

"Not yet. Any ideas?"

"I take my titles out of thin air," he said.

"Sounds like a typical Ben Vogelhut idea."

"I don't need any ideas from his degenerate tiny mind."

They sat quietly observing the tables fill up when Scott suddenly bent down under the table to tie his shoelace in order to avoid the owner of the pair of large flat feet he now saw on the ground near his chair.

"Hello Sterling," said Ben Vogelhut. "Did you hear that Louis Saint died? They found him drowned under the Pont Neuf a week ago. No doubt dead drunk. Didn't you know?"

"No, oh no," Sterling said. "No, I hadn't heard. How frightfully shocking. I've been away in the country visiting with old friends and then I was busy moving to my new apartment. I'm so, so sorry. When is the funeral?"

"It was yesterday in Montmartre. That's where he lived. He was poor. Never made much money playing the piano or teaching a few students."

"I didn't quite realize."

"The funeral was a strange affair."

"Who was there?" Scott said and emerged from under the table.

"Oh, hello, I wondered how long you'd be hiding," Ben said. "I only recognized a few. Orgoloff was there. You can always count on him to be loyal. And Pyotr Vasilevich without Bernice. There were people from the bars he frequented, and a surprising number of neighbors from up and down his street."

"I'm glad he had friends," Sterling said.

"We went back to his rooms afterwards," Ben said, "and had the surprise of our lives."

"What do you mean?"

"A *poule* was there with what she claimed was his child. Four years old."

"No!"

"Yes!"

"How extraordinary. I can't quite take it in," Sterling said. "What will she do now?"

"She was packing up her few belongings about to move downstairs to live with a friend, a scrap-dealer."

"The end of the line," Sterling said.

"Pyotr Vasilevich is planning to go ahead with their concert. Alone."

"We must all attend," Sterling said.

"Well, old chap, thanks for stopping by," Scott said when Ben Vogelhut pulled out a chair to sit. "We're about to leave."

"Just as well," Ben said. "I'm waiting for someone."

"So long, then," Sterling said, "we won't disturb you."

Scott scowled at her.

"Did you hear about Laura Waverley and her *Notes from Paris*," she said. "It'll be published in London and, possibly, in New York. But you probably know all about it already."

"I heard," Scott said. "It'll bring in some money and I hear she could use it. Poetry doesn't pay much."

"Her poems are beautiful."

"Yes, but she may do better writing for magazines."

"Which reminds me," Sterling said, "I must get home to my writing."

"Fine, I'll see you later?"

"Sure thing."

"So long, kid," Scott said with a weird expression on his face as he watched Sterling get into her expensive *Quadrilette*.

The *pneu* which awaited her at the concierge's lodge had her rush upstairs, take a quick bath, roll and fasten her stockings, step into a blue silk Poiret and twist on her long strand of pearls.

She hurtled the car across the river towards the Rive Droît and arrived fifteen minutes later in a quiver of excitement.

Chapter 20

Simone called me in the early morning.

"Meet me at the Café de la Paix this afternoon at five and we will have tea," she said.

"Do you have news for me?" I said.

"I will tell you when we meet."

By five I had poured myself into a white Hugo Boss suit, stepped into high Ferragamo heels which lifted me to six feet five well above Simone, twisted a series of silver and gold chains around my neck, and wore my Cartier tank watch, the one with diamonds. You wouldn't catch me like that at five in the afternoon in downtown Washington, but Simone, as always, had brought out the worst in me.

Traffic around the Opera House was frantic as usual, the ubiquitous police sirens lent a very Parisian air to the sounds of motor scooters and Smart Cars. Citizens on bicycles wove in and out of traffic with baguettes sticking out of baskets on their steering wheels, others hurried along in between tourists thronging the sidewalks, and I hurried along the Avenue de l'Opéra to pick up a New York Times at Brentanos.

I was at the café perusing the menu, seated towards the back of the room. The place was full, the waiters bustled about, and I was admiring the colorful carpeting, the lush chandeliers, and the high ceilings, when a man sat down next to me.

He had lost most of his hair but in compensation had a stylish mustache above heavy jowls. He was running to fat around the middle.

"Roger?"

"*Ma chére Jamie.*"

"Simone," I said. "Where's Simone?"

"She sends her sincere apologies, she had a sudden engagement with her dentist and asked me to stand in for her. Hope you do not mind?"

His voice hadn't changed and neither had his eyes. His hands were well manicured and he wore a thin wedding band. He looked me over quite openly and I was supremely glad about my smart outfit and athletic body.

"Mind? No, of course not."

"You are looking well."

"You, too," I lied and addressed the waiter who had suddenly appeared. "Let me order. I will have the special house salad and a glass of Sancerre Grande Réserve. What about you?"

Roger smiled that small stubborn smile I suddenly remembered. I felt a familiar resentment rise deep within me.

"I'll have the canapés au saumon fumé and a glass of Chablis."

While we waited for the order to be served Roger took out photographs of his wife—the one who was supposed to look like me—and two children, a lovely French portrait from an expensive photographer.

"Élise and Marcel," Roger said, forgetting to introduce the wife. "They could have been yours."

God forbid, I thought, and thank God I left. Not that the children weren't beautiful.

I looked Roger full in the face, smoothed down my Hugo Boss jacket and stretched out my long legs in my Hugo Boss pants.

"And your wife," I said, "what does she do?"

"She does what a wife does. She's at home in the country, she entertains my clients and helps me with my career. I've gone into local politics."

His eyes bored into mine and his anger almost blew out the back of my head.

"I'm very sorry that I didn't work out for you," I said. "I'm glad you've found the perfect wife. And your children are lovely."

Roger stuffed the photos back in his pocket.

"And you? You have not remarried?"

"No, so far I am blissfully single."

Our forced repartee suddenly reminded me of Mel Kramer in New York and our easy relationship and my spirits lifted. Then I remembered that I was also dating a youngish sax player in Washington. Not that there's anything wrong with that. Isn't it possible to be interested in two men at the same time?

"Ah, here's the perfect salad," I said and dug into the shrimp, the avocado, the perfect little wedges of grapefruit and thin strips of onion. Then, just because of nerves, I drained the wine glass in a couple of slurps and beckoned for another. After which I crumbled up a perfectly fine roll.

"Mother said you wished to know about Victoria d'Auvergne's family," Roger said and eyed me and my new wine glass.

"Yes," I said and swallowed several small shrimp in one go. "There was talk of a couple of families who might know about her. The Vasseurs and the Robillards."

"Mother mentioned them but somehow I thought that Victoria's granddaughter, Suzette d'Alville, would be easier for you to interview."

"You've found her?" I exclaimed and felt heat rise in my cheeks.

"She lives on rue Wagram. She seems to be like you, blissfully single—with two cats—but otherwise I know nothing about her."

"I don't have cats."

"Fine," Roger said and his eyes looked cold.

"How did you find her?" I said.

"Called a friend, who called a friend. It was simple enough. Don't know why Mamán couldn't do it."

I put down my fork, took another brisk mouthful of wine under Roger's surreptitious stare, produced my notebook and wrote down the name and the address.

While I wrote Roger finished his saumon fumé and his wine. When I looked up from my notebook I found him looking at me with an expression that made me shudder.

"I am eternally grateful and tell your mother that I will give her a call before I leave," I mumbled.

"Never thought you'd turn out to be an *Agent Policial*," Roger said.

"Private Investigator," I said. "Private Investigator."

"*Bién sûr*."

I now couldn't wait to get away and decided to enjoy my cappuccino at the hotel, alone.

As we left through the outdoor terrasse I hovered well above Roger—thanks to the Ferragamos—and was gratified by the many admiring eyes which followed me into the Place de l'Opera. Childish but satisfying. We parted with me fervently hoping that we would never meet again.

I sauntered down the avenue at the foot of tall buildings where dormer windows in four-sided mansard roofs glowed golden in the late evening sun. At the top of his mile-high column in Place Vendôme, a dwarfed Napoleon peered down at the masses or, maybe, towards Austerlitz, oblivious of Dior, Cartier, Chaumet, or Bvlgari, now installed in luxury boutiques under white awnings all about the square.

At my hotel the concierge informed me of the arrival of several overnight shipments which he was having delivered to my room tout de suite. They turned out to be from Topsy and contained some fifteen books all heavily marked with yellow Post-It notes.

Spread out on the desk by the window they represented a formidable amount of homework. I gazed at the titles in amazement. Biographies of acknowledged and supposed acquaintances of Sterling Kirkland Sawyer with a short note from Topsy saying 'read these and call me in the morning'.

Since it was now too late to look up Victoria Huddersfield's granddaughter, Suzette d'Alville, I went to my high-ceilinged bathroom, turned on the gold-plated faucet, filled the bathtub to the brim, poured in some delicious bubbles, took a luxurious bath, toweled off in a thirsty bathrobe, got wrapped in a silk pyjamas, switched on all the lights—since even at the finest hotels the bedside lamps are not for reading—and settled down with the first book, picked randomly. It turned out to be about Roland Lee Rainier.

I decided to read the bios only as far as the 1930s or the task would have been too formidable. I wasn't even sure all this reading would help me find Sterling. At best it would give me a feel for the places and times in which she lived.

Next I read about Laura Waverley, Louis Saint, and Claire Garcia-Bonsonwell. By the time I came to the end of their lives in the 1920s I was pretty much out of energy and barely managed to keep my eyes open to consume a late dinner delivered by room-service. I savored the sea scallop carpaccio with cauliflower cream and Imperial caviar— served richly at a table with fine linen and a rose in a single-stem vase—accompanied by sparkling Evian and followed by coffee and pastel-colored macaroons.

Thus revived, I flipped through the materials on Ben Vogelhut, Roland Lee Rainier, Scott Winteride, Bernice Boch, and Pyotr Vasilevich. They had all lived in Paris, or had visited lengthily, in the 1920s. They had all known one another and their bios were full of names of their mutual acquaintances.

They all had connections to the arts and literature, some had become famous—others not so much—but none had mentioned Sterling Kirkland Sawyer.

Chapter 21

I arose at the crack of dawn and called Topsy in Washington.

"Thanks a bunch," I said.

"You read them all?"

"No, silly, I only read about their activities in the 1920s and somewhat into the 1930s."

"Which ones did you read?"

"Strangely enough I began with the one I recognized the least but who turned out to be most interesting. Roland Lee Rainier, born in Iowa in1880," I said.

"And one of my absolute favorites. If CAT was Sterling then she mentions him in half of her articles. He was married to a temperamental woman. Seems they quarreled incessantly but stayed together for nearly fifty years."

"Someone said it only worked because they led separate lives," I said. "She had her friends and he had his but she supported his writing and he enjoyed her soirées. How ideal."

"Yes, I knew that would appeal to you. Which reminds me, how's Mel Kramer? You two could have the same kind of relationship, you in Washington going about detecting —coming around at least once a week for some of my famous home-cooking—and he in New York selling his paintings and staying away from his many former girlfriends. You could meet on weekends, sail off on delicious vacations, and then go back to your separate lives."

"What," I said, "no longer setting me up with eligible—or, as it usually turns out, ineligible—men in Washington?"

"I'll admit I feel somewhat defeated on that score so let's get back to Roland Lee Rainier. Since he wrote for *The Bright Set* and must have known Pierre Fast-Brown, doesn't it stand to reason that he would have met Sterling? He was frequently in Paris."

"Yes, I've thought of that connection," Topsy said. "But, so what? I've not come across any mention of Sterling in any of his writings."

"But if Sterling was CAT then she certainly knew all of them, including all the small press publishers, especially Ben Vogelhut of *The Pyramid Press*," I said.

"And she would have known Scott Winteride," Topsy said.

"He was a strange character."

"Seems he was always ready to pick up his valise and move on. Here today, gone tomorrow kind of thing."

"That's exactly what I deduced."

"He bounced around from writing poetry, to moving to Paris, where he sat around in cafés and talked about writing but, apparently, didn't do much about it."

"I wonder why he was such a loser. Have you found out any more about him?"

"I have. He never became a published novelist," Topsy said. "The New York publishers had an unreasonable phobia against the so-called expatriates, especially if they were self-published as most of them were. Instead he moved to London."

"Still, it was a fabulous time in Paris, wish I could have been there."

"Listen, you wouldn't have enjoyed the cold-water flats, the slop jars, the bad smells."

"I'd have found indoor plumbing somewhere."

"Sure, plus a couple of servants. Then you'd have gone slumming on the Left Bank, attended the Ballets Russes or the Revue Négre with Josephine Baker."

"Hey," I said, "I noticed that CAT wrote about Alexandre Orgoloff, the Surréalist painter, how his studio looked, how fashionably he was dressed, and that his parrot spoke in Polish. She also mentioned the eccentric pianist, Louis Saint."

"Oh, I can tell you about them. Orgoloff was a moneyed Polish count who left his country because of a romantic entanglement with a married woman, fled to Paris, married more money, turned himself into a celebrated painter and hobnobbed with the rich and famous."

"A celebrated minor painter?" I said.

"Never minor. His prices are still high."

"What about Louis Saint?"

"He started out as a classical pianist but later was mostly known for playing avant garde music."

"Was he well-known?"

"Not in any real sense. As soon as his last concert—given after his death—was over his audience seemed to forget about him. He had never been good at self-promotion. He drank himself to death. Fell in the river and died in 1925. They found him in the waters one morning under the Pont Neuf."

"How shocking. CAT obviously knew him well."

"For sure. Her eulogy was very moving. Did you notice that CAT never said good-bye to the readers of her *Paris Diary*?"

"Yes, I did."

"Since we hear nothing more about Sterling's other writings," Topsy said, "I've come to the conclusion that she was either extremely publicity-shy, or that she didn't publish under her own name, or that she was a very minor talent in the company of some of the greats of the day."

"I don't believe a word of that," I said. "I'll find her writings if it takes me all year."

"It's strange that she didn't attend her friend, Victoria Huddersfield's, wedding. At least not as a bridesmaid. Even had she been there as a guest I imagine her photo would have been in *The Bright Set* given her close association with Pierre Fast-Brown."

"I have good news in that respect," I said and waited for a gasp from Topsy.

"You've found out something," she gasped.

"I met with Roger yesterday," I said.

"You met with Roger? I thought you wanted to avoid him like the proverbial plague? How did that come about?"

"It wasn't on purpose but I think he found an excuse to substitute for Simone. He turned up at the café instead of her, we had a kind of high tea with heaps of wine instead of tea, and he gave me the name and address of Victoria's granddaughter. So there."

I thought our telephone connection had been cut off.

"Hello, are you there?" I shouted.

"Yes, I'm here and I'm speechless. Stunned to learn that there's some kind of break in the case. What's her name?"

"Her name is Suzette d'Alville, she's single according to Roger, and lives on rue Wagram which probably means she's quite well off."

"When will you meet with her?" Topsy said.

"I thought of calling her first but, instead, I think I'll go to her address this afternoon and catch her in person, if possible."

"You mean a stake-out. And if I know your devious ways there's a concierge who'll give you the low-down for a consideration."

I laughed because Topsy can always read my mind.

After we hung up I googled Suzette's mother, Marie-Louise, whose last name should be d'Alville if her daughter, Suzette, was single. When I could find no entries

I gave it up. Instead I flung my arms and legs about in some serious Tae Kwon Do exercises—ax kicks, side kicks, and jumping front kicks—and cleared my lungs with some stertorous shouts.

Then I showered, got dressed, and took a taxi to rue Wagram.

Chapter 22

1925

The concert hall off the Place St. German-des-Prés sat prominently at the top of a street and was slowly filling up. The crowd of people became denser as Sterling and Stefan walked towards the hall where Pyotr Vasilevich would perform alone in honor of Louis Saint. The bookstores and antique shops were shuttered behind green facades. Night had fallen. The sky was dark blue and a few distant stars blinked off and on. Inside the foyer, beyond the several entrance doors, they met up with an excited group of friends.

Effie Rousseau, in a floor-length black dress, arrived under the tutelage of Roland Lee Rainier, dapper in a dark suit and a bow tie. His face glistened in the bright lights, his dark hair tumbled around his forehead, and his eyes looked feverish. He soon lost the grip he had on Effie's arm and was swept to the side. Stefan Oxenkranz—who towered well above most heads—rescued them and got them to their seats.

Stefan returned to find Sterling—clad in a low-cut yellow dress with rows of shimmering beads—clinging to the wall. He clutched her arm and carried her along, found their seats in the third row, and set her down next to Claire

Garcia-Bonsonwell. Claire was splendid in a red shift which ended well above her knees, a red fringed shawl, and a spectacular red rose behind her ear. Stefan sat down with them.

From the small balcony came the clamor of many voices.

"That's Scott Winteride," Sterling shouted to Stefan above the din, "he came back from London especially for the concert, and there is Laura holding hands with Auguste."

The noise in the small hall was deafening.

"Amazing turn-out," Stefan shouted. "There's that Russian chap, Stravinsky, with Diaghilev. Can Virgil Thomson be far behind?"

"They've come for Pyotr's violin and in homage to Louis Saint," Sterling said.

"Too, too frightfully sad that the dear man didn't live to play for the first time in this esteemed hall," Claire said.

"Here is one of your favorite people," Stefan said to Sterling and squinted at her in conspiratorial fashion.

Bernice Boch, bursting out of a voluminous dress—no flat-chested flapper she—swooped down on Sterling and sat down heavily in her seat.

"Absolutely frazzled," she shouted, "I'm leaving early in the morning for Venice, large slabs of Carrara marble await me."

"How long will you be gone," Sterling shouted back.

"Who can tell, maybe forever."

"Surely you don't mean that," Stefan said. "What about Pyotr?"

"What about Pyotr?" Bernice looked triumphant. "He can follow me if he so wishes."

"Now, you don't really mean that," Sterling said echoing Stefan.

"You just try me," Bernice said.

The curtain should have risen at eight but by almost nine something had yet to happen and the audience was getting somewhat out of hand. When the curtain rose at nine-thirty it took a while for the noise to abate and no one heard much of anything. They were waiting for Pyotr.

A grand piano draped in sorrowful black stood in the middle of the stage and occasioned nervous comments from the audience.

"Now," said Stefan. He looked expectantly at the stage when Pyotr Vasilevich entered, his red hair seemingly on fire, his violin in hand. He turned his head towards the black-clad grand piano and raised the bow.

Sweet, melancholy, tones filled the hall.

"That doesn't sound at all what Louis Saint would have played," Stefan whispered.

Everyone had come to witness a rumble of discordant noise amid thunderous crashes of percussion. Instead, Pyotr stroked his violin quietly, and after a while the audience settled into uneasy silence.

As the last tones filled the hall Pyotr Vasilevich spun around and signaled. Two small canons hidden behind fake shrubbery ignited and spewed volumes of white smoke across the stage and into the audience to coughs and shrieks from those in the first rows. The smoke drifted ominously towards the back of the hall and rose towards the balcony.

As suddenly as the pandemonium had begun it all died down. The canons went silent, the smoke dissipated, and Pyotr escaped into the wings.

There were loud shouts for the violinist and presently a rumpled Pyotr Vasilevich, squinting insanely, took his bows on the stage.

"Speech, speech," someone shouted.

He held up his hand to silence the audience.

"Dear friends," Pyotr said several times. "Dear friends. You were surprised. You expected noises like cascading marbles and scratches on washboards. Maybe you did not know the quiet nature of the other Louis Saint. It was that spirit I wished to honor. And, so, we are here tonight to pay tribute to that incomparable, humble and unique pianist, our sorely missed friend, Louis Saint."

"Hear, hear."

"He should have been here tonight to take a bow at my side. We will never forget him and his genius. Only the canons testified to the other side of his personality."

An appropriate silence followed Pyotr's speech as he bowed his head and walked slowly into the wings.

"Encore, encore," someone shouted.

No one reappeared and the stage lights dimmed leaving only a faint aura of smoke.

Laura and Auguste—looking immensely puzzled —appeared next to Sterling who had lost sight of Stefan.

"Very strange," Laura said. "Our dear Pyotr has immortalized Louis Saint although not in the way he may have wanted."

"The poor man. Not at all what he would have expected. Except for the canons."

"I rather think that was one of Pyotr's inventions," Claire said.

"Most likely," Sterling said.

"It's all too, too sad," Claire said and folded her red shawl about her.

They saw Roland Lee Rainier in a blur to the left, his hair in an uproar, his cheeks aflame. He was swept away by the crowd and out the door followed by Effie Rousseau.

"We will end the evening at the Deux Magots," Sterling shouted to Laura. "Will you come? Oh, please say that you'll both come."

"We will."

They were standing in the crowded foyer being pushed and pulled this way and that when Stefan appeared pursued by Wainwright Manners III.

Winny grinned at Sterling, bowed to Laura and Auguste, and turned around to beckon to the person behind him.

Victoria, the Comtesse d'Auvergne, née Huddersfield, strolled up—as near as she could stroll and still make an entrance—and embraced Sterling.

"Darling," she said in that brassy voice of hers, "darling, how divine to see you."

"Lovely to see you, too," Sterling mumbled and freed herself from the suffocating embrace. "You are looking very fit. How's your darling baby boy, he must be barely a month old."

"Oh, I'm sure he's fine, the nannies have him, I'm glad to have it over with and to get about again, this is my very first outing since that terrible ordeal. I'm never having another baby, it was too, too gruesome for words."

"I see you brought Wainwright, your emissary," Sterling said and she could hear the chill in her own voice. "I suppose you're quite familiar with the way *my* life is going. Nothing seems to get by Winny."

"But, of course, darling, I know you're quite the little writer moving in quite the minor artistic circles."

Winny smiled his knowing smile.

Sterling sensed her confidence slip. Victoria had never failed to pierce her most vulnerable spots. In Victoria's presence Sterling was no longer the Cat's Meow, she became again the shy sixteen-year old girl who was brought back to New York from her safe convent in Burgundy, from the secure environment created for her by the sisters and from the motherly warmth of Soeur Madeleine.

Victoria had been one of Pierre Fast-Brown's favorites among the young smart set and she had reluctantly taken on the social education of Sterling. With a blend of envy and exasperation because of Sterling's greater fortune, because of her innocent looks, and her vulnerable demeanor, Victoria had sent caustic needles at Sterling that undermined her self-confidence. She had also made sure that uncertain rumors about Sterling circulated among her set and their sly whisperings meant that Sterling did not make many friends.

Any young man attracted to her was swiftly brought back into Victoria's fold.

It was not until Andrew Blake had encouraged Sterling to write—and not until he had published her poems in his magazine—that she was able to shake off Victoria and to become her own person. That was when she began writing the first of the three novels which now lay at the bottom of her trunk not good enough to be published but representing her learning process. Lately, during moments of happiness, she knew that her fourth novel would be successful. She had found her voice.

"Vicky is quite the writer herself," Wainwrigh shrieked over the noise. "Watch out for her poems in *The Bright Set*. Her Uncle Pierre promotes her work."

"You haven't changed in the least since we last met," Sterling said and looked Victoria straight in the eye but she knew that Pierre would do almost anything for Victoria.

"Oh, I do believe I am more beautiful now than before the baby," Victoria said. "You wouldn't know about that, of course, dear Sterling, although I must say you don't look quite as drab as during your last year in New York."

She knows, Sterling thought. How could she know, no one got to know about it, no one but Andrew and herself. Sterling felt heat surge through her head, felt her vision blur. No, she thought desperately, Victoria was just being her usual degrading self. She clung to the curved stairway rail and thought, I need Claire.

"Sterling," Claire said, "we must get out of here this instant. I'm feeling faint."

Sterling turned to Stefan but he was looking off into the distance.

"Stefan, darling," Victoria shrieked over the din which enveloped the foyer. She leapt to Stefan Oxenkranz's side, took his arm and snuggled close. "How divine to see you again, you must come to the château next month for the ball. We're having all your favorite people."

Stefan looked around at Sterling and tried to step back from Victoria in the cramped space. Sterling stared at Victoria and Victoria eyed Sterling in triumph.

"My dear Countess," Stefan said. "Your husband did mention the occasion and that some of our business partners would be coming in from Switzerland but I told him I would be out of the country. I regret that I must decline your kind invitation."

Stefan stepped around Wainwright who was watching with eyes full of malice, turned to Sterling and took her arm.

"Let's go, my dear," he said, "or we'll be late for dinner."

"Smashing," Victoria cried. "We'll join you."

Stefan bowed stiffly.

"We would be pleased for you to join us at some future date," he said and averted his eyes, "but tonight we have a previous engagement."

Victoria raised her chin defiantly, stepped close to Wainwright Manners III, looked around, ignored Sterling, froze out Stefan, saw Alexandre Orgoloff and his dowdy wife come down the stairs and shrieked in delight.

"Felicia, darling, and darling Alexandre, we're headed to the Boeuf sur le Toit, everyone will be there, the jazz band is divine and so is Kiki, do come join our table, we'll have a smashing evening."

"Yes," Felicia said, "smashing."

"Alex, old boy," Stefan said, "you remember Sterling."

Alex's eyes twinkled when he looked at Sterling. He took her hand and kissed it in his most courtly manner.

"*Un plaisir*," he said

Victoria took Felicia by the arm, and snuggled up to Alex. Sterling smiled widely at him before turning away.

Laura and Auguste who had been silent observers at the unexpected scene hurried down the stairs with Sterling and Stefan. They walked along the narrow rue de l'Odéon to retrieve Sterling's car.

"A bientôt," Laura cried and hooked her arm around Auguste's. "Come with us, dear Claire, we will join you two at the Deux Magots, the evening must end on a happy note."

"How do you know Victoria?" Sterling asked from her driver's seat in the darkness of the Quadrilette. The arc-lights above the street did little to disperse the fog which hovered over the sidewalk.

"I have done some business with the Count. I have met Victoria only once. We do not socialize."

"She seemed to know you quite well."

Stefan took a deep breath and stared straight ahead.

"My dear, I assure you, she does not," he said. "It is you I adore."

Chapter 23

1923

"Your friend, Victoria, is very jealous of you," Alex said and added a blue brush stroke to the canvas.

He stood back and stared long and hard at the painting. Sterling had learned not to talk to him while he studied his work. He would seem to forget about her entirely. Then he would pick up the paint brush and add a color or change an outline. But not today.

"Enfin," he said. "I can do no more about your figure today. It will not come to me. You are not an abstraction, I cannot see through you, I cannot make you float in my dream world."

"I'm sorry," Sterling said.

Alex laughed.

"Why should you be sorry? It is better to be mysterious, is it not?"

"So it's a compliment?"

"Yes, *kiciu*, it is a compliment. Go sit, go wait for me, I still have a few hours of work, then we shall eat."

She had been surprised the first time she entered his studio. It did not look like the studio of any other painter she knew although now she found it inevitable that the floors were not littered with papers and paint, that tables were not brimming over with strange objects. Alexandre Orgoloff was a fastidious man. A large green parrot with red wings sat on a beam high above the floor and screeched loudly when she entered.

Today, the parrot was in his cage stepping anxiously back and forth on his perch, shouting at her.

"What is he saying?"

"He's angry that he must be in his cage."

"He speaks in Polish?"

"If you understood what he's saying you would be very embarrassed," Alex said. "He's being very uncomplimentary about you."

Sterling glared at the parrot and the parrot glared back with beady little eyes.

"May I talk today while you work?" she said.

"You wish to talk about Victoria?"

"Yes."

"She is jealous of you."

"It is more than jealousy."

"Yes?"

"She hates me."

"You mustn't be afraid of her."

"I'm not afraid. Just sad."

"When people are jealous of me, or hate me, I cut them out of my life. You must do the same."

"I have tried to do that. I made myself disappear when we arrived in Paris together, I did not go to her wedding, I never visit her, I never write."

"But she will not leave you to yourself?"

"No, she will not. Wherever I go these days, there she is. She even has people spying on me, then she tries to take away my friends."

"Your friends won't desert you if they are your real friends."

"Maybe. And now she writes short stories and poetry like I do and gets published in the same magazine."

"Ah," Alex said and turned to a second canvas. "If she is not a true poet she will not last. The painters who copy my style they do not last. You must not let it worry you."

He stood again for a long while looking at the painting, studying it from various angles, adding a color, rubbing it out, then shaking his head and moving on to a second unfinished, still wet, canvas.

Sterling now sat quietly. She had gone to rue du Colisée the day after their first meeting at Effie's dinner. She had known from the first moment that she would go to him. She had walked up the creaking stairs to the top floor and knocked on his door and he had let her in immediately.

He now put down his brush. "I, too, am a poet. A painter is a poet. I paint my pictures around a theme, the theme must be in balance and once it is, then the painting is finished."

"And when will your poem with my floating figure be in balance?"

"Next week. Or maybe next month. I am leaving for the Côte d'Azur in ten days. I need a new environment for a series of paintings I have in mind for my next exhibition."

"Shall I come back next week?"

"Yes, *kiciu*, you shall come back."

Sterling smiled and Alex smiled back

"And what about your tall, blond beau?" he said. "Are you in love with him?"

"He is very good to me."

"And he loves you?"

"He says he adores me."

"It is not the same thing, no?"

"Maybe, maybe not."

"Will he marry you?"

"Maybe, maybe not."

Alex laughed.

"How could he not? If I were free I would marry you. Then you could give up your stories and poems and be a wife. I would like you to look after me."

Not I, Sterling thought.

Alex stopped looking at his paintings, went across to her and pulled her up from the chair. He was wearing an immaculate white shirt totally devoid of paint splatter, and a pair of long pants, perfectly pleated. The reddish hairs on his chest were curly. When he moved close to her she could feel the passion of his eyes upon her face.

"Now," he said and his wiry fingers closed around hers.

Chapter 24

"Mademoiselle Suzette d'Alville?" the concierge said. "No, Madame, the lady is not at home."

She stared at me—not unfriendly but not exactly friendly, either—and I looked back, each of us evaluating the other. I knew quite well what she was thinking, that I looked respectable enough and probably moneyed based on my Hermés scarf and handbag, and I knew that she was for sale.

"My name is Jamie Prescott," I said, "I have a message for Mademoiselle d'Alville from a friend of hers in New York. And your name, Madame?"

The concierge dried her hands on her blue apron and smoothed back some stray wisps of hair from her forehead. Then she stepped back and opened the door a couple of more inches. A whiff of boiled cabbage greeted me.

"I am Madame Fournier," she said.

"I'm most anxious to speak to Mademoiselle d'Alville," I said. "Do you have any idea when she will be back?"

Madame Fournier tossed her head and I thought I read contempt in her eyes.

"Not until the early hours of the morning."

"What would she be doing until the early hours of the morning?" I said trying to look as if that sort of thing would never happen to me.

Madame Fournier sniffled but hesitated whether from an inability to tell me or an inclination not to.

I dug in my handbag and came up with an envelope prepared in advance.

"I would not impose on your kindness nor keep you from your duties," I said. "Please consider this a small token."

She let the envelope with my token disappear into the pocket of her blue apron.

"She entertains at the Boîte Noir in Montmartre," she said. "Not that a body is supposed to know but it has come to my attention, nevertheless. It is a nightclub."

"Ah," I said and looked at my watch.

"It is too early, Madame."

"Yes, I imagine it is," I said.

Madame Fournier showed me to the door and I had a feeling that my gratuity was about to expire.

"How would I recognize Mademoiselle d'Alville?" I said.

"Ah, Madame, very easily. She wears her hair in blond curls although she's a brunette and she is almost as tall as Madame herself. Very tall and very, shall we say, well-built."

Madame Fournier cupped her upper torso at the points where Suzette was well-built.

A telephone rang inside the lodge and Madame Fournier disappeared with a polite excuse but with a firm hand on the door handle.

"*Merci*," I said to the door and returned to the street to find yet another taxi.

Back at the hotel I checked my e-mails and found that my jazz player, Jon, missed me terribly in Barcelona and couldn't wait to get back to me, and I e-mailed him back cringing with a bit of guilt at still not telling him I was actually an hour and a half away from him by air.

Then I selected one of the books sent by Topsy and descended to the wood-paneled bar. There were few people there and I settled down in a green leather chair at a round glass table where I proposed to read until it was time to dress in some touristy clothes intended for the Boîte Noir. I ordered crab rolls and a serendipitous Martini consisting of apple juice, champagne, a squirt of Calvados and fresh mint.

Thus fortified I opened the biography.

Effie Rousseau had lived a full and interesting life since returning to Paris in 1918 at the age of forty-two, following a few years of inactivity and an unhappy love affair in New York. She set up her house and studio on rue du Berri and started painting in earnest. She drew on her society friends to pose for her and, later, on their patronage to get shown at prestigious galleries and salons. It was after she began painting voluptuous nudes that she caught the eye of Orgoloff and many other famous painters of the day. In the black-and-white studio photographs—taken by the fashionable photographer Pierre Fast-Brown of *The Bright Set* fame—she looked radiant with lustrous eyes and outrageously curly hair. I wondered if, maybe, her hair was red.

In excitement I gulped down the Martini and ordered another. Was this Sterling's family friend with whom she was supposed to stay in Paris? I leafed through the biography in extreme haste, three times, but found no portrait of Sterling. Nor was there any mention of her in Effie Rousseau's biography. Another dead end.

While reading I had glanced up only occasionally to enjoy my surroundings: the rich wood paneling, framed photographs of illustrious patrons dating from the early 20th Century to quite recent celebrities. There was vintage paraphernalia everywhere.

The black marble bar counter was crowded with cocktail shakers, artfully arranged napkins, and bowls heaped with nuts. Somewhat loud customers—local literati, no doubt expatriates, if the conversation was any indication—now inhabited the black leather stools at the bar.

There were color photos in the book of Effie Rousseau's paintings, with one of Bernice Boch, the writer, very pink and peach colored. There were portraits of Alexandre Orgoloff, Pyotr Vasilevich, and Louis Saint, and it was mentioned that they all—the famous and the soon to be famous—came to Effie's spectacular Thursday night dinners, the dinners CAT had mentioned in the *Paris Diary*.

It was fascinating reading but took me no closer to Sterling.

I left the bar at nine-thirty and was on my way to the elevators when a woman stepped out of the shadows from behind a pillar under the surreptitious gaze of a hotel attendant.

She was wearing leather pants and a black jacket covered in rhinestones. She had purple hair and black nail polish. Ms. Puigh of the green hair had changed its color but, otherwise, was herself down to a new tattoo on her right ankle.

"Ms. Puigh," I said. "What a surprise."

"Call me Val," she said. "Short for Valentina."

"What a surprise," I said again.

"I told the doorman that I was here to see you and he knew your name. Pretty fancy. Invited me to wait in the salon over there, the one with the mirrors and the twenty foot ceiling—a bit like Versailles, isn't it—but I came here to catch you at the elevator instead. I just got in from New York. I can stay three days."

"I'm very surprised to see you," I said without exaggeration.

"I had to give you the news in person."

"Give," I said.

"Sterling Kirkland Sawyer was CAT."

Chapter 25

"Seriously cool," Ms. Puigh declared and swirled around in my opulent room.

An appropriately faded, Bouchard-like tapestry above the gold leaf headboard of my king size bed with satin sheeting set the tone along with Louis XIV side tables, plush chairs and carpeting, crystal chandeliers. and triple layers of silk curtains.

"Wowie," said Ms. Puigh in a daze and sank down in a pale blue armchair still clutching a yellow manila envelope.

She looked at me and grinned under her new purple hair.

"You're a cool chick," she declared. "I like your style."

"Thank you," I said, "you're kinda cool yourself."

"Okay, now," she said and handed me the envelope, "these are copies of Sterling's letters to Pierre Fast-Brown from 1923 to 1925."

I wanted to take a crazy spin around the room. At last something tangible. Actual letters from Sterling, her own words from beyond the years. I removed the copies of the letters—some of the images looked faded and some were quite creased—and spread them out on the large white desk in front of the window.

"Were there no letters after 1925?"

"Strangely enough, just these few postcards."

"That could be because, apparently, her *Paris Diary* for *The Bright Set* was cancelled in 1925," I said and picked up the copies of three postcards. They all depicted the *Chat Noir* and all were inscribed with words which seemed strangely familiar: *'All is well here, love Sterling.'*

It was the same card Sterling had sent to her sister, Rose—the card which Rose's daughter, Marjorie Robinson, had given me in Washington—with the exact same greeting in the exact same precise handwriting.

"I'm amazed the library let you make copies," I said.

Ms. Puigh waved a dismissive hand as if to say, don't ask, so I let it slide. Ms. Puigh was my kind of snoop.

I picked up the first letter—very short and typed on plain paper without an address—dated October, 1923.

> "*darlingest Pierre,'* it said, *'I'm sending you the amusing captions for dear Angelo's drawings, I do adore them and thank you for letting me work with him. Please give them to the editors. I know I've taken too long to get started but I am working hard on the diary, I promise you solemnly that the first will be on the next boat from Le Havre, love, love, Sterling.'*

"No address," Ms. Puigh said. "Wonder how she received her mail?"

"Probably like everyone else at that time," I said. "At the American Express office."

"You're too clever by half," she said. "And, here you are, the *Paris Diary*."

The diary was a charming account of mornings spent writing, lunches at la Quattriéme République, forays to French bookstores, afternoons reading, evenings eating at Les Deux Magots and dancing at obscure *Bals Musettes* with two unknown writers by the names of Scott Winteride and Bernice Boch.

"The 'unknown' writer, Bernice Boch," Ms. Puigh said. "Imagine, Sterling knew her when she was unknown."

"Someone had to," I said.

I picked up the next letter. It was dated June, 1924.

"What happened to the letters between October, 1923 and June, 1924?"

"That's all I found but this one is really interesting."

"She put the address on this letter," I said. "Rue Jacob. Sounds familiar."

Ms. Puigh looked at me in triumph.

"Maybe she was at the famous Hotel Jacob. Lots of Americans stopped there in those days before moving on to private apartments."

"So that's where she lived," I said, "on the Left Bank, after all."

> '*darlingest Pierre*' the letter said, '*I'm sending this month's Paris diary with darling Roland who's returning to New York this Friday. I had a lovely time writing it, had a sumptuous dinner at Effie Rousseau's place, I couldn't possibly "tell all" in the diary but I met someone who could become someone in my life. I know that's what you've been hoping for. In haste (because Roland is waiting) love, love, Sterling.*'

"Here," Ms. Puigh said. "I put the letter together with the November issue of *The Bright Set*. She's very casual about her famous friends."

"She doesn't mention a special man. She writes about a dinner at an Effie Rousseau's place but the mention is squeezed in between some banter about a Louis Saint and compliments about Roland Lee Rainier's writing and she can't possibly mean that either one of them is now becoming the love of her life."

"Rather not," I said. "Louis Saint apparently was not a ladies' man—except for the woman with whom he had a child—and Roland Lee Rainier was married in New York. I can't see her taking up long-distance with a married man."

I picked up the last letter—the address had been typed in the left hand corner—dated September, 1925.

> *'darlingest Pierre, no need to be sorry for me and my Paris diary, the writing of it took a lot out of my days, days that I should have spent writing on my short stories and poems and, especially, on my novel. Did I tell you I'm being published by The Pyramid Press, and quite possibly by Lane's in London—he's one of Claire's many influential friends. I am happily installed in my new apartment at 351 quai des Grands-Agustins. Do come to visit when you're here next month, love, love, Sterling. P.S. Stefan sends regards.'*

"Stefan," Ms. Puigh said. "Stefan, the special someone?"

"A first name only. Impossible to trace. Sounds Polish, somehow. Haven't run into a Stefan in any of the books I've read so avidly."

"I'll keep an eye out," she said.

"How do we get a hold of *The Pyramid Press* after September 1925? We should be able to find her short stories or at least figure out—by a process of elimination—what her pseudonym might be if she didn't publish under her own name."

"I'll get on it when I return," Ms. Puigh said.

"She moved to the quai des Grands-Augustins," I said. "The building must still be there."

"Yes, and the diary she sent must have been the last. She seems to be very buddy with Claire Garcia-Bonsonwell, even describes a visit with her to London, then talks a lot about the exposition at the Grand Palais—the one that established the modernist Art Deco style—and then she writes about trips to the country and the pleasure of writing in the shade of a peach tree. Very charming. Her swan song even though she never says so."

I thought of Sterling and wondered about this Stefan who had captured her heart. I wondered about her short stories and if they were ever published. And I knew I must take a look at the building on quai des Grands-Agustins.

"Where do you think Pierre Fast-Brown's private correspondence is archived," I said. "Sterling must have written him again after these letters. Maybe to his private address."

"I'll find out," said the unflappable Ms. Puigh.

Which made me think of Marjorie Robinson and the e-mail report I owed her. It would wait until the evening.

"Where are you staying?" I asked Ms. Puigh.

"Guess?"

"No idea," I said.

"On rue Jacob."

"At Sterling's hotel?"

"If we assume she stayed there."

"And if that's not exciting, I don't know what is," I said with feeling.

"I invite you to see it."

Ms. Puigh shuffled Sterlings letters and her Paris diaries back into the yellow envelope and handed them to me. Then she grinned at me happily. Her front tooth had a purple stain on it.

"Need the loo," she said, and I pointed her to the entrance hall where I lit a chandelier in the tall ceiling and opened the door to the bathroom.

"Oh, Jesus," Ms. Puigh shrieked, "look at that."

She stepped onto the pink marble floor, went to one of the double sinks, turned on the faucet and watched the water pour out of the gold-plating. She looked at herself in the beveled mirror and stuck out her tongue.

I closed the door behind her but could still hear her exclaim over the peach colored slippers and the fluffy bathrobes.

"I wanna be rich," she said when she came back out.

"Come on," I said, "let's go have dinner at the Deux Magots."

Victoria's granddaughter would have to wait.

Chapter 26

1926

"He kissed her," Sterling said.

"On the lips?"

"N-no, he wouldn't, they were in the street outside his house. He kissed her on both cheeks."

Claire stretched out in her garden chair and slowly lit a cigarette. They were under the peach tree in Sterling's garden.

"Did you recognize her?" Claire asked.

"No."

"What kind of a woman was she? Was she a *poule*?"

"No. She was well dressed. She looked rich."

"Did she have a car waiting?"

"No, a taxi came up as if someone had gone to get it."

"And you just arrived at that moment?"

"Yes."

"Did Stefan know you were coming?"

"No, I wanted to surprise him."

"Did he see your car?"

"No, I had it around the corner."

"Did he see you?"

"No. As soon as the woman left in the cab he went back inside."

"Good."

Sterling got her glass of wine from the garden table and took a solid sip.

"Good, you say. Good?"

"Yes, good, you poor dear, it'll give me a chance to find out who she might be—and I already know how to go about that—before you make a fool of yourself by showing him you're jealous."

"I am not jealous."

"What would you call it?"

"Rejected. I feel rejected."

That's how it had always been. The memories caught hard in her throat. The garden, the peach tree, a bird in the grass, Claire in her lawn chair, the wine glasses in their hands, all disappeared in a fog. Her mother's face, her hands caressing her, were now faint recollections, brought to life only because of the many times she had thought of them.

Claire filled their glasses to the brim, lit one more cigarette for herself and one for Sterling.

"I was always being sent away," Sterling said and inhaled deeply.

"Your father was still there, surely."

And there it was again, the image of her father at the train station in New York, seating her in the first class wagon, disappearing for a moment and returning with a tall blonde woman clasping the hand of a blue-eyed child with hair in ringlets, in a frilly dress, holding a small white parasol. The woman bent down to Sterling and blew a perfumed kiss across her face, saying that Genevieve and Sterling must become best friends. Sterling's father said that she must consider Genevieve her future sister. Sterling watched them disappear down the platform walking close together with Genevieve between them, and then the train set out for Boston where Sterling must stay with her grandmother while Genevieve took her place with her father.

"He was going to marry some rich widowed woman with a daughter. He was replacing me and my sister, Rose. Well, Rose probably never knew since she had already been shipped off to Cincinnati. But I was six and I remember it well. I felt horribly rejected."

"Where is your sister Rose now?"

"Still in Cincinnati. I send her an occasional postcard but we never saw one another again."

"What happened to Genevieve and her mother?"

"I was never told what happened. My grandmother and my aunt always stopped talking the minute I walked into a room. I learned by listening at the door to the servants' quarters. I guess he didn't marry her after all. I was not replaced but I felt rejected nevertheless."

"I know what you mean. But you did have a lovely grandmother."

"I did. But I was a bashful child and no one was very demonstrative. I was lonely. And when she died I was banished to the convent in Burgundy."

"Yes, I know."

"It has been the only blessing in my life," Sterling said.

"What, dear lamb?"

"What I thought was a banishment became a blessing. I was finally happy at the convent with Soeur Madeleine and all the young sisters, I immersed myself in French country life, I found peace in the chapel, I was educated well."

The fog descended once more as Sterling thought of her return to New York to her vast new apartment and to the social whirl of life with her Uncle Pierre. And Victoria. And Andrew Blake who had first loved her and then deserted her and who was exceedingly sorry.

Sterling crushed her cigarette brutally under her heel and ground it into the sod. Claire lit her another and filled up their glasses.

The sun was setting, no breeze wafted through the air, a bird chirped in the peach tree, and they both looked off into the distance at the silhouette of the town with the ancient basilica perched at the top of the hill.

"Your Soeur Madeleine is still a wonderful old nun and we must go visit her again when I return from Paris," Claire said.

"Yes."

"And your new country house is absolutely adorable, it is so much you, this is a great little town and so deliciously ancient. Promise me you won't feel lonely and that you will write on your novel every day before you return to Paris next month. Then you will come to see my new dance studio."

"You are going to have a dance studio? Where? How?"

"This is a secret," Claire said.

"I can keep a secret."

"I've found a swell little house in Montmartre and have rented it to use as my dance studio. I already have ten students and I'm giving up my apartment in town."

"Frightfully splendid news," Sterling exclaimed. "I just know you'll be marvelously successful. Spanish dancing is becoming quite the rage."

"It's my passion," Claire said.

"Scott must be pleased for you."

"Haven't seen him in a while. He went on a walking tour towards the South. Very strange fellow."

"Except you are really very fond of him, aren't you?"

"Of course, I am."

"And you are, nevertheless, discarding him for someone more exciting, old kid?"

The fog had lifted as it always did when she talked to Claire and Sterling took a good swig of Chablis and sent forth a cascade of laughter.

"Scott and I are too much alike to be comfortable," Claire said after a while. "We are both restless but when he wants to travel one way I want to go in the opposite direction."

"So sorry," Sterling said.

"And now, don't laugh," Claire said and laughed. "It just so happens that I've fallen in lust. A certain Russian violinist with a red goatee—I do adore the Russians, they're so passionate and rough around the edges—dressed in outrageous velvet jackets over white shirts. It speaks to my Spanish soul."

"Pyotr Vasilevich? How can you? You shouldn't."

"There'll be fireworks," Claire said.

"And he has suddenly erased any thought of Scott and of everyone else?"

"Exactly." Claire pulled furiously at her cigarette.

"What about poor Bernice? Doesn't she happen to be his wife?" Sterling said.

"You haven't heard the latest?"

"Judging from your lunatic smile, I assume not."

"Bernice left him."

"Jeepers," Sterling said, "I hadn't heard but I can't say I'm surprised. All I know is that she planned to go to Italy to search for marble."

"She found plenty of marble and she found the material for a new husband. An American banker with plenty of loot. They were married in Venice two weeks ago."

"She got a quick divorce from Pyotr?" Sterling said.

"No, my silly pet, Bernice and Pyotr were never really married. She just called him her husband to fool her mother in Buffalo."

"I had absolutely no idea."

"Where have you been, my pet? Everyone is whispering about it."

"I've been away," Sterling said and traced blue circles above her head.

Claire fixed her somber eyes on the horizon, then on the sunburned walls of the house, on the faded blue door and the weathered shutters. She stood up, threw back her head, re-arranged her shawl and stretched her skinny frame.

"This calls for more wine and the food I see coming on a tray carried by your no doubt fabulous cook."

They sat down to dry chicken with a lumpy sauce and watery vegetables.

"My dear," Claire drawled, "if I closed my eyes I'd think I was back in England. You must get rid of your cook tout de suite. And I mean before you invite other guests, my pet."

"But she cleans the house and washes my clothes and she's the only one I could find in the village."

"Toddle back and find another."

"I guess I will," Sterling said and knew she probably wouldn't.

Instead of trying the dessert which had the same color and consistency as the lumpy sauce they finished another bottle of Chablis. When that bottle was empty they slumped back in their chairs unable to get up.

Claire lit their cigarettes and giggled.

"What about Alex Orgoloff?" she said from the depth of her seat. "I hear his marriage, too, is suffering from irreparable estrangement."

Sterling drained her glass and looked off into the distance.

"Darling, I am his muse. I inspire him. Alex is still in his period of painting dreamy figures on a blue background. He works for hours while I watch."

"Doesn't sound like Alex but it sounds a lot like you. No little nudie escapades?"

Sterling widened her eyes at Claire and bent her head.

"But you pose for him. It must be intoxicating. He's a very virile man, women can't resist him, and his marriage to Felicia is in name only."

"Oh, Claire."

Oh, Claire, Sterling thought, I will not tell you everything.

"But then we both know that you fall for married men," Claire said and her eyes reflected the setting sun. "I wonder if it's to avoid making a commitment?"

"Is that Sigmund Freud I hear from your lips?"

"Maybe."

"Fine, then let this be the end of the subject," Sterling said.

"We should go inside," Claire said, "the morning dew will be falling soon."

"Let's," Sterling said.

Chapter 27

The outdoor terrace of the Deux Magots was chock-full of people enveloped in the ubiquitous Parisian cigarette smoke.

Ms. Puigh leapt at a front table being vacated by a slow-moving couple and we sat down to contemplate the crowd on the sidewalk close to the terrace. An enclosure with additional tables obscured the vista of the ancient church across the place Saint-Germain-des-Prés.

"That weird cage wasn't there when Sterling lived here," Ms. Puigh said. "Where we sit they would have had a perfect view of the church and of the full plaza."

"Pity," I said. "But not that unusual. Witness the pyramid which completely ruins the view of the lovely buildings at the Louvre."

"How true. Feels like an obscene sock in the eye." She pulled out a pack of cigarettes. "Mind if I smoke?"

"Go right ahead," I said. "What's one more cigarette."

A harried waiter—wrapped in a foot-long white apron over black pants—his long face without expression, his eyes sunk into deep hollows, took our orders of salmon filet and a green salad accompanied by a bottle of Sancerre.

"So," I said, "this is where they all hung out in the 1920s, here they sat—and I've seen the photographs by now—the men in their fedoras and shapeless dark suits, the women in their cloche hats and long strings of pearls, flat-chested in their flapper dresses."

"Yes, can't imagine how a big-busted woman was supposed to fit into them. Wonder what Sterling looked like and how she dressed, and what were her favorite foods and wines." Ms. Puigh heaved on her cigarette and her purple hair stood on end.

"She had money," I said, "that we know, and the woman she mentions most in her Paris Diary is Claire Garcia-Bonsonwell who was half-Spanish, exotic looking, and clicked her heels in Flamenco dances. The two of them must have sat here—maybe even in our exact same place: just imagine—and Claire was described as very elegantly dressed but somewhat eccentric. Ergo, I assume that her friend, Sterling, was also robed in Poiret and Vionette dresses, even Chanel, that she had bobbed hair as did Claire, although we don't even know if Sterling was a blonde or a brunette. In the photos in *The Bright Set* she looked very slim not to say thin."

I also remembered the photo in Paul Wainwright Manner's album in which Sterling—and I assumed it was her although her head had been turned away from the photographer—looked very elegant indeed seated in a small expensive car.

Our acne-scarred waiter plonked our plates and glasses onto the tiny round table. The salmon was a bit dry but the salad was good with black olives and a sprinkling of Feta cheese and it all washed down perfectly with the white wine.

"If it's true you can tell who you are by the friends you have then Sterling could have been quite promiscuous," I said.

During my last phone conversation with Topsy she had filled me in on the life of Claire Garcia-Bonsonwell. Her mother came from a famous dynasty of dramatic actors in London and her father was a Spanish Don who had departed for Madrid early on. Claire had inherited a marked sense of the dramatic expressed in her singular attires. She had attended dance classes in Madrid and was an accomplished Flamenco dancer. She had set up a successful dance studio in Paris and gave lessons for a couple of years.

"Are we having dessert?" Ms. Puigh crushed her cigarette into the ashtray. "How about a créme brûlée?"

I scanned the menu.

"I'll have an apple crumble, it doesn't sound very French but I don't know where you get a better one."

"Let's get the waiter's attention. Isn't it weird how difficult it is to catch his eye. Ah, here he comes."

We had the dessert with coffee.

Our waiter was suddenly eager to see us leave so I paid and we got up and walked along the square towards rue Bonaparte and rue Jacob.

"Don't turn around now," Ms. Puigh said, "but I believe we're being followed by a man in a blue velvet jacket and orange shoes."

"Oh, great," I said, "I've noticed nothing and I'm supposed to be the detective. Let's stop right now and look into the plate glass window of this lovely shop and see what happens. Tell me what he looks like. Young, old, middle-age?"

"Youngish."

"Long hair, short hair, blond, black?"

"Longish black hair."

"And how do you know he's following us?"

"He was outside your fancy hotel when we left."

"Could be a coincidence."

"Why would he be waiting around here?"

"He could have just arrived. Maybe he lives in this neighborhood."

"Then what was he doing outside your hotel?"

"Are you quite sure it's the same man?"

"It's the same. You can't miss that blue velvet jacket and those orange suede shoes."

"Doesn't sound like a good outfit for a man who should want to melt into the background."

We stared into the shop which happened to be almost in the dark and displayed antiquarian books. No one went by.

"He crossed the street," Ms. Puigh whispered.

I turned around just in time to see the man in the blue jacket and really, really orange shoes disappear into the Ladurée *patisserie* at the corner of rue Jacob. I took off my jacket, handed it to Ms. Puigh, pulled out my scarf, tied it around my head and put on my tinted glasses, the ones I use for driving.

"Gee, you look different," said Ms. Puigh in admiration.

"It's the best I can do in a hurry," I said. "I'm going to leave you here. Turn back, then double about to your hotel on the parallel street, I'll see you there as soon as I can."

"What are you going to do?"

"Follow him."

Chapter 28

While I studied the menu board outside the Bistro Pré aux Clercs the man in the blue velvet jacket and the orange shoes stood in an interminable line at Ladurées across the street where the window display was a symphony in pink, yellow, green and white confections.

He emerged carrying a large pink box containing, no doubt, some delicious macaroons and *baiser* kisses and then, without looking either to the left or to the right, he walked swiftly back down rue Bonaparte, past the Deux Magots and stopped at the traffic light with me right behind him.

He hurried across Boulevard St. Germain-des-Prés, veered sharply right and, before I could catch up, he had hailed the only taxi at the stand. He got in and slammed the door in my face. The taxi driver raised his hands in a Gallic expression of regret before taking off. The back of the cab was in darkness and all I saw was the shadow of a blue velvet sleeve and a square green button.

I removed my glasses, shook off the scarf, and laughed out loud. The situation was what Bob Makowski, in his ironic voice, would have called the luck of the Irish even though neither he nor I have any connection to the Emerald Isle.

As I trekked back to rue Jacob I thought that, at the very least, I had seen his face close up—long and narrow with a loose-hung mouth—and should be able to recognize him if I ever saw him again even in different clothes and shoes.

At the hotel, Ms. Puigh, with a grand flourish, invited me to her room on the third floor. Now, ninety years after Sterling had stayed here, the rooms were refurbished in gold tapestry and the bathroom was covered in marble tiles. There was a desk in front of one of the double windows where she might have sat at a less opulent one and I got a good feeling.

"Sit at the desk," said Ms. Puigh, and I did while I told her that her imagination must have run wild about the man in the velvet jacket and orange shoes.

"I can't for the life of me imagine why he would be following us," I said even as a small nagging thought began to build. "He may simply have come to buy macaroons. After all, Ladurée is that famous."

"He could more easily have gone to Ladurée on the Champs-Élysée if it was macaroons he was after."

It's especially annoying when people use my own kind of logic.

"I'd better be going," I said.

"Oh, no, please have a glass of wine with me downstairs before you leave. They have a lovely indoor court where we could sit."

We walked down the curved staircase to the lobby, ordered two glasses of Sancerre at the small bar and carried them outside. White curtains fluttered from several of the hotel windows facing the courtyard and a couple of tourists sat at the far end at a small table among potted plants.

"They tell me that the declaration of independence from England was signed by Benjamin Franklin, John Adams, and John Jay, on September 3, 1783, at a house just down the street from here," said the knowledgeable Ms. Puigh.

"I had no idea."

"There's a plaque on the wall to prove it."

"I'll take a look on my way back to my hotel," I said.

"Will I see you tomorrow?" Ms. Puigh said.

"Let me call you," I said diplomatically because the next day I needed to hunt down Victoria Huddersfield's granddaughter. Alone.

I took a right from the hotel and gazed in the dim light at the plaque on the wall at number 56, crossed the street and continued down to Place St. Germain-des-Prés.

I was debating whether I should have a coffee at the Deux Magots, maybe even a crêpe, when my heart lurched against my ribcage.

At a table towards the back of the terrace sat my jazz saxophone player, Jon Douglas, the one who had just sent me an e-mail supposedly from Barcelona lamenting that we had to be separated for so long and assuring me he missed me.

Jon Douglas was staring deeply into the eyes of a sultry black-haired very young woman and, as I stood paralyzed by surprise, they kissed unmistakably.

I quickly dismissed the idea of coffee on the terrace and hurried to the corner crossing the boulevard at the same point where I had earlier followed the man in the blue jacket and orange shoes. I sank into a taxi.

The streets flew by in a blur, my head was against the back of the seat, my thoughts sorted themselves out slowly, suppressed tears flowed briefly relieving the pressure in my chest whereupon my heart resumed its normal beat.

Back at the hotel I called Topsy in Washington.

"Guess what," I said, when she picked up the phone. "Guess who came to Paris."

"Don't know. Who?"

I told her.

"Oh, my God."

"He kissed her."

"On the mouth?"

"Yes, and half way down her throat."

"Did you recognize her?"

"No, looked like some Spanish floozy."

"Did he see you?"

"No, I was behind a bush planted in a huge flowerpot."

"Good."

"Did you say 'good'?"

"Gives you the upper hand. You can call the shots."

"Shots sound good."

Topsy laughed and I tried to do the same.

"I don't want to say I told you so, but you're not a Cougar at heart," Topsy said, "you need someone who's your equal."

"I know, I know. But honestly this has nothing to do with age, it has to do with character. I'm not really surprised, just mortified. He was so charming and warm and passionate to be with and I enjoyed that even as I knew this would happen. Just hadn't counted on seeing it up close and personal."

"We'll put it down to a good run, nothing ventured, nothing gained, tomorrow is another day, and all that kinda rot," Topsy said.

"The water is running in the bathtub," I said. "I'm going to lie in the bubbles and deal with my humiliation. I've ordered a late dinner, I'll swill a bottle of wine, send off some e-mails and go to sleep."

"Goodnight, Irene," Topsy said and we hung up.

Chapter 29

1927

Sterling turned in her narrow bed. The cell was bare except for the cross above her head and the small wash-stand at the opposite wall. Her dress hung limp on a wooden peg behind the massive door.

The only window let in an early sliver of dawn, a bird stirred and rustled its wings, a dog barked in the far distance. Sterling swung her feet to the floor, slipped into a pair of sandals, washed her face, brushed her hair and pulled the faded blue dress over her head. It felt precious to be unadorned, free of jewelry and silk hose, free of face powder and lipstick. Free.

She tip-toed down the narrow hallway and opened the door to the garden where Soeur Madeleine's three cats lay asleep in a basket. The dew shimmered on the grassy bank which led towards the vineyard and a small spring with crystal clear water.

Sterling walked slowly under the great oak trees stirring up twigs and leaves until she reached the water. It was seeping up in merry bubbles and she scooped it up in the hollow of her hand and drank. Around her on the forest bed small critters were getting busy, narcissus and hyacinths were about to open their crowns and silvery mushrooms with pink underbellies hid in the shadows.

She lay down in the grass and closed her eyes. The sounds of the forest intensified in the stillness and she remembered her childhood when she would get up early in the morning and creep down to the spring before anyone was up. She opened her eyes as the sun cast its first rays through the patchwork of the oak leaves.

The day had begun.

When she returned to the courtyard she heard hurried steps, a muted voice was joined by another, the iron pump screeched, water splashed into a wooden bucket, and lay sister Jeanne-Marie raised her cheery face to greet her.

"Bonjour, Mademoiselle," she said and giggled. She was barely fourteen and had yet to decide if she would stay on at the convent and take her vows.

"Bonjour, chérie," Sterling said and followed Jeanne-Marie into the pantry.

The two long tables in the cool dining-room had been set the night before with bowls for porridge, spoons and cups, and plates for bread. Sterling hurried to the kitchen to the large stove where the smoldering embers had been fed with great logs of wood. The flames sputtered and sparkled when she pried open the iron door and poked at the fire.

Sterling stirred the great iron pot on the stove where the porridge was beginning to simmer. She had signed up for early kitchen duty as she usually did. After early Mass and breakfast she would spend an hour peeling potatoes for the main meal at noon. Later she would take sister Jeanne-Marie with her to the market, buy fish, and upon their return help prepare the food for the twenty-two nuns and six lay sisters.

Soeur Madeleine—followed by Soeur Daphne, her young, impetuous, second-in-command—sailed into the dining room at precisely seven o'clock. She surveyed the sisters around the main table with her pale blue all-observing eyes and waited until Soeur Daphne had taken up her position at the head of the other table.

Then, with a slight nod of her head she folded her hands across her stomach, closed her eyes in a tight squint and blessed the food they were about to eat. Soeur Daphne, as well, folded her hands but did not close her eyes. Instead, she looked straight at Sterling who was next to Soeur Madeleine, and winked. Her brown eyes twinkled and she hastily brushed aside a lock of reddish hair from her plump cheek.

Sterling bent her head and suppressed a smile just as Soeur Madeleine opened her eyes and gave the signal to the sisters to tackle the stiffening porridge, to spread thick layers of butter and boysenberry jam on chunks of baguette and drink great big swallows of coffee. There was a determined clatter of porcelain and utensils, there was a murmur of subdued conversation and stifled laughter and a relaxation of stiff postures as Soeur Madeleine turned her attention to Sterling.

"We were very amused by the visit yesterday of Madame Rousseau and that young writer, Scott Winteride, and your friend, the Polish painter. He seemed very attentive to you, my dear. I do know he is quite famous."

Soeur Madeleine's pale eyes bulged.

"I was surprised by their visit," Sterling said. She had indeed been surprised when the three showed up at her house where she had gone from the convent to pick up an extra sweater.

Alexandre Orgoloff, his hair rumpled and his face flushed, his immaculate white jacket dusty, jumped out of Effie Rousseau's majestic Ford autocar and embraced Sterling closely. He looked in surprise at her plain dress and naked face and put two elegant fingers under her chin.

"This is how I will paint you when you come to sit for me again," he said and turned her face this way and that. "This time I will make you a portrait."

Sterling shivered and nodded faintly.

"Effie drives in the middle of the road," Alex stage-whispered. "She charges around corners with eyes closed, she drives in the middle of the road and takes no notice at all of other drivers. A frightful experience!"

Alex guffawed and shouted that he was never, never again being a passenger with Effie Rousseau at the wheel.

"But I do know how to change a tire," Effie said. "Come on, Scott, let's go see Sterling's new house."

Scott presented Sterling with a large basket of strawberries and wild flowers and followed the others through the black iron gate set in the low stone wall, into the garden and to the old wooden door to the kitchen.

"We will be leaving almost immediately, we're on our way south but Alex insisted on a detour to see you," Scott said.

"Charming, charming," Effie said when Sterling had put the basket on the kitchen table—painted blue like the open shelves stacked with faience plates—and placed the flowers in a vase with water.

Effie looked around approvingly and proceeded to the living room where she sat down in the largest chair and put her feet up on a footstool.

"You have no paintings on your walls," she said. "Alex, you must give her some."

"Of course," Alex said and winked at Sterling.

A fresh breeze came through the two windows facing the garden and blew at the sheer curtains. The ceiling was low, the walls were white-washed, the rug in the middle of the floor was striped in white and blue. Nothing looked like the expensive furniture at the apartment on the quai des Grands-Agustins.

"Charming, charming," Effie insisted.

Sterling invited them to afternoon tea at the convent and they all sat around the table in Soeur Madeleine's private living room where Alex engaged Soeur Daphne in conversation about her Persian cat and Scott held forth to Soeur Madeleine about the travails of writing while traveling. Effie admired the cross-stitching on the piano stool which depicted two plump angels soaring heavenwards. Seems like a sacrilege to be sitting on angels, she said in a loud voice to Sterling whereupon she looked tellingly at Soeur Madeleine's broad behind.

"I'm the only one who plays the piano these days," Sterling said, "and the angels don't seem to mind."

After tea Effie had steamed off in her tall open car with Scott clinging to his hat and Alex hanging out the back waving his arms frantically.

"Most amusing," Soeur Madeleine had said and closed the wrought-iron gate behind them.

Sterling had waved until the car disappeared around the bend, already missing them.

"And where is your young man these days," Soeur Madeleine now said.

"He is in Switzerland for a couple of weeks," Sterling said, "on business."

"We will miss you, my dear child. Are you sure you must return to Paris tomorrow?"

"I must. I do wish I could stay but Uncle Pierre is arriving from New York tomorrow evening."

What Sterling didn't say was that Stefan Oxenkranz was the one she wanted to see, nor that she was anxious to talk to Claire about the woman in the street outside Stefan's house.

She concentrated on spreading a thick layer of strawberry confiture on her bread and avoided Soeur Madeleine's searching look.

"I will be happy to accompany you tomorrow on your visits to the parishioners," Sterling said.

"We will start at ten o'clock," said Soeur Madeleine.

At exactly ten o'clock the next morning the two set out from the convent. The gate squeaked on its hinges and snapped shut behind them with a sharp click. On the other side of the narrow graveled road was a long stone wall topped by red tiles and behind it the vineyard belonging to the convent spread up the hill in straight lines.

A little further on lay the small village cemetery behind a tall stone wall and as they passed it Soeur Madeleine crossed herself and mentioned several names under her breath. Sterling bowed her head.

They walked along the dusty road up the steep incline towards the town. A profusion of pale stone houses with red tiled roofs and white shutters climbed up the hill and merged with the basilica at the top.

Half-way up the hill Soeur Madeleine and Sterling entered a narrow house of two floors where the plaster had peeled off the outer walls and exposed the ancient bricks underneath. From two tall windows upstairs hung pale pink begonias in white flowerpots and the entrance door was of rough-hewn wooden planks under a Romanesque arch.

Inside the door stretched a cobblestoned courtyard where two small children stuck their fingers in their mouths at the sight of the stately sister in her billowing black habit and her tall bare-legged companion. They scrambled indoors shouting *Maman, Maman.* This brought out a young woman in a blue dress and white apron on which she quickly dried her hands before greeting them.

"Bon jour, Soeur Madeleine," she said and then, "Mademoiselle."

"Bonjour, Gabrielle," said Soeur Madeleine.

Gabrielle motioned without another word and they followed her inside. The tiled hallway was cool and, at the end, led into a small room with a window towards the hills and the vineyards. A young very pale woman lay in a narrow bed under a thin blanket, her eyes closed. Out of a small bundle at her side peeked the tiny face of a newborn baby.

"My sister will not get out of bed," Gabrielle whispered. "She says her heart cannot endure the death of another baby."

Soeur Madeleine bent over the bed and picked up the baby, took her to a small table near the window and unwound the clothing. The baby cried weakly.

"This baby looks blue," she said to Gabrielle. "You must quickly find someone else to nurse her."

"I will," Gabrielle said.

"Now," Soeur Madeleine said sternly. "Go!"

She put the baby back in the bed with the mother.

"Louise," she said and gently shook the young mother's shoulders. "You must get well quickly, you must eat and drink so that you can nurse your baby. In the meantime someone else will do it for you. May God bless you and give you strength."

Louise Le Duc opened her eyes and looked at Soeur Madeleine in a panic.

"I'm going to fetch that husband of yours from the bistro, he needs to do his part now and must abandon the wine bottles."

A half hour later the baby had been taken to a neighboring house for nourishment and Gustave Le Duc, the hapless father, was chopping vegetables for soup in the kitchen while Gabrielle helped her sister get washed and fed.

"I will be back tomorrow," Soeur Madeleine warned sternly when she and Sterling left.

"The rest of our visits must wait until later," she said and walked briskly down the road back towards the convent with Sterling following.

When Sterling was ready to leave that afternoon Soeur Madeleine embraced her and held her close against the steady beat of her heart.

"Go with God, dear Minou," she whispered and repeated the pet name she had given Sterling when she first arrived at the convent as a child.

Sterling held tight to Soeur Madeleine who had always been her protector, the one person she trusted.

"I will see you very soon," she promised.

A few minutes later she was in the Quadrilette on her way back to Paris.

Chapter 30

It wasn't until the following evening that I got a look at Victoria's granddaughter.

The Boîte Noir in Montmartre was packed with several busloads of tourists intent on experiencing *la vie bohéme* and get a glimpse of the naughty which could be recounted back home with sly winks and suppressed smirks or, alternatively, in shocked whispers.

Suzette d'Alville—announced as Fifi, but clearly identifiable to me from the description given by Madame Fournier, the concierge—was the last act before the intermission.

She was tall, statuesque, near-naked, sexy and athletic. She strutted back and forth on the small stage while she belted out Edith Piaf's *La vie en rose*, no less, and then, in English, her very own version of Maurice Chevalier's popular song from Gigi about "Leetle girls" who grow up in the most delightful way.

I had a hard time sitting still but had to wait until after the intermission for Suzette to give another few displays of her body and her voice before she was through for the evening.

On my way backstage to the dressing rooms no one stopped me or asked what I was doing there which suited me well. I was just wondering what the New York heiress, Victoria Huddersfield, would have thought of her granddaughter's performance as a burlesque queen when I heard Suzette's voice calling out quite nearby.

I knocked on her door and was told to come in which I did.

The air in the dressing room was blue from cigarette smoke and I can't say I was getting used to it. Suzette was sitting in front of a round mirror taking off her make-up.

"Oh," she said in surprise when I walked in.

"Hello," I said, "I'm sorry to barge in like this but I wanted to be sure to catch you before you left."

"And who are you and why would you need to catch me," she said most pleasantly and in very good English. I thought that notwithstanding her athletic body she must be closer to fifty than to forty.

"My name is Jamie Prescott, I'm here for a couple of days visiting from the United States in search of information about someone who was a friend of your grandmother, Victoria nee Huddersfield. I believe her daughter, Marie-Louise, was your mother?"

Suzette stared at me for quite a while and shook her head.

"You mean Isabelle. My mother's name is Isabelle. Marie-Louise was my aunt. Let me get dressed," she said, "and we'll go somewhere to talk. It sounds fascinating and I enjoy a good mystery."

As do I, I thought. Google had not told me about Isabelle.

I waited outside Suzette's dressing room to give her privacy and after a few minutes heard her speak on her cell phone.

When she came out she looked quite respectable, her face clean of make-up except for her eyes which were blue with tiny crow's feet at the corners and lined in gray shadow. Her forehead was high and unlined, her hair obviously bleached but cut short with curls on top.

"I am so sorry," she said, "the mystery must wait until tomorrow, I have to be somewhere in half an hour. Please come by my apartment tomorrow for lunch and we will talk, yes?"

"Yes," I said, "it really is getting very late."

She fished out a card from her handbag, she wrote her address on rue Wagram on the back and gave it to me. It was a card from the Boîte Noir and under her name it said "Proprietor".

"You are the owner?" I said.

"Yes, Madame. I am the owner. Quite a nice business, eh?"

Yes, indeed, I thought, but why was it necessary for her to deck herself out as a *poule* and perform almost naked in front of flocks of leering tourists? Of course, who knows why anyone does anything anymore.

"You amaze me," I said, "and I look forward to seeing you tomorrow."

Back at the hotel I went straight to the bar where I ordered my serendipitous Martini. I pulled out my cell phone and texted my false-hearted suddenly erstwhile, lover, Jon Douglas.

I went straight to the heart of the matter and wrote simply: "*Paris, yesterday. Les Deux Magots. Good-bye.*"

I sat there several minutes, sipping the Martini, trying to determine my feelings—no, it wasn't jealousy, I decided, it was the rejection that stuck its pins in me mixed with a dose of wounded pride. When push comes to shove I'm the monogamous type. I knew I needed to press the 'Send' button and be done with it. Which I did.

The next day Madame Fournier, with an air of suppressed curiosity, escorted me to the elevator which took me up to the third floor and Suzette d'Alville's apartment.

Suzette led me into her large living room which continued into a dining room through an arched doorway. Her slap-dash make-up was very Boîte Noir but otherwise she was barefoot, dressed to her knees in a multi-colored t-shirt, her hair in a riot of curls. She looked as if she'd just tumbled out of bed and not on a good day.

"What can I get you," she said and her voice was hoarse. "A red Burgundy or maybe a Sauvignon Blanc, or something stronger?"

"The white wine will be perfect, thank you."

"I'll be right back."

I sat down between a half dozen pillows on a faded couch from which a furry cat escaped with an expression of disdain. White walls, tall ceilings with 19th Century moldings, ornate chandeliers, a formerly fine carpet, a still rich fireplace with a beautiful blue painting above.

"Orgoloff?" I said when Suzette returned with the wine.

"Yes, I never get tired of looking at it. I love the Surrealists. They say that the figure floating to the far right was his mistress."

"How lucky you are to own it," I said.

"It came to me from my grandfather," Suzette said. "Now what did you want to ask me?"

"I want to ask you about Sterling Kirkland Sawyer who I believe was a close friend of your grandmother, Victoria, the American heiress," I said. "But before we start let me tell you a bit about my own background and how an old acquaintance led me to you."

I gave Suzette an account of events up until the present and of CAT's descriptions of the famous people she had known in Paris in the 1920s.

"This Sterling disappeared completely by 1930?"

"Yes, and I would like to know if your grandmother, Victoria, ever talked about her."

"Well, first of all let us start lunch—a plate of cold cuts and an omelette aux fines herbes—which will not require a great effort on my part and I can concentrate on our conversation."

We served ourselves on chipped blue faience plates which I imagined had not originated with Victoria and refilled our glasses.

"Let me rather begin with my mother, Isabelle."

"Is she still living?"

"Oh, yes, but in the country."

There we go, I thought, that's the one I must talk to.

"Where exactly does she live?" I said.

"North of here. We no longer speak. She does not approve of my 'depraved lifestyle' as she calls it. Can you imagine, in this day and age."

I can very well imagine, I thought. How would my own mother have reacted if I'd become a go-go girl downtown Washington? Well, actually, she would probably have tried to accept me while at the same time wanting to rescue me and introduce me to some worthwhile boring citizen with marriage in the suburbs in mind.

"I can imagine," I said.

"In any case, my mother never cared about me. She sent me off to boarding school in Switzerland when I was nine. I ran away from school when I was twelve and she sent me to live with my grandmother. It's true that I was a difficult child but she didn't have to send me away."

"I'm so sorry," I said.

Suzette drained her second glass of wine.

"Nice legacy, mine," she said.

"What was your grandmother like? All I know about her is that she came from a very wealthy family in the States, that she was a debutante in New York in 1914, and that she came over to Paris in 1921 and married the following year."

"Here," Suzette said and heaped a second helping of the omelette aux fines herbes on my plate. "Yes, that is all true. I might add that she was unhappily married and that she—according to my sainted mother—went through liaisons with more illustrious men of her time than you could count on two hands."

"Wow," I said.

"You can say that again," Suzette said and laughed.

"Your aunt Marie-Louise, did she marry and have children?"

"No, she never married, she lived at home with my grandmother and did what society women did in those days. Nothing."

"And your uncle Henri?"

"Uncle Henri was the skeleton in the family closet. It seems that he seduced the neighbor's under-age daughter, ran away with her to the Côte d'Azur where my grandmother's emissaries found them and brought them back home. Seems he never got over it, never married, drank a lot, and died in 1975."

"What happened to the young girl?"

"She was later, much later, married off to a very common man in Paris who, they said, knew nothing of the upper classes, nor of her disgrace, and who had made his fortune in steel during the war and was immensely rich. They had one child, a son, whom, curiously enough, I ran into when I came to Paris twenty years ago. Poor Roger, his young American wife had just deserted him and returned to America. All he had to remember her by was the car she left behind at the airport."

The room spun around as I heard my marriage to Roger described in caricature. The omelette aux fines herbes stuck in my craw, the wine-glass shook in my hand, and I felt heat suffuse my cheeks.

"You knew it was me?" I managed to say above the noise in my ears.

"I realized it when he called me to say his ex-wife was looking for me," Suzette said. "However, Roger doesn't know about his mother, so don't you tell him. It's our special family secret."

"Of course not, he adores his mother," I said. "Most likely I won't be meeting him again. Ever."

"Poor Roger, he's stuck in his petit bourgeois life with his petite wife and petite children but he doesn't know he's stuck and it's a good thing you left. You would have made him very unhappy."

"Not to talk about how unhappy he would have made, and did make, me."

We stared into each other's eyes and burst out laughing and Suzette poured some more wine and we sat on the faded sofa in the living room and admired Orgoloff's mistress floating on a blue background above the fireplace.

"Tell me more about Sterling Kirkland Sawyer," Suzette said and I told her as much as I knew about her Paris days and all the famous people she wrote about, including Alexandre Orgoloff.

"I wonder if Orgoloff ever painted her," Suzette said just as a bell rang and she went to open the door.

I heard a man's deep voice, a babble of French, whispers and laughter and, then, from my low vantage point on the sofa I saw his orange suede shoes approach and, further up, his blue velvet jacket with four square green buttons.

"Meet my brother, Jacques," Suzette said.

He looked me in the eye and enjoyed the commotion in my face.

"You followed me," I said.

He scratched the beginnings of a black beard.

"Guilty."

"Let me see if I can figure this out," I said. "You were lurking behind a door and heard me talk to the concierge and having nothing better to do you followed me."

"Very true. I was curious so I followed you to your hotel where you met with the girl in the purple hair, and from there to the rue Jacob and to the Deux Magots."

Jacques scratched again, this time the back of his head.

"I'm sorry you had to go to so much trouble," I said, "it would have been simpler if you had asked me."

"But not as much fun," he said.

"I had no idea," Suzette said and looked at him without too much disapproval. "You must try to act your age."

He grabbed her and swung her around on the floor until they capsized into the sofa.

"You will have to take Jamie to see Maman," Suzette said and straightened her clothing.

"Oh, please," I said, "I'm sure I can find your mother's place on my own. No need to inconvenience your brother."

"You don't know Maman."

"Very true."

"She could decide at the last moment not to invite you in. Quite unpredictable."

"Fine," I said. "If you put it like that I will certainly appreciate your help."

"Here's my mobile phone number," Jacques said and grinned at me revealing two vampire-like eye-teeth.

"I'll call you," I said with a distinct sense of foreboding.

Chapter 31

1928

"I'm amazed," Sterling said and looked around Claire's new Flamenco dance studio. "It will all be a tremendous success with your many students and the Spanish musicians. How lucky for you to find them."

"I have been blessed," Claire said.

"You deserve it."

"I'm getting a stove," Claire said, "for the cold months."

"A lovely space," Sterling said, "I'm very happy for you. And to think you will perform next month in Madrid. Your Papa must be proud of you."

"He has always been proud of me," Claire said and lit a cigarette. "And I am proud of *you* getting your short stories published. The pen and ink drawings by Effie Rousseau will be divine."

"She started out as an illustrator before she went into oils," Sterling said. "She has been very good to me."

The studio was on the top floor of a two-story building on a busy street around the corner from the Sacré-Coeur, with a large kitchen and a combined sitting and dining area on the ground floor, and two bedrooms towards the back.

"This does not look terribly Claire," Sterling said when they sat down in the front room. The walls were painted white, the rustic furniture was included in the rent, the floors were bare and the mood decidedly plain.

Sterling eyed Claire in some concern and wondered how long this experiment would last.

"You can help me get some antiques and low divans with an abundance of pillows," Claire said, "we'll create a sinful den. Then we'll invite the artistic neighbors in."

"You are learning to be sociable," Sterling said. "It'll do you good."

"I doubt it," Claire said.

"What have you found out," Sterling said when they had moved to the rustic kitchen table with their wine glasses.

"Ah, yes," Claire said. "Stefan's mysterious lady visitor. I had dinner in Montmartre with the Berglin sisters, those British friends of mine."

"Who are they, should I know them?"

"Probably not, they don't mix with the Americans, don't come to the Deux Magots, keep to the British and the French, and frequent the Boeuf sur le Toit."

"As you know, I don't much like the Boeuf. So what are they? Writers, painters, what?

"They are mimes."

"They are mimes? You mean in face paint and costumes?"

"Exactly. White paint and brilliant red lips. Very exotic. And then there are two of them. Too exotic for the English so they flew to Paris." Claire looked at Sterling and laughed at her incredulous expression.

"They didn't!" Sterling said. "You mean they learned to fly? Like Lindbergh?"

"They did. A favorite uncle of theirs instructed them and off they went through the air having sent a trunk with their costumes ahead by sea."

"Can't believe I've never heard of them," Sterling said.

"I bet you've seen them. They were friends of Rolf de Maré and appeared in his Ballets Suedois."

"Of course," Sterling said. "That was the ballet company Orgoloff never liked so I didn't go."

"Their grandparents are neighbors of Stefan's family in Switzerland and that's how they know him."

"Tell me, then, what you found out," Sterling said.

"The woman you saw with Stefan is his cousin and not in any way about to abscond with your precious man. She is some kind of an artist."

"What is her name?"

"Natasha something, something, never caught her last name."

"Is she still in Paris?"

"That I do not know, why don't you ask him?"

"Oh, no, I couldn't, I will let it pass, it was a silly notion of mine to feel threatened."

"Quite right, my pet, wasn't it a good thing you waited?"

"Of course."

The last rays of the sun were fast disappearing behind the trees and Claire lit some of the candles scattered on tables across the room.

"When are they arriving?" Claire said. "How long would it take them from Giverny?"

"Here they are now," Sterling said just as a melodious claxon was heard in the street.

They went outside to the sidewalk.

The black Delage, its hood down, its shine covered with white powder, the spoked wheels clogged, crunched to a stop in front of the house.

Stefan Oxenkranz and Scott Winteride were windblown and dusty. Next to Stefan—the six-foot tall blond giant who was filling out around the middle—Scott was short, wiry, and a little seedy. They jumped out of the car and Stefan retrieved a large picnic basket from the red leather seat in back.

"Here," Stefan said to Claire, "brought you food which I aim to cook."

"And I brought the liquor," Scott said and started for the house, "which I aim to drink."

Stefan looked at Sterling where she stood in one of her simple blue dresses which she always wore in the country, and which she had deemed appropriate for the artistic environment in Montmartre.

"There," he shouted and ran to pick her up in his arms, "you look like a milk-maid. How delicious."

"A milk-maid," she said. "A bit of a come-down from your cousin Natasha."

"What?" Stefan swung Sterling around some more. "What do you mean?"

"Put me down, put me down," Sterling cried, "and don't laugh at me."

"Put the child down," Claire said. "I'm the one who told her about the mystery Swiss woman. Sterling wasn't supposed to show her hand like this. Do, pray, tell her all about Natasha."

Stefan put Sterling to the ground and kept his arm firmly around her waist. She squirmed but stayed and Scott shook his head at them.

"Natasha," Stefan said, "is a scribbler of verse and a tinkerer with watercolors. She is married in Zurich with two adorable children but once in a while she needs freedom and blows into Paris to see old friends. Occasionally she even comes to see *me*."

"Oh," Sterling said.

"She was here a few weeks ago and I wanted to introduce you but she left almost before she arrived. Some message from back home made her hurry back. Poor girl, her husband is the jealous type."

"Yes," Claire said and pried Sterling away from Stefan, "and none of us can abide jealousy *or* proprietary behavior. We need everyone to be free."

"Absolutely," Stefan said.

"Hear, hear," Scott exclaimed.

"Sorry," Sterling mumbled.

"Did you say you would cook for us, old chap," Claire said to Stefan.

"Absolutely."

An hour later Stefan, in a huge white apron, wiped his hands on a napkin hanging from the waistband, walked from the stove to the table and back to the stove juggling platters and bowls and sauce boats.

"Here," he said, "in the bowl are boiled new potatoes with butter and dill and on the platter herrings turned in breadcrumbs, fried with butter and topped with thick slices of lemon."

"But, first, smoked salmon," cried Claire who ate more than her usual small nibbles, "with an unbelievable mustard sauce."

"Not smoked, dear ignorant soul, this raw salmon has been marinated and then cured with a whiff of Akvavit. Our Swedish cook called it 'gravad lax'."

"How quaint."

"The salad," Sterling said, "just the way I like it. Green beans, white asparagus, sweet carrots."

"And dessert?" Scott's sallow cheeks were flushed while he filled their glasses, not for the first time.

"My universal fruit cup of wild berries picked as we sojourned in a stretch of forest on our way here," Stefan looked benevolent, still in his white apron, spreading out on the bench next to Sterling, "with sweet cream directly from a cow at the roadside."

"Hrmmph," Sterling said.

"Where did you learn to cook," Claire said. "I'm in awe, I who can't boil an egg."

"I learned from Marita, our svelte young Swedish cook who came to us when I was 16."

"Aha," Claire said.

"My mother was a great chatelaine who could not, like you, boil an egg, but she knew how to hire and how to keep her staff devoted to her. She never had to set foot in the kitchen and didn't know I spent hours there during my vacations from boarding school being initiated by Marita and also learning how to cook. Not, mind you, the food served upstairs but rather what they ate downstairs. Thus this simple meal."

"How utterly romantic," Claire said, "and alarmingly depraved."

"Hear, hear," Scott sighed.

Stefan looked pleased, served himself another heaping plate-full, poured a shot glass of akvavit which the others had hastily refused after one sip, and sent it down his throat in one gulp which infused his cheeks with color.

"Down the hatch," he said.

"Oh, my," Sterling said. "Did you know that I also learned how to cook—not in the same depraved way as you but rather by a couple of efficient nuns—when I was barely ten. By the time I left at sixteen I could whip up dinners for thirty or forty people in no time at all."

"My love," Stefan said, "we have more in common than that. Do you love me again?"

Sterling looked at him steadily for a long moment. Do I love him, she thought. I want to but I don't know how.

"Absolutely," she said using his own catch-word.

Chapter 32

1928

"Rats," Scott said and shook the whisky bottle. "Last drop."

Stefan had gone upstairs with Claire to the studio and explanations about Andalusia, dance steps, rhythms, guitar playing and handclaps trailed behind them.

Sterling sat in a small sofa opposite Scott.

"I'm sure Claire has a bottle stacked somewhere," she said.

"Never mind. Gin fizz will do."

He went out and came back with new bottles and glasses and sat down looking detached.

"I've bummed around a lot," he said.

"I didn't have a chance to be a rebel," Sterling said with a tiny laugh. "I was safely tucked away at the convent learning how to cook for forty people and then imprisoned in a fine apartment in New York City with a maid and a cook until I came out."

"Came out," Scott said scornfully. "I came out in the orphanage. My father died when I was two, I was an only child and my mother couldn't cope, gave me up. They didn't spare the rod at the orphanage."

"Oh, Scott."

"Couldn't get the devil out of me, though. I became pretty depressed." Scott reached for his glass. "Left when I was sixteen."

"You were terribly young."

"No, I was terribly old," Scott said. "Didn't belong anywhere. Didn't care for anyone. Always solitary. Bummed around, enjoyed the outdoors, drifted, learned to drink, learned to survive. Started to write."

"And your mother?"

"Gone," Scott said and re-filled his glass.

"How long before you straightened yourself out?"

"Who says I'm straightened out?" Scott almost smiled.

"I think so, your friends think so."

"I've got more enemies than friends," Scott said and stared into the bottom of his near-empty glass.

"Oh, Scott," Sterling said again.

"I've never told anyone all this before," Scott said. "I tried to return to high school but couldn't cut it. I don't take well to discipline, it was beaten out of me early."

"When did you get to New York?"

"1919."

"I was there," Sterling said. "Strange to think we walked around the same streets."

"Hardly," Scott said. "I was in Greenwich Village and you were on the Upper East Side. Your pictures were in *The Bright Set.*"

"True."

"And I lived in a garret and bar-tended at night."

"Oh, Scott, did you really?"

"I did, really. I wrote about it in my first short story."

"I remember. I thought it was fiction."

"Oh, Sterling, did you really," Scott mocked.

"I read your poems in *Poetry Magazine.*"

"Rats," Scott said. "That's when I learned."

"What?"

"That publishers are only in it for the money. Look at me now in Paris. American publishers look down upon us 'expatriates.' They will never touch me now."

"You will be published if I have anything to say about it," Sterling said.

"Live and learn," Scott said.

"Here," Sterling said, "Claire and Stefan are back."

Scott got up and went out the door to the kitchen.

"Where's Scott," Claire said.

"He'll be back in a minute," Sterling said.

"A most unpredictable fellow," Stefan said.

"Most irritating," Claire said.

"You must be kind to him," Sterling said.

"I'm as kind as I know how." Claire stood in the doorway, tall and straight as a stick, her eyes pools of black, her red lips as full as Scott's were thin and tight. "He finds me imperious and condescending and his despair and depression is an intolerable burden to me."

"But you're fond of him, nevertheless," Sterling said.

"Undoubtedly."

"Speaking of love," Stefan said, "Orgoloff has a new mistress, everyone is talking about it. She has a body like Venus and a face like a Madonna."

"You must have taken a very good look," Claire said and watched as Sterling shrank into herself and got up.

"I happened to come by his studio while he was painting. He was euphoric."

Stefan looked around.

"Where did Sterling go?"

"Probably out to find Scott."

"Orgoloff is completely besotted," Stefan continued. "He's painting in a new style."

"Fine, fine," Claire said. "Why don't you and I go clean the dishes."

They had no time to leave the room before Sterling, her face pinched, returned with Scott who looked pale and sick.

He wiped his mouth, looked around for the bottles, found one, poured liquid in a glass and drank it down.

"Opera singer," he said. "That's me."

He looked at them without seeing, jumped up, tore off his shirt, and draped it around his shoulders.

"Oh, no, Scott" Sterling said. "Not one of your performances."

Scott paid no attention. He opened his mouth, let out a series of lamentable sounds before he stumbled, clutched his head in both hands, sank to the floor and passed out.

"Oh, no," Sterling cried again. "Let's help him to bed."

"How did I know he would ruin our evening," Stefan said. "He was in a foul mood the whole car ride here."

"He'll be all right in the morning," Claire said.

But when Claire greeted Sterling and Stefan for breakfast Scott was gone.

"He took his rucksack, his hat, and his hiking boots," Sterling said. "How very sad."

"Has he found out about Pyotr Vasilevich?" Sterling said.

"Yes," Claire answered.

Chapter 33

My flight touched down at Reagan National Airport early in the afternoon and I found that my townhouse in Georgetown had survived my absence except for two wilted plants. I threw them out blaming Topsy for their demise.

Bob Makowski's phone call from Washington had come as I was reading my email from Jon Douglas in Barcelona.

"What's new in Paris," Bob had said, "and whatever it is the news here is more somber. I need you back, the big Henderson case in San Antonio is coming to a head, I'll be out of town for a week or more and you have two would-be clients clamoring for action."

I had stared in amazement at the email from Jon Douglas. "*Sweet pumpkin,*" it began and went on to explain away with unconvincing artistry his appearance at the Deux Magots.

"Why are you laughing," Bob had asked.

"If you must know, I'm laughing because a friend of mine has written a fictitious memoir and I'm supposed to believe it is fact."

"Is it by that fellow Joyce?"

"It might as well have been but, no, it's by a fellow named Douglas."

"About time you got rid of him."

"Yes, Bob," I had said. "It's done and I'll be at the office first thing in the morning."

Jon Douglas, I thought, the happy-go-lucky, passionate, perfidious jazz player with a cousin in every port. Not one of my better choices but fun while it lasted.

I dusted myself off, made a cup of black coffee and had it with some dry biscuits which was all I could find in my depleted kitchen cabinets.

Upstairs I took a nap, showered and dressed and at a few minutes before seven walked the two blocks to Topsy and Martin's place.

"Sterling Kirkland Sawyer has invaded our spare time, our thoughts, not to mention our home with particular emphasis on the study," Martin said when we sat in the front room.

"Don't be silly," Topsy said. "You're not here all day and when you return from your office in the evening, there I am in my little black dress with dinner on the table, cocktails cooling on the sideboard, and humorous conversation about the political shenanigans of the day."

Martin winked at me.

"Except when she's in sweats and running shoes, grilling cheese, serving beer, and gossiping about shenanigans that aren't political."

"It's true about the study, though," Topsy said. "Books do tend to pile up but don't forget it's *my* study and you are really very comfortable with your computer in the den."

"As you see, married life is agreeing with us," Martin said and winked again.

"Even the bickering agrees with you," I said.

"Where did we leave off," Topsy said. "About Sterling, I mean."

"I met with Victoria Huddersfield's granddaughter, Suzette d'Alville, two days ago but didn't have time to email you before I left Paris."

"And?"

"She's a stripper."

"A stripper!" Topsy guffawed.

"In her own nightclub, the Boîte Noir, in Montmartre. And Victoria had one more child, Isabelle, in addition to the two, Henri and Marie-Louise, we knew about, and she's Suzette's mother."

I told them the story Suzette had recounted and about her obnoxious brother, Jacques, in his orange shoes and blue jacket.

"That's what you must do next," Topsy said. "Get rid of the weird Jacques and go talk to Isabelle alone."

"Exactly."

"Too bad you had to return home at this very point."

"Bob's desperate," I said. "I'm staying five days and no more."

"Even though we haven't found Sterling's publications anywhere—and, believe me, it's not for want of trying—I've rather enjoyed getting back to Joyce, Fitzgerald, and Hemingway's books and reading them with a more mature eye than twenty years ago," Topsy said.

"Interesting, that's exactly what I was thinking," I said.

"I've also enjoyed Roland Lee Rainier's three books, a bit dated, of course, but they give a good picture of the way people behaved in the 1920s," Topsy said.

"Not to mention Bernice Boch's wonderfully naughty descriptions of bohemian life in Paris. She obviously hung out her friends to dry. Wonder how many she still had when she left."

"She married a wealthy banker who bought her a gallery in New York and set her up with a studio in which to produce her enormous Rodin-like sculptures. They had three children in quick succession and, as far as I know, remained married for the rest of their days," Topsy said.

"Before her marriage she had lived for several years with the Russian violinist, Pyotr Vasilevich. Whatever happened to him?"

"He was enormously successful, played concerts in all the major cities in Europe and had an on-again, off-again affair with Claire Garcia-Bonsonwell, the one CAT mentions so frequently in her Paris diary," I said. "Once he got over her it seems he married a very young Russian ballet dancer and had one son."

"Would that be the eminent film director, Oleg Pyotr Vasilevich?"

"The very one," Topsy said.

"Some summing up," Martin said as he came into the room with a tall stranger in a dark suit with a fine crease in his pants, totally shined shoes, and a discreet tie.

"Look who came to dinner," Topsy said and stared me down as if I was going to mention that she's not to introduce me to any more Washingtonian men without my go-ahead.

"This is Neil Robinson," Martin said. "Your client, Marjorie Robinson's, son."

"I came straight from the State Department," Neil said, pumped my hand and smiled into my eyes. His were brown and he had white sprinkles at the temples. "Otherwise I would have dressed more informally. I've been looking forward to meeting you."

"How is your mother," I said hoping she hadn't complained to him about my haphazard reporting.

"Busy as ever," he said, "I haven't actually been following what you are doing for her in Paris, she gets these things into her head and then rather drops them. You are looking for a long-lost great-aunt of mine?"

"Sterling," I said as if speaking of a close friend. "I must get back to Paris next week to follow a very promising lead."

"I took an intensive semester at the Sorbonne," Neil said, "and, because I'm fluent in French, State sends me on missions to Korea and Japan."

"While those who speak Japanese are sent to Paris?"

"You got it."

I laughed and Topsy mimed "divorced" behind his back.

"I was actually told by my mother to look for this Sterling while I was a student in Paris but, of course, at that time it didn't interest me. Now I'm suddenly interested," Neil said and smiled at me again.

Topsy mimed "charming" and I got up and followed her to the kitchen.

"Will you stop doing your Marcel Marceau routine," I said, "he could probably see you reflected in the glass door."

"Oh, God, you think he saw me?"

"If he did, it serves you right."

"Did you send Jon packing?"

"I did and I informed Mel in New York that I'm now a free agent. He's about to shed his long-legged model."

"You didn't! He isn't! And just as I thought Neil would be perfect for you."

"Perfect? We would commute between Japan and Washington?"

"What's this about commuting," Martin said and grabbed some empty glasses from the kitchen counter.

"Nothing," we said.

The dinner was not French cuisine but I thoroughly enjoyed a home-cooked meal for once. The dessert wasn't bad either. Actual créme brulée. Topsy knows how to handle a blow-torch.

"Between them, Topsy and Jamie have read about a hundred books in a month," Martin said to Neil. "Your mother's little obsession has gripped the entire household. We also get constant messages on the machine from Reginald Fletcher at the bookstore announcing more discoveries of the antiquarian variety."

"Whatever happened to Ben Vogelhut after he closed down *The Pyramid Press*?" Neil said. "I still have some holes in my knowledge."

"Enough, enough," Martin said and got up from the table. "It's getting a wee bit too literary for a poor constable like myself who spends his days tracking down those who must be served papers under the law. A most prosaic occupation and although I don't mind getting educated I suggest we take a break over coffee."

"Oh, poor baby," Topsy cried. "Don't believe a word he says. He's just as caught up in this mystery as everyone else. But do let's have the coffee right now."

Our conversation sagged somewhat over the de-caf and, with jet-lag setting in, my eyes began to itch and close involuntarily.

"She's falling asleep," I heard Topsy say and woke up with a start.

"Let me walk you home," Neil said. "I gather you live not far from here. Then I'll get a cab to take me to the Watergate. I have an early morning meeting."

"Good luck," Topsy whispered and shooed me out the door with Neil.

"Lovely evening. I'll call you tomorrow," I said to her.

"Could we have dinner some night this week," Neil asked when he stood on the stoop and watched as I opened my red front door. "I'd like to hear more about Sterling."

"Of course," I said. "Why don't you come by Tuesday night at seven and we can take it from there."

"See you then," Neil said and walked briskly to the corner where I saw him hail a cab.

I unplugged the phone, turned off the cell, reminded myself to e-mail my mother who was cruising on the rivers of Eastern Europe and set the alarm for six. I would put in an hour at the gym to perfect some Tae Kwon Do exercises before going to the office.

Chapter 34

"Where did we leave off," Neil Robinson said when we had both ordered wild mushroom ravioli and Chianti at my favorite Italian restaurant in Georgetown.

"Ben Vogelhut," I said. "And let's throw in Scott Winteride for good measure."

"Never actually heard of either of them until the other night."

"About Scott Winteride," I said, "we have a biography by one of his contemporaries. Seems that he was a nettlesome character who fell out with most of the other writers at the time. He resented their success, whenever they had any, and complained endlessly about being rejected by New York publishers for being a so-called 'expatriate'."

"What a waste of talent," Neil said.

"I think no one then knew who would be successful and who would fizzle out. Many of them had equal talents but not sufficient drive to do the hard work or, obviously, the ability to promote themselves," I said. "But Scott Winteride was unable to finish his novel and his obnoxious behavior put a stop to any hopes of publication. Which brings me to Ben Vogelhut. He ran his private press for several years and published some of the better writers in Paris in the 1920s."

"You mean like Ezra Pound and Joyce?" Neil said.

"Precisely."

"Heady stuff."

The ravioli and the wine arrived and we dug in with equal appetite both of us having spent the day at work and I, at least, having had no time for the one-hour plus lunch break usual in the life of the hard-working bureaucrats of official Washington.

"What about Scott Winteride's writing, was he any good?" Neil said. "Did you say that you read his book of short stories?"

"I actually did."

"What were the stories about?"

"He railed against the so-called pillars of society and described the horrors of the orphanages of the day, in positively Dickensian terms. Apparently it was autobiographical."

"What happened to him after Paris?"

"He roamed around in Europe until the Germans invaded France. He fled to England where he continued to write without getting published and died there in 1948."

"A very sad story."

"Yes," I said, "CAT mentioned him in lots of the Paris diaries and praised his short stories. Strange how completely he has disappeared from the records."

The ravioli gone and the bottle of Chianti empty we ordered no dessert but went straight for the cappuccinos.

"One more thing," Neil said and stirred sugar vigorously around in his coffee cup, "whatever happened to Claire Garcia-Bonsonwell?"

"She was quite celebrated in Spain as a Flamenco dancer and had a dance studio in Montmartre for a couple of years before moving to Spain definitively."

"You said that my great-aunt Sterling Kirkland Sawyer praised Effie Rousseau's pen and ink drawings as well as her oils in her *Paris Diary*. Did you find out if Sterling ever got published? Maybe Effie illustrated some of her short stories."

"I haven't found anything yet. It's all very frustrating, Sterling is like a shadow that slips through my fingers at every turn."

"I feel quite confident that you will solve the mystery," Neil said, "and so does my mother. Which reminds me that I haven't heard from her today although she said she would call me."

"I e-mailed her earlier to let her know I'll be in New York on my way back to Paris next week," I said.

"Here," Neil said, "let me try her cell phone again. I told her I was having dinner with you and she insisted on an immediate report."

"I can imagine," I said.

"No reply," Neil said and texted her instead of leaving a voice mail message. "I told my mother about your surreptitious visit to the grandson of Wainwright Manners III in New York."

"Martin told you?"

Neil looked at me a bit sheepishly.

"Yes."

"He really shouldn't have," I said and couldn't conceal my irritation.

"Very sorry," Neil said. "I can tell from your face that you resent the interference if that's what it is."

"My own fault," I said. "I'm not used to dealing with a case in which my close friends become involved. I usually keep the progress of my investigations quiet until I'm sure of the outcome. Sorry if I seemed rude."

"I'm afraid my mother said that she was planning to do some sleuthing herself."

"I hope she didn't contact Paul Manners," I said, again more sternly than I had intended.

"Ah," Neil exclaimed. "That's her phone now. Hello, Mother?"

He then sat up abruptly and stared towards the street above my head.

"What?" he looked about him wildly, white of face and shouted into the phone. "What do you mean? When?"

He listened for a few tense moments and slumped down in his chair slowly.

"Yes, of course," he said, "yes, I understand, I'll leave right away, I'll drive, I'll be there in about four hours."

"Neil," I said.

He looked around in a daze.

"That was my uncle."

"I thought you called your mother?"

"He has her phone. He's at the hospital. He was just about to call me. My mother was in a hit-and-run accident on Central Park West not far from her home."

"Is she all right?"

"No. She's dead."

Chapter 35

1929

The windows sparkled with lights from a thousand stars, shadows moved languidly behind sheer curtains, and upon entering Sterling was met by a steady hum of voices and occasional laughter wafting from the main salon across the marbled foyer.

Stefan Oxenkranz's elegant home on the rue de la Paix was tucked in between two larger houses but still consisted of three floors with salons and bedrooms with paneled walls and reception rooms with flowers in Louis XIV vases. A grand winding staircase swept upwards from the foyer.

Two Venetian chandeliers glittered above white-gloved waiters and added their luster to the distinguished guests. Two long tables stood laden with porcelain and silverware, tall center-pieces fashioned from waxed fruits and live orchids, platters brimming with Stefan's favorite marinated salmon, new potatoes, thin blood-red sliced roast-beef, all manner of pâtés, caviar galore, and silver chafing dishes with lobster and shrimp and mussels and plump escargots with garlic butter, and hearts of artichokes in wine sauce.

Sterling stood at the entrance and surveyed the opulent scene. This evening she was dressed in a white sleeveless

Chanel—with a low-slung belt and a profusion of pleats, the perfect backdrop for her long string of pink pearls. A happy smile brightened her face as Stefan came towards her and she offered him her cheek. He pulled her to him and embraced her and whispered in her ear. She smiled and nodded.

He took her by the hand and drew her into a circle of foreign ambassadors and ministers and their wives, French counts and their countesses, painters and writers, gallery owners and museum curators and, towards the middle in a small huddle, Alexandre Orgoloff, Claire Garcia-Bonsonwell, and Scott Winteride.

"Thank God," Claire gasped and circled her ivory cigarette holder above her head tracing smoke in the air. She was in one of Elsa Schiaparelli's more outrageous creations having abandoned Spanish red for a rainbow of colors. "Thought you'd never come."

"My dear," Alex said and kissed Sterling's hand, not once but twice. "I am telling darling Claire that Elsa has taken her divine surrealist inspiration from me."

"Of course," Claire said and winked at Sterling. "Alex inspires us all."

"And you, my dear," Alex said to Sterling "you look divine in white satin, from the Mademoiselle on rue Cambon, I fancy. You are ravishing, there is a wondrous glow to your face."

"Stefan brings out the best in Sterling," Scott said and stared at Orgoloff without quite concealing his disdain.

"Ah," Alex said, "and I presume that you believe you bring out the best in Claire."

"Now, my pets," Claire said and circled her cigarette once more, "now is not the time for small jealousies being aired."

"Jealousies?" Alex exclaimed and laughed.

"We have different opinions about painting and writing, that's all," Scott said.

"Cubism, Dadaism, Surrealism," Sterling said breezily. "Let us forget the isms, this evening is not for quarrels or differing opinions, this evening is for celebration and happiness."

They looked around for Stefan and Claire eyed Sterling through another burst of smoke.

"Is he really forty," she said and threw ashes to the wind. "Doesn't look a day over thirty-nine although he needs to curb his culinary appetites. I can't abide voluminous men."

"I never threw a birthday party for myself," Orgoloff said. "No need to celebrate getting old."

"Old?" Stefan said. "Talking about me behind my back?"

"I do it to your face," Claire cried, "but you know I love you."

"Not as much as Sterling does, I hope," Stefan said and looked around for her. "Where did she go?"

"Over there," Claire said. "I believe she has met your friends, the Berglins. Better catch her before they tell her all about your Swiss girlfriends back home."

"Ah, the beautiful Berglin sisters," Orgoloff said and made his way across to the new group on the heels of Stefan.

"Who are the beautiful Berglin sisters," Scott said to Claire.

"Where have you been, old chap," Claire looked irritated. "They're now with the Ballets Russes. They flew themselves from London to Paris, they look quite fabulous in white face paint and red lips, they frequent the Boeuf sur le Toit where they mime to the Charleston."

"Never go there, myself," Scott said.

"They were friends of Rolf de Maré," Claire said. "He of the other wonderful ballet."

"The Suédois," Scott said. "Closed four years ago."

"Oh, you've heard of the Ballets Suédois," Claire said.

"Must you always make me feel bad?" Scoptt stared at her angrily.

"No, I don't always 'must'."

"Maybe you would rather continue here without me?"

"That would be entirely pleasant."

"Then I'm going."

"Go, and good riddance."

"I won't be back this time."

"I hope you won't."

Claire charged across the floor to the Berglin sisters just as Sterling was pulled away by Stefan and steered towards the food-laden table.

"They're at it again," Sterling said to Stefan.

"She's rotten to him," he said.

Claire stood suddenly at their side clasping her glass.

"Talking about me, my pets?"

"The men will stick together," Sterling said.

Their plates filled they went to one of a dozen round tables set with white tablecloths and pink roses in crystal vases. The walls were a pale green and the large Matisse painting hanging on the far wall dominated the room with its bright greens, reds, yellows, and purples.

"The *Chér Maître,*" Orgoloff murmured to Sterling as he sat down next to her. "When will your *chér amour* hang mine?"

"Would that be a painting of your new mistress?"

"My leetle *kiciu* is showing her sharp claws tonight. Why should you be jealous, you who have the attention of our magnificent host?"

"I am not jealous," she murmured back.

"Come sit for me tomorrow, then? Your face has grown more beautiful since I saw you last in the country. It has a transparency that I would like to catch."

Stefan sat down on the other side of Sterling.

"What are you whispering about," he said to Alex. "How is your sensuous Venus with the Madonna face? That is one painting I would buy. I have the perfect space for it in the next room where it would hang above the fireplace, by itself, without any competition."

"You are too gracious, mon ami," Orgoloff said. "Come around to the studio next week and we shall see."

"Maybe tomorrow," Stefan said, "I leave in three days for Switzerland for at least a month."

"It is business before it is pleasure," Orgoloff said. "You must not leave your lovely Sterling alone for so long. Why not take her with you?"

"I would not be able to pay sufficient attention to her," Stefan said. A slow flush had come over his face and he got up from the table.

"Come around to see me next week, *ma chérie*," Orgoloff whispered and Sterling looked long into his eyes and smiled.

"I will be going to the country," she said.

When the small jazz band played up at the back of the salon the floor was soon filled with an ever more noisy group kicking up their legs, raising their arms high, shaking their shoulders in the performance of the latest Charleston and Bunny Hop variations.

The waiters carried in the bombe glacée, the musicians finished with a prolonged flourish and the dancers drifted back to their tables. The conversations wound down and by two in the morning the last guests walked towards the staid Place Vendôme to limousines and taxi cabs. The night was luminous with stars, a full moon glowed in a dark blue sky, and morning in Paris was about to stir.

Upstairs in Stefan's small sitting room adjacent to his bedroom suite, on a table, sat an exquisite velvet-lined box from Cartier.

"What is this," Stefan said.

"Happy birthday," Sterling said. "I love you."

Stefan looked at her and a strange shadow fell over his half-closed eyes.

"Do you know this is the first time you have ever told me that you love me."

"But you have always known that I do."

"It is not the same thing."

"Open your gift," she said.

Stefan stepped to the table, picked up the box, and opened it to a Cartier wrist-watch.

"The perfect gift for the perfect gentleman," he said and fastened the watch on his left arm, "I shall wear it always."

"I am happy you like it."

Sterling sat down at the edge of his large double bed. "I feel dizzy," she said, "your champagne was too, too, delicious."

"Then give me the best present of all," Stefan said and sat down beside her. "Let's not stay at your place tonight. Stay here with me."

Chapter 36

1929

"Uncle Pierre," Sterling exclaimed and ran towards him where he disembarked from the Le Havre train.

"You received my telegram," Pierre Fast-Brown said. "This trip was a sudden decision, I had no time to write you a letter."

"No matter," Sterling said, "I am only too delighted to see you, I've missed you sorely."

"If you missed me so sorely you could have come home to see me," he said. His tone of voice was dry but he beamed at her in his usual way. "You have been in Paris since 1921 and here we are in September of 1929 and you are still here."

She beamed back and hugged him exuberantly.

"It seems both a short time and a long time. So much has happened."

"Well, well, what is this," Pierre said when Sterling hugged him again and held her at arm's length. "I must say you look uncommonly well."

"Oh, I feel uncommonly well, I'm making the very last revision to my novel and I've almost finished the book of poems which Effie will illustrate."

"You must tell me all about it later."

"I hired a touring car, my little two-seater would be too small," she said, "do you have a lot of valises? We will go directly to the Ritz."

Fast-Brown sat back in the rear seat of the touring car and closed his eyes.

Sterling looked at him in concern. He seemed tired not only from the journey but deep creases had formed in his face where she had noticed none before, his hair had turned white and was cut close to the scalp.

"Are you feeling quite well?" she said.

"Yes, yes," he said with a touch of impatience, "but I'm concerned about that dear child, Victoria. I had a letter from her saying that you are now her enemy and that you are setting your friends against her."

"What?"

"I am only repeating what she writes. Naturally, I don't believe a word of it."

"I can assure you that I have done nothing of the kind. We move in completely different circles and, in fact, we never meet and I hardly ever think about her."

"It would mean a lot to me to have my two favorite girls be close again," Pierre said.

"I will make an effort," Sterling murmured.

"That's a good girl." He beamed at her. "And now, let me freshen up at the hotel and I will pick you up for dinner at seven."

"No, why don't I pick you up instead, we will dine at the Deux Magots and you can meet some of my dearest friends."

"Although my preference is for the Café de la Paix where all I have to do to meet friends is sit at a corner table, it would be better if we dine somewhere quiet with no friends at all around," Pierre said. "I have something serious to discuss with you."

"Are you ill?"

"No, no, nothing like that but I would still prefer a quiet place where no one will interrupt us. May I suggest that you come back to the hotel and we will dine in my suite."

Fast-Brown smiled but looked pale and pre-occupied.

"Of course," she said quickly, "I will come back at seven o'clock."

When they sat over coffee and a cognac three hours later Sterling leaned back in her chair and put out her cigarette.

"Now, Uncle Pierre, what is it?"

"I was in such a hurry to get here that I would have flown in one of those Zeppelin airships they used to have," he said.

"Intrepid, indeed," Sterling said and looked at him anxiously.

He looked back at her and narrowed his eyes.

"I want you to instruct your stockbroker to sell all your stocks," he said. "I want you to send an order by telegram right now. Here, I have prepared a draft for you."

"My portfolio has increased five-fold in the past year," she said. "Why would I sell? What have you learned? What is wrong?"

"My dear child, everything is wrong. I have it on the best—and quite confidential—authority that you must get out of the stock market right now."

"Is that what you are doing?"

"No, I have invested my monies in paintings and real estate and such like. I do not believe in stocks."

"Have you come all the way to Paris to tell me this?"

"I have."

"Then I will do what you advise although my portfolio seems to be in the best of shapes. Not that I really need all that money. Give me the draft and the telegram will be sent tomorrow morning."

"I promised your dear departed grandmother that I would look after your interests. Thank you for heeding my advice, dear child."

"I trust you implicitly."

"Have you discussed investments with Stefan?"

"No, we never talk about money. He takes care of his and I take care of mine. But I will talk to him when he returns from Switzerland in late October."

Pierre stayed in Paris ten days during which time he bought paintings for himself and a trunk full of gifts for his staff back home, dined with Sterling several nights at the Deux Magots where he joked with Claire Garcia-Bonsonwell, admired her scarlet and silver outfits, praised her mother's latest triumph on the stage in London. and managed a tête à tête with Alex Orgoloff to whom he was heard describing the new Museum of Modern Art in New York. On his last night before leaving for London he invited everyone to the Boeuf sur le Toit for oysters and Champagne. They were all heart-broken to see him leave.

Two days later there was a telegram from her stockbroker in New York asking Sterling for final confirmation of her order to sell and she, without hesitation, confirmed.

"Claire," Sterling said when they stood together at the Galerie Surréaliste where Orgoloff was exhibiting his latest paintings.

"I must get back to the dance studio although I'm getting tired of my boarders who stay up all night," Claire said. "What I need is a visit to my Papa in Madrid."

"Claire," Sterling said again, "are you invested in stocks?"

"What?" Claire burst out laughing. "Stocks? My dear old girl, I depend solely on my allowance from my father. No, I don't own stocks. Why do you ask?"

"I was advised to get out of the stock market and I did," Sterling said, "so I thought you should, too, but now we'll forget all about it."

"Loved your Uncle Pierre, my pet, in a platonic kind of way. I don't think he's that interested in women although he loves to see us dress fabulously well and enjoys our girlish gossip."

"He never steps out without a woman on his arm."

"Not the same thing. But speaking of fabulous, when is your man returning from Switzerland?"

"In a few weeks."

"You're blushing," Claire said.

Claire looked steadily at the heightened color in Sterling's cheeks and at her bright eyes.

"I've been wondering when you would capitulate," she said drily, "wondering when you would tell me. You will marry him, then?"

"The die is cast."

After Sterling left Claire and the gallery she strolled slowly through the streets to her apartment on the Grand-Agustins. She sat down in front of her traveling Corona and stared at the blank page for several long minutes but nothing came to her mind. She shivered and put away the machine.

She went to the den and opened her trunk, placed the manuscript of her novel and poems under the removable tray together with James Joyce's *Ulysses* and her two signed Bernice Boch books. Then she re-read her latest letter from Stefan and placed it in the trunk before locking it.

Chapter 37

"You mean your client died?" Bob Makowski slapped his pencil down hard on the desk. "I've had suspects die but never a client."

"The police told Neil Robinson that they have two witnesses, one swears she saw a yellow cab swerving, hitting, and taking off."

"Don't tell me. The second witness saw a dark blue sedan doing the same thing."

"Just about."

"What's the plan now?"

"Well."

"You're going back to Paris," Bob stated. "To the crêpes and the champagne."

"Listen," I said. "I have a gut feeling that I'm getting close to finding out what happened to Sterling."

"Okay. I'll admit that I'm getting somewhat caught up in the case myself—not a whole lot mind you—how long will you be gone?"

"About ten days," I said.

I put in a call to Ms. Puigh's office in New York. I hadn't heard from her since leaving Paris and my text messages and e-mails had gone unanswered. Instead of her voice on the line I got a taped message to the effect that Ms. Puigh was no longer employed at the company.

Trying to settle the sudden butterflies in my stomach I dialed the main number and asked for Human Resources.

"Val Puigh," a pleasant woman said. "No, we cannot disclose her whereabouts or her phone number or address."

"I understand," I said. "Instead, may I leave a message with you for her to call me?"

That could be arranged the pleasant woman said although there was no telling when the message could be delivered.

Several likely and some unlikely reasons for her sudden departure from her job occurred to me. She had found a better-paying job. She had returned to Paris. She had gone back to school. She had painted her hair orange and had departed for India in search of a guru.

As a last measure I sent yet another e-mail to Ms. Puigh hoping for an imminent reply.

Not planning to put in supplies in my empty refrigerator for my short sojourn in Washington I invited myself to dinner at Topsy and Martin's house. Imagine my surprise when I arrived at seven to find my mother, the lawyer, installed with a drink on the living room sofa.

"Hello, my dear Cassandra," she said, "figured this was where I could catch you and here you are."

"Cassandra?" Martin exclaimed.

"An abominable middle name which serves strictly as my middle initial," I said and looked sternly at my mother, "and which I want everyone in this room to forget instantly on penalty of a painful death."

"Sorry," my mother said. "But you really are quite unreasonable about it. It was my own mother's name."

"Can't help it," I said. "I thought you were on a river cruise in Eastern Europe."

"Got back yesterday, still jet-lagged."

She patted the seat next to her and I sat down with a glass of wine supplied by Martin.

"I was telling Martin about your mother growing up in Denmark," Topsy said."

"I thought you were Swedish," Martin said.

"Back a generation," my mother said.

"A Swedish great-great grandfather was knighted in the early 1800s," I said. "He built a sturdy mansion south of Stockholm complete with a moat and a watch-tower. The family prospered and my grandmother grew up there in the 1930s quite pampered and wilful."

"Well," my mother said.

"That's what you told me," I said. "Your mother fell in love with a lowly engineering student from Denmark who was completing an internship in Stockholm."

"True," my mother said.

"She defied her parents' wishes, eloped with him to Copenhagen, was forevermore disowned by her family, and gave birth to my mother the following year," I said. "She was nineteen and he was twenty-two."

"You mean your grandmother never got to see her Swedish family again," Martin said to me.

"She was often quite sad and I never knew why," my mother said. "My father was the one who told me and he felt very guilty. Then, when I was sixteen, my parents were killed in a car accident."

Martin looked horrified.

"Both of them?" he said. "What happened to you after that?"

"I went to live with my father's family for two years until I graduated. That's when I came into my own money and decided to put it all behind me and come to this country to study."

"She enrolled at Georgetown University where she met my father who was a law professor there," I said, "and the rest is history."

What actually happened was that she was married at nineteen to my father who was thirty-five and I was born a year later. Twelve years ago when my father died my mother went back to law school and is now a partner in a small law firm in downtown Washington.

"Dinner's ready," Topsy said and we trooped to the dining room and sat down to another home-cooked meal. While Martin poured an aromatic red Beaujolais Topsy passed around her renowned Boeuf Bourguignon.

"Straight out of one of my favorite French cookbooks," Topsy said. "The one Bernice Boch wrote a year after her weird detective story—and after her last novel—shortly before she abandoned writing and took up sculpture."

"Never read her books but I love her sculptures," I said. "Rodin-like without being bombastic."

"Please pass Bernice's *Artichokes á la Normande*," Topsy said. "They were cooked with olive oil, carrots and chopped onions, then white wine, garlic and rosemary were added."

"And, voilà, delicious," I said and began plucking the tender leaves.

"I hear you're involved in a quest for a missing hundred and fifteen-year old woman in France," my mother said.

"How word gets around," I said and told her some of what I'd found out.

"Seems you still have a lot of ground to cover," my mother said after which she bid us a jet-lagged goodnight and promised to call me. Martin took her to her parked car around the corner and returned to the kitchen to rattle plates into the dish-washer.

"Before I forget," Topsy said and went to the den, "I have a tote full of books for you from Reginald Fletcher, don't know what's in it. Let me know what you find."

"Will do," I said and accepted another cup of coffee. "And now Ms. Puigh has disappeared."

"She sounds like a lot of fun," Topsy said. "I hope she won't be in any danger through her association with you?"

Topsy, herself, got involved in one of my cases when we attended a travel agent conference in San Francisco a couple of years ago. She ended up in jeopardy of her life and decided then and there that she's not private investigator material.

"No, it's not that kind of a case," I said. "But Ms. Puigh is the flighty type and I never know quite where I have her. At the moment I don't have her anywhere at all."

"Check your e-mail."

And there it was, a message from 'SnakeVal'.

"*Imagine my surprise,*" the message said, *"when I arrived at your hotel in Paris and discovered that you had checked out. You're back in Washington, I assume? I have lots of news, completed my research for you, was fired from my job in New York for being AWOL, will stay in Paris at least ten days at my small hotel thanks to the generous check you sent me for the work I've accomplished so far. I'm off on a short vacation in Nice. Call me!"*

Topsy was reading over my shoulder.

"Her name is SnakeVal?"

"No, her name is Valentina but she uses Snake in homage to her tattoo."

"Of course."

"At least now I know where she is, more or less," I said. "I must return to Paris tout de suite."

"Of course," Topsy said.

Chapter 38

Jacques was waiting for me in the doorway to his apartment building on rue Cardinal Lemoine. He was dressed in tan pants, a white shirt, a dark blue Armani blazer, and shiny black loafers *sans* socks.

He waved to me without enthusiasm.

I had arrived the day before after a short stop in New York where Neil Robinson had confirmed to me over lunch that my quest for Sterling Kirkland Sawyer should continue—albeit on an even tighter budget than that imposed by his late mother, if that was possible. This had not prevented me from checking back into my five-star hotel. I would give up my vacation to Turks and Caicos. Mel Kramer had taken me to dinner in SoHo and we had enjoyed a night-cap at his apartment where all signs of a long-legged model had disappeared. The next morning he drove me to the airport for my flight to Paris.

I was still jet-lagged and in a very uncommunicative mood.

Jacques got into my rental BMW with a surly hello and I snaked the car around Place Contrescarpe amid tourists and locals spilling over from the sidewalks, around bicyclists wobbling on the cobbled stones, past a street musician accompanying a blaring CD player on his violin, and downhill towards Place Maubert.

I ventured a look at Jacque's conservative outfit.

"What," I said, "no orange suede shoes or blue velvet jacket with big buttons to go to the country?" I said.

"My Maman is old-fashioned. She thinks me too eccentric. She does not approve of poetry and I am a poet."

"Ah," I said in a flash of illumination, "that's why you're dressed like Ezra Pound."

"You know about Ezra Pound?"

"I do, and I've always admired the way he dressed."

"Well, thank you. I have read all his *Cantos,* he was a genius, and I aspire to write like him."

"I hope you will stick to poetry and not copy his fixations on economics and politics."

"I know nothing of economics or politics," Jacques said. "I stay aloof, you understand."

"I am very relieved," I said, "but if you'd rather not go to the country I can easily find your mother's place by myself. I could call you later and let you know how my meeting went."

"I would be immensely thankful," he said. "I came only because I thought you would bring the one with the purple hair."

"She is not in town right now."

"Who is she?"

"Val is my gofer."

"Go for?"

"Yes, she fetches for me. Quite invaluable. She's a perfect Francophile like myself."

Jacques stared at me, his face blank.

"Maybe you'll introduce me."

"Sure," I said and thought, in a pig's eye.

I circled back to Place Contrescarpe where he sprang to the pavement, waved gallantly, and skipped the few steps to his front door on Cardinal Lemoine. I felt sure he would soon be dressed again as a poet immersed in his personal *Cantos*.

A few minutes later I was on my way out of town towards Reims very much thankful to be alone. Traffic was heavy with fumes hanging low above small Peugeots and Citröens and French vans pursued by large trucks from other European countries.

After clearing a few tunnels lined with gleaming white tiles I emerged unscathed on a two lane road. The scenery soon changed to long stretches of low brush and occasional trees huddling around scattered houses. Then the landscape opened up to red poppies in yellowing fields with solitary farm houses, rolled hay bales, and allées of ramrod-straight poplars.

Soon the soil became chalky and luxuriant vines rose in razor sharp rows from the sides of the road. In small villages sand-colored houses with red tiled Mansard roofs nestled around corners while an occasional larger house was set well back from the road.

After taking a couple of wrong turns, conferring with a few helpful shopkeepers, and reversing to get back on track, I found a wide country lane and, at the end of it, a wrought-iron gate. I parked in front of the entrance and went inside to the cobbled courtyard. The mansion sat there as a golden jewel at the foot of lush vineyards. Champagne country with Chardonnay, Pinot Noir, and Pinot Miniére grapes.

As soon as I stepped up to the door it was opened wide by the chatelaine herself. Isabelle d'Alville had been expecting me but I had not imagined what I found. Having judged by her children—the common stripper and the dissipated poet—I had pictured a hard-faced, thin-bodied, judgmental old witch.

Instead, here stood a country woman with an ample body in a loose-fitting dress, a halo of formerly blond hair, a rosy face with eyes of gray, and very sturdy bare legs in up-dated Mary Janes. She must have been close to eighty but didn't look a day over seventy.

"Come in, come in," she said in English with an indefinable accent. "I have been looking so much forward to meeting you."

"It is very good of you to take the time to see me," I said equally politely, "I realize that you are probably very busy this time of year."

"Champagne has kept me busy all year round almost all my life," Isabelle said. "My husband's great-grandfather started the house back in the late 1800s and his many sons and grandsons and great-grandsons and sons-in-law continued the company into this century."

"What a wonderful family enterprise," I said.

"But not any more," Isabelle said. "My husband died some years ago, I carried on with the help of two of his nephews."

"Very successfully, I can tell."

"Yes, yes, very successful. But now the nephews are both retired, their children are lawyers and dentists and I am alone carrying on. You have met my children and I am sure you realize that they are not cut out for the champagne business."

"Well."

"I am in the process of selling this ancient house of champagne to a consortium from Paris and I will soon retire to my mansion and my rare collection of Limoges porcelains."

"Maybe you will have time to do some traveling," I said.

"Mais non, Madame, that is not my wish. I do not care for travels except around my vineyards. Have you seen how green and straight they reach for the hilltops? We have the best soil, very chalky, the best grapes, the finest wine casks, the finest experience for the palate."

Isabelle looked animated and proud.

"Come," she said, "I am on my way to the caves and, if you wish, we have time for a brief tour before the tourist groups arrive."

We took a short walk from the mansion to an immense building with a reception area, a souvenir shop, a tasting bar, and an exhibit of champagne bottles from magnums to Jeroboams to absolutely humongous.

"We will enter here," Isabelle said and I followed her down to the cellars. "We are not the largest house in the area but we are one of the best."

Isabelle took me through the caves with explanations at every step, from hand-picked grapes, fermentation, the process of turning each bottle daily for a period of six to eight weeks to rid them of yeast formations, stacking the bottles for several years until finally opening them carefully to disgorge the deposits of yeast to produce a drink for the gods.

We had a taste of several glasses of white Brut, Brut rosé and Demi-Sec and Demi-Sec Rosé, until I felt my eyes glaze over and my knees begin to buckle. Champagne goes first to my head and then to my legs.

Isabelle laughed—she, wisely, had taken only small sips—and took me by the arm back to the mansion.

"Time for coffee, I believe," she said and I followed her through a hall furnished with country chests and trestle tables on a vast tiled floor into an equally vast living room with chintz-covered sofas in cheery colors of poppy-reds and grass-greens and cornflower-blues, with a large painting in similar colors—by Matisse, without a doubt.

Isabelle d'Alville beckoned me to a side-board where she poured coffee from a percolator and filled our plates with small pastries and eclairs.

"Now," she said when we had settled down each in a sofa with a coffee table in between. "Tell me about this woman you have lost."

"It seems she was a friend of your mother's from way back in New York in the early 1900s," I began. "They both came over to France in 1921 and then, of course, your mother married and moved away from Paris while Sterling—the woman I'm looking for—stayed in the city and became a writer. Then, inexplicably, from around 1930 we can find no trace of her."

"How very strange," Isabelle said. "After my daughter called I began to search my memory and also some of my mother's papers which I haven't seen in at least forty years. And look what I found."

"Yes?" I said and actually felt a little faint.

Isabelle went to a chest-of-drawers and brought back a photograph in an ornate silver frame and a book in a light blue cover.

"First the book," she said. "It's by a James Joyce whom I do not know and it was signed and dedicated."

I held in my hand a first edition of *Ulysses*—printed by Darantiére—and opened it to the front page. The dedication was dated 1922.

"*To a fine fellow writer,*" it said.

"Your mother was a writer?" I said.

"I believe she had some poems published," Isabelle said. "But I wouldn't have called her a writer. The book was at the bottom of the box where I found the photograph. It was covered by some old newspapers."

She handed me the photograph.

"I wonder if this could be your Sterling together with my mother? On the back it says 'we came out together'. What do you think that means?"

"That would have been in the year 1914, when they were 18," I said, "and 'coming out' meant they were presented to high society for the purpose of finding a husband."

"Sounds like mother," Isabelle said and handed me the framed black and white photograph signed in the corner by Pierre Fast-Brown. "She was a frightful snob. She's the one on the right."

My eyes blurred.

Sterling, posing on the left in the photograph, smiled at me enigmatically from across the years.

A lovely smile that opened her eyes wide. They looked light, maybe blue? Her lashes were long, her lips full and well-defined, her teeth small and even. Her face was heart-shaped. Her hair was long and curly and pulled back closely around her head. It looked blond with a couple of light streaks.

She was beautiful and young and striking and my heart went out to her.

Sterling was leaning away from Victoria who looked into the camera imperiously as if she owned the world. Her long black hair was without curl, her eyes very dark, her lips thinly stretched over large teeth, her chin pointed.

"Tell me about your mother," I said while I kept looking at Sterling in the photograph. "Did you ever hear her speak about Sterling Kirkland Sawyer?"

"Do you think she was the one they called 'Sissy?"

"Yes."

"Then I remember my mother throwing temper tantrums about her."

"When was that?"

"I must have been ten, it would have been around 1942 at the time we all went to Switzerland to live during the war."

"Do you remember what your mother said about Sterling?"

Isabelle d'Alville slumped back in the sofa and suddenly looked her age. Her hand fluttered across her face as if to wipe off something painful.

"My mother once said that she hoped Sissy would rot in hell. She was quite irrational about her."

What could have brought on such venom, I wondered.

"Do you happen to have any letters sent to your mother from those years?" I said.

"No. My mother burned all her personal papers before she died. She never wanted me to know anything about her. My sister Marie-Louise and my brother Henri were a few years older and we had nothing in common. Marie-Louise hated me. I was my father's darling and she was unspeakably jealous of me. After I married we never met again."

"I'm sorry," I said and handed the photograph of Sterling and Victoria back to Isabelle.

She pushed the frame back at me.

"Take it," she said, "you may have it."

"Are you sure? I thank you so much."

"Marie-Louise took her revenge on me for having fallen in love and married successfully while she was an old maid living with Mother. She coaxed my daughter, Suzette, away from me and made her come live with her and Mother. It was a great tragedy for me. And you see how she turned out. A stripper in Montmartre. Mon Dieu."

"Did your mother ever say where Sissy was living?"

"In Vézelay."

"Vézelay in Bourgogne?"

"Bién sûr. She had become a religeuse."

"You mean she was in a convent?"

"One cannot know. It is possible."

"Did your parents divorce?"

"No, no, even if my father wanted to he couldn't leave her because she had the money and he did not."

The champagne haze having been dissipated by several cups of coffee I took my leave of Isabelle with profuse thanks and some regret for having stirred up bad memories for her.

"You are going to Vézelay?" she asked before waving goodbye. "Will you let me know what you find out?"

"Bién sûr," I said with feeling.

Chapter 39

1930

The sleek boat was moored on the right side of the river, it had a canopy on the upper deck under which the guests thronged around a mahogany bar with a white-clad bartender. He mixed the Sidecars—cognac, Cointreau, lemon juice, and ice—shook the concoctions vigorously and served them with a lemon rind.

"Perfectly perfect, my dear man," Claire exclaimed and downed a second glass before following Sterling to the buffet on the lower deck. A slim, young man with a pencil mustache played the piano, everyone was dressed to the hilt, Effie Rousseau in a shimmering blue sequined dress, Claire in red from the bandeau with osprey feathers to the buckles on her shoes, and Sterling in a rose-colored Sciaparelli.

The host—one of Effie's numerous admirers and a great connoisseur of, and investor in, modern painting—moved around his boat smiling incessantly at his guests.

"He's not too bright but I rather like that," Effie whispered to Sterling, "takes the pressure off the relationship and his parties are *always* successful. He thinks he's a poet but between you and me he has no facility for writing in verse. He will no doubt be published soon."

"Here come Laura and Auguste," Sterling said and waved. "Over here, over here, Laura, old girl, I was excited to see the display in Auguste's window of your beautiful book of poems illustrated by Effie. Soon I hope my own book of poems will join the distinguished company."

"Scott Winteride isn't here tonight," Claire said. "Just as well, his jealousy is tiresome."

"I would be jealous of you, too, my pet, if I had to watch how Pyotr pursues you so shamelessly," Auguste said.

"Really, Auguste," Laura said, "what do we know about it."

"Oh, pooh," Claire said and blew smoke.

"Sales are slowing down at the shop, people are leaving Paris in droves, their money is gone thanks to the greedy men on Wall Street," Laura said.

"I saw your special friend, Wainwright Manners III, yesterday at the Deux Magots," Auguste said to Sterling. "He is on his way back to the States, I gather his father lost everything during the crash and now there's no allowance for Wainwright. He said he had to borrow money for the boat. Steerage class."

"Sorry about that but good riddance, nevertheless. You know very well that he is no special friend of mine," Sterling mumbled, feeling self-conscious about heeding Pierre Fast-Brown's advice and saving her skin while so many others were suffering.

Up the narrow gangplank came Bernice Boch, her bulk as usual draped mysteriously in a flowing gown. She was followed closely by a tall, handsome man in a somber business suit and an even more somber tie.

"The new husband," Claire whispered to Sterling. "The banker dripping with loot."

"Meet Juniper," Bernice said when she had her feet balanced on the deck and a firm hand on the husband's arm. "You may congratulate me. I am now Mrs. Juniper Osborne III."

"The Third?" Claire mumbled. "How divine for you."

Congratulations floated about, the women embraced the new Mrs. Osborne warmly and the men shook the lucky man's hand vigorously.

"We sail tomorrow," Juniper Osborne said.

"We'll settle in New York," Bernice said. "Paris and Europe are shot to pieces."

"Everyone says that les Beaux Jours are coming to an end," Sterling said.

"Speaking of leaving," said Bernice who was now a sculptor, "is it true that Ben Vogelhut is bound for Germany and that Scott Winteride is off to London again?"

"Everyone is talking about it," Claire said.

"And, I believe, everyone is talking about you and Pyotr," Bernice said when her new husband was out of earshot. "Good luck with that."

Claire laughed out loud and turned away.

"Dear Laura," she said instead, "you look tired."

"What she needs," Auguste said, "is a long vacation in the mountains, maybe in Spain."

"It would do you good," Sterling said. "I, too, will be going to the country."

"Talking about losing money," Bernice said to Sterling, "your blond beau, Stefan, looked very pale and distraught the other night at the Dingo, not at all his boisterous self. Did he bring back bad news from Switzerland?"

The room swirled around Sterling, she wanted to shout, no, no, Stefan is still in Switzerland, he has not come back yet or he would have let me know, and she hardly heard Claire's voice through the fog in her ears and the tears pressing against her lowered lids.

"Oh, you are mistaken," Claire said, "Stefan is perfectly all right, I do believe he's a financial genius."

"He did look pale and not his usual self," Bernice insisted.

"Come along," Claire said to Sterling. "So sorry, you chaps, a perfectly delightful party, the food was divine, dear Effie, and the company superb but I must get my beauty sleep and Sterling is driving me in her little Quadrilette."

Sterling never knew how she got down the wobbly gangplank to the pier, or how she got into her car and drove Claire back to Montmartre, then herself home, or how she got up to her apartment or how she found her bed and tumbled into it.

She lay there wide awake until the early morning sun glowed through the curtains.

Chapter 40

"You mean you had in your hand the positively first edition of *Ulysses*? I am so, so envious," Topsy said and I could hear her gasp of air on the phone.

"I was amazed, too," I said, "and even more amazed that Joyce had dedicated it to 'a fine writer'."

"Victoria was a fine writer? That's certainly news to me," Topsy said. "Tell me, was the outside of the cover blue and the inside white?"

"Yes, how did you know and what does it mean?"

"Just a curiosity," Topsy said. "Something to do with the difficulty of finding a particular color blue that Joyce insisted on and the printer having to improvise. What else did you find?"

"At the risk of making you even more envious," I said, "please be informed that I now know exactly what Sterling looked like."

"Don't tell me. You got a photograph."

"Their official 'coming-out' picture."

"Was she lovely?"

"She was and you will see for yourself when I get back. Isabelle gave it to me, didn't even want to keep the silver frame, said she didn't want to be reminded of her mother."

"Wow, doesn't speak well of Victoria. What did *she* look like?"

"Not nearly as pleasant and innocent as Sterling. I'm beginning to form a very negative picture of her."

"On a different note," Topsy said, "what was in the tote of books Reginald Fletcher gave you before you left?"

"Books about Laura Waverley, August Metier, and James Joyce, plus some dull-looking fiction from the 1920s."

"Laura Waverley lost her money in 1929, had to sell her car and a lot of her first editions. But she was the type of person who always bounced back which she did in quite a spectacular way," Topsy said. "She suddenly got a bee in her bonnet and left Auguste to take up with a Spanish Flamenco dancer whom she met on a vacation to Spain. She wasn't heard of for a couple of years."

"Wow," I said. "I didn't know that. Wonder if Claire Garcia-Bonsonwell had something to do with that. What happened next?"

"She returned from Spain and went back to Auguste."

"And lived with him happily ever after?" I said. "And, please, don't say 'not exactly',"

"I won't," Topsy said. "I don't know exactly what happened to them after that. All I know is that she was buried at the Pére Lachaise cemetery in the 1960s."

"I'm amazed," I said.

"Unfortunately, I must cut this delightful conversation short," Topsy said. "I've got a deadline for my grammar column and need a good question for my 'Letters from the Readers.' You wouldn't have one, would you?"

"I can think of only one right now," I said and gnashed my teeth at the thought. "It drives me bonkers when people from ordinary folks to TV analysts and commentators sprinkle their observations with 'like' 'you know' and 'I mean' before and between and after every other sentence. Like I mean, you know?"

"I know," Topsy said, "but it won't help."

"They don't realize how annoying it is, and how sadly inept it sounds."

"I know," Topsy said, "I'll use it," and on that happy note we rang off.

Reading about the writers in Paris in the 1920s gave me no comfort. Many were alcoholic, got into brawls, were unfaithful to their husbands or their wives or their girl-friends, had illegitimate children, went broke, couldn't get published, got writer's block, caught tuberculosis or worse, landed in prison, had to teach English to make ends meet, tried to settle in Italy or Switzerland, or went home in disgrace, or committed suicide. Except for the few—those of great talent, perseverance, money, and luck—many were failures. Maybe I wouldn't have wanted to be a part of it, after all?

My e-mails now informed me that Mel Kramer planned to visit me in Washington two weeks hence, that Jon Douglas wished to do likewise, that Neil Robinson wanted me to rent an economy car and to stay at small cheap bed and breakfasts in Burgundy during my quest for a nunnery. It was obvious he had no idea what makes me tick.

In the meantime, Ms. Puigh had not reacted to my inquiries and was not back at her hotel. Jacques d'Alville had left several messages inquiring when he could meet her. It would be over my dead body.

The bar now seemed to be my best destination which is where I settled down with my books and ordered my serendipitous drink accompanied by crab rolls.

A party of British swingers entered the bar and made admiring remarks about current expatriate writers of whom I knew nothing, and I hastily finished my drink.

I closed the last book I intended to read about the writers of the past—and about their sad fates—and prepared myself for my real quest: Finding Sterling Kirkland Sawyer.

I rented the BMW to take me to Vézelay in the morning planning to find the best hotel there and then shook off the exertions of the last few days by going to the gym.

Chapter 41

Driving on the highway to Auxerre took me through a landscape of barren fields with clumps of trees and a few allées of those ubiquitous poplars. Occasional churches showed their Romanesque towers in the distance in isolated villages with red-tiled roofs atop buff-colored houses.

In Auxerre I parked the car outside the town wall and walked through the portal with the ancient astronomical clock which showed both sun and moon time if only I had known how to read it. After a hasty lunch with a view of the river Yonne, in the shadow of great houses with wattled walls and bright red and yellow mosaic roofs I topped off the meal with a café crème and continued on my way towards Vézelay.

Soon the road wound its way higher and higher, rain oozed down in a steady stream—I had been informed that here it rained one hundred days out of the year—soaking the haystacks and making the two-lane road extremely slippery. Cows and sheep stood dumbly in the fields without moving, their heads down.

Dark, dense forests now appeared on both sides of the road and up the mountains and down the valleys. The only convent I had been able to find in the vicinity of Vézelay lay outside the town on a road veering off to the right a few miles south. However, it was getting late and I decided to look for one of Neil Robinsons's bed and breakfast places hoping it wouldn't be too devoid of amenities.

And so I got to the town up a steep slope to a small square where tourist buses and private cars parked haphazardly. The Basilica of Saint Mary Magdalene rose in a sudden burst of sun at the top of the hill surrounded by a tapestry of ancient buildings. The houses were brown, gray, golden, with red tiled roofs, most with white shutters, amid a forest of chimneys. The one road in the middle—leading straight to the front portal of the Basilica—wended its way steeply upwards.

It took me about fifteen minutes to negotiate the short road since I stopped several times at a crêperie, at a bookstore, at a gift shop, to enquire about the bed and breakfast place I had found on the net. Everyone was solicitous, everyone was kind, but no one recognized the place I was looking for until I got to the antique store three houses short of the Basilica.

"Ah, but yes, Madame," said the proprietor at my enquiry, "my daughter has an excellent hotel de chambres next door to me. I shall take you."

While two nuns in black flowing habits passed us on the road—their arms hidden within their wide sleeves and their eyes determinedly fixed on the ground—Madame Duval took me next door to her daughter's excellent bed and breakfast where I was greeted as a member of the family. They sat me down in the kitchen to partake of what Madame Duval described as a necessary refreshment consisting of crêpes and coffee. Then I deposited my bag in a very small bedroom upstairs next to a shared bathroom—shared only, I was assured, with one other guest—I was given a small stack of clean-scented towels and a large piece of soap and told that dinner would be served at eight.

Madame Duval returned to her antique shop and her daughter, Lizette, told me all about the convent outside of town.

"Only one of the old nuns is still alive," she said, "she is very ancient but they have plenty of help from the young ones."

"How old do you suppose she is," I said.

"Maybe a hundred."

"Really?"

"Or maybe eighty."

"Okay," I said. "Do you imagine I can pass by and drop in or do I need an introduction?" I realized that my knowledge of convents and nuns was very scant.

Lizette eyed me as if those were exactly her thoughts.

"But yes, you can drop by any time except during Mass."

"Of course," I said and felt foolish because I didn't know when Mass was held except for the one in early morning which I'd heard about but didn't imagine that I would interrupt especially if it happened to be at five a.m.

"Do you think ten o'clock would be appropriate," I said.

"Oh, *absolument,* Madame," Lizette said happily.

I walked the half block up the road and had stopped before the great entrance to the Basilica when a voice rang out behind me.

"Ah, Madame," said an enthusiastic Madame Duval and peered at me from her short height of about five feet, "I have now closed my shop and will be delighted to show you our great Basilica."

"How very kind," I said and meant it although at the same time deciding to return the next day to contemplate the exceptional Romanesque features in solitude.

"You know, of course, of the legend about Mary Magdalene's relics in our crypt. We recognize that three Marys have been rumored to be the sainted one and that the story is said to be a fabrication."

"What do you believe," I said.

"If God willed it then everything was possible," said Madame Duval. "It is said that the Sainted Mary Magdalene was sent to sea by devoted followers in the Holy

Land after the crucifixion of Our Lord, that she reached Marseilles, where she lived to an old age. Her relics were brought here by circuitous routes."

"And did she have a daughter?"

"Madame!" she looked quite scandalized. "Who would say such a thing?"

"Several writers with fabulous imaginations."

"I understand. Writers of fiction." The dismissal was total. "A church was built to our Saint and from here the pilgrims set out for Jerusalem and for Compostela in Spain."

We had entered the Basilica and stood before the great doors at the entrance to the church, with the grand figure of Christ in the middle, arms outstretched, bare feet with gnarled toes, with depictions of Mary Magdalene and Lazarus gazing upwards. Stepping inside the nave I was struck by the beauty of the soaring multi-colored arches and tall capitals with stone sculptures of scenes from the Old Testament.

The church was free of tourists the buses having departed several hours ago, the quiet was profound, and while Madame Duval was busy lighting candles I took the opportunity to sneak off towards the crypt. Going down a narrow staircase I arrived at the foot of an altar with the famous relics. It was said that here sins were forgiven by God. I sat for a while on a wooden bench and imagined Sterling sitting there similarly some eighty years ago.

When I returned to the nave I found Madame Duval in a frenzy thinking she had lost me and happy to reclaim me.

After dinner a short walk around town was quickly accomplished since there was only the one main road and no side streets whatsoever. It was not difficult to imagine Sterling walking this very road. Nothing had changed here in the last hundred years—let alone in the last thousand—the church and the relics and the early Mass would have held meaning for her as a Catholic, very devout for all I knew, while I, as a tepid Protestant, felt mainly historically inspired.

Had Claire Garcia-Bonsonwell ever visited her friend Sterling here, I wondered, she had been a devoted walker of country-sides in addition to being a gifted dancer.

I walked back to my humble bed and breakfast abode in the near darkness and ruminated on the friendship I hoped Claire and Sterling had enjoyed. And thinking of great friendships I returned to my computer to send an exhaustive e-mail to Topsy in Washington.

By ten I fell into a heavy sleep in my single bed with two lumps to the mattress in the smallest of bedrooms. Neil Robinson would have approved.

Chapter 42

The elderly nun—she could easily have been eighty and just as easily a hundred—looked up at me from her stooped position at the convent vegetable garden.

When she straightened up she was quite tall and quite thin, she had very white hair that curled at the ends, blue eyes, a small protruding stomach, and a lovely smile.

"Americaine," she said and looked at my jeans, t-shirt, and sneakers.

"Jamie Prescott," I said, "and, yes, I'm an American."

She wiped dirt off her hand and shook mine.

"I am Soeur Jeanne-Marie," she said. "If you have come on a retreat we have one space left and you are very welcome to stay with us for as long as you wish."

"That would have been lovely," I said quite truthfully because it had just occurred to me that a couple of weeks in the country doing nothing might suit me very well.

"But?" She smiled and took my arm so we could walk together up the garden path towards a tall wrought-iron gate in the stone wall and through that to the convent house.

"Some other time, perhaps," I said, "I am here on a different errand."

"You are here on an errand for someone?"

"For Sterling Kirkland Sawyer."

Soeur Jeanne-Marie let go of my arm, stood quite still and looked at me with very startled eyes. Her smile faded, her cheeks flushed an alarming red, and her hands shook so that she had to grasp one with the other to keep them still.

"For Sterling?"

"Do you remember her? Did she live here with you?"

"Who are you?"

Her hands stopped shaking but the flush in her face intensified. Her eyes were now watering.

"I'm so sorry if I startled you," I said. "I am here on behalf of Sterling's family in the United States. They lost touch with her around the year 1930 and never heard from her again. Her grand-nephew has asked me to find out what happened to her."

"Oh," she said in a small voice.

"And here I am," I said. "Is this where she lived?"

"You had better come back to my rooms," Soeur Jeanne-Marie said, "it is time for one of my little white pills."

"I am so sorry. I've given you a shock. I should have been more careful."

She took my arm again and hurried me through the gate to the two-story building where the doors and windows stood open and voices were heard from within amidst the rattling of pots and pans. Inside, in a small tiled foyer, she opened a door at the back and called to someone.

Out hurried a very young sister clad in a checkered dress, a kerchief, and a white apron and handed Soeur Jeanne-Marie her little white pill.

The sister looked at me with a less than happy expression and I hurriedly repeated my apologies without revealing exactly what I was apologizing for. The little white pill had an instantaneous and amazing effect on Soeur Jeanne-Marie and she waved away her protector, opened a second door and shooed me inside with quite a firm hand. Then she made a quiet request for refreshments to be brought to her rooms for her and for her American guest.

"They look after me," she said with a mischievous smile, "not that I usually need looking after. I'm only ninety-six."

"Again, I'm sorry," I said, "but you are looking wonderfully well again. I should have guessed eighty-two at the most."

"Really? You think so? Yes, that is how I feel most of the time. Eighty-two. So someone has come to find our dearest Sterling. I am very much shocked. She never mentioned any family in America. She was an orphan."

"She had a sister, Rose, who heard from Sterling only once shortly after she moved back to Paris. Rose had a daughter, Marjorie, who had a son named Neil."

"It is all a very great surprise," Soeur Jeanne-Marie said. "We didn't call her Sterling, of course, to us she was Minou, that is what Soeur Madeleine named her when she came here as a young child and later on—when she came here as a young woman—we kept the name for her."

"She came back in 1921," I said. "Were you here and did you know her?"

The refreshments were brought in on a tray by the same young sister who still eyed me with some hostility, not very holy of her, I thought, but what do I know about being holy.

We helped ourselves to the obligatory crêpes and, thank the Lord, two pitchers with coal-black coffee and hot, hot, milk, from which I concocted an enormous helping of café crème while Soeur Jeanne-Marie took herb tea.

"Oh, yes, I was here," she said and watched with obvious pleasure how I swilled down my coffee. "Minou used to drink it like that, very hot and very strong. She was wonderfully lively and fun, we used to go to the market together in the early mornings and she would race me to the gate every time. I sometimes won but she was awfully fast."

"You must have been very young," I said.

"I was fourteen when I first came here. I did not know yet if I would give my life to the Lord. I had been orphaned and Soeur Madeleine, our Mother Superior, took me in and I loved it here. I was told to try the outside world and I did try to be a chambermaid at a house in Auxerre."

"But you decided to become a nun instead."

"It was a better life for me. I could be with Soeur Madeleine, she was a very saintly person, loving and kind. She was happy when Minou returned from America and to think that Minou bought a house quite near here and came to stay very often."

"She had a house here? Did she have a peach tree?"

"Yes, how did you know?"

"She wrote about it in a magazine."

"Yes, she would always be writing, sometimes in French and then she would read it aloud to me. And sometimes when her great friend, Claire, would visit they laughed and laughed and would not tell me what they laughed about. I was holy, you understand. They drank many bottles of wine." Soeur Jeanne-Marie doubled over with laughter at the memory.

"Sterling was happy?"

"Oh, yes, Minou was happy when she was with Soeur Madeleine."

"I'm glad," I said.

"My Soeur is long gone," she said, "and I have been alone all these years. I do not know why God would give me such a long life."

"Did Minou come here in 1930?"

"Yes, that must have been the year she came back to live at the convent."

"Had she lost her money and had to sell her apartment in Paris and her house in Vézelay?"

"Oh, no, she had her apartment in Paris, very beautiful I was told, and she gave the country house to the convent so we could rent it out and use the income doing God's work for the poor. Come with me," Soeur Jeanne-Marie said.

She got up quite suddenly, retrieved a walking stick at the front door and motioned for me to follow her. We walked back the way we had arrived, past the vegetable garden and out the wrought-iron gate to the road.

The cemetery hid behind a tall stone wall making the headstones within invisible from the road. We walked through yet another gate which squeaked bitterly on its hinges and Soeur Jeanne-Marie slowed down and crossed herself frequently as we passed the old cemetery plots.

We stopped before the smallest of gray moss-covered headstones on the smallest of plots and Soeur Jeanne-Marie knelt down and smoothed the earth around it with trembling hands. I bent down to read the faint inscription.

Madeleine Edwige Bourdon, it said, born 1872 and died 1933.

"She came from such a fine family in Auxerre," Soeur Jeanne-Marie said, "they gave her a better education than girls received at that time, they wanted her to marry well and have her own fine family but she wished only to serve God. Minou became her first child and I became her second."

"I am very sorry that you lost her so early," I said.

"It happened so quickly, we had no time to prepare ourselves. We buried her in the winter when the ground was quite cold. Then Soeur Daphne became the Mother Superior, she lived on until 1949 and you can see here that we buried her next to Soeur Madeleine. That is what they would both have wished."

"I'm very sorry," I said and helped Soeur Jeanne-Marie up from her kneeling position.

"Thank you, my dear," she said. "When Minou returned in 1930 we did not know what would soon happen. At first she stayed at her own house but presently she decided to stay in her small room at the convent to live the life we all lived, simple and austere. She worked in the vegetable garden, the same garden where you found me today, she liked to get up early in the morning even before the sun rose, I sometimes followed her at a distance when she went to the small brook. She would drink a sip of the water and lie down in the grass with her eyes closed. I would leave very quietly and after a while she came back to the house and we started breakfast together. It was the way it had always been."

"How lovely," I said.

"It was the best time."

"Yes," I said.

"After a few weeks Minou left for Paris. She was waiting for her special beau to return from Switzerland. She was happy and said she would soon be married."

"Sterling was getting married?" I stammered.

"Oh, yes."

Soeur Jeanne-Marie suddenly looked quite ashen.

"Is it time for one of your pills," I said, thinking it was a pity she didn't carry them with her on her walks.

"Yes," she said.

We reached the convent just as her holy assistant came out the door and, with a withering look at me, ushered Soeur Jeanne-Marie inside.

"May I return tomorrow?" I asked.

The holy one shook her head as in 'No,' but Soeur Jeanne-Marie nodded a faint 'Yes.'

Chapter 43

"Sterling got married?" Topsy exclaimed when I reached her on the phone.

"That's what Soeur Jeanne-Marie told me."

"Tell me more. Where, when, and to whom?"

"I don't know. My little nun had to return to the house to get one of her white pills, and I had to leave."

"She isn't dying, I hope."

"No, don't say that, I've grown quite fond of her in the short time we've been together. She said Sterling, or Minou as they called her here, returned to Paris to wait for her special beau to return from Switzerland and that she was happy because she was getting married. That was in October of 1930."

"Well, gee whiz, Jamie, you're on the brink of solving the mystery. Did she, you think, marry and go off to Switzerland to live, changed her last name to that of her husband's, and then simply lost touch with everyone in the States?"

"I will learn more when I visit with Soeur Jeanne-Marie this afternoon. The big question is, who was Stefan and what was his last name."

"Well, call me day or night, never mind if you wake up Martin."

"Will do."

"And speaking of Martin, he has had some disturbing news about a Ponzi scheme unraveling in our lovely capital. People have lost their savings left and right and the jails will soon be full of hedge fund managers. You haven't invested with a firm called Roulette Equities, I hope?"

"Not personally but now you have me worried. I'll have to get in touch with my financial adviser, he has invested for me the last several years and secured some quite extraordinary results. Did you lose something in this scheme?"

"Well, unfortunately, Martin had some Roulette Equities and that money may be gone. My money, thank God, is separate and I am the prudent one, as you know."

"Yes, I know."

My call to my financial adviser's office phone went straight to his voice-mail, his cell phone did likewise, and my e-mail to him went unanswered.

Feeling immensely uneasy at the prospect of losing a third of my investments—the rest being in conservative instruments, cash, and real estate—I called Bob Makowski in Washington and got him on the first ring.

"When are you coming back," he said before I'd said more than hello.

"Bob, I'm on the brink of closing this case. I'll be home very soon."

"What a relief. I don't mind telling you work is piling up. So, what else is new?"

"Bob, I need you to do me a personal favor. You've heard of Roulette Equities, I assume?" I said.

"Now don't tell me you were fool enough to give them your money?"

"I don't know and I can't get a hold of Tom Abbott, my financial adviser. Here, write down his number and address and please, please find him. I'll e-mail him again and tell him you're authorized to learn if he invested my money with Roulette Equities. And then tell him to contact me immediately."

"Will do, I'll let you know and I'll have him call you, how's that."

"You're an angel," I said with feeling.

"You bet."

My e-mails had been piling up and I answered them in the order they'd come in. Mel Kramer said he was contemplating a trip to Paris if I didn't show up in New York soon. Jon Douglas was eagerly awaiting my return to Washington and, apparently, did not understand that we'd broken up. Neil Robinson inquired about my expenses and forgot to ask about the Sterling search. Ms. Puigh was back from Nice sojourning at her hotel in Paris and unable to locate me at mine.

I reached Ms. Puigh on her cell phone.

"Finally," I said. "Why did you disappear?"

"Look who's talking."

"Sorry. I'm in Burgundy for a few days. How long before you return to the States?"

"Getting fired was the best thing that ever happened to me. I was rotting away in the archives. I've decided to take a sabbatical as you might call it, for as long as my savings last."

"And your research at the university? Did you find any letters from Sterling to Pierre Fast-Brown?"

"I found four. From 1921, 1924, 1929 and 1930." Her voice was breaking up.

"What? Just four?"

"Sorry to say. There was no other private correspondence in his files from anyone."

"Bummer," I said with feeling. "I was afraid of that. Lots of people destroy their personal papers. I guess I would, too."

"At least there were four and I made copies," Ms. Puigh said and after a few agonizing moments we were cut off.

Letters, I thought. Letters in Sterling's hand, written to a person who must have been very important in her life. I wanted to shout the news to someone but there was no one there.

Instead, I sprinted down the steep hill from my hotel des chambres to the parking lot to get rid of my pent up excitement, no doubt looking like a demented tourist, got the car, and headed back to the convent and Soeur Jeanne-Marie.

Chapter 44

1930

Sterling stood for a long time across the street from Stefan's house on the rue de la Paix. A few weeks ago the lights had blazed behind the window-panes and music and laughter and animated conversations had been heard within. Now the tall windows were dark although shadows flickered and moved within the rooms. The front door stood ajar.

She moved in a daze across the street, pushed open the door and crossed the threshold, waiting. Slowly her heartbeat increased until her head felt light and her throat tightened. The foyer was empty of furniture and the precious rugs and the Murano chandeliers were gone.

A door opened on the upper floor and onto the curved staircase staggered two men in large aprons carrying a Louis XVI chiffonniere. Behind them came another two carrying Stefan's large double bed now broken down into several pieces. And behind these four movers Stefan appeared in a pair of old pants and an old shirt. He carried his very favorite Orgoloff painting.

"Sterling," he said.

"When were you going to tell me," she moaned. "Have you lost everything?"

"Everything."

"And you didn't come to me for help?"

"I cannot ask a woman for help."

Sterling stormed up the stairs and met him halfway up.

"Not even the woman you are going to marry?"

Stefan continued down the staircase with the painting, leaned it against the wall, and turned to her.

"It's only furniture," he said, "I'm keeping the paintings and the silver and everything is not yet lost. It is a matter of re-organizing my life, of re-assigning my assets, of selling the house, of returning to Switzerland for a while."

"Returning to Switzerland?"

"Until I get my affairs in order. Here," he said to the movers, "put it down in the foyer and continue moving the bedroom furniture, then the parlor and dining room furniture, roll up the rugs but leave the paintings on the walls."

"To Switzerland?" Sterling repeated.

"Come," Stefan said, "the kitchen is still functioning, I will be staying until Sunday, we will have something to eat and drink. Come."

She followed him down a narrow staircase to the basement and into the kitchen. It was dark and damp but Stefan bustled about busily and soon produced some of his 'gravad lax', an omelette, a salad with a few green leaves and a couple of tomatoes, a stale baguette, and two huge tumblers of Vin Ordinaire.

"There," he said to Sterling who sat on the edge of a kitchen chair. "We need food."

"I'm not hungry," she said.

"Nonsense," he said, "you should eat, I've worked up an appetite moving all that furniture. Sorry to see some of it go but c'est la vie, as they say."

"I suppose next you will say no use crying over spilt milk?"

"Come on," he said, "more likely easy come, easy go, don't look so downcast, everything will turn out for the best. Life's a gamble and I still have a few options left."

He took her by the arm, moved her to the table and sat her down with one of the large tumblers of wine.

"Down the hatch," he said and lifted his glass. He leaned his head back and emptied it in a few large gulps. Color suffused his cheeks. He coughed hard then laughed uproariously.

"Have you been drinking all day?" she said.

"Yesh, I have."

"So you're really quite drunk?"

"Yesh, I am."

"Let me help. How much money do you need?"

"You wouldn't have that much."

"I believe I might."

"Everyone lost their money in New York. And in Zurich. And in Paris."

"But I didn't."

"You didn't?"

"I sold my stocks a few weeks before the crash."

Stefan threw his head back, laughed, got up unsteadily and poured another tumbler of wine.

"You don't need to drink any more," she said.

"Oh, but I do." He poured the wine down his throat.

"Come home with me now."

Stefan dug into the omelette, tore off a chunk of baguette, cleaned up the salad and the salmon, and wiped his mouth unceremoniously with a kitchen towel.

"I'll come home with you," he said, "seeing that I no longer have a bed."

"Can you safely leave the packers here by themselves?"

"I'll send them away."

Stefan threw the porcelain and glasses in the sink, doused it all with a bucket full of water, and followed Sterling up the stairs.

The packers had moved everything to the foyer and stood waiting to be paid. Stefan emptied his pockets, gave them all he had and bowed them out the door. Then he sat down on the bottom stair and looked long and hard at his furnishings which would soon belong to other people.

Sterling's ancient Quadrilette—which she had not bothered to replace because it was still serviceable—was parked at the curb. She maneuvered Stefan into the passenger seat and took to the wheel. He leaned his head back and began to snore. She drove sedately towards the river and across the bridge to the Grands-Agustins.

"We've arrived?" Stefan sat up suddenly, almost sober.

"Yes, we've arrived," Sterling said.

Upstairs she made some very strong coffee which he gulped down and she sat in her apple-green sofa and looked at him. She looked at his thinning hair, at his blurred eyes, and at his flushed cheeks. And she thought, is it pity or is it love I feel at this moment. It must be, it had to be, love.

"How long will you be in Switzerland?" she said.

"Hard to say."

"Shall I come with you?"

He looked at her in surprise.

"Come with me? No, my dear, you are much better off here."

"I wouldn't mind. I would get to know your country."

He got up and moved to the window where he looked down at the Seine, across to the houses on the other bank, to the barges on the slow-moving water.

"I will be much too busy to take special care of you there," he said without turning around.

"Yes, I imagine I would be rather in the way."

Stefan still didn't turn around but coughed long and hard.

"Could you not wait a while?" she said. "If you took instruction now and converted, we could be married in Vézelay within a few months."

Stefan turned around slowly, his eyes straining, his lips trembling.

"My dear," he said.

He moved towards the sofa where Sterling sat very straight, her eyes bright and trusting. He looked into those eyes and closed his.

"Stefan?"

"My dear, how can I tell you this without hurting you. I never meant it to end this way. I am already married. I have a wife in Switzerland."

Sterling felt the ground shift and heard the moan that rose in her throat.

"Married," she whispered.

"I never thought you wanted marriage so I didn't think it mattered."

"Married." Her voice was dull.

"We hardly ever see each other," Stefan said. "She lives her life and I live mine."

"Is that your 'cousin' Natasha? The one who visited you a short while ago and who is quite artistic?"

Stefan rearranged the corner of the carpet with his foot.

"No, that's her sister. Natasha is my sister-in-law."

"And do you have children?" Sterling's voice faltered.

"Two," he said.

"And every time you have been traveling to Switzerland you really went to see them?"

"Yes."

"And the story about her 'husband' who was jealous, was that really about you and your wife? Do you love her? And are you jealous of the private life she lives without you? Is that the real truth?"

"No, it's not like that."

"You've been quite good at deception."

"Yes," he said. "Did you sleep with Orgoloff every time I went away?"

Only that once, she thought. It was between Alex and me, it had nothing to do with anyone else.

"You no longer have a right to ask," she said.

"People have been talking."

"People here are always talking."

"And he does not excite you?"

Yes, he excites me, she thought, but stupid me, I waited for Stefan.

"I'm sorry," Stefan said.

"Exceedingly sorry?"

"Oh, yes, yes, darling Sterling, I am exceedingly sorry. I didn't mean to hurt you. You've never talked about marriage in all the years I've known you. I didn't think you wanted that. I don't know what to tell you."

"There is nothing you can tell me. Even if you obtained a divorce, as a Catholic I couldn't marry you."

Stefan sat down next to Sterling on the apple-green sofa and took her hand.

"That's a lot of nonsense," he said. "In any case, a divorce is out of the question. She would never let me see the children. And, as for money, it all belongs to her, the mansion in the country, the house in Zurich, the summer place in the mountains, the horses, everything."

"You own nothing?"

"She came from a rich family and she and Natasha inherited it all. My father's estate went to my older brother. There was nothing much left for me. And now I've lost what I made in the stock market."

"You are leaving then?"

"On Sunday."

"I see," she said and sudden tears filled her eyes and ran down her cheeks.

Stefan jumped to her side and wiped away the moisture from her face.

"I'll be back," he said. "No need for tears."

It was true, Sterling thought, her tears had been shed many years ago when she was very young and very trusting.

"Everything will turn out all right, you'll see," Stefan said. He put his arms around her and kissed her.

It would never be all right, of course, she knew that, and a terrible void opened up in front of her, she looked into the darkness and saw herself, saw the past and the future, saw her sinfulness and waited for the forgiveness, the forgiveness which might never come.

"I am pregnant," she said and her voice was hollow.

"Oh, my dear, I am exceedingly sorry," Stefan said. The flush in his cheeks ebbed until his face was quite white and pinched. He pressed the fingertips of both hands to his eyes. "This is a very bad moment for it to happen."

"Yes." Sterling said. "It has become a very bad moment."

"I will postpone my travel to Switzerland but I must still go there as soon as possible."

"Yes," she said. The darkness did not recede but she felt a quiet resolve within. She was now alone but she would be strong.

"Right now there is only one way out of this," Stefan said. "I will arrange it for you."

Sterling got up from her apple-green sofa and walked to the front door.

"I need to be alone," she said and opened the door for him.

"Where will I sleep," he said.

"Wherever you wish. Just not here."

"I'll come back tomorrow," he said as she closed the door behind him.

Chapter 45

1930

It was early morning when the sky was still a pale blue sliver over the rooftops with traces of pink from the rising sun, when water splashed rapidly towards the gutters and shopkeepers rolled up the metal shutters and set out tables and chairs on the sidewalks.

Down at the river a few early barges tugged away with their cargoes while the *bouquiniste* stalls on the embankment were still covered with dark canvas shielding their books from the dampness of the October night.

The stands at the morning markets were emerging and horse carts laden with fruits and flowers and vegetables rattled across the cobbled stones ready to be unloaded.

The Cathedral of the Notre Dame rose mightily above the dark river supported by the gray stone wall where green ivies hung down towards the water. Across the Pont Neuf, on the Île St.-Louis, the buildings stood tall, some leaning forward, some pushed back, with a single horse-cab passing slowly by. The stone wall stretched out along the embankment shadowed by dusky leaves.

The lights were on behind the shutters on the Boul' Mich and books and magazines and periodicals were taken from mailing boxes and placed in the window and on bookshelves inside the shop. In the art galleries along the quais lights came on and shadowy figures moved silently between the paintings at the back and the windows at the front. Inside the tall buildings the early morning activities began.

Late night revelers wound their way towards the Rotonde and the Select in search of a coffee and a brioche if not a cognac to chase away the remnants of the debauched night. Someone cackled a hoarse, smoke-infested laugh, another stumbled over a chair and invoked a sour smile from a fatigued waiter.

The building was on a street off the Champs Elysées. The entrance with its slender columns flanking the wooden door sat in shadow, a discreet brass plate with black lettering reflected the morning sun, while the lofty windows behind wrought iron rails and red flowers in pots looked blind.

The taxi cab stopped at the corner, Stefan grasped her hand and raised it to his lips.

"It is for the best," he said.

She pulled her hand free.

"Go," she said. "I will be on my own."

"I will return in two hours."

"Do not," she said. "I have made other arrangements."

"As you wish but I will come around in the afternoon."

She gave no reply, gathered her gloves and her handbag, adjusted her string of pearls and her cloche hat, opened the car door and stepped to the sidewalk.

She started towards the entrance.

"I am so sorry," he said. "Please forgive me."

She shook her head. She looked at the brass plate briefly, shuddered violently and pushed the door open. She went inside, her head bent.

She never looked back.

Chapter 46

"Did Sterling marry her beau?" I asked when Soeur Jeanne-Marie and I were seated in her rooms over the protests of the holy lay sister.

It was two in the afternoon and the sun shone bright, the clouds high in the sky were tufts of cotton drifting on a blue carpet.

"We had a difficult year, the year Minou returned from Paris. She looked very ill when she arrived and Soeur Madeleine took her to the hospital in Auxerre," Soeur Jeanne-Marie said in a voice almost inaudible.

"What was wrong?"

"They never told me but when they returned a few days later Minou looked very pale. She stayed in her cell many days until Soeur Madeleine forced her to come with her to the vegetable garden and on longer and longer walks. Then, little by little, we had our dear Minou back, she spent some time in her own house, her friend Claire came to be with her, other friends came to visit especially the *chér Monsieur* Orgoloff who had become quite famous and, in the end, she had mended."

"What happened to her beau?"

"They never told me, he never came to see her, and Minou never married him."

"I have learned that his first name was Stefan. What was his last name, do you know?"

"No, I never even knew that his first name was Stefan."

"It is no longer relevant," I said. "Is Minou's house far from here? Would it be all right for me to go see it?"

"Take a right from the convent, at the fork in the road take a left and about half a mile down that road you will see a cottage behind a low stone wall with a large peach tree on the front lawn. That is the house and you may go in, the door is not locked. We sometimes lend it to visitors but no one is staying there right now."

The holy one burst into the room without knocking.

"It is time for your afternoon nap," she said to Soeur Jeanne-Marie while completely ignoring my presence.

"Do not go far away," Soeur Jeanne-Marie said to me and I thought she winked her blue eyes. "We will have an early supper together at five and after supper you will accompany me on my evening walk."

"My dear," she said to the holy one, "I would like supper for two served in my rooms."

The holy one looked right through me, and held the door open to indicate my immediate exit.

The walk to Sterling's country house took little more than fifteen minutes.

The peach tree was there in the small front garden with a white bench under it and further in towards the house stood two gnarled apple trees. The walls were white-washed, the shutters pale green and the door leaned down on its black hinges.

I sat for a moment on the white bench and imagined the Sterling I now had a good picture of sitting here with Claire Garcia-Bonsonwell, drinking wine, trading outrageous gossip, and laughing uproariously. A car would arrive and Alexandre Orgoloff would jump out and join them. I imagined that his hair would tumble over his forehead and the sensuous look from his gorgeous eyes would envelop Sterling. Had they been lovers? They must have had a loving relationship if he came to see her in her hour of sadness. Had he known this beau of hers, this Stefan whom she didn't marry after all?

A sudden burst of wind made me get up and approach the door. Feeling like an intruder into Sterling's sanctuary I went inside with hesitant steps. There was a fresh scent of apple in the room coming from a large wooden bowl on a trestle table. Someone took loving care of Sterling's house. My throat tightened as I sat down in a plain wooden chair and looked at a framed picture on the wall. A line-drawing of a peach tree with a woman, seen from the back, in a garden chair under it. It wasn't signed but I guessed who had drawn it. Imagine, here it hung, unacknowledged, in a country house in Vézelay. Sterling's house.

The kitchen had a wood-stove and blue faience plates in a wooden rack above the sink. Sterling would have had a good wood fire burning on cool evenings. She probably had a woman from the village cooking for her and serving up delicious omelettes and onion soups and other savory dishes on the blue plates. In the dusk she would have been looking out the window which faced the apple orchard and, further away, the convent vineyard.

The small bedroom had a single bed with an iron headboard and the only other furniture was an iron washstand. The wooden peg behind the door was empty but I imagined Sterling hanging up a plain summer dress before going to bed. There was no chest-of-drawers or a closet for clothes. It seemed that Sterling was a different person in the country from her sophisticated self in the city. I liked the person she had been in the country.

Upon my return to the convent an hour and a half later Soeur Jeanne-Marie greeted me outside the door. She was dressed in her black habit and a well-worn rosary hung from her black woolen belt. A white wimple made her look taller and held her round face severely.

"Come," she said and folded her hands into the wide sleeves of her habit. "Our supper is in my rooms."

"I loved Sterling's house," I said. "And I loved her garden, especially the peach tree."

"It is not the same tree, of course," Soeur Jeanne-Marie said. "Peach trees last not much more than ten or fifteen years. I have planted at least six new trees in the very same spot over the years because Minou adored peaches."

"How very lovely of you," I said with feeling.

Chapter 47

1930

"I packed my bag as soon as I got your message," Claire said, "and here I am in my sturdy, second-hand Ford coupe. Love the yellow color, don't you know. It's the 1928 model. Bought it from Bernice Boch."

"Exactly your style, old chap," Sterling said and helped Claire unstrap her valise—mud-splattered from the precarious country roads—from the open rumble seat.

"A frightful experience," Claire said and tried in vain to rearrange her wind-blown hair and red scarf. "I do believe I did more than twenty-five miles an hour bumping over every single rock in the road. Hideously fast speed, but, if not, I'd have arrived only tomorrow. It took me several cans of petrol."

"How long will you stay?" Sterling said and helped heave the valise through the house to the guest room.

"For as long as you need me."

"How lovely."

"You said you were ill after you left Paris but you're looking quite well now," Claire said.

"I wasn't well at all when I arrived but between Soeur Madeleine's prayers and the sisters at the convent and the country air and the good food, I've recovered."

"This will cheer you up no end. Tremendously audacious. Colette's *Aventures Quotidiennes* with her Figaro articles. It will remind you of CAT," Claire said and dragged the book out of her bag.

"Thanks awfully. She's my absolute favorite. She has cat's eyes and beautiful legs. Remember when we saw her in *La Vagabonde* with poor Paul Poiret as the unfortunate lead. As Pierre Fast-Brown said, he should have stayed with his dress designs."

"Devastating spectacle," Claire howled.

They sat down outside in their customary garden chairs, Sterling poured white wine for Claire while she, herself, drank a glass of Evian. Claire lit her cigarette and blew a long streak of blue smoke into the air.

"Don't tell me," she said, "you've given up cigarettes as well as this nectar of the gods?"

"I've given up a lot of things," Sterling said, "it is no longer to my taste. I spend so much time with the sisters at the convent and I do not wish to offend them by smoking."

"I should probably become holy and give up all of my delicious vices," Claire said, "but you have become holy enough for the both of us."

They looked at each other and started giggling.

"Except that I partake of Soeur Madeleine's sinful Kir. She's devoted to her after dinner drink."

"Now for the gossip," Claire said. "I had a letter from Bernice in New York, her new husband has bought her a studio and a gallery and she's big, even bigger than usual, with child."

"Bernice is having a baby?" Sterling said and bowed her head.

"You mustn't worry about yourself," Claire said. "One beautiful day, when the time is right, you will have your own, I feel quite sure."

"Of course," Sterling said. She lay back in her chair and stared at the sky where the clouds had turned rose-colored from the setting sun. Her eyes were large and shiny. "I'm happy for Bernice."

"Yes, she has written the news to absolutely everyone except, I imagine, to Pyotr Vasilevich."

"I presume he has been in good hands and shouldn't mind too much."

"Yes, he was in my hands for a little while but you know how it is, I've moved on."

"You merciless woman."

"I confess."

"Have you seen Scott Winteride?" Sterling said. "And how about Laura and Auguste?"

"Scott has left for Italy once more, seems to believe he can write there, and Laura is on vacation in Spain. She was quite exhausted, poor pet."

Claire stubbed out her cigarette and inserted a fresh one into her long amber holder.

"Alex Orgoloff came back from the Riviera full of enthusiasm with a stack of new paintings and full of gossip about the beauties bathing in the sun in daring décolleté. Seems not to worry about the lack of money all around—not to mention the paucity of Americans—he's having an exhibition next month. He asked me about you."

"And what did you tell him?"

"What you asked me to tell him. That you're incommunicado in the country and don't want to see anyone. Needless to say, he didn't believe a word of it. You may expect his unannounced visit at any time."

"Oh, no."

"I did my best but, with Alex, one's best is not good enough."

"Fine," Sterling said and sank further down in her chair.

They sat a while in silence while Claire finished most of the wine and several more cigarettes. Sterling absently poured her Evian into the grass and reached for the wine.

Paris seemed far away. She had not been back to the Grands-Agustins since that fateful day when she had left the clinic and gone to the apartment for the valise she had packed in advance. She had left in the Quadrilette within the hour and had settled into her house in Vézelay by the late afternoon.

During the next few weeks she had a long talk with Soeur Madeleine, after which she had sent the pneu to Claire and asked her to visit.

"I did what you asked," Claire said. "I got your mail from the American Express and put the letters in your trunk at the apartment. Let me know if you want me to bring any of it here?"

"No," Sterling said. "I've told Pierre Fast-Brown to write me care of the convent."

"And you don't expect to hear from anyone else?"

Stefan's name hung heavily in the air while Claire gazed solemnly at Sterling and Sterling gazed back.

"It serves no purpose," she said.

"Fine," Claire said and got up. "Battle on. I'm ready to follow you to the convent and indulge in some convent food for dinner. How bad can it be?"

"Behave yourself."

Claire stayed two weeks. They went to the market and stocked up on a few food items. Dinner was taken at the convent. The wine bottles—full and empty—piled up on the kitchen counter and the dishes often sat unattended in the sink. It was a leisurely and happy two weeks.

When Claire sat in her newly washed and polished yellow Ford coupe with a picnic basket on the back seat, her red shawl around her shoulders and her hair firmly secured by a scarf, Sterling hugged her for the longest time and all but cried.

"Come back soon, won't you?"

"As soon as I get back from Spain," Claire said. "In a couple of months or six. I must spend some time with my Papa."

"Write to me," Sterling shouted through a cloud of dust above the thunderous noise of the motor.

When she could no longer see or hear the car she walked down the road, past the convent, past the cemetery, to the foot of the road leading up to the Basilica.

The air inside the church was cool and Sterling sat down in a pew to rest. She leaned back. She rested her head and looked up at the tall, multi-colored columns and at the capitals with their small groups of sculptures. She sought out the one in which St. Benedict brought a child back to life. She sat for a long while in the silence of the church.

"You have not been here for several weeks," a gentle voice said.

"Dear Pére Dionysius," Sterling said. "I have had a guest from Paris."

"Are you feeling quite well?"

"I am feeling fine," Sterling said and stood up. "I will return to speak with you in a little while."

She went down the narrow stone steps to the crypt where the relics of the blessed Mary Magdalene rested on a small altar. Sterling had sat on the front bench innumerable times in silent prayer to the Saint whom God had forgiven because of her great love for his Son. Sterling knew well the story of the three Marys whom history had fused into one but this did not detract from her feelings of peace whenever she sat in the crypt.

She recited in a whisper the familiar words meant for yet another Mary: 'Hail Mary, full of grace, the Lord is with thee,' and her voice quavered when she came to the last phrase.

She crossed herself and went upstairs in search of Pére Dionysius who was old and other-worldly and whom she had known almost her whole life.

He turned to her in his kindly way and blessed her. A ray of sun shone through the tall windows in the nave and illuminated her face. She sank down on her knees and accepted her state of grace feeling pure and forgiven.

Chapter 48

I followed Soeur Jeanne-Marie inside once more and a very young lay sister served us *oeufs en meurette* accompanied by crisp baguettes and a small salad with greens from the vegetable garden. We had sparkling Evian in heavy tumblers without ice and never once did the holy one appear. We didn't speak while we ate and Soeur Jeanne-Marie looked pre-occupied. At the end of the meal she swallowed one of her little white pills. When at last she got up and motioned that we were leaving, she walked more slowly than before.

We stopped in her small garden and she picked a bouquet of white anemones and blue-bells and one single red poppy which she gave to me. She took my arm and we walked back down the garden path to the gate, and from there to the cemetery. Again, she crossed herself and bowed her head when passing certain graves and we made a circle to Soeur Madeleine and Soeur Daphne's headstones. Then we crossed a small lawn to the very back of the cemetery where Soeur Jeanne-Marie knelt by a stone lying flat on the ground. She wiped off a few twigs and leaves and small stones and pointed for me to kneel down as well.

The small headstone had a simple cross at the top and one simple name: Minou.

Under the name were her dates. Born 1896. Died 1931. Sterling had lived thirty-five short years.

Although I had gradually understood what awaited me at the cemetery, the reality was still devastating. Sterling had died young, she never married, she never lived a full life, and there was no mystery to be solved anymore. My search was over and I felt immense grief as if I had lost my only sister.

I placed the bouquet of red, white and blue flowers next to the small stone. Soeur Jeanne-Marie, still on her knees, had closed her eyes and ran her rosary gently through her fingers. I was down beside her, cheeks wet, eyes closed. The Lord's prayer of my childhood came back to me forcefully. I prayed for Sterling.

"How did she die?" I asked when we had somehow collected ourselves and sat on a stone bench under a nearby tree.

"She had a fever," Soeur Jeanne-Marie said and crossed herself. "She had been with us for about six months, she was very serene and happy, her friend Claire visited with her once at the beginning but she saw no one else.

"Claire was her true friend," I said.

"Yes, they went for long walks, Minou laughed when Claire was here but she never drank wine or smoked those strong cigarettes again. She no longer walked up the hill to sit in the chapel at the Basilica. Instead she attended Mass here at the convent with Soeur Madeleine and Soeur Daphne and after Mass her eyes were bright and she stayed in her room for several hours."

"She was happy," I said more to myself than to Soeur Jeanne-Marie.

"She was at peace but she had lost her will to live. She was what you would call depressed. Soeur Madeleine worried much about her. There was some paperwork signed with a lawyer from Auxerre,"

"Yes?"

"The doctor from Auxerre was called when Minou developed a fever," Soeur Jeanne-Marie said. "She was ill for a week and slowly recovered but it was a false hope and two weeks later Minou left us. We buried her here according to her wishes, without her real name, just 'Minou'."

Her eyes were clouded with sorrow.

"I wished that God had taken me instead of her," Soeur Jeanne-Marie whispered. "She has been in my prayers every day for these many years."

She stood up, unbent her back, took my arm and led us towards the convent, from the cemetery down the road, through the heavy gate, and up to her small garden patch. There, once again, we sat down on a bench.

"Soeur Madeleine swore me to silence," Soeur Jeanne-Marie said. "But I believe that now, so many years later, she would forgive me for speaking so freely to you. There are some particulars which must be set right. I have always felt guilty about my vow. And, now God sent you to me so that I might atone if I have done wrong."

When we were back in her rooms Soeur Jeanne-Marie sat down heavily in her high-backed chair, her feet up on a small stool embroidered with faded yarn, and closed her eyes.

I waited, sitting uncomfortably on a plain wooden chair without upholstery, on a well-worn seat which sloped forward so that I was forced to scoot back occasionally. During one of these maneuvers Soeur Jeanne-Marie opened her eyes and looked me straight in the eye.

"You are the first one to come here," she said. "No one came after the *chér Monsieur* Alex laid white lilies on her grave, he came one day in a big touring car with Minou's friend, Claire, and they both cried."

I wiped at my own tears.

Soeur Jeanne-Marie had closed her eyes again.

"I was not supposed to talk about it," she said, "and I didn't. But I knew."

"What did you know?"

"This is what I swore not to tell anyone and may the blessed Mother forgive me for the sin I am about to commit."

"She forgives you," I said, "I am quite sure."

"I heard the cries in the middle of the night and I became very afraid. I left my room and went to Minou but Soeur Madeleine bade me return to my bed and never to speak to anyone of what I had seen."

"Yes?" I said.

"The child was taken away to the village to be nursed."

"A child was born?" I heard my voice rising. "Sterling had a baby?"

"Yes."

"And the baby lived?"

"Yes, the darling baby lived."

Chapter 49

This was not the only news that sent my world into a crazy spin.

When I returned to Paris I was greeted by a slew of text messages and e-mails from Bob Makowski and Topsy with ominous news. It appeared that my financial adviser had invested my money unadvisedly and that I was now in the company of a multitude of fine citizens who'd been scammed in a Ponzi scheme soon to be making headlines from coast to coast. The short of the long of it was that I'd lost a substantial sum of money likely never to be retrieved and, in quite a panic, I felt compelled to tighten my belt immediately until I could assess the actual loss.

I looked around at the satin sheets, the silk curtains, the crystal chandeliers, and the antique chairs, tucked my feet into the peach-colored slippers, filled the bathtub with hot water and bubbles and lay there until the water was tepid and I felt quite drained. I toweled off, put on the thirsty dressing gown for what I knew would be the last time in a while, ordered my last dinner with a superb bottle of Chablis, ate and drank slowly and deliberately and shortly thereafter fell into bed where I passed out.

Bright and early and hung over, I explained to my concerned friends at the reception that I must check out this very day due to unforseen circumstances whereupon

I had a sumptuous breakfast at the in-house café, went upstairs to pack my bags, declined the use of a private limo to the airport, entered a lowly taxi under the solicitous stare of the doorman, to whom I gave a last handsome tip, and confided my new address to the taxi driver.

Twenty minutes later I arrived at my new hotel on rue Jacob where I had secured a room on the second floor facing the inner courtyard. There I settled down on the bed since the room contained no cozy armchair and called Washington.

"Sterling died," I said when I got Topsy on the line.

"Yes," she said, "we knew that or she would have been a hundred and fifteen by now."

"No, I mean she died in 1931, in Vézelay, when she was thirty-six."

"She died in 1931," Topsy shouted to Martin who was making noises in the background.

"It made me feel really sad," I said.

"Oh, me too, me too, I was so much hoping she lived a long, happy married life in Switzerland."

"So was I."

"But you've done what you set out to do, you've solved the mystery."

"Not exactly," I said. "Soeur Jeanne-Marie was a very reluctant eye witness weighed down with guilt at revealing Sterling's story to me. In a way that story is only now beginning."

"Tell me this minute," Topsy said.

"There was a child," I said.

"There was a child," Topsy shrieked to Martin.

"Yes, there was a child," I said. "Sterling had a daughter and named her Edwige Claire—Edwige after Soeur Madeleine's middle name and Claire after Claire Garcia-Bonsonwell—and she was known by the last name of Le Duc, the name of her foster parents."

"Unbelievable."

"I know. I'm still in shock."

"Tell me, tell me."

"She was born on April 20, 1931."

"Where?"

"Right there at the convent."

"Unbelievable."

"She was delivered by the two Soeurs Madeleine and Daphne who, it turns out, were respectively a midwife and a nurse."

"What a wonderful act of charity and love."

"Yes," I said. "When the baby was only a few hours old they both knew that Sterling was too weak to nurse her. They took the baby to a young mother in the village who had just lost yet another baby and who was able to nurse Sterling's."

"Unbelievable."

"Sterling died two weeks later. I went to the cemetery with Soeur Jeanne-Marie and saw the stone, quite small, just inscribed with the dates and the name they had for her. Minou."

Topsy sniffled quite loudly.

"Did the baby stay with the woman who nursed her?"

"She did. She was brought up as the Le Duc's own daughter but apparently everyone knew that Edwige Claire was not their real child but was born to a single mother somewhere."

"She was born 1931 and would be about 80 today. Did you find her in the village?"

"I wish that things were finally that simple. No, I didn't find her in the village, Soeur Jeanne-Marie had not heard of or from her in sixty years and did not know what had happened to her. When Edwige was twenty-one she left."

"What did the Soeur think happened?"

"She said that Edwige had never been happy in the village—she was bullied by the local children and even shunned and called names by the grown-ups."

"In those days so-called illegitimate children were horribly stigmatized."

"Exactly. And it took me quite a while to pry the rest of the story out of Soeur Jeanne-Marie. Before she died in 1933, Soeur Madeleine had given Soeur Daphne a letter to pass on to Edwige when she reached the age of twenty-one. That would happen in April of 1952. Before Soeur Daphne died in 1949 she gave the letter to Soeur Jeanne-Marie who delivered it to Edwige three years later."

"Did your Soeur know what was in the letter?"

"She never read it but guessed from what happened next that the letter revealed everything. Edwige went to Auxerre to the law firm which had managed her trust fund, she found out about her heritage, she came into the money which gave her freedom to leave Vézelay. And that is what she did. She came back, packed her bag and left that same afternoon without a word to anyone."

"Where did she go?"

"No one knew."

"What do *you* think happened?"

"I've been thinking quite hard," I said, "and imagined what *I* would have done."

"*You* would have traveled toute de suite to Paris, *you* would have found Claire Garcia-Bonsonwell and even Alexandre Orgoloff, and *you* would then have moved into Sterling's apartment on the Grands-Agustins and lived happily ever after."

"Sounds about right."

"Did your Soeur tell Edwige about Claire and Orgoloff?" Topsy said.

"She said that she told Edwige all she remembered. Of course, by that time she knew that Alexandre Orgoloff was dead—he was on a visit to Poland in 1949 when his heart gave out. She couldn't tell Edwige about Claire since she didn't even know her last name and she knew nothing of Sterling's relatives in America."

"But she told Edwige everything else. Good girl, your Soeur."

"Absolutely. Soeur Madeleine had not intended to hold her to the vow after Edwige reached the age of twenty-one."

"That must have taken care of your Soeur's guilt feelings."

"Yes, she finally agreed that the truth could be revealed to me. I think she's longing to know what happened to Edwige and, maybe, to see her again."

"She never tried to find Edwige on her own?"

"I asked her if she ever wrote to Edwige at the address in Paris but she was still reluctant to tell me everything."

"If I know you, you pried it out of her?"

"Well," I said.

"Well?"

"Soeur Jeanne-Marie did write and her letter was returned as undeliverable."

"Don't tell me. Sterling had sold the apartment?"

"That's what I would guess."

"Then how will you find Edwige?"

"I'll start from scratch."

"And when will you come back home?"

"It's anyone's guess," I said, ignoring my guilt feelings at deserting Bob Makowski and my many duties in Washington. "And, furthermore, guess where I'm now staying."

"Where?"

"Due to unforseen circumstances I'm now at Ms. Puigh's small hotel on the rue Jacob."

"That's quite a let-down," Topsy said with feeling.

"Funny thing is that I feel quite relieved to be in a less pretentious hotel. Quite comfortable, in fact. More down to earth."

"Hrmmp," said Topsy who knows me better than I know myself.

Then I told her about Tom Abbott and Roulette Equities.

"Martin," I heard Topsy shout again, "she lost her money."

"Not all of it," I shouted back. "And one last thing. I need you to do me a favor."

"Anything at all."

"Please keep what I've told you about Sterling confidential. I want to inform Neil Robinson before anyone else hears about it."

"Not to worry, you're the boss, I won't breathe a word to anyone and I'll make sure Martin doesn't either."

After we hung up I was still left with the feeling that I was losing control of my own case.

Chapter 50

Ms. Puigh had sent me Sterling's four letters to Pierre Fast-Brown. They were brief and the quality of the copies was not that good. The ink must have faded over the years. I read them sitting with a glass of house wine outside the Café Pré aux Clercs across from my hotel.

> *Paris, 2 August 1921*
>
> *Darling Uncle Pierre, thank you, thank you, thank you for seeing me off in such style—what else could I expect from my best uncle and best friend—the pearl necklace is divine, the diamond clasp with the red ruby makes it all the more special since I know it belonged to your mother. It's a precious heirloom and I will wear it often and treasure it always.*
>
> *Love, love, yours ever, Sterling*

These were the pearls I had seen Sterling wear in the photograph in Paul Manner's scrapbook. I applauded her silently for not hiding her pearls away in a box but wearing them on a daily basis.

351 quai des Grands-Agustins
15 November 1929

Darlingest Uncle Pierre, we did have a lovely time when you were here and I miss you immensely and want you to know that I took your valuable advice about my stocks. No one helps me as much as you do. Did I ever really thank you? If not, let me do it now. I love you and am most grateful to you. You saved me when I was young and lost and you are still saving me now even though I am no longer that young and not quite as lost. Stefan loves me, Claire loves me, Effie loves me. Alex loves me and all the sisters love me. I feel very blessed. But to answer your question, no, I no longer see Victoria. It is better for me and I don't want you to worry about it any more.

Love, love, Sterling

I read the letter three times. What was that about her stocks, did she salvage her money during the crash? If so, then Edwige would have been sitting pretty in 1952. Stefan was still without a last name, everyone loved her, and it warmed my heart to know that she had cast Victoria Huddersfield aside.

351 quai des Grands-Agustins
2 February, 1930

Darling Uncle Pierre, life is so full of wonderful events right now and it makes the burglary—which happened two weeks ago while I was in Vézelay—seem almost irrelevant were it not for the fact that the thieves took my two most darling paintings, the one by dear Matisse and one of my Derains. Fortunately, the other two paintings, the ones Effie Rousseau made me buy, were still in my trunk awaiting framing. The thieves seemed not to be interested in my three Orgoloffs on the wall, a fact I have not told dear Alex. He might feel slighted by the thieves! All I have left of the paintings is the photograph you took of me standing next to them. Great pity. The police are not overly concerned about my loss which is probably permanent.

Did I tell you that Scott Winteride has deserted his Paris friends and has gone to Venice and Rome for a prolonged visit. I miss him a whole lot. Also, as I think you know, Effie Rousseau is now painting in Rome and Claire is talking of Spain again. Alex is painting on the Côte d'Azur, and Bernice Boch married a new man and went home last month. Alas, soon all I have left is Stefan.

Always yours, Sterling

Sterling seemed very casual about being burgled and losing valuable paintings but, of course, in 1930 prices had not gone up to their later astronomical heights.

Effie Rousseau, I had found out, was a French portrait painter who had worked in Rome before returning to Paris in the late 1930s. During the Second World War she had been a fervent resistance fighter, was interned in a concentration camp in France and, tragically, died there a few days before the end of the war.

351 quai des Grands-Agustins
11 June, 1930

Darlingest Pierre, my only regret right now is that my writing is still blocked, I have not finished the book of poems although Effie has already given me her illustrations, my second book of short stories needs revising and I can't get to it, and the novel is finished except for the last two chapters. The end of a book, they tell me, is the most difficult to write and I want it to be perfect. I feel quite desperate about it. So wish me luck.

Yours forever, devotedly Sterling.

How very sad, I thought. Sterling had not seen her stories, her poems, her novel, in print. Two months after writing the last letter to Pierre Fast Brown she was pregnant and eleven months later she was dead. And today, eighty years later, I was on my way either to find Sterling's daughter or to discover that I had reached the end of the road.

A taxi from the stand on Boulevard Saint-Germain-des-Prés got me to the quai des Grands-Agustins. The building sat next to an antiquarian bookstore, a real estate office, and a café with small tables and red tablecloths. I sat down and ordered and paid for a crème and a brioche in lieu of a much needed lunch which I felt I must forgo in order to be prepared for a hasty exit.

The entrance door to number 351 had a security panel with six buttons and no names attached. Only two people entered in the next half hour, the first a tall, white-haired gentleman, the second a young student with a backpack. Two tenants exited, one a woman with two small children in tow, and the other a youngish woman carrying a white laundry bag.

Having long finished the coffee and my brioche I ordered and paid for a glass of Kir with white wine. No sooner had the waiter served the drink than an elderly woman emerged from number 351 and approached the table next to me.

"Madame Brisson," the waiter said and pulled out her chair. She ordered, took out a book and a pair of glasses and proceeded to read. She never once looked up. When her *Crocque Madame* and half bottle of wine arrived she ate and drank without taking her eyes from the book. She was dressed in a black skirt and a white blouse with feet in comfortable walking shoes. Her hair was braided and hung down her back. Her face was quite lined, her eyes a faded gray. Was she sixty, seventy or more? Was she Edwige Claire Le Duc?

I was about to approach her when Madame Brisson stuffed the book in her pocket, stood up, paid, and walked briskly up the street before I could get my act together. She was carrying a tote and I imagined she was on her way to the Mono Prix a couple of blocks away.

Having sat at the café for the better part of an hour I now left to set up my observation post outside the real estate office from where I could keep an eye on number 351. While there I studied—and more or less memorized—the apartments for sale in the neighborhood at quite exorbitant amounts of Euros. When Madame Brisson appeared up the street, her tote brimming with food items, including a long baguette, I stood before her door, waiting.

She put down her bag on the sidewalk and looked at me questioningly.

"Madame Edwige Brisson?" I said.

"Madame Brisson, *Oui*," she said. "Edwige, *Non*."

"*Pardon*," I said. "I am looking for Edwige but I'm afraid I must be mistaken about her last name. It may be Le Duc. I believe she lives in this building."

"And who wishes to see her?" Madame Brisson had a beginning look of anxiety in her round face.

"My name is Jamie Prescott and I am here as an emissary from her family in the United States."

"Edwige has no family in America."

"But her name is Edwige?"

"Yes, but her last name is not Le Duc."

Madame Brisson looked triumphant and punched in her code to open the door.

"Her last name could be something else." I raised my voice in desperation. "Could you tell her I will be at the café for another hour and would like to speak to her?"

It wasn't clear if Madame Brisson had heard me because she slipped through the door with her tote leaving me on the sidewalk.

I returned to the café and sat down at a different table but the waiter wasn't fooled.

"Another café and brioche," he inquired, "or another Kir?"

I took the only way out and smiled.

"I'll take a *Crocque Monsieur*," I said. "I was talking to Madame Brisson and am now waiting for Edwige to join me."

"Madame Edwige will not be home until five," my waiter said and looked quite as triumphant as did Madame Brisson when she informed me that Edwige's last name was not Le Duc.

"Do you by any chance know her last name?" I said.

"No, Madame," the waiter said and moved away hastily.

It was now two in the afternoon and since I could not very well stay at the café three more hours, I ate my lunch, paid, and hurried back to rue Jacob.

Eighteen new e-mail messages awaited my attention and I ploughed through them in half an hour. Most were from Bob Makowski sounding impatient in Washington. Mel Kramer sounded impatient in New York and I reassured him. Topsy sounded impatient in Washington and I related the contents of Sterling's letters. Ms. Puigh was having a spectacular time in Nice. And, surprise, Neil Robinson had been posted to Tokyo and would be leaving Washington within a week. He expected me to wind up his case by then. I can do that, I thought.

At ten to five I was back in front of the entrance to 351 quai des Grands-Augustins, not a second too soon. A woman was about to punch in her code on the panel when

I arrived. She was tall with a good haircut, dressed in a black suit and a white silk shirt and carried a briefcase as if she'd just come from a business meeting. Was she sixty or seventy? Could she really be eighty? I'm notoriously bad at guessing anyone's age.

"Madame Edwige?" I said.

"Yes?"

"I have greetings for you from Soeur Jeanne-Marie in Vézelay," I said.

Edwige dropped her briefcase and leaned against the wall, closed her eyes briefly and then stared at me with a deepening frown.

"Jeanne-Marie?" she said. "You have spoken to her? She is still living?"

"She is ninety-six and still living."

"A ghost from the past." Edwige looked considerably ghostly herself. She bent down and picked up her briefcase.

"I'm sorry if I startled you," I said.

"Who are you and how did you find me?" Again she steadied herself against the wall.

"My name is Jamie Prescott," I said. "Soeur Jeanne-Marie sent me to find you. She is hoping to see you one last time. If you invite me in I will tell you everything. It is a very long story."

Edwige Claire took another good look at me and nodded. Then she punched in her code and let me in.

Chapter 51

The end wall was painted red with faint silvery stripes, over the fireplace hung an unmistakable Derain, the fine carpets were charmingly worn and faded, on a glass-topped side table stood a dainty statuette of a bronze and ivory Charleston dancer on a marble base. And on the black coffee table rested a tall thin statue which could only be a Modigliani.

I was floored and quite dizzy. I felt like taking a spin around the room and shout to the roof tops that I was in Sterling's apartment with Sterling's daughter, that I was at the end of the quest—it felt like the holy grail—but the triumph was tempered by the knowledge of Sterling's sad fate and the fact that she had never seen her child grow up within a happy marriage to her Stefan.

Edwige said for me to wait while she changed and I walked to the tall windows from where I had a splendid view of the River Seine. I watched a barge move along slowly in the wake of a tourist-laden *Batobus* and knew that Sterling had once stood here enjoying the same view. My heart was very full.

"Now," Edwige said and offered me a seat in a chinz-covered sofa between the fireplace and the black coffee table. I could hardly take my eyes off the Modigliani. "Now tell me who you are, how you found me, and why you're interested in me. Normally, I would not have invited a total stranger to my home but you could not have invented Soeur Jeanne-Marie."

"Thank you," I said, "It's a long story."

"I've arranged for us to have some tea," she said, "it will be served in a few minutes. In the meantime, do start from the beginning."

"Your mother had a sister in America," I said. "Her name was Rose Kirkland Sawyer, she had a daughter whose name was Marjorie. Marjorie married and lived in New York City until earlier this year when, very sadly, she was the victim of a traffic accident and died."

"I never heard of an aunt named Rose," Edwige said, "or someone named Marjorie."

"Marjorie would have been your cousin," I said. "She was the one who came to me—in my capacity as a private investigator—and asked me to find your mother, Sterling Kirkland Sawyer. Her son, Neil Robinson is with the American Foreign Service, or the State Department as we call it, and lives in Washington, D.C. After his mother died he asked me to continue the search for your mother."

The door to the living room swung open and in came a tea tray carried by Madame Brisson who was now dressed in a dark blue dress and a white apron. She looked at me in surprise mixed with suspicion and put down the tray in front of Edwige.

"Anything else," she said to Edwige.

"Thank you, no, just leave the supper in the oven and I will see to it myself. Goodnight, my dear."

Madame Brisson left the door ajar and Edwige got up to close it.

"She lives in the apartment downstairs and helps me out a couple of hours every day. She is possessed of a very healthy curiosity and I'm sure she's burning up to know who you are," Edwige said.

"That would be my guess."

"I, myself, am still in shock," she said. "I had quite forgotten about everyone. It has been so many years and I have never been back to Vézelay. Tell me how you went about your search to find me. It interests me. I am a retired history teacher, I taught at the Sorbonne and have done my share of research. You speak French very well, how did that come about?"

"Twenty years ago I lived in France, in the countryside, married for a few years. I divorced the husband but still love France. A different story all together."

"Yes," Edwige said, poured the tea from a silver teapot and offered me a dry biscuit.

"I take it that your name is no longer Le Duc," I said and nearly broke a tooth on the biscuit.

"No, it is not. My last name is Gerard. From my late husband."

"If you hadn't stayed on in this apartment I would never have found you," I said.

"How *did* you find out where I live?"

"From your mother's letters to a friend of hers in America. I have copies of those letters which I would like you to have."

Edwige shied away from the envelope I offered her as if it held noxious material. I placed it on the coffee table.

"This was your mother's apartment was it not?" I said.

Edwige Gerard got up from the sofa and walked to the window, from the window to the fireplace, from the fireplace back to the sofa where she sat down and closed her eyes.

I waited for her to speak and looked at her face as she sat there next to me. I tried to see Sterling in her. But since all I had was an image from a photograph of a young Sterling from 1914, it was impossible now to see a resemblance close to a hundred years later.

I took out the photograph from my purse.

"Here," I said and Edwige opened her eyes. "This was your mother at eighteen."

She didn't reach for the photograph and I placed it on the coffee table next to Sterling's letters to Pierre Fast-Brown.

Edwige spoke as if I wasn't there.

"I learned about her when I was twenty-one years of age," she said. "From my childhood I do not recall Soeur Madeleine, Soeur Daphne I would see from a distance, and only Soeur Jeanne-Marie ever came to visit. My parents, Louise and Gustave Le Duc, were very strict and I was punished for every little misdeed. I would get into fights with the other children when they called me names which I did not understand."

"Yes, Soeur Jeanne-Marie told me," I said.

"Oh, she did, did she?" Edwige said in a voice that would have withered my Soeur if she had heard. "Then why didn't she tell *me*? All she did was hand me a letter on my twenty-first birthday which made my whole previous life a lie. A lie in which everyone had conspired."

"She had taken a solemn vow not to tell anyone."

"And no doubt feels tremendous guilt."

"Oh, she does, she does, you have no idea."

"And now that she's close to the end of her life she felt so guilty that she had to tell a total stranger?" Edwige said.

"She felt that God had brought me to her."

"Well, you can tell her I will never forgive her and that her God will not, either."

"She will accept that as her just punishment," I said, "she is a very saintly person but I don't know what else she could have done. She was only a child of fifteen when you were born, she was completely obedient to the nuns at the convent and she was relieved that she could give you the letter when you turned twenty-one. She did tell you everything she remembered about your mother when you returned from the lawyers in Auxerre. Is that not true?"

Edwige got up and went to the fireplace where she turned her back to me.

"She did try to find you later," I said. "She wrote a letter to this address which was returned with the notation 'undeliverable'."

Edwige nodded.

"I returned it myself. I was that angry."

"I understand," I said, and I suppose I did.

"I know my anger may be misplaced," she said at last. "That is what my therapist would have told me, I'm sure. I have been angry all my life, first at the children in the village, then at the parents who turned out not to be my parents at all, then at the sisters who could have told me, and at God who had deserted me."

"How about Sterling, your real mother. She provided for you, she loved you from the moment you were born and certainly before you were born or she could have made sure she didn't have you. Abortions were frequent even in those days. Instead she chose to give you life. She couldn't have known she would die from puerperal fever. I feel quite sure she would never have abandoned you had she lived."

What I didn't say was that Sterling left Edwige very well off and that she was lucky to have inherited this apartment and a sizeable trust fund and to have lived here all her life.

"She didn't tell me who my father was," Edwige said, "she could have left me a letter. His name was absent from the birth certificate. In those days, if a woman was not married the father could not appear on the child's certificate."

She looked at me with a great deal of anger.

"Therefore," she said, "I was illegitimate. An ugly word with which to punish an innocent child. It was a curse until the laws changed in the 1970s but that was too late for me. I was told by the lawyers in Auxerre that my last name was Sawyer after my birth mother but I never used it. I remained Le Duc until I married a fellow student at the Sorbonne and took his last name, Gerard."

"She would have told you if she had lived. She didn't know she would die."

"Yes, I thought of that," Edwige said. She was close to tears.

"Your father's first name may have been Stefan," I said, "and if it's the last thing I do I will find out who he was. Soeur Jeanne-Marie never knew either his first or his last name."

"Then how do *you* know?"

Over supper in the dining room I told Edwige everything I had discovered about Sterling Kirkland Sawyer from the moment Marjorie Robinson stepped into my office on K Street in Washington. How I found Victoria Huddersfield, how Ms. Puigh found the letters Sterling had sent to Pierre Fast-Brown, in which she mentioned a special man in her life named Stefan.

I told her how we read CAT's *Paris Diary* and found out that CAT was Sterling, how my ex-husband, Roger, told me about Victoria's granddaughter, Suzette D'Alville, and how I visited with Victoria's daughter, Isabelle, how she gave me the photograph of Sterling and told me about the convent in Vézelay and how I found Soeur Jeanne-Marie.

"You are quite the investigator," Edwige said and stretched out her hand for the photograph of Sterling which I had taken from the coffee table in the living room and placed on the sideboard in the dining room. She looked at it for a long, long time.

We had finished supper and were sitting over black coffee—black because Madame Brisson had neglected to buy the requisite milk—into which we both stirred heaps of sugar. On the dining room wall facing me hung two large Surrealist paintings with dream-like figures floating on a blue background.

The third painting was a portrait of a young woman, her hair cut short under her ears and curling forward on her cheek, her wide eyes looking at me with a smile that went to her slightly parted lips.

"All three paintings are by Alexandre Orgoloff, the famous Surrealist," she said.

"Your mother mentioned him several times in her *Paris Diary* in the same breath as Matisse and Picasso."

We looked from the photograph to the painting and back. There could be no doubt.

"It's an Orgoloff of Sterling," I said. "Now we know what she looked like as an adult."

"Beautiful," Edwige said and then her tears flowed. "I never imagined she would have known Orgoloff and that he would have painted her. Thank you."

She looked around the dining room at her three paintings and smiled at me.

"Tell me about your life," I said.

"When Soeur Jeanne-Marie gave me the letter I had finished my entrance exam to the university in Auxerre," Edwige said. "My parents were not educated people but I never questioned how they could afford to send me to a boarding school in town. Later I understood that my schools had been paid from the portion of the trust the lawyers in Auxerre administered. I also learned that the Le Ducs had been paid quite handsomely all through my childhood. I understood then that they never loved me for myself, they loved me for the money."

"I am so sorry," I said.

"In Auxerre I learned that my real mother had died when I was born, and that she had left me this apartment in Paris and a fortune invested in New York which was being administered by a law firm in Paris. As Soeur Jeanne-Marie told you, I returned to Vézelay, packed a small suitcase, and left for Paris that very evening. I lived in a hotel for several months until my new lawyers paid the renters to evacuate the apartment and I've been here ever since."

"And you pursued your studies at the Sorbonne and married. I am very glad. I am only surprised that you never tried to trace your family in America?"

"Soeur Jeanne-Marie told me that my mother had no family there and I took that to be true. All I wanted was to be free, to leave and never speak to anyone in Vézelay again. And that vow I have kept. I erased the past from my memory."

"I'm sorry," I said. "I've reminded you of the bad times."

"My dear, I had a wonderful life with my husband—he died two years ago—with my work and my friends, we traveled in Europe, and I still have an apartment in Venice. My husband and I collaborated on several history books and I am quite well-known in scholarly circles."

Edwige hadn't mentioned children and I didn't ask.

"You must have inherited your talent from your mother," I said instead. "She was in the process of having a book of poems published with illustrations by Effie Rousseau. Your mother may also have finished a novel she was working on up until she died. And, of course, Claire Garcia-Bonsonwell, the English-Spanish dancer, was your mother's best friend and you have her name, Claire."

"I never knew. Do you know why she named me Edwige?"

"For the woman she loved as a mother. The Mother Superior at the convent. Her name was Madeleine Edwige."

"I never knew that, either."

Edwige stood up and invited me to do the same. She picked up her mother's letters to Pierre Fast-Brown from the coffee table.

"I am feeling suddenly quite tired. I will read the letters later," she said. "Will you return to see me tomorrow for lunch? We will speak of Soeur Jeanne-Marie and how I can meet her."

On my way down the stairs I heard the door to Madame Brisson's apartment click shut.

Chapter 52

1931

"Your shipment from New York has arrived," Soeur Madeleine said when Sterling returned from her afternoon walk to her house.

"It's the layette from Bloomingdale's. I knew I could count on them to hurry this to me," Sterling exclaimed and excitement colored her voice and put heat in her cheeks.

"I took it to my rooms," Soeur Madeleine said. "Shall we look at it now or later?"

"Oh, now," Sterling said, "now. Let's not wait another minute."

Half an hour later she sat on the floor next to the large carton surrounded by little garments, fluffy blankets, yellow booties, tiny socks, and flowery bonnets.

"Look, look," said Soeur Madeleine, "our little daughter, and I feel sure it will be a daughter, will eat out of these tiny plates with these beautiful silver spoons. You must have them engraved."

"She will drink from this silver cup and she will be very pretty, and she will laugh when I hold her and spin her around the room. I already love her vastly. I will take her to my beautiful house, we will sit under the peach tree, and

I'll show her the apple orchard from my bedroom window. I will open up the wooden trap under the kitchen floor for her to feel the fresh scent of yesteryear's apples stored underneath."

Soeur Madeleine smiled at Sterling.

"She will look in a few years just the way you looked, my dear Minou, when you first arrived to the convent so many years ago. Her hair will be long and golden, her eyes will be blue and radiant, her hands will be very slender."

"You made me feel very pretty," Sterling said. "I had never felt pretty and wanted before."

"My dear, you were the prettiest little girl we had ever seen, and so clever to learn French so quickly."

"I know what we shall call my little daughter," Sterling said. "She will be named after you, because you are my beloved mother, she will have your middle name, she will be Edwige."

"I am very honored and delighted. Will you not give her a second name as well?"

"Yes, of course. She will be Edwige Claire because Claire is my loveliest friend."

"How very perfect." Soeur Madeleine beamed at her.

Soeur Madeleine looked long and searchingly at Sterling where she sat encircled by her baby's clothes. Soon her condition would be a difficult matter to conceal but it is of no importance, she thought, we will not be afraid of anyone's opinion. Minou is my beloved daughter and I will stand by her always.

"I will accompany you to your apartment in Paris as soon as you and your baby are ready to move," Soeur Madeleine said. "Or you may wish to stay at your house through the summer so we can look after you here. Then we will find a competent nanny to help you and to live with you in Paris for as long as you find it necessary."

"Yes," Sterling said. "I confess I feel quite incompetent to take care of a new baby but I will learn. It will be a wonderful time for us all. I do hope Claire will come back soon. I have not told her about the baby yet."

"She will be happy for you," Soeur Madeleine said and smiled.

Claire's letter arrived the following day.

Madrid, Spain, March 1, 1931

Darlingest, how brutish of you not to write me a single letter, yes, I know, I've been moving about in the most dashedly muddled way since arriving here and your missives may have been following me around just steps away from finding me. However, dear old girl, we will make up for everything and have a bottle and a laugh when I return although it may be a while. I am quite relieved that I've given up my studio in Montmartre. My Papa insists on keeping me here a while longer, his horses are heavenly and I am riding about the countryside with my second cousin, Don Carlos, a divine man. And you know how I adore divine men. My dance recitals went swimmingly, I am getting quite famous. Be well, old chap, write soon,

Claire

Sterling wrote a loving letter back—without revealing her condition—hoping it would reach Claire. Then, resolutely, she put aside all thoughts of the past and of the future beyond the birth of Edwige Claire, she blocked out all thoughts of Stefan, Stefan who had a wife and two children in Switzerland. This baby would be hers alone. What the world would think, how the tongues would wag, how she would meet the challenges, she refused to contemplate. She thought of no one in Paris, not of the opulent life at dinners and concerts and exhibitions and night-clubs, not of jewelry and couture dresses and silk hose, not of friends and fellow writers, except for Claire.

She wrote only one more letter.

Vézelay, March 14, 1931

Darling uncle Pierre, how very boring for you to be laid up in hospital but I'm glad to know that when you receive this letter you will be home convalescing albeit on a strict diet. Please, darling, get well very soon.

What is new with me, you asked, and why haven't you heard from me for so long. I do know that I have been terribly remiss in writing my customary letters to you and I hasten to remedy this omission. Dearest uncle Pierre, I have left behind the glamour and the glitter of Paris and have retired to the convent and my house in the country to be with dear Soeur Madeleine and the sisters.

Wish you could see me in my old blue dress with my face devoid of powder and lipstick and my neck without jewelry. In another month I will write you again to tell you more about my new life and what I plan for the future. Be well and rest up so that you may visit me very soon, all my love, darling,

Sterling

By the time the daffodils appeared in the garden in late March, her walks up the hill to the Basilica had ceased, and she stayed at the convent and went to her house only a few more times. Soeur Madeleine delegated most of her own daily duties to Soeur Daphne and they both kept a keen eye on Sterling's health. When the time came they were there with their learning and wisdom for several long hours. Ether was administered and when Sterling awoke the baby had been cleaned and wrapped in a pink flannel.

Soeur Madeleine placed the bundle in Sterling's arms. Sterling, her eyes misty, her smile joyous, gazed into the tiny face with its rosy cheeks, a high forehead, an upturned nose, and full lips. The hands with the fine pink nails are mine, she thought. The baby suddenly opened her dark eyes with the long lashes that curled at the ends ever so finely and gazed back at Sterling.

"She sees me," Sterling said and kissed the little face, "she knows I love her. Darling Edwige Claire."

Chapter 53

"I knew you would find her," Topsy said from Washington. "Tell me, tell me."

I told her.

"When are you returning? You've found Sterling, you've found her daughter, what else is there to do?"

"Just the impossible. The identity of Edwige's father."

"You can't mean that," Topsy wailed. "Let her do her own research, and what difference can it make at this point?"

"You surely know me by now, I can't give up until a mystery is completely solved. Wouldn't you like to know?"

"Oh, all right, I suppose. It seems impossible, though."

"I'll get back to Victoria's daughter, Isabelle. She'll have to search her memory or to have another look at Victoria's boxes. Or I must talk to Suzette, she lived with Victoria, she must have picked up something she's nearly forgotten. I have no other sources left. What if it turned out to be Alexandre Orgoloff? Did Claire know and tell him, after all? Could he have left letters behind? Maybe to Effie Rousseau?"

"How would you ever find out?" Topsy moaned. "It sounds much too complicated."

"I know," I said and I knew I must soon give it up.

"Please do come home soon," Topsy said, "we're all desperate to see you."

My e-mails were full of messages from all those desperate people. Bob Makowsky actually sounded the least desperate, he was mainly exited about his new girlfriend whom I had not yet met and didn't mention the office at all.

The most surprising message was from Mel in New York who informed me he was negotiating a partnership in an art gallery in Washington and would I think that a good idea? He would, of course, still keep his apartment and his art gallery in New York.

I had to smile because he knew exactly how to make sure he didn't crowd me and I smiled some more because at the same time he was sure not to crowd himself. I e-mailed him that I thought it was a splendid idea.

Neil Robinson had departed for Tokyo earlier than anticipated and told me he was elated to learn that I had found his second cousin, Edwige, and to tell her he would visit with her on his first leave. He even recommended a three-star hotel for me in Paris and raised my per diem. Ms. Puigh would be returning from Nice the next day and looked forward to seeing me at our hotel.

Before I left my lovely hotel I had instructed the concierge to return to Topsy the two parcels of books she had sent me and which I had read and had no more use for. I had held back two novels, both taking place in Paris in the 1920s, which might be fun to read. I settled down for the evening with one of them. Poorly written, very dated, with an improbable plot, albeit a first edition in hardcover, with a worn dust-jacket. It soon put me to sleep.

The next day Edwige Claire Gerard greeted me with a big smile and an extravagant lunch.

"I went to my small storage room downstairs and found some items I haven't seen in years," she said. "The lock on this old steamer trunk was broken when I moved into the apartment in 1952 and the trunk was put in the basement. We never used the storage room. I was able to twist the lock open just before you arrived."

"It must have belonged to your mother," I said. "I'm surprised you never opened it."

"You may be surprised but you don't understand how I felt about her all these years. I put her away."

I understood but thought that my natural curiosity would have gotten the better of me. And contemplating the fine furniture, the paintings, and the Modigliani, it occurred to me that Edwige had been somewhat selective in her efforts to banish her mother.

I looked at the fine-looking, albeit very dusty and a bit scuffed, Louis Vuitton trunk of the kind that rich passengers used when traveling by train and by steamship at the beginning of the 20th Century.

"I waited for you to arrive to look closely at it all," Edwige said.

She knelt down beside the trunk and I, numbed by anticipation, took my place beside her. She removed several jewelry boxes from the inset trays and put them on the coffee table. Then came several unframed paintings. We both knew there was a Matisse and a Juan Gris and two more Orgoloffs. They were all signed.

One ink drawing on paper showed a man in a bulky jacket, protruding ears and a pince-nez, bent over an upright piano. In the right-hand corner stood a slender figure of a woman in an elegant dress twirling a long string of pearls.

Six pen and ink drawings signed by Effie Rousseau lay at the bottom of the trunk. 'For your poems,' a small note said. Under the artwork was an envelope with black and white glossy photographs of Sterling next to her fireplace looking up at two paintings. The photos were signed by Pierre Fast-Brown.

Then came the books all signed and dedicated. Several from Roland Lee Rainier, one from Scott Winteride, two from Bernice Boch, and the list didn't end there.

Here was a cedarwood box with letters written on fine linen stock in distinctive handwritings with the blackest of inks which had not faded in all those years. I spread them out on the carpet. Some were still in envelopes with their return addresses, many were not.

I knew, of course, what I was looking for. A letter from Sterling's elusive beau, Stefan. Would that his letters were in envelopes with a last name and an address or this last source of information would be useless. He most certainly would not have signed his last name to love letters.

I riffled through several dozen letters signed by friends whose names I knew mainly from CAT's *Paris Diary* and some whose names I had learned only recently. There were short and long missives from Claire, from Soeur Madeleine, from Scott Winteride, from Laura Waverley, and from Alex who would have been Orgoloff, and a short handsome note from Effie Rousseau.

And, then, there they were. The letters from the elusive special man in Sterling's life.

Unceremoniously, I dropped the letters from her famous and distinguished friends to look in awe at the three in my hand.

The first envelope had a Swiss stamp still attached and his name and address on the back written in a beautiful cursive hand. It was addressed to Mlle Sterling Kirkland Sawyer at 351 quai des Grands-Agustins.

Stefan von Oxenkranz had written from an estate called Schloss Obern, Switzerland. Seemed like a very vague address but maybe the small crest above the name made a more specific mention of place unnecessary.

Stefan, then, had been Swiss and not Polish as I had long thought.

The other two envelopes also had stamps from Switzerland and his name on the back followed by the name of a hotel in Zurich.

Edwige had continued emptying the trunk while I stared at Stefan von Oxenkranz's three envelopes. These were letters written to Edwige Claire's mother from her father.

She must open them and read them privately. This was no longer my mystery to be solved. It was her life to be revealed.

"Edwige," I said. "I believe we have found your father."

"My father?" she said.

"His name was Stefan von Oxenkranz and he was most likely a nobleman from Switzerland."

"From Switzerland," Edwige said.

"Here," I said and handed her the three letters, "you should read them in private. I will sit in your dining room until you call me."

She took the letters in both hands and bore them to the chinz-covered sofa in front of the fireplace where she sat down with her back to me.

I tip-toed to the dining room longing to get back to the hotel and my computer to google Stefan von Oxenkranz. It was a great inconvenience that my cell phone while in France did not get me into the Internet. Alas, I would have to contain my curiosity.

Twenty minutes later Edwige handed the three letters back to me.

"They are in English," she said. "and I will confess that my English is not very fluent. I read them as well as I could but maybe you could translate them for me."

The first letter from Switzerland was dated May 1928.

> *. . . . my darling,"* it said, *"our visit to Claire's studio in Montmartre made me happy because I think you do love me and I will attempt to return earlier than planned to be with you. You enjoyed my gravad lax and fine new potatoes, did you not? If only Winteride had not so misbehaved, he is not fit for polite company. I kissed your sweet face in my dreams last night and did I tell you that I never remembered my dreams before I met you. Now I awake every morning with you in my thoughts and almost in my arms. Je reviens! Forever, Stefan*

"So beautiful," Edwige said when I had read her the letter in French. "He loved her. What could have happened?"

"Soeur Jeanne-Marie said that he never came to visit your mother in Vézelay. We will never know what happened between them."

Or, maybe, I thought—and I was afraid that Edwige had the same suspicion—maybe Stefan was not the father at all. Could it have been Alexandre Orgoloff? Didn't my Soeur say that he visited Sterling's grave soon after she died? Had he learned about the baby and simply fled? After all, he was married.

The second letter from Switzerland was dated August 1930.

> *My dear*, it began, *thank you for helping me prepare for my soirée next week, I need the butler to make sure enough champagne is in stock for fifty guests, both the Brut rosé and the Demi-Sec Rosé, I enjoy the fruity taste. The Beluga caviar will be delivered by the Swiss ambassador's chauffeur on the day of the dinner and I will prepare the salmon as soon as I return in ten days. Fondly, Stefan*

Rather business-like, I thought.

"I wonder where he lived," Edwige said. "Sounds very opulent."

"Yes, it does, doesn't it, somewhere on the Rive Droît I assume."

The third letter, also from Switzerland, was dated October, 1930.

> "*My dear, dear Sterling, I came to your door later that same afternoon but you either wouldn't open it or you were not there. You can imagine how worried I became, maybe you were ill and had been taken to hospital. I have heard that these operations can be*

> *risky although I had found you the very best place. I went around to Orgoloff's studio and he told me he'd had a pneu saying you had gone to the country and would be back in a week. I was very much relieved. He promised to tell you that I had to leave for Switzerland in the morning."*

What operations, I thought. Was he talking about an abortion? Didn't he realize she had not gone through with it? Obviously not at that moment. Did that mean he never learned about the baby?

> "*I wanted to tell you,*" the letter continued, "*that my divorce will be final in one year from now. We have worked out an arrangement about the children but I had to give up everything else. So when next you see me, and it won't be until next spring, I will be without money, without a Schloss, without a riding horse, or a house in the city. Do you think you will still have me? We will live as husband and wife unless you will give up your Catholic ways and agree to marry me at the Mairie instead of in the church? You will see, you will have other babies and we will live happily ever after. I kiss your sweet face in my dreams whether you wish me to or not, yours forever, Stefan*

He had been married already, in Switzerland, he had children, he was getting a divorce but seemed acutely unaware of Sterling's deep religious beliefs. I surmised that she would never have assented to live in so-called sin with Stefan.

"He never saw her again," Edwige cried. "He must have returned to Paris long after she died. Do you think she answered this letter without telling him about the baby, about me?"

"We'll never know," I said. "She must have broken off her relationship with him which is why he never came to Vézelay. Maybe he got the news of her death from Alexandre Orgoloff or from Claire Garcia-Bonsonwell. Now I wonder if Claire knew about the baby—about you—or not. My guess now is that Orgoloff didn't know. Therefore, Stefan couldn't learn about you from him."

"I wonder if he returned to Switzerland," Edwige said.

"If his divorce had gone through he had kind of burned his bridges. Seems he gave up his property in return for rights to his children there. Maybe he went to Switzerland and recovered some of his wealth. We don't know what business he was in."

"We'll never know," Edwige said, "and I don't mind that too much. What I learned from his letters was that he loved my mother but that her faith prevented her from being happy with him. Religion has a lot to answer for."

We went back to sit on the floor in front of the Louis Vuitton steamer trunk which suddenly looked very distinguished. Soon the floor around us was filled with manuscripts, some still with carbon paper attached, others tied together neatly with string. One batch containing poems was marked *Beautiful Musings* and another batch was marked *Paris Diary*.

Into my hands came a slim volume, beautifully bound in red leather with gold lettering, entitled simply, *Short Stories* by Sterling Kirkland Sawyer, illustrated by Effie Rousseau. I swallowed the lump that came to my throat at the realization that Sterling did see one of her books in print.

"Look," I said to Edwige, "your mother's book."

We looked at the foreword by Ben Vogelhut of the *Pyramid Press* in which he praised Sterling as one of his most distinguished and talented writers. It was dated Paris, May, 1929.

The last batch we pulled out was a thick manuscript marked *Novel* in Sterling's distinctive small script. I couldn't resist, I opened the novel to the first page and read the first paragraph.

> *Paris at night,* it said, *was not the same as Paris by day. At midnight we dressed up in men's clothing, outrageous cravats and shiny buttoned boots, and went to roam the streets, venturing into bars where no man bothered us the way they would have if we had been women. Freedom, Marie shouted and slapped me on the back. I felt a true rush of power and strength. Vive la France, I shouted as loudly but no one paid attention. I was simply another man at a bar. The year was 1875.*

Sterling had written a novel about women's emancipation, she who lived in an era where women in America had only recently obtained the right to vote and where French women had to wait twenty more years. I always knew she was my kind of woman.

"Look," Edwige said and opened a jewelry box lined in dark blue velvet.

We looked in stupefaction at the glitter, the platinum, the diamonds, the gold. A diamond-studded pendant had a quadrant-shaped watch at the end.

"It's a Cartier," I said, "one of those famous lapel watches. And look at the rings. Your mother must have had very slender fingers if those fit her."

Edwige looked at her own slender hands and nodded.

"This is gorgeous," I said and picked up a silver cigarette case with red flowers on black lacquer. The lock sprang open without the slightest effort. "Look, it still has three Dunhills inside. She smoked them in this long amber holder."

We looked at each other feeling delirious.

Edwige pulled out a very long string of pink pearls with a rectangular diamond clasp with a large red ruby at the center.

We gasped in unison.

"That's her gift from Pierre Fast-Brown," Edwige said. "I read her letter to him."

"It must have reached to her waist," I said, "and she wound it a couple of times around her neck. She was a fabulous flapper, I can just imagine her with Claire out on the town lunching at the Ritz, dining at the Café de la Paix or at the Boeuf sur le Toit with Alexandre Orgoloff or Pierre Fast-Brown."

"She would have worn this," Edwige said and brought up an emerald-green cloche hat with a black velvet band and a diamond clip. Silk and crêpe de chine dresses in pink and white and blue were enclosed in tissue paper. "What an era, what dresses, what hats, what jewelry. It had all changed when I arrived in Paris in 1952."

"It must have," I said and got up although reluctant to leave all the glitter behind. "I should let you have a good rest."

"Tomorrow we will discuss how to meet with Soeur Jeanne-Marie," Edwige said.

Chapter 54

"All right, so *now* you're coming home," Topsy said. "I congratulate you. You must be feeling pretty fine at this moment. Swiss, not Polish after all, huh?"

"Google had nothing," I said. "There was a family tree with Stefan von Oxenkranz's ancestors going back to the 1500s. He was born in 1889 with a question mark in the column of death. He, too, has disappeared from the records."

"There must be some better sources in Switzerland," she said. "Not that I want you to keep looking."

"I suppose not."

"Hope you're not contemplating another search," Topsy said again, and I could sense her making a face over the phone.

"You're making a face," I said, "but not to worry. This is the end of the road and I'll be returning in a couple of days."

"When exactly?"

"In a couple of days."

"What two, three, four?"

"Hard to tell. Tomorrow I'm off to Champagne country to visit with Isabelle, Victoria Huddersfield's daughter. She called me this morning and I promised to come and tell her the whole long story. I owe her."

"And another taste of her champagne won't hurt you either. Bring me some!"

"Will do," I said.

The road to Reims was familiar but I never do get tired of the French countryside with its small villages nestled deep in the fields with the tree-lined allées and the vineyards stretching up the hills. On the way I had a cup of coffee at a small café and sat outside in the sun watching the locals, the old men nursing their wine glasses at nearby tables and the women hurrying along carrying mile-long baguettes.

Isabelle d'Alville greeted me on the steps of her fine mansion with a warm embrace and a kiss on each cheek.

"My dear young friend," she said, "I have looked forward to your visit and to hear your news."

She sat me down in her cozy living room, a young girl—whom she introduced as her fille-a-tout-faire—brought in plenty of black coffee and hot milk and Isabelle poured and served and gave me a running account of her business activities.

"The consortium is having some trouble agreeing on their financing," she said. "My people tell me I must hold firm but the pressure is wearing me down. Suddenly, I don't care that much, I just want to be relieved of the day to day exertions."

"Guess you're ready to retire after all," I said. "You really should travel somewhere, not necessarily abroad but right here in your own country."

"Perhaps," she said. "but they still want to keep me on in an advisory capacity and I look forward to that. Telling everyone how they should perform their work without the responsibility. Does that not sound ideal?"

"It certainly does," I said and, seeing that I had missed lunch, chose a tartelette aux fruits with raspberries fresh from the garden.

"Now," Isabelle said, "tell me everything from the beginning, from the time you left for Vézelay. What did you find out?"

"First of all, I found a convent close to the Basilica of Saint Mary Magdalene, and I found a great small hotel des chambres in the town itself."

"I visited there many years ago with my husband. He enjoyed an occasional short vacation."

"If you remember the drive leading up to the town then you might have seen the convent to the right of the road. I invited myself to meet with the sisters."

"I can imagine."

"The first nun I met turned out to be the only one I needed. Her name is Soeur Jeanne-Marie and she has white hair and blue eyes. She is ninety-six years old but lively and energetic except when she forgets about her little white pills."

"She has a heart condition?"

"Yes, but seemingly under control. She was very startled when I first mentioned the name Sterling Kirkland Sawyer and it took her a while to tell me the story."

"And?"

We sat there for the better part of an hour while I told her. We consumed more coffee and more tartelettes while Sterling came to life in the telling of her story, how I visited her small cottage a short walk from the convent, how I learned about Soeur Madeleine and her loving care of Sterling, how Sterling spent many months in a small room at the convent with just a narrow bed and a wash-stand.

I told Isabelle how Effie Rousseau and Scott Winteride and Alexandre Orgoloff had visited with the sisters at the convent. I told her about the great friendship between Sterling and Claire and how Soeur Jeanne-Marie who was only fourteen years old at the time used to hear them laugh and gossip, smoke cigarettes, and drink untold bottles of wine.

"What a marvelous adventure for you to discover everything you were looking for," Isabelle said. "But you haven't told me what happened to Sterling. I remember she was a writer. Did she publish her books to great acclaim? Did she marry and have children, did she live a happy life?"

"Oh, Isabelle," I said on the verge of tears. "My adventure wasn't marvelous, it was very sad up until the last few days. Sterling never realized her dreams of becoming a published writer. She never did marry. She didn't live a long, happy life."

Isabelle got up hastily from the sofa and came to sit next to me.

"My dear, what did you find out that would make you so upset? I am almost afraid to hear the end of the story. Come, let us take a stroll around my flower garden. A bit of fresh air will do us good."

Outside in the potting shed Isabelle stuck her feet into a pair of Dutch-looking wooden shoes and offered me a pair. I got out of my sandals and put on the comfortable clogs. We donned wide-brimmed straw hats and were ready to tackle her country garden. And a true country garden it was with tall grasses wafting in the breeze, with climbing sweet peas, clumps of lavender lupin, with irises, red geraniums and pink rose bushes. We passed a burgeoning white lilac bush and fruit trees where birds were tasting ripe cherries. Some unseen critters rustled the ground cover. I ate more red raspberries straight from the bush.

We sat on a wooden bench facing Isabelle's vineyard.

"Sterling died in 1931 at the age of 36," I said at last. "She was buried in Vézelay."

"My dear," Isabelle said. "Was it the influenza or some other terrible illness?"

"No, it was puerperal fever. She died a few weeks after her baby was born."

"A baby! Puerperal fever! Sanitary conditions were not what they are today. Women died after childbirth. But my dear, she wasn't married? Did all this take place at the convent? How very extraordinary."

"The sisters were quite extraordinary," I said with feeling.

"And the baby lived?"

"Yes, the baby lived and I found her in Paris a few days ago."

"How very amazing of you," Isabelle said. "How did you manage?"

"It was luck," I said. "She inherited Sterling's apartment on the quai des Grands-Agustins and I found her there. She's about eighty years old but in great shape."

"Just a couple of years older than me," Isabelle said. "Let's go back inside, I want to hear all about it."

"Well," I said and got no further because we were interrupted by a loud voice calling his chère Maman.

Isabelle got up quickly, her straw hat fell off her head and slid to her shoulders, held by two thin ribbons, and she teetered in her wooden shoes.

"My son," she said and shook her head impatiently. "He never gives me notice before arriving. A very bad habit. I do have a telephone."

We walked towards the house with Isabelle hurrying several steps in front of me.

Jacques stood in the open door in his blue velvet jacket with the big square buttons and on his feet the loud orange suede shoes. His hair stood straight up in the air supported by hair-spray and he had grown a remarkable goatee.

"Mon Dieu," Isabelle whistled under her breath, "he is wearing his masquerade outfit again, and what did he do to his hair? And to his face?"

"Chère Maman," Jacques said again and Isabelle lent him both cheeks to kiss but pulled away quickly.

He turned his eyes to me and threw up his hands in mock surprise.

"You are here again," he said.

"Hello, Jacques," I said.

"Maman, I've brought my new girl-friend to meet you."

He turned and stretched out his hand to the girl-friend behind him.

She stood before us in hair which had turned white blond and spiked, in a green mini-skirt and yellow leg-warmers.

"I am Valentina Puigh," she said.

"Mon Dieu," Isabelle said.

"Bon jour, Madame," Ms. Puigh said.

"You speak French," Isabelle said.

"Studied at the Sorbonne."

"Really?"

Ms. Puigh turned to me and grinned.

"Got back from Nice three days ago," she said, "and here you are all dressed up as a milk-maid."

"Thank you," I said. "What's going on?"

"Jacques found me at the hotel. Isn't he adorable?"

"Do you know each other?" Isabelle said to me.

"Yes, indeed. Ms. Puigh was my research assistant during my quest for Sterling."

"I didn't realize. Did you introduce this woman to my son?" Isabelle said.

"Not really," I said. "It just sort of happened."

"We came to say good-bye," Jacques said.

Chapter 55

"You came to say good-bye?" Isabelle said. "Pray, tell, where are you off to?"

"Val and I are departing for Rapallo tomorrow morning. In Italy we will walk in the footsteps of that famous American poet, Ezra Pound, it will be a great inspiration."

"Jacques has written some marvelous poems in the style of the Cantos," Val Puigh said to me. "It's all on his web-site. You must look him up."

She raked up her spiky hair until it stood totally on end.

"I'll do that," I said weakly.

"I suppose you studied poetry at the Sorbonne, Miss Puigh?" Isabelle said.

"I took French language and civilization," she said. "The poetry I have from my master's degree in New York. Don't mind my hair, I may turn it green tomorrow, but you shouldn't judge the book by its cover."

Bravo, I thought, no one talked down to my Ms. Puigh.

"How long do you plan to be on this vacation?" Isabelle said frostily to Jacques.

"For as long as the money lasts."

"Yes, I can imagine. And how much money *do* you have?"

"I am hoping for an advance on my allowance."

Isabelle walked very fast towards the house and I could tell she was angry. I hurried two steps behind her with Jacques and Ms. Puigh close on my heels.

Inside, Isabelle continued in a straight line down a hallway into what I realized was her office, with Jacques in her wake. The door closed and Ms. Puigh and I sat down in front of the fireplace.

"I had no idea his mother was this loaded," she said and took the last raspberry tartelette from the coffee tray. She wolfed it down while looking around the room, appraising the paintings, the silver, the rugs, the antiques. "Maybe we can still travel first-class."

"Don't get your hopes up, his mother is getting tired of supporting him."

"He lost his part-time job at the bookstore on rue de l'Odéon. On the other hand, if he has a job he can't write his poetry full-time."

"And wouldn't that be a pity," I said. "Have you actually read anything he's written? The truth now."

She giggled.

"Truthfully, no."

"So you're in it strictly for a trip to Italy?"

"Truthfully, yes."

"How did you get here?" I said.

'The train to Épernay, only an hour and a half. Great town, I'd been there before. We came the rest of the way on rented bikes hoping to be invited to dinner by his mother. That hope is diminishing fast. Marvelous country-side, though, isn't it, and you see so much more from a bicycle."

She was chewing on the last of the macaroons from the tray when Jacques returned looking flustered, with Isabelle right behind looking furious.

"Say goodbye," he said to Ms. Puigh, "we're leaving."

"I guess you'll be going third class," I whispered to Ms. Puigh.

"I'll e-mail you," were her last words.

"My son is not at all like my husband, or like me," Isabelle said and sat ram-rod straight and seething in the sofa. "He is spoiled and irresponsible and untalented. However, he's my son. I will continue to pay his rent and utilities but the monthly allowance will end. He must go to work."

"They're still going to Italy?"

"Maybe Miss Puigh will pay."

"What a lovely thought," I said.

"Will you now tell me the rest of the story about Sterling's daughter, Edwige Claire? Was she very much surprised that you found her? And what could she tell you about her mother?"

"She told me a good deal about her own life but very little about Sterling. She never knew her."

"*Dommage,*" Isabelle said.

She straightened up some framed photographs on the side-table and picked up one of a man in a formal suit with a boutonnière in the wide lapel, looking directly and charmingly into the camera. It was a black-and-white photo but his wavy hair still looked blond. The pouches under his eyes and the jowls under his chin spoke of an appetite for good food and drink. Nevertheless, a very attractive man.

"My father," Isabelle said and forgot all about Edwige Claire. "I adored him. He died two years after my mother, Victoria, but during those two years I spent much time with him and we became closer than ever. I miss him every day."

"I thought your father died in 1950," I said. "Long before your mother."

"Where did you get that?"

"From the Internet," I said. "That's where I first traced your grandmother."

"Ah, the Internet. I don't go there. It leaves no privacy for anyone, not for my family, not for my business, not for my children and, God knows, the world does not need to know anything about them."

"But your mother died in 1967?"

"Yes."

"Tell me more about her life in France. Did she ever return to the States? Did your father accompany her? Being a count, she must have wanted to show him off in New York."

"My father was not exactly a count and he never wanted to accompany her to the States. I told you they had a very unhappy marriage."

"The Google item said that Victoria Huddersfield married Henri, le Compte d'Augverne in 1921, and that he died in 1950. I'm quite sure I remember this correctly."

"But my father was not the count d'Augverne. My mother divorced him in 1932, after which she re-married, and I was born a year later."

"So, Henri and Marie-Louise were your half-siblings?"

"*Bién sûr.*"

"I'm amazed," I said, "Google kept that a secret. Tell me how it all came about, if you don't mind, that is. I shouldn't really be prying into your private life since it has nothing to do with my search for Sterling."

"Not at all, my dear Jamie, if I may call you by your first name. As a child and as a young woman I never knew anything about my mother's life, only that for thirty-five years she made my father miserable. In the last two years of *his* life he told me his story. He had lost his money during that horrible stock-market crash in 1929, he had lost his fiancée in an accident—a woman he didn't want to talk about but whom, I gathered, he had loved very much—and he was quite destitute and desolate and lonely when he met my mother. She, of course, was in the process of being divorced from the Count d'Augverne—she had been cited as the 'other' party in a divorce scandal. She was going to marry that other man but he deserted her at the last moment. Instead, she married my father."

It sounded a lot like the plot from a romance novel and it sounded a lot like my image of Victoria. No wonder Sterling had wanted to cut all ties to her.

"Your poor father married her for her money," I said. "That never turns out well."

"The only good thing to come of it was me, he always said. He was the best father anyone could have and my mother was insanely jealous of me and of him. He, of course, found consolation from the horrors of his marriage with other women. I understood this even as a child."

"You loved him very much."

"I did. He was a fun-loving man, he adored good food and good wine, and good company, he took me traveling to Switzerland and Italy and, once, to Venice by train on the Simplon-Orient Express. What luxury. It was a hotel on wheels. And the food, my dear! I've always dreamed of repeating that journey. I was only seven but I remember it well. My father was my idol. He even took me to Holland to visit with a cousin of his, a diplomat."

Isabelle wiped imaginary dust from her father's picture frame.

"Your father was from Holland?"

"No, no, but he loved to visit there. He always lived in France. He never quite told me the whole story but I believe he had a wife who divorced him when he lost his money. She took him for everything except this banner with his family crest. He was very proud of it."

I looked up at the wall to a pennant embroidered in faded red and gold.

"That's my Swiss family crest," she said. "I believe he came from a noble family but that he did not inherit any great wealth. His older brother came into the entire Oxenkranz estate."

I swear I felt the earth shift under me.

"Oxenkranz?" I said when the room stopped spinning. "Your father's name was Oxenkranz?"

"Yes, my father's name was Stefan. Stefan von Oxenkranz."

Chapter 56

"Victoria married Stefan?" Topsy shouted from Washington. "Sterling's Stefan?"

"Yes, I was in total shock."

"Me, too. Me, too. Let me see if I got all this straight," she said. "He returns to Switzerland believing Sterling's has had an abortion, he writes that his divorce will be final in a year, says he will return to her, that they will live together or marry in a civil ceremony if her religion will not let her wed a divorced man."

"But Sterling dies and her baby is given to foster parents in the village," I said, "Stefan learns about her death when he returns to Paris but doesn't learn about the baby. He now has nothing left in Switzerland, he has lost his money and probably his children, he's completely at sea, Victoria grabs him—she would have taken pleasure in taking something of Sterling's—he marries her in desperation and, voilá, the tragedy is perpetuated."

"Or worse. Victoria gets pregnant on purpose and he must marry her. He's trapped."

"His lack of money must also have played a role," I said. "At first."

"Yes, once the situation stabilized he probably made more of his own. Did he strike you as a man without resources who wouldn't have bounced back?"

"No, he didn't—and Isabelle didn't say—but he took her traveling around Europe to meet his diplomat friends. He must have been used to luxury hotels and first-class transportation. I got the feeling that Victoria wouldn't have given him money for that, so, yes, he must have recovered somehow. I can't tell you how much I detest that woman in retrospect."

"Why would he have stayed with her?"

"No doubt because of Isabelle," I said. "He adored her and he would have lost her in a divorce. He'd lost two in Switzerland already. Fathers didn't get custody in those days."

"Or maybe Victoria was too jealous to let another woman have him?"

"Sounds about right."

"What was Isabelle's reaction? She suddenly has a half-sister she knew nothing about. Some people would be upset."

"Isabelle was thrilled and happy. Didn't feel threatened at all. It will take her mind off her disappointing children. She wants to meet Edwige as soon as possible."

"And *you* will be making the introduction. Will you ever return home?"

"I have a reservation early next week. I'm stopping off in New York to see Mel on my way to Washington."

"Of course," Topsy said and sighed deeply in anticipation of a great romance unfolding. Topsy who has only recently won in the romance department with Martin has her own baggage. In fact, much more than I do. She has an ex-husband with a new wife in Florida, a twenty-something daughter in Los Angeles— whom she sees once a year if she's lucky—and a son in Seattle who calls once in a great while.

"Mel e-mailed me that his Uncle Gus—the one in the retirement home in the Bronx—has done some sleuthing in the so-called Sterling Case."

Hard to imagine what Uncle Gus could have unearthed but by now a half dozen would-be investigators were stepping on my toes—not that I wished to dismiss all of their excellent in-put—and I decided to take this one in stride. I would treat him as a secret informer. Got a feeling he would like that.

"What could he have discovered?" Topsy said.

"Nothing. Mel was apologetic but feels he owes his Uncle Gus. Probably guilt-ridden at not visiting him more often at the retirement home. I don't want to let Mel down."

"That's what your relationship will be all about," Topsy said, and she knows whereof she speaks. "Give and take, whether you like it or not."

"Did you have any reactions from your readers to your, that is my, complaint about the sprinklings of 'you know' and 'I mean' in such rampant usage by all and sundry?" I said.

"You have no idea. Hundreds of irate readers complained saying they switch TV channels in retribution to such sloppy speech. Some readers got positively menacing."

"There you go, I feel vindicated."

"When will Edwige and Isabelle meet?"

"The day after tomorrow."

"And when will Edwige visit your Soeur in Vézelay?"

"That's the more difficult part. Edwige says she's not yet up to seeing all the distant familiar places although she wouldn't mind seeing Soeur Jeanne-Marie."

"Yes?"

"I'm leaving for Vézelay in the morning to bring the Soeur to Paris."

"I was afraid of that. Does that mean you've postponed your return?"

"For a day or two," I said. "I've simply got to see this through to the happy end."

When I arrived at the convent the next afternoon Vézelay and its surroundings were drenched in one of those one hundred annual days of rain. I parked outside the stone wall, pulled on the rain boots I'd purchased in Auxerre, got out the folding umbrella, but still arrived at the front door soaked and muddy.

As I was dripping on the entrance floor the Holy One came to my rescue and relieved me of outerwear and muddy boots, propped up the umbrella in a stand, took my small over-night bag and escorted me in silence—following a solemn bon jour—down the hall to a small cell. The narrow bed had a white bed-spread and a wooden cross on the wall above. Two towels sat on a spindly chair by its side. The pitcher on the washstand had fresh water and, on the side, a bar of soap in an enameled dish. There was a wooden peg on the inside of the door. A small window looked out on the fields.

"Hope you'll be comfortable, the bathroom is next door," the Holy One said. "My name is Belle."

"Thank you very much, Belle," I said.

"Soeur Jeanne-Marie is sleeping but she will have tea with you at four."

"I'll rest here until you fetch me," I said, hung my jacket on the wooden peg, washed my hands in the bowl with water from the pitcher, and stretched out on the narrow bed. I could feel the wood through the thin mattress. My purgatory, which I probably deserved, I thought, and remembered that I owed Neil Robinson a progress report.

"Tell me all about it," Soeur Jeanne-Marie said at four-thirty after the tea things had been cleared and Belle had left us. "You've found darling Edwige Claire and you are taking me to see her tomorrow. I am all packed."

"She's expecting us for lunch," I said. "And you will be staying in her guest room overnight."

"You said on the telephone that Edwige still lives in dear Sterling's apartment in Paris. Then the letter I sent long ago was returned to me by mistake?"

"That would seem to be the case," I said. I felt pretty sure that Edwige Claire was not the type to offer a full confession.

"We will never know, and it is better that way." My Soeur looked me in the eye until I blushed.

"You will be very surprised at everything I've found out," I said.

"A half sister," she exclaimed when I came to the end of the story. "And Sterling's beau was Edwige Claire's father after all? But he never came to visit. Only the chér Monsieur Orgoloff ever came to see her while she lived and once after she died. I am sure we suspected that he was the father but, of course, we could never speak of it. He was never told about Edwige and he never returned to visit us."

"That's what I figured," I said.

"And the beau, he was from Switzerland and his name was Stefan? I never knew his name. I knew about Victoria, though. I heard Minou and her friend, Claire, talk about her and Claire said Minou was well rid of her friendship."

"I can imagine," I said.

"And then Victoria married Minou's beau? It all sounds very strange."

"It was a strange time," I said. "The one good thing that came of it was their daughter, Isabelle. You and Edwige will both meet her tomorrow for the first time."

That evening we had dinner in the hall at a single long table where Soeur Jeanne-Marie sat at the head and twelve young and old nuns and lay sisters took their seats and scrutinized me from under lowered lids.

It was French country fare at its best with bean soup, goat's cheese and olive oil in the salad, and a Boeuf Bourguignon that beat anything I'd ever had, including Topsy's. After dinner my Soeur and I retired to her rooms for half an hour and she sprang on me the last surprise of the evening.

"Many years ago," she said, "I found these letters among blessed Soeur Madeleine's papers. I do not read English but the letters were from New York. In your country."

She handed me the letters. One was from Pierre Fast-Brown to Sterling. One was addressed to Soeur Madeleine from a law firm in New York. Inside that envelope was a letter addressed to Pierre Fast-Brown at an address on the Upper East Side.

"Please read them," Soeur Jeanne-Marie said. "I believe the time has come."

New York, April 20, 1931

My darling girl, how glad I was to hear from you at long last. I am not sure at all that I will recognize you without your Chanel dresses and your Cartier watch and, especially, without wearing my mother's lovely pearl necklace! Are you contemplating joining the convent and leaving us all entirely behind? Where is that brute of a beau? Why does he not return to sweep you away from the country and from the sisters, charming though it all is and however much you think you are happier there?

Much as I would wish to visit you and make you see sense, I am sorry to say that my doctors will not allow me to travel for a while yet and I, meek as I have grown, must heed their advice. How I wish you would jump on the next boat from Le Havre and surprise me with a visit! I love you, my darling girl, Pierre

The second letter was written in a shaky hand which was hard to read.

Vézelay, May 15, 1931

Esteemed M. Pierre Fast-Brown, it is with the deepest sorrow and the most inexpressible pain that I have the obligation to inform you that your darling

Sterling, our beloved Minou, closed her eyes forever several weeks ago to rest eternally with our Lord and in the care of the sainted Mary Magdalene to whom she had prayed so often in the last months of her life.

I believe that Minou would have wanted me to tell you about the secret which she had held close to her heart, the miracle of the birth of her darling daughter, Edwige Claire. We, at the convent, have sent the baby to live with a good family in town while we await instructions from you. In the meantime, you will be relieved to know that Minou made a will with a respectable firm of lawyers in town in which she made the proper provisions for her child.

I remain, dear M. Fast-Brown, with my deepest sympathy, your devoted servant.

Soeur Madeleine, Mother Superior, the Convent of the Blessed Heart, Vézelay.

The third letter was typewritten on letterhead from a law firm in New York City.

New York, June 1, 1931

Excellent Mother Superior, it is with great regret that we must inform you that Mr. Pierre Fast-Brown passed away two weeks ago after a long illness. Your letter, unfortunately, arrived too late and we take the liberty of returning it to you, unopened.

Very sincerely yours, Joseph D. Granger, Esq.

"I will give the letters to darling Edwige Claire in Paris," Soeur Jeanne-Marie said.

"No one in the United States learned of Sterling's death," I said. "I feel pretty sure that Pierre Fast-Brown would have informed Sterling's sister, Rose, who, in turn, would have told her daughter, Marjorie Robinson."

Life might have turned out quite differently for Edwige Claire, I thought. If Pierre Fast-Brown had not died he would certainly have come to Vézelay to take care of Edwige Claire. He would no doubt have hunted down the brute of a beau, as he called him, the father, Stefan Oxenkranz, who would then not have married Victoria, and who would then not have had his other daughter, Isabelle. Edwige Claire would have been spared a difficult childhood in Vézelay, instead she would have been a pampered Daddy's girl, she would have been the one to travel on expensive trips in Europe, she would have married someone quite different from her Sorbonne fellow student, she would have visited with her American family, Marjorie Robinson would have come to know her cousin. Best, or worst, of all, Marjorie would have had no need of my services. An almost intolerable thought from my selfish perspective which I quickly dismissed as quite unworthy.

I expressed some of all this to Soeur Jeanne-Marie and she nodded and smiled and nodded and shook her head and, in the end, looked a little bewildered.

"It was God's will," she said, but somehow I couldn't make myself believe that.

We sat silently with our different thoughts until the spell was broken when Belle brought in a tray with two glasses and a bottle.

"We prepare our own Crème de Cassis," my Soeur said, "our black currents are abundant and I—as was dear Soeur Madeleine's custom—always enjoy a small glass of Kir with white wine before bedtime."

"I will join you," I said.

"You are sleeping in darling Minou's room," was the last words that followed me on my way to my narrow bed. "She would have been well pleased."

Chapter 57

"Imagine Paris," Soeur Jeanne-Marie said. "Imagine sitting in darling Minou's living room with darling Edwige Claire. My heart is full of God's blessed love."

Isabelle looked at my lovely Soeur in fascination, Edwige observed her as if seeing a ghost from the past. And I? I felt happier than I could have imagined.

Our trip from Vézelay had taken a little less than three hours and Soeur Jeanne-Marie had not said much the entire time but had her nose pressed against the window commenting now and then on the country views which flew by in haste.

Soeur Jeanne-Marie had exclaimed over the traffic in the streets, the Parisians, the bicycles, the cars, the river, the Eiffel Tower, and the blessed Cathedral of Notre Dame which we had driven past slowly. At the quai des Grands-Augustins she had clutched my arm as we crossed the street between parked cars and hurrying pedestrians. She had closed her eyes when we ascended in the small, squeaky elevator.

The meeting between my Soeur and Edwige Claire had been a little awkward and I think they were glad to have me there as a buffer. My Soeur had taken Edwige's hand and pressed it to her lips upon which Edwige had cried out with tears in her eyes and embraced the little nun.

The ice thus broken we had a mid-morning snack, Soeur Jeanne-Marie took a little white pill and a short nap, after which she was ready for her big adventure.

Isabelle had arrived shortly before lunch. She and Edwige Claire now stood together near the fireplace, under the Derain painting, next to the side tables with the Charleston dancer and the Modigliani sculpture, both of them tall, both of them with wide shoulders and good legs, with high foreheads, very straight noses, and full lips. In age they were two years apart, both intelligent, well-educated women. Half-sisters. Looking alike yet different. Topsy had told me I should feel proud at having brought them together, and I did.

I sat down with Soeur Jeanne-Marie in the bright chintz-covered sofa opposite the fireplace and she took my hand. In her black habit, her face encased in starched white, she looked like a strange bird in a gilded cage.

"Let me tell you about your father," Isabelle said to Edwige. "He was very tall and very good looking. Charming, as you can imagine. When he was thirteen his parents sent him to England to be educated at Eton and Oxford, that is why he always spoke English with that special accent the British have."

"I never knew his name was Stefan," my Soeur said. "And imagine him being Swiss. I wish I had met him. I think darling Minou loved him very much. It was a great tragedy."

"You are the only one here who knew my mother in person," Edwige said. "Will you not tell us more about her?"

Soeur Jeanne-Marie let go of my hand and shifted around in the soft cushions.

"You would have liked the way she walked," she said and her face softened. "She had long legs and took big steps, I was always trying to keep up. She also ran very fast and when she did I never could catch her."

"I, too, walk fast," Edwige said. "My husband was always two steps behind me."

"Your mother was tall for a woman, like you, and always very elegant in those slim dresses of hers. Her back was straight, her neck was long—the *chér Monsieur* Alex painted her into many of his pictures—and she had a trick of turning her head quickly when she talked to you. Her hair was very blond, she said she got that from her mother."

"Mine was blond," Edwige said.

"When she smiled her blue eyes would shine and open up wide. She could suddenly look very happy and carefree. She spoke in a low voice but very distinctly and from her French you could never tell that she was an American. She was a loveable person but solitary. It took a while for others to get to know her but once she was your friend she never deserted you. Oh, how I miss her."

Soeur Jeanne-Marie suddenly looked as if she needed one of her little pills. I took her hand and she relaxed and regained her color.

"In any case," Isabelle said hastily, "in any case, after Eton and Oxford my father came to study at the Sorbonne and he always told me he loved France best, the countryside, the people, the history, the literature, the arts, the theater. There was nothing he loved more than good company, good food and, especially, good wine."

"Charming," Edwige said.

"Sterling did, too," my Soeur said.

"I don't have to tell you that he was a great favorite of the ladies." Isabelle smiled. "He introduced me to some frightfully delicious salmon with which he drank a frightfully evil Swedish drink—apparently his family had a cook from Sweden—it was colorless like Vodka and with the same devastating effect. Nothing at all like Champagne."

"It was served at an informal dinner to which we were invited at the Swedish Embassy many years ago," Edwige said. "My husband took an interest in the influence of the early church on Viking life and got to know the ambassador. He tried the akvavit and, immediately, his face turned first red and then white. After that he spoke quite unintelligibly about the Vikings."

"Sterling and Claire would drink bottles and bottles of wine," my Soeur said. "They would sit under the peach tree in two lawn chairs and gossip and laugh. I quite envied them and wondered what it was like to be dressed in silk dresses, wear diamonds and pearls and rings on every finger and high heels and lipstick."

"My dear," Isabelle said, "I'm sure *we* should be the ones to envy *your* life serving the poor, helping the needy."

"Of course. I could never have been anything but a nun," my Soeur said, "but I did have curiosity about the world when I was young."

"My father made friends with everyone," Isabelle said. "He knew painters and actors, musicians and dancers, he loved fine furniture and antiques, he loved traveling to foreign places. He loved nothing better than to prepare delicious food for guests and watch them eat. He could have been a professional chef, he could have been anything at all."

"He sounds very charming," my lovely Soeur said.

"My father admitted he relished making the money he needed for the luxuries he enjoyed," Isabelle said. "He traveled a great deal to Switzerland and bankers from there came to meet him in Paris where he had a small pied-à-terre away from my mother who had her own amusements in the country. But he never told me exactly *how* he made his money."

The picture of these two people—Sterling and Stefan—was as complete as it would ever be to me. It struck me how very different they had been. Maybe not that compatible after all? Religion had ruled Sterling's life. Had it made her moralistic and even judgmental? Stefan had been quite the opposite. Worldly, fun-loving, attractive to women, maybe not entirely fastidious in money matters, easily veering from the moral path that Sterling was on. Their love was frozen in time. Would they have lasted? I could almost predict it in my mind.

"He must have been a wonderful father to you," Edwige Claire said. "I wish I had known him."

"Oh, so do I, so do I," Isabelle said and patted Edwige's arm. "Now I understand the sadness I saw in him from time to time. I believe he was thinking of your mother. I believe she was the love of his life and that he missed her for as long as he lived."

"Do you think he knew about me?" Edwige Claire said in an anguished tone of voice.

"Oh, no. I'm sure he did not. He would never have abandoned you, he was such a kind, loving person. He would have loved you the same way he loved *me*."

Soeur Jeanne-Marie tried to get out of the soft-cushioned sofa and needed my help to escape from its grip.

"Thank you, my dear," she said, "it is a beautiful sofa, but I am used to plain wooden chairs."

She moved to the tall windows and gazed out at the river and the barges and the tourist boats. From the street came the noise of cars, blaring police sirens, and whiffs of exhaust fumes. It was a very long way from the convent in Vézelay.

"I brought you this," Isabelle said to Edwige.

"A photograph of my father," Edwige said.

She beamed at Isabelle and Isabelle beamed back. I, myself, felt I had a silly grin on my face.

"Since we are giving gifts," Edwige said to me, "here is something I want *you* to have.

When I unwrapped the pink tissue paper I had in my hand Sterling's Cartier lapel watch.

"It's better than Christmas," I said in a weak voice. "I will wear it forever and make everyone I know terribly envious."

"Darling Soeur Jeanne-Marie," Edwige continued, "I want you to have this prayer book which belonged to your Minou. I know you will treasure it."

"It would be good to lie down for an hour," my Soeur said and clutched her gift, "it has been a long day but I don't want it to end. A short nap will revive me."

"Dearest Soeur," I said. "It is time for me to return to my hotel and pack my bags. I will be leaving for America the day after tomorrow. Please be well and I will write to you."

I embraced her and she kissed me on both cheeks.

"Go with God," she said, "and thank you for making all this possible."

While I wiped my eyes Edwige took Soeur Jeanne-Marie to her guest room and returned after a few minutes.

"She is not sure she can sleep on such a soft mattress," Edwige said, "I hope she doesn't take it into her head to sleep on the floor."

"I must go, too, I intend to visit with my daughter," Isabelle said and looked at her wrist-watch. "This watch belonged to my father, he gave it to me just before he died. I never saw him without it, it must have meant something very special to him. He told me it was a gift. It's a Cartier and I wear it always."

When Isabelle had gone Edwige beckoned me into the dining room where Sterling's Louis Vuitton trunk stood in a corner.

"Come," she said, "I want you to choose one of these paintings. I think my mother would have wanted you to have one of them."

"I couldn't possibly," I said.

"Do not protest. Please. You will make me very happy. I can never thank you enough for everything you've done for me. Without you we would not have been here today."

"In that case I'll take the Orgoloff with a million very humble thanks. Only, how will I get it back to the States?"

"I have known you just a short while," Edwige said and chuckled, "but I'm sure you'll think of something."

My head was spinning as I tried to solve the transportation problem.

"You'll be taking the Soeur back to Vézelay tomorrow," I said. "How long will you stay?"

"I won't be staying. Only to visit my mother's grave but I promise to stay in touch with Soeur Jeanne-Marie."

Chapter 58

Back at the hotel I was on my way to the elevator when a familiar voice reached me from the bar.

"Ms. Puigh," I said and walked across the foyer. "What a surprise."

Her hair was still white blond but had collapsed somewhat for want of sufficient hair spray.

"What a beastly mother," she said. "We never even had lunch. We biked back to the train and went third class to Paris."

"You are not going to Rapallo?"

"No, Jacques and I are not compatible after all."

"You mean he wanted you to finance the trip?"

"Yeah. I'm returning to the States next week. How about you?"

"Leaving the day after tomorrow," I said.

"I guess you found Sterling?"

"I did," I said and told Ms. Puigh almost everything.

"Wow," she said. "Some story."

"It is."

"Are you free tomorrow morning?" Ms. Puigh said.

"For a couple of hours, yes."

"How about joining me on a short pilgrimage?"

"What?"

"To Père Lachaise with roses."

"Really?"

"There are a few people we should visit."

"Good idea, I guess. Sure, I'll go with you."

The concierge called a taxi and we left at nine-thirty in the morning. As Ms. Puigh said, an early start saves the day. We directed the taxi to the far entrance at the Pére Lachaise cemetery on rue des Rondeaux. It was now ten in the morning and we were among the very first visitors.

We took a detour to Marcel Proust straight down the path from the gate—Sterling might have met him, he frequented the Ritz in the late evenings swathed in furs and woolens and died in 1922. On to the poet, Guillaume Apollinaire, beloved friend of Pablo Picasso whose bust of Guillaume stood in a small park next to my favorite church in Place St. Germain-des-Prés.

On the way we passed the grave of the painter, Marie Laurencin, Apollinaire's mistress. Then to Gertrude Stein—her name was in Greek lettering—and Alice B. Toklas whose name was on the back of their headstone.

"Her name is on the back supposedly because she didn't want to intrude on Gertrude's genius but I don't see where else her name could have gone," I said.

"I'm giving one rose to Alice," Ms. Puigh said.

She placed the flower close to the stone and I did the same for Gertrude.

"Look," said Ms. Puigh, "I didn't know that Laura Waverley was here and Auguste Metier is right next to her. He died two years after her."

"I had wondered if they stayed together," I said and placed two roses for them. It was turning out to be quite a pilgrimage. I wished Topsy could have been here.

We went on to Oscar Wilde who had died in Paris, impoverished and vilified. Around the corner were Edith Piaf of the sonorous voice, and the Surrealist poet, Paul Élouard, Alexandre Orgoloff's friend. Then to Amadeus Modigliani, one of whose tall, sinuous statues stood in

Edwige's apartment, and back to the main path looking for Alexandre Orgoloff.

"Here he is," Ms. Puigh said. "Division number ninety-eight."

The vault in front of the stark, elegant granite headstone had white gravel with dead leaves blown in by the wind, and a few weeds. I bent down to pick up a piece of stray paper and removed the leaves. There were no flowers.

"Even though he died in Poland his painter friends in Paris brought him back to be buried here," I said. "He was very well loved."

I gave him the rest of my flowers as a token of love from Sterling and to thank him for the painting I now owned. We had wrapped the flower stems in cotton wool soaked in water and covered in plastic.

"The flowers will last a few days," I said as we walked away, still the only visitors there, feeling subdued but gratified with our visit.

"You're quite the romantic," Ms. Puigh said.

I smiled and walked a little faster.

"Oh," I said, "consider it a momentary lapse."

We left the cemetery in search of yet another taxi to take us back to the hotel where I took leave of Ms. Puigh. I shook off the slight depression which had beset me at the cemetery —romantic and unlike a conventional burial ground though it was—and set out on a farewell walk through the Luxembourg Gardens. There I sat for a good half hour on a bench watching an assortment of Parisians stroll past with no one in a hurry, and young children on a run towards the water.

I returned to the hotel feeling relaxed and accomplished. I had given everyone what they wanted with the one regret that Marjorie Robinson had not lived to learn of the outcome. It had been an emotional experience unlike any other case I'd been involved in. The people I'd met had touched me, I had learned more about their past than I had anticipated at the start and I felt reluctant to let it all go. As Topsy would no doubt point out: I now suffered from withdrawal symptoms. The case was solved. I had nothing more to do.

It was at this dispirited moment that Bob Makowski reached me on my cell phone.

"Been trying to call you forever," he shouted as if he didn't trust my phone in Paris to respond to his normal voice. "Got some news for you."

"Give," I shouted back.

"I've had someone in New York follow up on the hit-and-run accident that killed your client."

"And?"

"They found the guy. A third witness had noted down the licence plate but didn't come forward until a couple of days ago. They pulled in the perp and are waiting for him to come up with a twenty thousand dollar bail. Seems he has no assets and can't find a bondsman."

"Got a name?"

"Lucifer Wahnschafft."

"You're kidding me. Lucifer?"

"Apt, wouldn't you say?"

"I imagine they've informed Neil Robinson but I'll email him just in case. He'll be relieved."

"I guess."

"Got Lucifer's address?"

"No, but I can get it."

"Might as well," I said and we hung up.

Chapter 59

"An honest-to-goodness Orgoloff?" Topsy hollered from Washington. "Signed?"

"Signed," I said. "Sterling must have bought it since he, like most of the other famous artists, never signed a painting until it was ready to change hands for money."

"How did you get it?" she hollered again and I told her.

"You lucky dog."

"That's what I've been telling myself."

"How will you get it back to Washington?"

"I'm still working out that small detail. Edwige gave me a notarized gift certificate which should ensure that I'm not accused of transporting stolen goods."

"How would she prove the painting is hers to give?"

"I don't know. Swearing that she found it after ninety years in her mother's trunk? It would certainly hit the news and provide me with my fifteen minutes of fame. I will cross that bridge if ever I get to it."

"You're definitely leaving Paris the day after tomorrow and stopping over in New York?"

"Definitely."

I'd forgotten to tell her about the Cartier lapel watch and decided to buy her a huge bottle of Chanel No.5 at Charles de Gaulle as compensation for all the riches that had been bestowed upon me.

Wednesday morning I sank into my first class seat on Air France and ordered a Mimosa for breakfast. An hour into the flight I pulled out the copy of the manuscript of Sterling's novel which Edwige had made for me. It had no title but I clearly remembered the first paragraph beginning with *Paris at night was not the same as Paris by day.*

Two hours later and bleary-eyed I turned the last page of the novel. It was an amusing—and very well-written—romp by two best friends disguised as men during their adventures in the night-life of Paris in the late 1800s. Underlying the fun was the reality of the limitations women faced and their struggles for equality in a man's world.

"*As men we were accepted everywhere,*" I read. "*Women deferred to us in bars and bals musettes, and in the streets they grew fearful if we walked too closely behind them. Masquerading as men, we felt powerful and superior. We could go anywhere at any time. It was a heady experience and we became addicted to our adventure and hardly an evening went by that we did not disguise ourselves and go out on the town.*"

At the moment when I was ready for a first-rate ending in which the women conquered the world not as women disguised as men but in their own right, the manuscript stopped abruptly in the middle of a sentence. The two protagonists in the novel were on the brink of deciding on their futures. I shouldn't have been surprised that the manuscript ended where it did. Didn't Sterling write to Pierre Fast-Brown that the last chapters of a book were the most difficult to write and that she suffered from writer's block?

Mel was at the airport and transported me in style to his apartment in SoHo. We had bagels with cream cheese and lox for lunch sitting on bar stools facing his stainless steel equipped kitchen. His sauna now had new *his* and *her* bathrobes and the bathroom two new toothbrushes. Was I ready? Probably, if Topsy's plans for us were practicable and we could live our lives separately during the week and get together at week's end.

"An antique Cartier watch," Mel said and stared closely at my lapel. "With diamonds. I always knew you had style and exquisite taste but this is incredible."

"It was Sterling's," I said and told him the whole long story. When I came to the end we were stretched out in luxurious chairs facing an early red and orange Rothko with the coffee in our mugs long gone.

"Barcelona," Mel said.

What? How did he know about Jon and Barcelona? Loose lips in Washington?

"What?" I said more loudly than intended and sat up abruptly.

"We're sitting in Mies Van der Rohe's Barcelona chairs," Mel said. "Bought them at auction last week."

"Barcelona. Of course," I said. "Wonderful chairs."

"Never thought I'd say this but you make my life seem tame," Mel said and eyed me under hooded lids. "I trust you don't have any more rabbits to pull out of your hat."

"I should unpack," I said.

When I came back out I had the Orgoloff under my arm, wrapped in a monogrammed towel from my hotel. I sat it down carefully on the coffee table next to the Giacometti.

"What?" Mel said. "What is it? Do you steal towels from hotels?"

"I hardly know how to tell you. It's my last rabbit from my last hat."

Mel stood up next to me, the towel came off slowly, and I clasped the painting in my arms. Mel's art dealer eyes went first to the quite recognizable figures in the painting and then down to the distinguished, unmistakable signature.

"No," he shouted. "I can't believe it. Did you rob a museum? How the hell did you get it and how did you transport it?"

"Rolled up at the bottom of my suitcase, the one I checked in," I said, and then I had to tell him the rest of my story. By the time I finished Mel poured a stiff drink for himself and mixed a Kir Royal for me—the champagne is to keep you in your Paris mood, he said—and together we stared for the umpteenth time at the Orgoloff.

"It's from his blue esoteric period," Mel said. "Couldn't be clearer. He put the date on the back. 15-8-24."

"Sterling bought it," I said. "Or he gave it to her as a gift."

"You're sitting pretty," Mel said. "This should easily take care of the hit you took in the Ponzi scheme."

"I could never sell it," I said.

"I thought that's what you'd say. At the very least, let me display it at the gallery here and at the new gallery in Washington?"

"Okay," I said. "Let's make a splash and get a little famous. In the meantime I'll wrap it up and put it back in my suitcase. When are we meeting your uncle Gus?"

"Shit," Mel said and grabbed his cell phone.

"Uncle Gus, we're on our way. Don't leave."

"Come on," he said and handed me my jacket on the way out the door. "They're waiting at the tavern around the corner. Probably drunk as skunks by now."

"They?"

"Yeah, Uncle Gus brought along an old pal of his who wants to meet you."

Uncle Gus was everything I had expected and then some. Granted, he was a little drunk but he got up as a true gentleman, shook my hand and bowed his head over it.

"Charmed, I'm sure," he said and grinned at me. His teeth were a little yellow but he seemed to have all of them.

"Well?" Mel said.

"Just as pretty as you told me. Probably smarter than you, my boy. You hold on to her."

"Who's your friend," Mel said and shook hands with an elderly specimen with a bald head and a grizzled beard.

"Alistair Truck," the specimen said, "Yes, like truck on wheels. They call me Al."

"What will you have?" Mel said. "We're famished."

We consulted and discussed and decided on platters and dishes with a seafood casserole for us and thick steaks with fries for them. The beer foamed in the Steins and we dug in.

"Ahh," Uncle Gus declared and smacked his lips. "Where were we?"

"You wanted me to tell them what I know about that s.o.b. Wainwright Manners the Third," Al said.

"You knew him?" I said and ignored Mel who ordered coffee for me without asking.

"You might say so. Cheated me out of a small fortune at cards. Wouldn't let me off the hook even if he knew I didn't have the money. Had to borrow to get him off my back. Sleazy character. Always boasting about his great career as a writer in Paris, France. Mind you, I knew him in the 1960s and he could brag and boast and no one would have known the truth after thirty years."

"Sounds exactly the way I imagined him," I said.

"Fancied himself a ladies' man, always talking about some Countess in France for whom he did great favors."

"Victoria," I said.

"Who?"

"Never mind. Wainwright lived at 1550 68th Street from 1934 on," I said. "Did you ever visit him there?"

"Once. I came to his door begging him to give me some relief. His apartment was full of expensive paintings and silver and such like. He was drunk when I got there and he lurched around his living room and pointed to his famous paintings—Matisse and Derain he said they were—and I asked him how he could have afforded to buy them. He was really drunk by then and said, and these were his very words: 'Went in and grabbed them from a disagreeable girl who owed me big time. She thought she was God's gift to literature but I showed her. I only took what should have been mine', he said."

"Sterling's paintings," I said.

"The next time I saw that son-of-a-bitch he threatened me and said someone would break my bones if ever I revealed what he had told me."

"So, you didn't tell anyone?"

"Nah, wasn't worth my while. He forgave me the rest of the money I owed him and I figured we were even."

"Are you willing to make a deposition to this effect?" I asked.

"A deposition? You mean to swear that this is the truth and nothing but the truth?"

"Something like that."

"Sure thing. It's the truth, ain't it?"

An eye-witness, I thought. An investigator's dream.

Uncle Gus was triumphant and Al looked flushed with success.

"Thanks, guys," Mel said when they'd finished their apple strudels.

"I can't tell you how grateful I am," I said.

"We'll be in touch," Mel said. "Here, take a cab back to Brooklyn, it's on me."

"Can you believe it," Mel said when we were back at his apartment. "Uncle Gus came through. I told you, salt of the earth, and old, grizzly Al wasn't bad either. What will you do now?"

"Pay a visit to Paul Manners," I said. "I need some additional information from him for my articles in the Washington Post and the San Francisco Chronicle. I'm Betty Johnson, free-lance reporter from Albany."

"I think I love you," Mel said.

We still don't know a lot about each other. In particular, only Bob Makowski knows about my so-called investi-kit which I carry around with me in my oversized satchel. It contains binoculars, two pairs of handcuffs, pepper spray, a Swiss army knife, Duct tape, a flashlight, batteries and chargers, my fake business cards, and a few more odds and ends.

As it happened, Mel didn't know yet that I can't sleep without reading for at least half an hour or until my eyes close and I hadn't known until that evening that Mel must go for a run before turning in no matter how late or how early it gets.

So, we now followed our habits.

Mel went running for forty-five minutes around the dangerous streets of the neighborhood and I took a shower and settled down with the only book I still hadn't read from the treasure trove Reginald Fletcher, our antiquarian, had left for me with Topsy not that long ago.

The cover had the title—*They came to Paris*—above a drawing of two gorgeous flappers in black sheaths, cloche hats, and long strings of pearls.

I turned to Chapter One.

"*Paris by night was not the same as Paris by day. At midnight we dressed up in men's clothing, outrageous cravats and shiny buttoned boots.*"

I stopped reading.

"Oh, my God. Oh, my God." I heard myself but didn't even know I was shouting.

The book dropped to the floor. I rushed to the front door when I heard the key turn. My cheeks burned, my eyes watered, the air had left my lungs.

"What the hell's going on?" Mel was dripping wet from his run.

"This book is Sterling's novel," I shouted and didn't care who could hear me. I ran to the bedroom and came back out with Sterling's manuscript.

"Show me," Mel said.

We read the first pages of the novel together and compared them to the manuscript. Word for word they were identical.

"Who's Paul Bentley?" Mel said and stared at the name of the author.

"I have a pretty good idea," I said. "Look, the publisher is *Universal Publishing* and the book was published—and copyrighted by the author, for shame—in 1932 a year before they went out of business."

"And look at the two flappers on the dust cover. They were afraid to show the women dressed as men," I said.

"I'm taking my shower now," Mel said. "Don't go away."

"I can't possibly sleep now," I said when he returned to the living room. "I have to read the entire book just to be certain."

"Sure, sweetie, I'll keep the coffee percolating."

We double-checked every page together.

The last few chapters were disappointing in the sense that the two women in the novel—so emancipated in the beginning—ended up quite conventionally. They both married men who acted manly and to whom they deferred.

"That doesn't strike me as the same style as the rest of the book," Mel said.

"That's where Sterling left off because of her writer's block," I said. "Her imposter finished the book for her."

"Wainwright Manners III?"

"You bet."

Chapter 60

"Who did you say?"

"Betty Johnson, Sir," I said. "If you remember, we visited a couple of weeks back about your grandfather's company, *Universal Publishing*."

"Ah, yes, Miss Jones."

"Johnson, Sir. Betty Johnson."

"What do you want now?"

It was eleven in the morning and Paul Manners was already slurring his speech.

I had spent the previous day putting together the notarized deposition from Alistair Truck and copying Sterling's manuscript and her letter to Pierre Fast-Brown about the theft of her two paintings. I got a declaration faxed over from Edwige Claire in Paris to the effect that the carbon copy of her mother's manuscript had only recently been found in her trunk which had not been opened since 1931. It had been stored in a vault with Sterling's other furniture and paintings until 1952. Edwige Claire had also over-nighted one of the black-and-white glossies of Sterling shown with her Matisse and her Derain. I brought along Paul Bentley's book *They Came to Paris*.

I was ready to go.

"Mr. Manners," I said, "I have something to show you."

"I thought you said it would take several months," he slurred.

"Would it be convenient if I drop by your apartment this afternoon, Sir?"

"Fine, fine. Come after lunch. At 2 o'clock."

This time Paul Manners hadn't shaved, his clothes looked as if he'd slept in them, and his cheeks were flushed.

He didn't shake my hand.

He let me into the living room reluctantly. Upon entering my eyes went automatically to the paintings on the back wall.

They were gone.

My heartbeat increased considerably.

"You're moving?" I said.

"No, but I've moved my paintings to a safe place," Manners said.

"To your bank vault?" I said.

"That would be telling, wouldn't it?" he said. "Did you know that your business card doesn't have a telephone number? How do you expect people to get in touch with you? Very unprofessional."

"I'm very sorry. Must've given you the wrong card," I said quite truthfully. "Why did you want to get in touch with me?"

"About my paintings. Did you tell someone about them?"

"No, most certainly not."

"I got some strange phone calls and a strange visitor. Thought it had something to do with you."

"Nothing to do with me," I said. "You had a visitor?"

I had a fleeting thought of Uncle Gus and Al.

"Never mind," Manners said. "What did you want to show me?"

I sat down on the couch, placed my briefcase on the floor beside me and brought out its contents.

"Here," I said and handed Paul Manners Al's declaration.

He read the statement several times and each time his face flushed more deeply. He looked closely at the notary seal.

"What's this garbage?" he said and pushed the statement back across the table to me.

"We have credible proof that in 1929 your father stole the Matisse and the Derain—now removed from your wall—from the apartment of one Sterling Kirkland Sawyer at 351 quai des Grands-Augustins in Paris."

"That statement isn't credible proof. All the notary did was attest to the signature not to the veracity of the contents," he shouted. "I remember that lying bum, Al Truck, he cheated at cards and owed my father money. And now you believe this statement he made against my father who's dead and can't defend himself?"

Paul Manners got up and walked towards the hall. Seemed he wanted me to leave. When I didn't budge he returned and glared down at me.

"Sit down," I said, "we need to talk."

He remained standing.

"My name is Jamie Prescott," I said and handed him my real card. "Private Investigator."

"You're not Betty Jones, free-lance journalist?"

"Johnson," I said as if it mattered. "No, I'm not."

"Bitch." Paul Manners said and sat down looking somewhere between bewildered and terrified.

"I represent the heirs of the woman who owned your paintings," I said.

"You don't have any proof."

"Take a look at this, then," I said and handed him the black-and-white photograph.

He sat pressed into his armchair, his mouth open, his sparse hair on end. He looked at the paintings in the photo and then looked up at the empty spaces on the wall.

"They are not the same," he said.

"Yes, they obviously are," I said. "Even though the photos are in black and white and the paintings are no longer on your wall, I know they're the same. Any court will rule against you."

"My father told me he bought the paintings directly from the artists at a discount," Manners said.

I handed him Sterling's letter to Pierre Fast-Brown from 1929. Paul Manners read it with a pained scowl on his face and gave it back to me. Then he got up and filled his glass to the brim with Jack Daniels. He didn't offer me any. Not that I needed whisky this early in the afternoon.

"My father said that he had known Derain personally and that he kept the painting for sentimental reasons. Same with Matisse."

"Did your father ever exhibit the paintings or have them evaluated?"

"No, he kept them under wraps, didn't want the notoriety."

No wonder, I thought.

"He had stolen the paintings," I stated flatly, "and I believe that you have known all along. I believe he told you in order to prevent you from revealing them to the world once he was gone."

Manners stared at me fearfully.

"You had nothing to fear until now," I said. "Not until this moment when Sterling Kirkland Sawyer has come back to life quite miraculously."

"It will be your word against mine," he said.

"Hardly," I said. "I will give you until tomorrow to bring the paintings back."

"What will you do if I refuse? Sue me?"

I was on somewhat shaky ground. Maybe he knew that cases of stolen paintings notoriously take forever to resolve? Years, sometimes. Maybe I hadn't scared him sufficiently?

"The police will be on your doorstep," I said.

"I'm not about to hand over a fortune in paintings," he said in a weaker voice.

"You can and you will," I said. "The paintings belong to Sterling Kirkland Sawyer's daughter who still lives in the apartment in Paris from where they were stolen."

"*I* didn't steal anything," he said, rallying.

"But you kept stolen goods knowingly all these years."

"Didn't know nothing about it," he shouted. "Go ahead, sue the hell out of me."

Paul Manners got up unsteadily and pointed to the door.

"You get out of here right now," he said, "I'll defend my right to the paintings and it'll take your precious woman in Paris forever and will cost her a fortune to the lawyers. So, there."

"Believe me," I said, "you'll regret it."

I knew it would now be an uphill battle and decided to move on until I could come up with a new strategy.

"One more thing," I said.

"There's more?"

"Afraid so."

I took out the Paul Bentley book and handed it to him.

"My father's book," he said. "It's been out of print fifty years. How did you find a copy?"

"Got it from an antiquarian book store in Washington," I said. "Your father wrote under the name Paul Bentley?"

"What are you trying to pull?" he said. "There's nothing wrong with using a pseudonym. My father used his mother's maiden name of Bentley and his uncle's first name of Paul. This was his only novel, he wrote it in Paris—except for the last two chapters which he finished here—I still have his manuscript."

"Are you sure?" I said.

"Of course I'm sure. My grandfather's company published the book just before they went bankrupt in 1933. It was a New York Times bestseller for six weeks. Very popular at the time even though it was about two degenerate women. I can show you what the critics thought of it. Not all opinions were favorable, of course."

"I can imagine," I said. "The subject must have seemed upsetting for the times."

"I've always been very proud of his novel," Paul Manners said seeming to forget our adversarial situation. "It was the best thing he ever wrote. Especially the first line in the first paragraph, the one about Paris at night was not the same as Paris by day. I liked that."

He drained his glass and reached for the bottle.

"I have one more piece of bad news for you," I said.

I handed him the copy of Sterling's manuscript.

"My father's manuscript!" he shouted and pointed at me with an accusing finger. "How did you get a copy?"

"This is not your father's manuscript."

He sat down abruptly and looked at the first sentence of the first paragraph.

"I don't understand," he said.

"The book was written by the same Sterling Kirkland Sawyer who owned the Derain and Matisse paintings. Your father didn't write the novel. He stole her manuscript."

I didn't want to confuse the issue by agreeing that he did write the last two chapters.

"You're lying," Paul Manners shouted.

"The evidence is overwhelming," I said.

Sterling's manuscript fell from his hands to the floor and I picked it up.

"You're making it up," he shouted.

"No," I said. "Your father stole her manuscript from her trunk—in which she kept special books and mementos—at some time after she moved to the convent in the country. She left everything in her apartment intending to return. Instead she died and her home was broken into one more time."

In my mind's eye I saw Wainwright Manners III sneaking back to Sterling's place, finding her manuscript—but missing the carbon copy—and then, for good measure, taking James Joyce's signed *Ulysses* and, out of spite, giving it to Victoria, Sterling's worst friend. I remembered wondering why the dedication had not been more specific. Victoria must, somehow, have erased Sterling's name.

"This Sterling was a nun?" Paul Manners said having seemingly forgotten all about his problems with the stolen paintings.

"No," I said, "she was not a nun but she was extremely religious and had spent her childhood at that same convent."

"I don't believe any of it," he said. He filled up his glass and downed most of it in one audible gulp.

He looked at me with red-rimmed eyes.

"You leave now," he said and swerved towards the front door.

This time I did as bidden. I left without another word. I stayed outside the door and listened as Paul Manners stumbled about in the hallway. Then I took the elevator down.

There aren't many hiding places on Central Park West for someone of my ilk to perform surveillance but I stationed myself behind a hotdog stand on the other side of the street.

Paul Manners came rushing out from his building six, seven minutes later. His arms were flailing, his coat flapped in the wind, and he steered himself down the street at half a gallop. I rushed along on the opposite side without bothering to hide. Manners was oblivious to the world.

We continued our speedy walk down one street to another, across avenues, around corners, and down an alley. When I emerged from the alley we were back on a side street and Paul Manners had a key in the lock of the front door to a townhouse with a black iron fence and five steps up. I stayed on the other side of the street until he disappeared inside.

I took a leisurely stroll over and looked at the name on a grubby brass plate. L. Wahnschafft, Conservator, the plate said.

L. for Lucifer? The hit-and-run driver who was at this moment in jail on suspicion of killing poor Marjorie Robinson? A conservator of paintings? The picture was suddenly crystal clear.

I walked up the five steps to the front door and rang the bell. I peeked in through the bay window to my right but saw nothing.

I rang the bell again.

"Yes?" The door opened a sliver and a fat face with long blond hair appeared in the opening.

My foot was inside the door, my hands pushed it open and I was in. The fat face was attached to a muscular body with broad shoulders and long arms bursting out of cut-off sleeves.

"Stanley," Paul Manners shouted. "Who is it?"

"That woman," Stanley shouted back a second before I took a deep breath and raised my arms to within an inch of my face. The shout released the air from my lungs and propelled me forward. Two chops and the knife which had appeared in Stanley's right hand slid across the floor and rattled into a far corner.

He was heavy, but off-balance, as he came towards me. His surprise was instant as was his scream when I stepped up, grabbed his arm, twisted him around, kicked his legs out from under him, and in two seconds got him on the floor with his arm tacked behind him. His nose hit the floor in a move I had not anticipated and spewed blood all over the tiled floor. He tried to kick his legs about but to no avail. I hadn't been in combat for a while but was pleased to know that I hadn't entirely lost my Tae Kwon Do touch. In case that was not enough I dug in my roomy satchel for the handcuffs in my investi-kit and snapped them on Stanley's inert wrists. He lay in the corner moaning and put up no resistance.

"What the hell are you doing," Paul Manners shouted in the doorway and launched himself weakly against me aiming a blow at my head. I took him by the scruff of the neck and marched him back into a study of sorts with canvasses stacked against the walls. Sterling's two paintings were on separate easels in the middle of the room destined, maybe, to be painted over or simply hidden in plain sight.

"Sit," I said to him and planted him in an armchair. He sagged and covered his face with both hands.

"You are an accessory to murder," I hissed at him. "You sent Lucifer after Marjorie Robinson."

"No, no," Paul Manners whined. "It was Stanley's idea, it wasn't me. I had nothing to do with it."

"It was Stanley, not Lucifer?"

"Yes, yes."

What a disgusting bunch.

"She came to your apartment, didn't she?" I said.

"Like a fool I let her in. She was a pushy woman. Thought she could trick me. Said that her aunt and my father were friends in Paris, wanted to know if he'd told me about her aunt. Said she was a writer. Wouldn't say how she found me."

Paul Manners blew his nose violently.

"Then she went across and looked at my paintings, asked all kinds of questions. Wouldn't leave. Stanley was there, heard the whole thing. He's not quite right in the head, Stanley, never was. Very protective of me, always was. He must have followed her when she left. I know nothing about it. Never heard about the accident until they arrested Lucifer. He's Stanley's father but he didn't do it although it was his car."

I didn't believe him. I knew in my heart that he was an accomplice. I felt like an accomplice myself. What had I told Marjorie that made her act on her own? Certainly nothing about the paintings. Had I given her Paul Manner's address? I didn't think so but it wouldn't have been difficult for her to find him. Had she become impatient with my haphazard reporting? Or was she simply the kind of impulsive person who meddled without thinking? I would never know. Here I suddenly heard Bob Makowski's voice telling me to stop equivocating and get on with the job at hand.

Stanley was still moaning in his corner and although I didn't want to waste a good pair of handcuffs I decided to keep him cuffed. He didn't even notice. I returned to Paul Manners and pulled him up from his chair.

"Help, help," Manners shouted weakly, "Stanley, help me."

But Stanley, moaning, his nose still bleeding, was in no position to help anyone and in three seconds flat I had Paul Manners' right arm handcuffed and attached to the old-fashioned radiator.

"You can't do that," he shouted. "It's illegal."

"Sue me," I said.

It may be a fallacy that possession is ninety percent of the law but it sounds good to me so I stepped up to the two easels, removed the Matisse and the Derain, bundled them under my arm and stepped back into the foyer.

"Hey," Paul Manners shouted. "You can't do that."

"Sue me," I said.

Outside on the sidewalk my luck was still with me. A taxi swerved to the curb and skidded to an abrupt halt. I opened the door before the car had half stopped, slid the paintings onto the back seat and got in beside them. I slammed the door with a satisfying thud and told the driver to take me to SoHo to Mel's loft.

Then I called the authorities.

Chapter 61

Mel arrived from New York in the late afternoon and we were awaiting guests for drinks in honor of my Alexandre Orgoloff esoteric blue period painting.

"We're not eating here?" Mel said.

"No, I'm having dinner catered at Topsy and Martin's place. My treat."

"Catered? Seriously, you can't cook at all?" he said.

"Can you?"

"I can do bagels and cream cheese and lox."

"I can do a fabulous omelette."

"We won't starve, then," Mel said.

"We won't," I said. "I can also set a table and fold napkins."

"I hear you."

My table usually has Royal Copenhagen porcelain—given to me by my mother when she moved to smaller quarters after my father died—glittering Orrefors glassware and some really fabulous George Jensen silverware enfolded in white linen napkins. Not tonight, though. I'd been coming home from the office at ten every night and had no time for domestic pursuits.

"All you need is a waiter," Mel said just as Philippe came through the door dressed in his best gear—a starched white jacket over black pants—carrying canapés to the sideboard.

"Bonjour, Monsieur," he said and Mel sank down in a chair and started laughing.

"Are you doing all this to impress me?" he said and wiped his eyes.

"No, it's for my Orgoloff."

"You're going to an awful lot of trouble for a few guests."

"That's how it may seem."

"Hey," Mel said, "catering is what I do at the gallery on opening nights and this is one stupendous opening night."

"Thank you."

My fabulous Orgoloff—in a frame designed not to over-shadow the subject—had replaced a Préfète Duffaut over the fireplace and looked quite at home. The party was about to begin.

Topsy and Martin arrived at six, my mother and Bob Makowski a few minutes later. They immediately gathered in awe in front of my painting.

"You lucky dog," Topsy repeated and, in great waves of enthusiasm, exuded Chanel No.5 from Charles de Gaulle.

"I like blue but who are all those figures floating about," Bob Makowski said. "Hard to believe that people pay money for such pictures. Is that a starfish? No offense, but I wish someone would explain this to me."

"I'll do it," Martin said and pulled Bob with him to the kitchen. They stayed there about thirty seconds and came barreling back out looking chastised.

"Who the hell is the guy in the kitchen," Bob said. "He threw us out."

"My waiter," I said. "Philippe."

"And I suppose you have a cook as well?"

"François," I said, "over at Topsy and Martin's preparing dinner."

"I knew Paris would go completely to your head," Bob said.

"I'll explain art to you some other time," Martin said just as Philippe appeared with the drinks and served the artfully arranged canapés.

We sipped wine staring at the Orgoloff. The blue background was not entirely blue but had feathery strokes of aqua and gray and white. The surrealistic human figures had fantastical eyes and transparent moth-like wings, a large fish with bulging eyes fled from a villainous starfish who pursued a headless woman's stark, white body.

"Oh, boy," Bob Makowski said and moved around the room in a frenzy, "look at those twisted legs. And is that an eye in the middle of her stomach. Or worse?"

"Tell everyone about the other paintings, the Derain and the Matisse. The ones that Wainwright Manners III stole from Sterling and which *you* liberated from Paul Manners," Martin said. "Another of your stories to dine out on."

"She incapacitated one man—I believe he was felled by two chops and a twist—intimidated Paul Manners into a catatonic state, hand-cuffed him to the radiator, and arrived at my loft in a taxi clutching the priceless pictures in her arms," Mel said.

"And lost two good pairs of handcuffs," I said. "The paintings are now stashed in a bank vault in New York awaiting shipment to Paris. Edwige may donate both to the Louvre."

"Good for her," Martin said.

"Paul Manners has given up his claim to the paintings in a notarized letter through his lawyers. Probably thinks it will help his case," I said.

"If I were Edwige I'd keep the paintings and enjoy them," Topsy said.

"Think of the insurance," Mel said.

"And think of the publicity," Martin said.

"Of course it will be news anyway when the prosecutors in New York call Jamie as a witness against Lucifer, Stanley, and Paul Manners in the death of Marjorie Robinson. They are busy accusing each other and the State will need Jamie to sort it out."

"I'm afraid there's no way around it," I said. "In for a penny, in for a pound. I'll be summoned as a witness and I'll have to appear. If the case gets to that point."

"All in a day's work," Topsy mumbled. "For Jamie, that is, not for the likes of the rest of us."

"I'm starving." Bob finished off the last of the canapés.

"Let's go," I said.

We found our places around Topsy and Martin's large dining table and Philippe was there to serve François's signature onion soup.

"Watch out now," Topsy exulted later when Philippe swung through the door from the kitchen and placed before us a huge blue serving platter with a reddish starfish laid out in majesty, its eyes, at the very ends of its five hefty legs, staring indignantly at a baked trout.

The creature glistened with a *court-bouillon* dressing of dry white wine with whole peppers and bay leaves. It didn't make it look more palatable.

"Starfish for Orgoloff," Philippe said.

We stared in some disgust and cried out in unison.

"Too strange to eat," Mel said.

"I'm certainly not having any."

"Better exhibit it at the gallery."

"Thank God for the spinach soufflé."

"And white asparagus."

"That sounds more like Bernice Boch."

"With a *Sauce Mousseline* made with eggs, butter and whipped cream. Voilá."

"Bernice was not on a diet."

"Neither are we."

We toasted Orgoloff and, reluctantly, the starfish and one another in a fine Mercier Demi-Sec champagne and talked and laughed and devoured the baked trout and the salad, then the scrumptious paper-thin crêpes Normandes served for dessert.

"Tell us about Sterling's book," Martin said.

"We found her notes for the last two chapters in the trunk. They were clear. One of the women would go on to University and become a scientist. She would turn down a marriage proposal to pursue her career. The other woman would become a successful published writer living 'in sin' with a married man."

"Talk about wishful thinking." Mel said.

"A writer has wonderful powers to manipulate her characters and make them good or evil, and live or die," I said. "Edwige is talking about getting the book reissued with the last two chapters ghostwritten to reflect Sterling's intentions."

"Paul Manner's name will be mud," Bob Makowski said.
"Again," Martin said.

"Did I hear you say that Sterling is up for an honorary degree at your alma mater?" my mother said.

"It was Sterling's alma mater, as well, and they are thrilled at the thought. They loved her short stories," I said, "and they will surely love her novel."

"You're working very hard on Sterling's behalf," my mother said.

"Edwige and Isabelle will be here for the ceremony in three months time."

"I thought Isabelle did not like to travel," Topsy said.

"She has become a different woman," I said. "She also wants to recreate the journey she made as a child with Stefan, her father. She and Edwige will be traveling on the Orient Express from Paris to Venice where they will stay at Edwige's house."

"Wow," Topsy said looking dreamy-eyed.

"Oh, no, we won't," Martin said.

"Now," Topsy said to my mother when we sat over coffee and a fine old Grand Marnier in front of the fireplace in the living room. "Now, tell Jamie."

"Tell Jamie what?" Mel said.

"There's always more," Martin said.

"About Stefan von Oxenkranz," my mother began. "My colleague in Switzerland e-mailed me while you were on your way back from Paris."

"You'll love this," Topsy said.

"Seems that the owner of the *Schloss*—that would be Stefan's ex-wife—sold it in 1932, re-married and moved away with the children. Court papers showed that Stefan was accused of abandoning them by moving to France. He may never have seen the children again."

"Which is why he was so devoted to Isabelle and stayed in an unhappy marriage with Victoria. He wasn't about to lose another child to divorce," I said.

"What happened to those children? Are there descendants in Switzerland who would be related to Edwige Claire and Isabelle?" Martin said.

"Not according to my colleague's investigation," my mother said. "Stefan's son died in 1942, without issue, and his daughter never married. Even she died early on."

"You should go there," Topsy said.

"Oh, no, the case has been resolved," Bob Makowski said, "and we can get back to work. Chasing real criminals."

"Stefan von Oxenkranz," Topsy said, "he sounds so glamorous. The way Isabelle described him made me wish even more fervently that I had lived at that time."

"No," I said, "the ones I really, really would have wanted to meet were Sterling and Claire. I wouldn't have cared about anyone else."

"Maybe just Laura and Auguste?"

"Maybe."

"How about Bernice Boch and Pyotr Vasilevich and Scott Winteride?"

"Oh, okay."

"And Roland Lee Rainier?"

"Sure."

"Whatever happened to Claire?" Martin said.

"Oh, no," Bob Makowski moaned.

"She gave up her dance studio in Montmartre within a short time, apparently she never stuck with anything for too long. She went to Spain to join her father at his country estate, gave acclaimed dance recitals, fell in love with her second cousin, an illustrious equestrian, married him and settled with him in Madrid. They had no children. She established a famous dance studio there and continued to teach and dance into her old age."

"At least someone ended up with a good life," my mother said. "Sterling would have been happy for Claire if she had lived to know about it."

"Yes," I said.

"How strange that no one in New York learned about Sterling's death," Topsy said.

"Pierre Fast-Brown was probably the only person who knew about her sister, Rose," I said, "and he died before he heard from Soeur Madeleine."

"I imagine that Roland Lee Rainier heard about Sterling from someone in Paris," Topsy said, "but he might not have known anything about Sterling's family. Remember how secretive she was."

"Effie Rousseau may have heard mention of Sterling's sister, Rose, when she lived in New York but she was then painting in Rome," I said.

"What about Claire?" my mother said. "She came back to the convent with Alexandre Orgoloff to visit Sterling's grave."

"She must have returned immediately to Madrid. Stefan Oxencranz would have learned about Sterling's death from Orgoloff once he returned from Switzerland," I said.

"Seems like a colossal conspiracy of unhappy circumstances. And, in the end, no one knew about Sterling's child," Martin said.

"Not even the evil Victoria," my mother said.

We sat around for another hour, hesitant to leave our recent adventure and take up our daily lives again. I wanted to stay with Sterling and Stefan and Claire and Orgoloff and my Soeur and Edwige and Isabelle. And Topsy wouldn't let go for the longest time of Joyce and Roland and Scott.

Chapter 62

"Here," Mel said and tossed me The Washington Herald, The Washington Post, The New York Times, and USA Today. "You're famous."

The headlines were not what I'd wished for, the notoriety was a pain with my phone off the hook, quite literally, my cell phone swamped, and what looked like a reporter with her photographer lurking on the sidewalk outside my front door.

I stared at the headlines but didn't read the rest.

Glamorous Private Investigator Uncovers Art Theft

"Nothing wrong with that," Mel said. "Let's face it, babe, you're glamorous."

D.C Investigator Finds 100-Year Old Paintings in New York

"Nothing wrong with that either," Mel said.

Unknown Matisse and Derain Discovered. Now at the Louvre

"Or with that," he said.

Spectacular Orgoloff To Be Exhibited At New Gallery in Washington This Week

"Free publicity," Mel said.

Intrepid Local Private Investigator Receives $10 Million Gift From Benefactor In Paris

"Hrmmp," Mel said. "How did they find out about that?"

"Reporters," I said, "worse than detectives. Wonder who spilled the beans. The world is full of blabbermouths."

"They're quoting so-called informed sources. One paper mentions a close associate of the benefactor in Paris."

"Madame Brisson," I said. "Edwige's inquisitive maid. Or, Jacques d'Alville who wouldn't be adverse to some reflected glory."

"Useless to speculate. The damage is done," Mel said. "How about some breakfast?"

I flipped two omelettes â la créme fraiche from the frying pan to our plates and added toast and orange juice to the tray. Mel carried it to the dining room table where it stood in the midst of the newspaper pile-up.

"It'll pass," Mel said. "It's your fifteen minutes of fame. The news channels will mention it tomorrow after which you'll be old news as long as you avoid the talk shows."

"Until I reappear during the trial," I said mournfully. "In the meantime, I may have to put the Orgoloff in a bank vault."

"Or hire round-the-clock armed guards."

"Ah, what I've always dreamed of."

It is true that we still don't know everything about one another. For example, Mel doesn't know that I sometimes carry a gun. It's in the office, in the safe, with Bob's. But I would take it home if I had the Orgoloff on my wall seeing that—thanks to the newspapers—my possession of it was now public knowledge.

"The omelette is as good as they come," Mel said. "I tried to find bagels but they don't have the right kind here. No real lox, either."

"I bet I can find you some."

"Babe," Mel said. "It can wait. We'll be in New York next weekend. And please let me call you Cassandra."

"Absolutely not," I said, "Martin told you, didn't he?"

I watched the photographer pack up her gear and leave my sidewalk with the reporter.

"He swore me to silence," Mel said.

"Okay, I'll let you call me Cassandra once a year. On my birthday. That's the best I can do."

Mel laughed and shook his head at me.

"The Islands are beckoning," he said.

"Turks and Caicos?"

"That's what I'm thinking."

"Great minds think alike," I said and brought in two cups of café-au-lait topped off with whipped cream and sprinkles of cinnamon.

"Fancy," Mel said.

"We'd better get down to the gallery," I said and went off to slink into my lacy Donna Karan dress, the one that exposed my right leg as high up as was decently possible. I now had to uphold my glamourous image.

At six o'clock that evening Mel's new gallery was jam-packed. The Orgoloff hung on the back wall, illuminated and gorgeous. Two guards—armed but not in obvious uniforms—loomed on the sidelines. The invited guests were dressed to the hilt, Washingtonian insiders, curators from the finest museums, all my friends and colleagues and many of Mel's friends from the art world in New York. No reporters or photographers. The catering, headed by Philippe and François, was flawless, the Champagne sparkled, the canapés were scrumptious.

When the guests had departed Bob Makowski was the last one left.

"The painting is not half bad," he said. "It grows on you. The color is the best thing about it. But what do I know about paintings. You're going to have a security problem with it. Better take home the Colt."

"Colt," Mel said. "You have a gun?"

"Well, it's not a horse," Bob said.

Mel's startled look told me that he also realized that we don't know everything about each other.

"It's part of the job," I said.

"Babe," Mel said, but I thought I'd better not tell him how often I carried it.

"See you at the office tomorrow," Bob said when he left.

"Yes," I said.

We left the Orgoloff at the gallery under the observant eye of one of the armed guards and went to meet Topsy and Martin for dinner.

"Spectacular evening," Topsy said. "The Orgoloff looked even better than I remembered it from your house."

"It's going to be a pain in the neck," Martin said. "You should sell it."

"Whoa, whoa," Mel said. "She can't do that. Remember who gave it to her."

"Nevertheless," I said, "it's become a pain in the neck."

"You wouldn't," Topsy said.

"You couldn't," Mel said.

"You should," Martin said.

Chapter 63

The next morning, after driving Mel to the airport, I parked my Jaguar in the K Street garage and brought up a coffee and a couple of croissants from the coffee shop on L Street.

My office looked unfamiliar. I'd been away in another century, in another time. The framed prints on the walls looked trivial, the large oriental rug seemed not as fine as before, the double curtains—brocade over sheers—looked no more than adequate. Only the silver tray with the silver coffee set looked stylish. I switched my coffee from paper to porcelain and added two lumps of brown sugar.

I took the cup to the hermetically closed window and looked down eight floors at the soundless traffic on K Street, mostly cabs going rapidly in both directions. The sun shone bright on the buildings on the other side, where disorderly paper stacks sat in the wide window sills and shadowy figures moved behind the shiny panes. Soon small groups of upscale executives would stream on to the sidewalks heading for quiche and red wine on L Street, a Martini and shrimp cocktail on Connecticut Avenue, or ethnic food at Dupont Circle.

I turned away from the window to add another lump of sugar to my coffee. My desk looked smaller than it did a month ago. Possibly because of the stacks of legal file folders—leaning like three towers of Pisa—awaiting my attention.

The envelope Marjorie Robinson had left me posed by itself in the middle of the desk. Feeling very sorry that she hadn't lived to know about Sterling I asked someone in the outer office to get me Neil Robinson on the phone at the Embassy in Tokyo.

"I saw the headlines in the New York Times on the Internet," Neil said. "And I received a full report from the police about the hit-and-run driver they have in custody. I'll be attending the trial whenever it happens."

"It will take time," I said.

"Thanks also for your several e-mails," Neil said. "You turned out to be quite as intrepid as I had imagined. And very lucky. Did my second cousin really give you a ten million dollar Orgoloff painting as a gift?"

"It was supposed to be a private matter," I said.

"A nice bonus," Neil Robinson said icily.

"I had no idea the painting was that valuable."

There was absolute silence at the other end of the line. I could feel the wheels spinning in his head picturing how a potential heirloom had escaped him. Always assuming that he would know the contents of Edwige's eventual will. Personally, I wouldn't be surprised if she left everything to the museums.

"I talked to Edwige last night," I said. "I have decided to lend the Orgoloff for a certain period of time to the Museum of Modern Art in New York. They will insure it and display it with a plaque saying 'In memory of Sterling Kirkland Sawyer, b. New York City, 1896, d. Vézelay, France, 1931'."

Edwige had insisted on giving me, instead, Orgoloff's sketch of Louis Saint at the piano and Sterling standing on the side twirling her long string of pearls. It had taken its place above my fireplace and pleased me greatly. I felt no obligation to tell Neil Robinson about this.

"Oh," he said.

"I hope that seems fair," I said.

"I suppose it's up to you," he said. "I'll be seeing Edwige in Paris next month."

"That's what she tells me," I said. "I hope the two of you will have many things in common."

"Thank you." he said and his voice had defrosted somewhat. "I'll visit the Orgoloff at the museum in New York. I'll be very curious to see it."

"I'll let you know when they hang it," I said.

"I'll see you at Topsy and Martins place, I hope, when I get to Washington."

"Absolutely," I said.

There was a sharp knock on my door, the handle rattled, our new research assistant burst into my office and made me spill coffee down the front of my silk blouse, just missing my Cartier lapel watch.

She was in purple hair with white highlights, Jimmy Choo boots, and a mini skirt to drive the Washington establishment crazy. She grinned at me in her New York kind of way.

"Found a fab retro-boutique in Georgetown," Ms. Puigh said.

"I bet," I said and went to get a fresh blouse.

Ms. Puigh sat down across from me and lit a cigarette which she put out hastily by throwing it into my fine porcelain coffee cup.

"Sorry," she mumbled, "a Parisian custom."

"Old habits die hard," I said.

"We'll go back there, won't we?"

"For sure."

"What's the next project?"

"Let's go see Bob."

"He's a doll," Ms. Puigh said.

"Yes, and no," I said. "Mostly yes."